"*Legend* is a damned good book. David Gemmell is a delicious writer—a master of fantasy with an edge; the rogue who's driven to heroism. One of the best pure reads in many a day."
—ALLAN COLE AND CHRIS BUNCH

"[Gemmell's] books strike me as heroic fantasy in the truest sense ... The settings are convincing, with the level of detail you'd find in a historical novel. The stories have a realistic feel and present the more mundane facts upon which idealized legends are later built. This reader will be looking for the next one."
—JULIE DEAN SMITH

"David Gemmell is very talented: his characters are vivid and very convincingly realistic. [*Morningstar*] kept my interest from the first chapter. Watching a common thief become engulfed in a growing legend was a fascinating experience. I'm very much looking forward to his next book."
—CHRISTOPHER STASHEFF

"*Legend* is a rousing tale, all primary colors: think of Robert E. Howard meeting David Eddings. If you like headlong adventure, this one's for you."
—HARRY TURTLEDOVE

"[*Legend*] is a powerful novel, intense and moving—military fantasy at its finest ... Sweeping in its scope ... The depictions of courage, honor, and fortitude are second to none."
—LAWRENCE WATT-EVANS

By David Gemmell
Published by Ballantine Books:

LION OF MACEDON
DARK PRINCE

KNIGHTS OF DARK RENOWN

MORNINGSTAR

The Drenai Saga
    LEGEND
    THE KING BEYOND THE GATE
    QUEST FOR LOST HEROES
    WAYLANDER
    IN THE REALM OF THE WOLF
    THE FIRST CHRONICLES OF
           DRUSS THE LEGEND
    THE LEGEND OF DEATHWALKER*

The Stones of Power Cycle
    GHOST KING
    LAST SWORD OF POWER
    WOLF IN SHADOW
    THE LAST GUARDIAN
    BLOODSTONE

*forthcoming

Legend

Book One of *The Drenai Saga*

David Gemmell

A Del Rey® Book
BALLANTINE BOOKS • NEW YORK

A Del Rey® Book
Published by The Ballantine Publishing Group
Copyright © 1984 by David A. Gemmell
Excerpt from *The King Beyond the Gate* copyright © 1985 by David A. Gemmell

Del Rey and colophon are registered trademarks of Random House, Inc.

www.randomhouse.com/delrey/

Library of Congress Catalog Card Number: 94-94194

ISBN 0-345-37906-3

Manufactured in the United States of America

First Ballantine Books Edition: November 1994

20 19 18 17 16 15 14

This book is dedicated with love to three very special people. My father, Bill Woodford, without whom Druss the Legend would never have stood on the wall of Dros Delnoch. My mother, Olive, who instilled in me a love of stories in which heroes never lied, evil rarely triumphed, and love was always true.

And my wife, Valerie, who showed me that life can be like stories.

Grateful thanks are also due to Russell Claughton, Tim Lenton, Tom Taylor, Nick Hopkins, and Stella Graham for their help throughout the project.

Prologue

THE DRENAI HERALD waited nervously outside the great doors of the throne room, flanked by two Nadir guards who stared ahead, slanted eyes fixed on the bronze eagle emblazoned on the dark wood.

He licked dry lips with a dry tongue and adjusted his purple cape about his bony shoulders. He had been so confident in the council chamber at Drenan six hundred miles south when Abalayn had asked him to undertake this delicate mission: a journey to distant Gulgothir to ratify the treaties made with Ulric, Lord of the Nadir tribes. Bartellus had helped to draft treaties in the past and twice had been present at talks in western Vagria and south in Mashrapur. All men understood the value of trade and the necessity of avoiding such costly undertakings as war. Ulric would be no exception. True, he had sacked the nations of the northern plain, but then, they had bled his people dry over the centuries with their taxes and raids; they had sown the seeds of their own destruction.

Not so the Drenai. They had always treated the Nadir with tact and courtesy. Abalayn himself had twice visited Ulric in his northern tent city and had been royally received.

But Bartellus had been shocked at the devastation in Gulgothir. That the vast gates had been sundered was no surprise, but many of the defenders had been subsequently mutilated. The square within the main keep boasted a small mound of human hands. Bartellus shivered and wrenched his mind from the memory.

For three days they had kept him waiting, but they had been courteous—even kindly.

He adjusted his cape again, aware that his lean, angular frame did little justice to the herald's garb. Taking a linen cloth from his belt, he wiped the sweat from his bald head. His wife constantly warned him that his head shone dazzlingly whenever he grew nervous. It was an observation he would have preferred to be left unspoken.

He slid a glance at the guard to his right, suppressing a shudder. The man was shorter than he, wearing a spiked helm fringed with goatskin. He wore a lacquered wooden breastplate and carried a serrated spear. The face was flat and cruel, the eyes dark and slanted. If Bartellus ever needed a man to cut off someone's hand . . .

He glanced to his left—and wished he had not, for the other guard was looking at him. He felt like a rabbit beneath a plunging hawk and hastily returned his gaze to the bronze eagle on the door.

Mercifully, the wait ended and the doors swung open.

Taking a deep breath, Bartellus marched inside.

The room was long, twenty marble pillars supporting a frescoed ceiling. Each pillar carried a burning torch that cast gaunt dancing shadows to the walls beyond, and by each pillar stood a Nadir guard bearing a spear. Eyes fixed firmly ahead, Bartellus marched the fifty paces to the throne on the marble dais.

Upon it sat Ulric, Warlord of the North.

He was not tall, but he radiated power, and as Bartellus moved into the center of the room, he was struck by the sheer dynamism of the man. He had the high cheekbones and midnight hair of the Nadir, but his slanted eyes were violet and striking. The face was swarthy, a trident beard creating a demonic appearance that was belied by the warmth of the man's smile.

But what impressed Bartellus most was that the Nadir lord was wearing a white Drenai robe embroidered with Abalayn's family crest: a golden horse rearing above a silver crown.

The herald bowed deeply.

"My lord, I bring you the greetings of Lord Abalayn, elected leader of the free Drenai people."

Ulric nodded in return, waving a hand for him to continue.

"My lord Abalayn congratulates you on your magnificent victory against the rebels of Gulgothir and hopes that with the horrors of war now behind you, you will be able to consider the new treaties and trade agreements he discussed with you during his most enjoyable stay last spring. I have here a letter from Lord Abalayn, and also the treaties and agreements." Bartellus stepped forward, presenting three scrolls. Ulric took them, placing them gently on the floor beside the throne.

"Thank you, Bartellus," he said. "Tell me, is there truly fear among the Drenai that my army will march on Dros Delnoch?"

"You jest, my lord?"

"Not at all," said Ulric innocently, his voice deep and resonant. "Traders tell me there is great discussion in Drenan."

"Idle gossip merely," said Bartellus. "I helped to draft the agreements myself, and if I can be of any help with the more complex passages, I would consider it a pleasure to assist you."

"No, I am sure they are in order," said Ulric. "But you do realize my shaman Nosta Khan must examine the omens. A primitive custom, I know, but I am sure you understand."

"Of course. Such things are a matter of tradition," said Bartellus.

Ulric clapped his hands twice, and from the shadows to the left came a wizened old man in a dirty goatskin tunic. Under his skinny right arm he carried a white chicken, and in his left hand was a wide, shallow wooden bowl. Ulric stood as he approached, holding out his hands and taking the chicken by the neck and legs.

Slowly Ulric raised it above his head—then, as Bartellus' eyes widened in horror, he lowered the bird and bit through its neck, tearing the head from the body. The wings flapped madly, and blood gushed and spattered, drenching the white robe. Ulric held the quivering carcass over the bowl, watching as the last of its lifeblood stained the wood. Nosta Khan waited until the last drop oozed from the flesh and then lifted the bowl to his lips. He looked up at Ulric and shook his head.

The warlord tossed the bird aside and slowly removed the white robe. Beneath it he wore a black breastplate and a belted sword. From beside the throne he lifted the war helm of black steel, fringed with silver fox fur, and placed it on his head. He wiped his bloody mouth on the Drenai robe and carelessly tossed it toward Bartellus.

The herald looked down at the blood-covered cloth at his feet.

"I am afraid the omens are not pleasant," said Ulric.

◊ 1 ◊

R EK WAS DRUNK. Not enough to matter but enough not
to matter, he thought, staring at the ruby wine casting
blood shadows in the lead crystal glass. A log fire in the
hearth warmed his back, the smoke stinging his eyes, the
acrid smell of it mixing with the odor of unwashed bodies,
forgotten meals, and musty, damp clothing. A lantern flame
danced briefly in the icy wind as a shaft of cold air brushed
the room. Then it was gone as a newcomer slammed shut
the wooden door, muttering his apologies to the crowded
inn.

Conversation, which had died in the sudden blast of
frosty air, now resumed, a dozen voices from different
groups merging into a babble of meaningless sounds. Rek
sipped his wine. He shivered as someone laughed; the
sound was as cold as the winter wind beating against the
wooden walls. Like someone walking over your grave,
he thought. He pulled his blue cloak more tightly about
his shoulders. He did not need to hear the words to know
the topic of every conversation: It had been the same
for days.

War.

Such a little word, such a depth of agony. Blood, death,
conquest, starvation, plague, and horror.

More laughter burst upon the room. "Barbarians!" roared
a voice above the babble. "Easy meat for Drenai lances."
More laughter.

Rek stared at the crystal goblet. So beautiful. So fragile.
Crafted with care, even love, multifaceted like a gossamer

5

diamond. He lifted the crystal close to his face, seeing a dozen eyes reflected there.

And each accused. For a second he wanted to crush the glass into fragments, destroy the eyes and the accusation. But he did not. I am not a fool, he told himself. Not yet.

Horeb, the innkeeper, wiped his thick fingers on a towel and cast a tired yet wary eye over the crowd, alert for trouble, ready to step in with a word and a smile before a snarl and a fist became necessary. War. What was it about the prospect of such bloody enterprises that reduced men to the level of animals? Some of the drinkers—most, in fact— were well known to Horeb. Many were family men: farmers, traders, artisans. All were friendly; most were compassionate, trustworthy, even kindly. And here they were talking of death and glory and ready to thrash or slay any suspected of Nadir sympathies. The Nadir—even the name spoke of contempt.

But they'll learn, he thought sadly. Oh, how they'll learn! Horeb's eyes scanned the large room, warming as they lighted upon his daughters, who were clearing tables and delivering tankards. Tiny Dori blushing beneath her freckles at some ribald jest; Besa, the image of her mother, tall and fair; Nessa, fat and plain and loved by all, soon to marry the baker's apprentice Norvas. Good girls. Gifts of joy. Then his gaze fell on the tall figure in the blue cloak seated by the window.

"Damn you, Rek, snap out of it," he muttered, knowing the man would never hear him. Horeb turned away, cursed, then removed his leather apron and grasped a half-empty jug of ale and a tankard. As an afterthought he opened a small cupboard and removed a bottle of port he had been saving for Nessa's wedding.

"A problem shared is a problem doubled," he said, squeezing into the seat opposite Rek.

"A friend in need is a friend to be avoided," Rek countered, accepting the proffered bottle and refilling his glass. "I knew a general once," he said, staring at the wine, twirling the glass slowly with his long fingers. "Never lost a battle. Never won one, either."

"How so?" asked Horeb.

"You know the answer. I've told you before."

"I have a bad memory. Anyway, I like to listen to you tell stories. How could he never lose and never win?"

"He surrendered whenever threatened," said Rek. "Clever, eh?"

"How come men followed him if he never won?"

"Because he never lost. Neither did they."

"Would you have followed him?" asked Horeb.

"I don't follow anyone anymore. Least of all generals." Rek turned his head, listening to the interweaving chatter. He closed his eyes, concentrating. "Listen to them," he said softly. "Listen to their talk of glory."

"They don't know any better, Rek, my friend. They haven't seen it, tasted it. Crows like a black cloud over a battlefield feasting on dead men's eyes, foxes jerking at severed tendons, worms . . ."

"Stop it, damn you . . . I don't need reminding. Well, I'm damned if I'll go. When's Nessa getting married?"

"In three days," answered Horeb. "He's a good boy; he'll look after her. Keeps baking her cakes. She'll be like a tub before long."

"One way or another," said Rek with a wink.

"Indeed, yes," answered Horeb, grinning broadly. The men sat in their own silence, allowing the noise to wash over them, each drinking and thinking, secure within their circle of two. After a while Rek leaned forward.

"The first attack will be at Dros Delnoch," he said. "Do you know they've only ten thousand men there?"

"I heard it was less than that. Abalayn's been cutting back on the regulars and concentrating on militia. Still, there're six high walls and a strong keep. And Delnar's no fool—he was at the Battle of Skeln."

"Really?" said Rek. "I heard that was one man against ten thousand, hurling mountains on the foe."

"The saga of Druss the Legend," said Horeb, deepening his voice. "The tale of a giant whose eyes were death and whose ax was terror. Gather around, children, and keep from the shadows lest evil lurks as I tell my tale."

"You bastard!" said Rek. "That used to terrify me. You knew him, didn't you—the Legend, I mean?"

"A long time ago. They say he's dead. If not, he must be

over sixty. We were in three campaigns together, but I only spoke to him twice. I saw him in action once, though."

"Was he good?" asked Rek.

"Awesome. It was just before Skeln and the defeat of the Immortals. Just a skirmish, really. Yes, he was very good."

"You're not terribly strong on detail, Horeb."

"You want me to sound like the rest of these fools, jabbering about war and death and slaying?"

"No," said Rek, draining his wine. "No, I don't. You know me, don't you?"

"Enough to like you. Regardless."

"Regardless of what?"

"Regardless of the fact that you don't like yourself."

"On the contrary," said Rek, pouring a fresh glass, "I like myself well enough. It's just that I know myself better than most people."

"You know, Rek, sometimes I think you ask too much of yourself."

"No. No, I ask very little. I know my weaknesses."

"It's a funny thing about weakness," said Horeb. "Most people will tell you they know their weaknesses. When asked, they tell you, 'Well, for one thing I'm overgenerous.' Come on, then; list yours if you must. That's what innkeepers are for."

"Well, for one thing I'm overgenerous, especially to innkeepers."

Horeb shook his head, smiled, and lapsed into silence.

Too intelligent to be a hero, too frightened to be a coward, he thought. He watched his friend empty his glass, lift it to his face, and peer at his own fragmented image. For a moment Horeb thought he would smash it, such had been the anger on Rek's flushed face.

Then the younger man gently returned the goblet to the wooden table.

"I'm not a fool," he said softly. He stiffened as he realized he had spoken aloud. "Damn!" he said. "The drink finally got to me."

"Let me give you a hand to your room," offered Horeb.

"Is there a candle lit?" asked Rek, swaying in his seat.

"Of course."

"You won't let it go out on me, will you? Not keen on the dark. Not frightened, you understand. Just don't like it."

"I won't let it go out, Rek. Trust me."

"I trust you. I rescued you, didn't I? Remember?"

"I remember. Give me your arm. I'll guide you to the stairs. This way. That's good. One foot in front of the other. Good!"

"I didn't hesitate. Straight in with my sword raised, didn't I?"

"Yes."

"No, I didn't. I stood for two minutes, shaking. And you got cut."

"But you still came in, Rek. Don't you see? It didn't matter about the cut—you still rescued me."

"It matters to me. Is there a candle in my room?"

Behind him was the fortress, grim and gray, outlined in flame and smoke. The sounds of battle filled his ears, and he ran, heart pounding, his breathing ragged. He glanced behind him. The fortress was close, closer than it had been. Ahead were the green hills sheltering the Sentran Plain. They shimmered and retreated before him, taunting him with their tranquility. He ran faster. A shadow fell across him. The gates of the fortress opened. He strained against the force pulling him back. He cried and begged. But the gates closed, and he was back at the center of the battle, a bloody sword in his shaking hand.

He awoke, eyes wide, nostrils flared, the beginning of a scream swelling his lungs. A soft hand stroked his face, and gentle words soothed him. His eyes focused. Dawn was nearing, the pink light of a virgin day piercing the ice on the inside of the bedroom window. He rolled over.

"You were troubled in the night," Besa told him, her hand stroking his brow. He smiled, pulled the goosedown quilt over his shoulder, and drew her to him under the covers.

"I'm not troubled now," said Rek. "How could I be?" The warmth of her body aroused him, and his fingers caressed her back.

"Not today," she said, kissing him lightly on the forehead

and pulling away. She threw back the quilt, shivered, and ran across the room, gathering her clothes. "It's cold," she said. "Colder than yesterday."

"It's warm in here," he offered, raising himself to watch her dress. She blew him a kiss.

"You're fine to romp with, Rek. But I'll have no children by you. Now, get out of that bed. We've a party of travelers coming in this morning, and the room is let."

"You're a beautiful woman, Besa. If I had any sense, I'd marry you."

"Then it's a good job you have none, for I'd turn you down and your ego would never stand it. I'm looking for someone more solid." Her smile took the sting from her words. Almost.

The door opened, and Horeb bustled in bearing a copper tray containing bread, cheese, and a tankard.

"How's the head?" he asked, placing the tray on the wooden table by the bed.

"Fine," said Rek. "Is that orange juice?"

"It is, and it'll cost you dear. Nessa waylaid the Vagrian trader as he left the ship. She waited an hour and risked frostbite just to get oranges for you. I don't think you're worth it."

"True." Rek smiled. "Sad but true."

"Are you really heading south today?" asked Besa as Rek sipped his fruit juice. He nodded. "You're a fool. I thought you'd had enough of Reinard."

"I'll avoid him. Are my clothes cleaned?"

"Dori spent hours on them," said Besa. "And for what? So that you can get them filthy in Graven Forest."

"That's not the point. One should always look one's best when leaving a city." He glanced at the tray. "I can't face the cheese."

"Doesn't matter," said Horeb. "It's still on the bill!"

"In that case I'll force myself to eat it. Any other travelers today?"

"There's a spice caravan heading for Lentria that will go through Graven. Twenty men, well armed. They're taking the circular route south and west. There's a woman traveling alone, but she's already left," said Horeb. "Lastly there's a group of pilgrims. But they don't leave until to-morrow."

"A woman?"

"Not quite," said Besa. "But almost."

"Now, girl," said Horeb, smiling broadly, "it's not like you to be catty. A tall girl with a fine horse. And she's armed."

"I could have traveled with her," said Rek. "It might have made the journey more pleasant."

"And she could have protected you from Reinard," said Besa. "She looked the part. Now come on, Regnak, get dressed. I've not the time to sit here and watch you break-fast like a lord. You've caused enough chaos in this house."

"I can't get up while you're here," protested Rek. "It wouldn't be decent."

"You idiot," she said, gathering up the tray. "Get him up, Father, else he'll lie there all day."

"She's right, Rek," said Horeb as the door closed behind her. "It's time for you to move, and knowing how long it takes you to prepare your public appearance, I think I'll leave you to get on with it."

"One must look one's best—"

"When leaving a city. I know. That's what you always say, Rek. I'll see you downstairs."

Once he was alone, Rek's manner changed, the laughter lines about his eyes easing into marks of tension, sorrow al-most. The Drenai were finished as a world power. Ulric and the Nadir tribes had already begun their march upon Drenan, and they would ride into the cities of the plains on rivers of blood. Should every Drenai warrior kill thirty tribesmen, still there would be hundreds of thousands left.

The world was changing, and Rek was running out of places to hide.

He thought of Horeb and his daughters. For six hundred years the Drenai race had stamped civilization on a world ill suited to it. They had conquered savagely, taught wisely, and in the main ruled well. But they had arrived at their sunset, and a new empire was waiting, ready to rise from the blood and ashes of the old. He thought again of Horeb and laughed. Whatever happens, there is one old man who will survive, he thought. Even the Nadir need good inns.

And the daughters? How would they fare when the hordes burst the city gates? Bloody images flooded his mind.

"Damn!" he shouted, rolling from the bed to push open the ice-sealed window.

The winter wind struck his bed-warmed body, snatching his mind back to the reality of today and the long ride south. He crossed to the bench on which his clothes had been laid out and swiftly dressed. The white woolen undershirt and the blue hose were gifts from gentle Dori, the tunic with gold embroidered collar a legacy of better days in Vagria, the reversed sheepskin jerkin and gold ties a present from Horeb, and the thigh-length doeskin boots a surprise gift from a weary traveler at an outland inn. And he must have been surprised, thought Rek, remembering the thrill of fear and excitement as he had crept into the man's room to steal them only a month earlier. By the wardrobe stood a full-length bronze mirror, where Rek took a long look at his reflection. He saw a tall man with shoulder-length brown hair and a well-trimmed mustache, cutting a fine figure in his stolen boots. He looped his baldric over his head and placed his longsword in the black and silver sheath.

"What a hero," he told his reflection, a cynical smile on his lips. "What a gem of a hero." He drew the sword and parried and thrust at the air, one eye on his reflection. The wrist was still supple, the grasp sure. Whatever else you are not, he told himself, you are a swordsman. From the sill by the window he took the silver circlet talisman—his good-luck charm since he had stolen it from a brothel in Lentria—and placed it over his forehead, sweeping his dark hair back over his ears.

"You may not actually be magnificent," he told his reflection, "but by all the gods in Missael you *look* it!"

The eyes smiled back at him. "Don't you mock me, Regnak Wanderer," he said. Throwing his cloak over his arm, he strolled downstairs to the long room, casting an eye over the early crowd. Horeb hailed him from the bar.

"Now, that's more like it, Rek my lad," he said, leaning back in mock admiration. "You could have stepped straight from one of Sieben's poems. Drink?"

"No. I think I will leave it a while yet—like ten years.

Last night's brew is still fermenting in my gullet. Have you packed me some of your vile food for the journey?"

"Maggoty biscuits, mildewed cheese, and a two-year-old back of bacon that will come when you call it," answered Horeb. "And a flask of the worst—"

Conversation ceased as the seer entered the inn, his faded blue habit flapping against bony legs, his quarterstaff tapping on the wooden boards. Rek swallowed his disgust at the man's appearance and avoided glancing at the ruined sockets where once the man's eyes had been.

The old man pushed out a hand on which the third finger was missing. "Silver for your future," he said, his voice like a dry wind whispering through winter branches.

"Why do they do it?" whispered Horeb.

"Their eyes, you mean?" countered Rek.

"Yes. How can a man put out his own eyes?"

"Damned if I know. They say it aids their visions."

"Sounds about as sensible as cutting off your staff in order to aid your sex life."

"It takes all sorts, Horeb, old friend."

Drawn by the sound of their voices, the old man hobbled nearer, hand outstretched. "Silver for your future," he intoned. Rek turned away.

"Go on, Rek," urged Horeb. "See if the journey bodes well. Where's the harm?"

"You pay. I will listen," said Rek.

Horeb thrust a hand deep into the pocket of his leather apron and dropped a small silver coin into the old man's palm. "For my friend here," he said. "I know my future."

The old man squatted on the wooden floor and reached into a tattered pouch, producing a fistful of sand, which he sprinkled about him. Then he produced six knucklebones bearing crafted runes.

"They're human bones, aren't they?" whispered Horeb.

"So they say," answered Rek. The old man began to chant in the Elder tongue, his quavering voice echoing in the silence. He threw the bones to the sandy floor, then ran his hands over the runes.

"I have the truth," he said at last.

"Never mind the truth, old man. Give me a tale full of golden lies and glorious maidens."

"I have the truth," said the seer, as if he had not heard.

"The hell with it!" said Rek. "Tell me the truth, old man."

"Do you desire to hear it, man?"

"Never mind the damned ritual, just speak and begone!"

"Steady, Rek, steady! It's his way," said Horeb.

"Maybe. But he's going a long way toward spoiling my day. They never give good news, anyway. The old bastard's probably going to tell me I shall catch the plague."

"He wishes the truth," said Horeb, following the ritual, "and will use it wisely and well."

"Indeed he does not and will not," said the seer. "But destiny must be heard. You do not wish to hear words of your death, Regnak the Wanderer, son of Argas, and so I will withhold them. You are a man of uncertain character and only a sporadic courage. You are a thief and a dreamer, and your destiny will both haunt and hunt you. You will run to avoid it, yet your steps will carry you toward it. But then, this you know, Longshanks, for you dreamed it yestereve."

"Is that it, old man? That meaningless garbage? Is that fair trading for a silver coin?"

"The earl and the legend will be together at the wall. And men shall dream, and men shall die, but shall the fortress fall?"

The old man turned and was gone.

"What was your dream last night, Rek?" asked Horeb.

"You surely don't believe that idiocy, Horeb?"

"What was your dream?" the innkeeper persisted.

"I didn't dream at all. I slept like a log. Except for that bloody candle. You left it on all night, and it stank. You must be more careful. It could have started a fire. Every time I stop here, I warn you about those candles. You never listen."

◇ 2 ◇

REK WATCHED IN silence as the groom saddled the chestnut gelding. He did not like the horse; it had a mean eye, and its ears lay flat against its skull. The groom, a young slim boy, was crooning gently to it as his shaking fingers tightened the girth.

"Why couldn't you get a gray?" asked Rek. Horeb laughed.

"Because it would have taken you one step too many toward farce. Understatement is the thing, Rek. You already look like a peacock, and as it is, every Lentrian sailor will be chasing you. No, a chestnut's the thing." More seriously he added, "And in Graven you may wish to be inconspicuous. A tall white horse is not easily missed."

"I don't think it likes me. See the way it looks at me?"

"Its sire was one of the fastest horses in Drenan; its dam was a war-horse in Woundweaver's lancers. You couldn't get a better pedigree."

"What is it called?" asked Rek, still unconvinced.

"Lancer," answered Horeb.

"That has a nice ring to it. Lancer . . . Well, maybe . . . just maybe."

"Daffodil's ready, sir," said the groom, backing away from the chestnut. The horse swung its head, snapping at the retreating boy, who stumbled and fell on the cobbles.

"Daffodil?" said Rek. "You bought me a horse called *Daffodil?*"

"What's in a name, Rek?" answered Horeb innocently. "Call it what you like; you must admit it's a fine beast."

15

"If I didn't have a fine sense for the ridiculous, I would have it muzzled. Where are the girls?"

"Too busy to be waving good-bye to layabouts who rarely pay their bills. Now, be off with you."

Rek advanced gingerly toward the gelding, speaking softly. It turned a baleful eye on him but allowed him to swing into the high-backed saddle. He gathered the reins, adjusted his blue cloak to just the right angle over the horse's back, and swung the beast toward the gate.

"Rek, I almost forgot," called Horeb, pushing back toward the house. "Wait a moment!" The burly innkeeper disappeared from sight, emerging seconds later carrying a short bow of horn and yew and a quiver of black-shafted arrows. "Here. A customer left this behind in part payment some months ago. It looks like a sturdy weapon."

"Wonderful," said Rek. "I used to be a fine bowman."

"Yes," said Horeb. "Just remember when you use it that the sharp end is pointed away from you. Now begone—and take care."

"Thanks, Horeb. You, too. And remember what I said about candles."

"I will. On your way, boy. Be lucky now."

Rek rode from the south gate as the watchmen trimmed the lantern wicks. The dawn shadows were shrinking on the streets of Drenan, and young children played beneath the portcullis. He had chosen the southern route for the most obvious of reasons. The Nadir were marching from the north, and the fastest way from a battle was a straight line in the opposite direction.

Flicking his heels, he urged the gelding forward toward the south. To his left the rising sun was breasting the blue peaks of the eastern mountains. The sky was blue, birds sang, and the sounds of an awakening city came from behind him. But the sun was rising, Rek knew, on the Nadir. For the Drenai it was dusk on the last day.

Topping a rise, he gazed down on Graven Forest, white and virginal under the winter snow. And yet it was a place of evil legends that normally he would have avoided. The fact that instead he chose to enter showed he knew two things: First, the legends were built around the activities of a living man; second, he knew that man.

Reinard.

He and his band of bloodthirsty cutthroats had their headquarters in Graven and were an open, festering sore in the body of trade. Caravans were sacked, pilgrims were murdered, women were raped. Yet an army could not seek them out, so vast was the forest.

Reinard. Sired by a prince of hell, born to a noblewoman of Ulalia. Or so he told it. Rek had heard that his mother was a Lentrian whore and his father a nameless sailor. He had never repeated this intelligence; he did not, as the phrase went, have the guts for it. Even if he had, he mused, he would not keep them long once he tried it. One of Reinard's favorite pastimes with prisoners was to roast sections of them over hot coals and serve the meat to those poor unfortunates taken prisoner with them. If he met Reinard, the best thing would be to flatter the hell out of him. And if that did not work, to give him the latest news, send him in the direction of the nearest caravan, and ride swiftly from his domain.

Rek had made sure he knew the details of all the caravans passing through Graven and their probable routes. Silks, jewels, spices, slaves, cattle. In truth he had no wish to part with this information. Nothing would please him better than to ride through Graven quietly, knowing the caravaners' fate was in the lap of the gods.

The chestnut's hooves made little sound on the snow, and Rek kept the pace to a gentle walk in case hidden roots should cause the horse to stumble. The cold began to work its way through his warm clothing, and his feet were soon feeling frozen within the doeskin boots. He reached into his pack and pulled out a pair of sheepskin mittens.

The horse plodded on. At noon Rek stopped for a brief, cold meal, hobbling the gelding by a frozen stream. With a thick Vagrian dagger he chipped away the ice, allowing the beast to drink, then gave him a handful of oats. He stroked the long neck, and the chestnut's head came up sharply, teeth bared. Rek leapt backward, falling into a deep snowdrift. He lay there for a moment, then smiled.

"I knew you didn't like me," he said. The horse turned to look at him and snorted.

As he was about to mount, Rek glanced at the horse's hindquarters. Deep switch scars showed by the tail.

Gently, his hand moved over them. "So," he said, "some-one took a whip to you, eh, Daffodil? Didn't break your spirit, did they, boy?" He swung into the saddle. With luck, he reckoned, he should be free of the forest in five days.

Gnarled oaks with twisted roots cast ominous dusk shad-ows across the track, and night breezes set the branches to whispering as Rek walked the gelding deeper into the for-est. The moon was rising above the trees, casting a ghostly light on the trail. Teeth chattering, he began to cast about for a good camping site, finding one an hour later in a small hollow by an ice-covered pool. He built a stall in some bushes to keep the worst of the wind from the horse, fed it, and then built a small fire by a fallen oak and a large boulder. Out of the wind, the heat reflected from the stone, Rek brewed tea to help down his dried beef; then he pulled his blanket over his shoulders, leaned against the oak, and watched the flames dance.

A skinny fox poked its snout through a bush, peering at the fire. On impulse, Rek threw it a strip of beef. The an-imal flicked its eyes from the man to the morsel and back again before darting out to snatch the meat from the frozen ground. Then it vanished into the night. Rek held out his hands to the fire and thought of Horeb.

The burly innkeeper had raised him after Rek's father had been killed in the northern wars against the Sathuli. Honest, loyal, strong, and dependable—Horeb was all of those. And he was kind, a prince among men.

Rek had managed to repay him one well-remembered night when three Vagrian deserters had attacked him in an alley near the inn.

Luckily Rek had been drinking, and when he had first heard the sound of steel on steel, he had rushed forward. Within the alley Horeb had been fighting a losing battle, his kitchen knife no match for three swordsmen. Yet the old man had been a warrior and had moved well. Rek had been frozen to the spot, his own sword forgotten. He had tried to move forward, but his legs had refused the order. Then a sword had cut through Horeb's guard, opening a huge wound in his leg.

Rek had screamed, and the sound had released his terror.

The bloody skirmish was over in seconds. Rek took out the first assailant with a throat slash, parried a thrust from the second, and shoulder-charged the third into a wall. From the ground Horeb grabbed the third man, pulling him down and stabbing out with his kitchen knife. The second man fled into the night.

"You were wonderful, Rek," said Horeb. "Believe me, you fight like a veteran."

Veterans don't freeze with fear, thought Rek.

Now he fed some twigs to the flames. A cloud obscured the moon, and an owl hooted. Rek's shaking hand curled around his dagger.

Damn the dark, he thought. And curse all heroes!

He had been a soldier for a while, stationed at Dros Corteswain, and had enjoyed it. But then the Sathuli skirmishes had become a border war, and the enjoyment had palled. He had done well, been promoted; his senior officers had told him he had a fine feel for tactics. But they did not know about the sleepless nights. His men had respected him, he thought. But that was because he was careful, even cautious. He had left before his nerve could betray him.

"Are you mad, Rek?" Gan Javi had asked him when he had resigned his commission. "The war is expanding. We've got more troops coming, and a fine officer like you can be sure of promotion. You'll lead more than a century in six months. You could be offered the gan eagle."

"I know all that, sir, and believe me, I'm really sorry I shall be missing the action. But it's a question of family business. Damn, I would cut off my right arm to stay; you know that."

"I do, boy. And we'll miss you, by Missael. Your troop will be shattered. If you change your mind, there will be a place for you here. Any time. You're a born soldier."

"I'll remember that, sir. Thank you for all your help and encouragement."

"One more thing, Rek," said Gan Javi, leaning back in his carved chair. "You know there are rumors that the Nadir are preparing a march on the south?"

"There are always rumors of that, sir," answered Rek.

"I know; they've been circulating for years. But this

Ulric is a canny one. He's conquered most of the tribes now, and I think he's almost ready."

"But Abalayn has just signed a treaty with him," said Rek. "Mutual peace in return for trade concessions and financing for his building program."

"That's what I mean, lad. I'll say nothing against Abalayn; he's ruled the Drenai for twenty years. But you don't stop a wolf by feeding it—believe me! Anyway, what I'm saying is that men like yourselves will be needed before long, so don't get rusty."

The last thing the Drenai needed now was a man who was afraid of the dark. What they needed was another Karnak the One-Eyed—a score of them. An Earl of Bronze. A hundred like Druss the Legend. And even if, by some miracle, this were to happen, would even these stem the tide of half a million tribesmen?

Who could even picture such a number?

They would wash over Dros Delnoch like an angry sea, Rek knew.

If I thought there was a chance, I still wouldn't go. Face it, he thought. Even if victory was certain, still he would avoid the battle.

Who will care in a hundred years whether the Drenai survived? It would be like Skeln Pass, shrouded in legend and glorified beyond truth.

War!

Flies settling like a black stain over a man's entrails as he wept with the pain and held his body together with crimson fingers, hoping for a miracle. Hunger, cold, fear, disease, gangrene, death!

War for soldiers.

The day he had left Dros Corteswain, he had been approached by one of the culs, who had nervously offered him a tightly-wrapped bundle.

"From the troop, sir," he had said.

He had opened it, embarrassed and empty of words, to see a blue cloak with an eagle clasp in crafted bronze.

"I don't know how to thank you all."

"The men want me to say ... well, we're sorry you're leaving. That's all, sir."

"I'm sorry, too, Korvac. Family business, you know?"

The man had nodded, probably wishing he had family business that would allow him to depart the Dros. But culs had no commission to resign; only the dun class could leave a fortress during a war.

"Well, good luck, sir. See you soon, I hope . . . we all hope."

"Yes! Soon."

That had been two years ago. Gan Javi had died from a stroke, and several of Rek's brother officers had been killed in the Sathuli battles. No message had reached him of individual culs.

The days passed—cold, gloomy, but mercifully without incident—until the morning of the fifth day, when, on a high trail skirting a grove of elm, he heard the one sound he disliked above all others: the clash of steel on steel. He should have ridden on; he *knew* he should. But for some reason his curiosity fractionally outweighed his fear. He hobbled the horse, swung the quiver to his back, and strung the horn bow. Then carefully he worked his way through the trees and down into the snow-covered glen. Moving stealthily, with catlike care, he came to a clearing. Sounds of battle echoed in the glade.

A young woman in armor of silver and bronze stood with her back to a tree, desperately fending off a combined assault from three outlaws, burly men and bearded, armed with swords and daggers. The woman held a slender blade, a flickering, dancing rapier that cut and thrust with devastating speed.

The three, clumsy swordsmen at best, were hampering each other. But the girl was tiring fast.

These were Reinard's men, Rek knew, cursing his own curiosity. One of them cried out as the rapier lanced across his forearm.

"Take that, you dung beetle," shouted the girl.

Rek smiled. Not a beauty, but she could fence.

He notched an arrow to his bow and waited for the right moment to let fly. The girl ducked under a vicious cut and flashed her blade through the eye of the swordsman. As he screamed and fell, the other two fell back, more wary now; they moved apart, ready to attack from both flanks. The girl had been dreading this moment, for there was no defense but flight. Her gaze flickered from man to man. Take the tall one first, forget about the other, and hope his first thrust is not mortal. *Maybe* she could take them both with her.

The tall one moved to the left while his comrade crossed to the right. At that moment Rek loosed a shaft at the tall outlaw's back that lanced through his left calf. Swiftly he notched a second arrow as the bewildered man spun around, saw Rek, and hobbled toward him, screaming hatred.

Rek drew back the string until it touched his cheek, locked his left arm, and loosed the shaft.

This time the aim was slightly better. He had been aiming for the chest—the largest target—but the arrow was high, and now the outlaw lay on his back, the black shaft jutting from his forehead and blood bubbling to the snow.

"You took your time getting involved," said the girl coolly, stepping across the body of the third outlaw and wiping her slender blade on his shirt.

Rek tore his eyes from the face of the man he had killed.

"I just saved your life," he said, checking an angry retort.

She was tall and well built, almost mannish, Rek thought, her hair long and mousy blond, unkempt. Her eyes were blue and deep-set beneath thick dark brows that indicated an uncertain temper. Her figure was disguised by the silver steel mail shirt and bronze shoulder pads; her legs were encased in shapeless green woolen trews laced to the thigh with leather straps.

"Well, what are you staring at?" she demanded. "Never seen a woman before?"

"Well, that answers the first question," he said.

"What does that mean?"

"You're a woman."

"Oh, very dry!" She retrieved a sheepskin jerkin from beneath the tree, dusting off the snow, and slipping it on. It did nothing to enhance her appearance, thought Rek.

"They attacked me," she said. "Killed my horse, the bastards! Where's your horse?"

"Your gratitude overwhelms me," said Rek, an edge of anger in his voice. "Those are Reinard's men."

"Really? Friend of yours, is he?"

"Not exactly. But if he knew what I had done, he would

roast my eyes on a fire and serve them to me as an appetizer."

"All right, I appreciate your point. I'm extremely grateful. Now, where's your horse?"

Rek ignored her, gritting his teeth against his anger. He walked to the dead outlaw and dragged his arrows clear, wiping them on the man's jerkin. Then he methodically searched the pockets of all three. Seven silver coins and several gold rings the richer, he then returned to the girl.

"My horse has one saddle. I ride it," he said icily. "I've done about all I want to do for you. You're on your own now."

"Damned chivalrous of you," she said.

"Chivalry isn't my strong point," he said, turning away.

"Neither is marksmanship," she retorted.

"What?"

"You were aiming for his back from twenty paces, and you hit his leg. It's because you closed one eye, ruined your perspective."

"Thanks for the archery instruction. Good luck!"

"Wait!" she said. He turned. "I need your horse."

"So do I."

"I will pay you."

"He's not for sale."

"All right. Then I will pay you to take me to where I can buy a horse."

"How much?" he asked.

"One golden Raq."

"Five," he said.

"I could buy three horses for that," she stormed.

"It's a seller's market," he retorted.

"Two, and that's final."

"Three."

"All right, three. Now, where's your horse?"

"First the money, my lady." He held out a hand. Her blue eyes were frosty as she removed the coins from a leather pouch and placed them in his palm. "My name is Regnak, Rek to my friends," he said.

"That's of no interest to me," she assured him.

◊ 3 ◊

THEY RODE IN a silence as frosty as the weather, the tall girl behind Rek in the saddle. He resisted the urge to spur the horse on at speed despite the fear gnawing at his belly. It would be unfair to say he was sorry he had rescued her; after all, it had done wonders for his self-esteem. His fear was of meeting Reinard now. This girl would never sit silent while he flattered and lied. And even if by some stroke of good fortune she did keep her mouth shut, she would certainly report him for giving information on caravan movements.

The horse stumbled on a hidden root, and the girl pitched sideways. Rek's hand lanced out, catching her arm and hauling her back in the saddle.

"Put your arms around my waist, will you," he said.

"How much will it cost me?"

"Just do it. It's too cold to argue."

Her arms slid around him, her head resting against his back.

Thick, dark clouds bunched above them, and the temperature began to drop.

"We ought to make an early camp," he stated. "The weather's closing in."

"I agree," she said.

Snow began to fall, and the wind picked up. Rek dipped his head against the force of the storm, blinking against the cold flakes that blew into his eyes. He steered the gelding away from the trail and into the shelter of the trees, gripping the pommel of his saddle as the horse climbed a steep incline.

24

An open campsite would be folly, he knew, in this freak storm. They needed a cave, or at least the lee of a rock face. For over an hour they moved on until at last they entered a clearing circled by oak and gorse. Within it was a crofter's hut of log walls and earthen roof. Rek glanced at the stone chimney: no smoke.

He heeled the tired gelding forward. At the side of the hut was a three-sided lean-to with a wicker roof bent by the weight of the snow upon it. He steered the horse inside.

"Dismount," he told the girl, but her hands did not move from his waist. He glanced down. The hands were blue, and he rubbed at them furiously. "Wake up!" he shouted. "Wake up, damn you!" Pulling her hands free, he slid from the saddle and caught her as she fell. Her lips were blue, her hair thick with ice. Lifting her over one shoulder, he removed the packs from the gelding, loosened the girth, and carried the girl to the hut. The wooden door was open, snow drifting into the cold interior as he stepped inside.

The hut was one-roomed. He saw a cot in the corner beneath the only window, a hearth, some simple cupboards, and a wood store—enough for two, maybe three nights—stacked against the far wall. There were three crudely made chairs and a bench table roughly cut from an elm trunk. Rek tipped the unconscious girl on to the cot, found a stick broom under the table, and swept the snow from the room. He pushed the door shut, but a rotten leather hinge gave way and it tilted open again at the top. Cursing, he pulled the table to the doorway and heaved it against the frame.

Tearing open his pack, Rek pulled his tinderbox free and moved to the hearth. Whoever had owned or built the holding had left a fire ready laid, as was the custom in the wild. Rek opened his small tinder pouch, making a mound of shredded dry leaves beneath the twigs in the grate. Over this he poured a little lantern oil from a leather flask and then struck his flint. His cold fingers were clumsy and the sparks would not take, so he stopped for a moment, forcing himself to take slow deep breaths. Then again he struck the flint, and this time a small flame flickered in the tinder and caught. He leaned forward, gently blowing it; then, as the twigs flared, he turned to sort smaller branches from the store, placing them gently atop the tiny fire. Flames danced higher.

He carried two chairs to the hearth, placed his blankets over them before the blaze, and returned to the girl. She lay on the crude cot, scarcely breathing.

"It's the bloody armor," he said. He fumbled with the straps of her jerkin, turning her over to pull it loose. Swiftly he stripped off her clothing and set to work rubbing warmth into her. He glanced at the fire, placed three more logs to feed the blaze, and then spread the blankets on the floor before it. Lifting the girl from the cot, he laid her back before the hearth, turning her over to rub her back.

"Don't you die on me!" he stormed, pummeling the flesh of her legs. "Don't you damn well dare!" He wiped her hair with a towel and wrapped her in the blankets. The floor was cold, and frost seeped up from beneath the hut, so he pulled the cot to the hearth, then strained to lift her onto the bed. Her pulse was slow but steady.

He gazed down at her face. It was beautiful. Not in any classic sense, he knew, for the brows were too thick and thunderous, the chin too square, and the lips too full. Yet there was strength there, and courage and determination. But more than this: In sleep a gentle, childlike quality found expression.

He kissed her gently.

Buttoning his sheepskin jacket, he pulled the table aside and stepped out into the storm. The gelding snorted as he approached. There was straw in the lean-to; taking a handful, he rubbed the horse's back.

"Going to be a cold night, boy. But you should be all right in here." He spread the saddle blanket over the gelding's broad back, fed him some oats, and returned to the hut.

The girl's color was better now, and she slept peacefully.

Searching the cupboards, Rek found an old iron pan. From his pack, he took out a pound of dried beef and set about making soup. He was warmer now and removed his cloak and jacket. Outside the wind beat against the walls as the storm's fury grew, but inside the fire blazed warmth and a soft red light filled the cabin. Rek pulled off his boots and rubbed his toes. He felt good. Alive.

And damned hungry!

He took a leather-covered clay mug from his pack and

tried the soup. The girl stirred, and he toyed with the idea of waking her but dismissed it. As she was, she was lovely. Awake, she was a harridan. She rolled over and moaned, a long leg pushing from the blanket. Rek grinned as he remembered her body. Not at all mannish! She was just big but wonderfully proportioned. He stared at her leg, the smile fading. He pictured himself naked alongside her . . .

"No, no, Rek," he said aloud. "Forget it."

He covered her with the blanket and returned to his soup. Be prepared, he told himself. When she wakes, she will accuse you of taking advantage of her and cut your eyes out.

Taking his cloak, he wrapped it around himself and stretched out beside the fire. The floor was warmer now. Adding some logs to the blaze, he pillowed his head on his arm and watched the dancers in the flames circle and jump, twist and turn . . .

He slept.

He awoke to the smell of frying bacon. The hut was warm, and his arm felt swollen and cramped. He stretched, groaned, and sat up. The girl was nowhere in sight. Then the door opened, and she stepped inside, brushing snow from her jerkin.

"I've seen to your horse," she said. "Are you fit to eat?"

"Yes. What time is it?"

"Sun's been up for about three hours. The snow's letting up."

He pushed his aching body upright, stretching the tight muscles of his back. "Too much time in Drenan in soft beds," he commented.

"That probably accounts for the paunch," she noted.

"Paunch? I've a curved spine. Anyway, it's relaxed muscle." He looked down. "All right, it's a paunch. A few more days of this and it will go."

"I don't doubt it," she said. "Anyway, we were lucky to find this place."

"Yes, we were." The conversation died as she turned the bacon. Rek was uncomfortable in the silence, and they began to speak at the same time.

"This is ridiculous," she said finally.

"Yes," he agreed. "Bacon smells good."

"Look . . . I want to thank you. There—it's said."

"It was a pleasure. What about starting again, as if we had never met? My name is Rek." He held out a hand.

"Virae," she said, grasping his wrist in the warrior's grip.

"My pleasure," he said. "And what brings you to Graven Forest, Virae?"

"None of your damned business," she snapped.

"I thought we were starting afresh," he said.

"I'm sorry. Really! Look, it's not easy being friendly—I don't like you very much."

"How can you say that? We've only said about ten words to each other. A bit early for character assessment, isn't it?"

"I know your kind," she said. Taking two platters, she deftly flipped the bacon from the pan and handed him a plate. "Arrogant. Think you're the gods' gift to the world. Footloose."

"And what's wrong with that?" he asked. "Nobody's perfect. I enjoy my life; it's the only one I've got."

"It's people like you who have wrecked this country," she told him. "People who don't care, people who live for today. The greedy and the selfish. We used to be great."

"Rubbish. We used to be warriors, conquering everybody, stamping Drenai rules on the world. A pox on it!"

"There was nothing wrong with that! The people we conquered prospered, didn't they? We built schools, hospitals, roads. We encouraged trade and gave the world Drenai law."

"Then you shouldn't be too upset," he told her, "that the world is changing. Now it will be Nadir law. The only reason the Drenai conquered was that the outlying nations had had their day. They were fat and lazy, full of selfish, greedy people who didn't care. All nations fall that way."

"Oh, so you're a philosopher, are you?" she said. "Well, I consider your opinions to be as worthless as you are."

"Oh, now I'm worthless? What do you know of 'worthless,' prancing around dressed as a man? You're an imitation warrior. If you're so eager to uphold Drenai values, why don't you get off to Dros Delnoch with the other fools and wave your pretty little sword at the Nadir?"

"I've just come from there, and I'm going back as soon as I have accomplished what I set out to do," she said icily.

"Then you're an idiot," he said lamely.

"You were a soldier, weren't you?" she said.

"What's that to you?"

"Why did you leave the army?"

"None of your damned business." He paused, then, to break the awkward silence, went on: "We should be at Glen Frenae by this afternoon; it's only a small village, but they do sell horses."

They finished their meal without speaking, Rek feeling angry and uncomfortable yet lacking the skill to pierce the gap between them. She cleared the platters and cleaned out the pan, awkward in her mail shirt.

Virae was furious with herself. She had not meant to quarrel with him. For hours as he slept she had crept about the cabin so as not to disturb him. At first when she woke she had been angry and embarrassed by what he had done, but she knew enough about frostbite and exposure to realize he had saved her life. And he had not taken advantage. If he had done so, she would have killed him without regret or hesitation. She had studied him as he slept. In a strange way he was handsome, she thought, then decided that although he was good-looking after a fashion, it was some indefinable quality that made him attractive—a gentleness, perhaps? A certain sensitivity? It was hard to pinpoint.

Why should he be so attractive? It angered her; she had no time now for romance. Then a bitter thought struck her: She had never had time for romance. Or was it that romance had never had time for her? She was clumsy as a woman, unsure of herself in the company of men, unless in combat or comradeship. His words came again in her mind: "What do you know of 'worthless,' prancing around dressed as a man?"

Twice he had saved her life. Why had she said she disliked him? Because she was frightened?

She heard him walk from the hut and then heard a strange voice.

"Regnak, my dear! Is it true you have a woman inside?"

She reached for her sword.

◊ 4 ◊

THE ABBOT PLACED his hands on the head of the young albino kneeling before him and closed his eyes. He spoke, mind to mind, in the manner of the order.

"Are you prepared?"

"How can I tell?" answered the albino.

"Release your mind to me," said the abbot. The young man relaxed his control; the image of the abbot's kindly face overlapped his thoughts. His thoughts swam, interweaving with the memories of the older man. The abbot's powerful personality covered his own like a comforting blanket, and he slept.

Release was painful, and his fears returned as the abbot woke him. Once again he was Serbitar, and his thoughts were his own.

"Am I prepared?" he asked.

"You will be. The messenger comes."

"Is he worthy?"

"Judge for yourself. Follow me to Graven."

Their spirits soared, entwined, high above the monastery, free as the winter wind. Below them lay the snow-covered fields at the edge of the forest. The abbot pulsed them onward, over the trees. In a clearing by a crofter's hut stood a group of men facing a doorway in which stood a tall young man, and behind him was a woman, sword in hand.

"Which is the messenger?" asked the albino.

"Observe," answered the abbot.

Reinard had not had things going his way just recently. An attack on a caravan had been beaten off with heavy losses, and then three more of his men had been found dead at dusk, among them his brother Erlik. A prisoner he had taken two days previously had died of fright long before the real entertainment could begin, and the weather had turned for the worse. Bad luck was haunting him, and he was at a loss to understand why.

Damn the speaker, he thought bitterly as he led his men toward the cabin. If he had not been in one of his three-day sleeps, the attack on the caravan would have been avoided. Reinard had toyed with the idea of removing his feet as he slept, but good sense and greed had just held sway. Speaker was invaluable. He had come out of his trance as Reinard had carried Erlik's body back to the camp.

"Do you see what has happened while you slept?" Reinard had stormed.

"You lost eight men in a bad raid, and a woman slew Erlik, and another after they killed her horse," answered Speaker. Reinard stared hard at the old man, peering at the sightless sockets.

"A woman, you say?"

"Yes."

"There was a third man killed. What of him?"

"Slain by an arrow through the forehead."

"Who fired it?"

"The man called Regnak. The Wanderer who comes here on occasions."

Reinard shook his head. A woman brought him a goblet of mulled wine, and he sat on a large stone by a blazing fire. "It can't be; he wouldn't dare! Are you sure it was him?"

"It was him," said Speaker. "And now I must rest."

"Wait! Where are they now?"

"I shall find out," said the old man, returning to his hut. Reinard called for food and summoned Grussin. The axman squatted on the ground before him.

"Did you hear?" he asked.

"Yes. Do you believe it?" answered Grussin.

"It's ridiculous. But when has the old man been wrong? Am I getting old? When a craven like Rek can attack my men, I must be doing something wrong. I will have him roasted slowly over the fire for this."

"We're getting short of food," said Grussin.

"What?"

"Short of food. It's been a long winter, and we needed that damn caravan."

"There will be others. First we will find Rek."

"Is it worth it?" asked Grussin.

"Worth it? He helped some woman kill my brother. I want that woman staked out and enjoyed by all the men. I want the flesh cut from her body in tiny strips from her feet to her neck. And then the dogs can have her."

"Whatever you say."

"You don't sound very enthusiastic," said Reinard, hurling his now-empty plate across the fire.

"No? Well, maybe *I'm* getting old. When we came here, there seemed to be a reason for it all. I'm beginning to forget what it was."

"We came here because Abalayn and his mangy crew had my farm sacked and my family killed. And *I* haven't forgotten. You're not turning soft, are you?"

Grussin noted the gleam in Reinard's eyes.

"No, of course not. You're the leader, and whatever you say is fine by me. We will find Rek and the woman. Why don't you get some rest."

"A curse on rest," muttered Reinard. "You sleep if you have to. We leave as soon as the old man gives us directions."

Grussin walked to his hut and hurled himself on his fern-filled bed.

"You are troubled?" his woman, Mella, asked him as she kneeled by his side, offering him wine.

"How would you like to leave?" he asked, placing a huge hand on her shoulder. She leaned forward and kissed him. "Wherever you go, I shall be with you," she said.

"I'm tired of it," he said. "Tired of the killing. It gets more senseless with every day. He must be mad."

"Hush!" she whispered, wary now. She leaned into his bearded face and whispered in his ear. "Don't voice your fears. We can leave quietly in the spring. Stay calm and do his bidding until then."

He nodded, smiled, and kissed her hair. "You're right," he said. "Get some sleep." She curled beside him, and he

gathered the blanket around her. "I don't deserve you," he
said as her eyes closed.

Where had it gone wrong? When they had been young
and full of fire, Reinard's cruelty had been an occasional
thing, a device to create a legend. Or so he had said. They
would be a thorn in Abalayn's side until they achieved justice. Now it was ten years. Ten miserable bloody years.

And had the cause ever been just?

Grussin hoped so.

"Well, are you coming?" asked Reinard from the doorway. "They're at the old cabin."

The march had been a long one and bitterly cold, but
Reinard had scarcely felt it. Anger filled him with warmth,
and the prospect of revenge fed his muscles so that the
miles sped by.

His mind filled with pictures of sweet violence and the
music of screams. He would take the woman first and cut
her with a heated knife. Arousal warmed his loins.

And as for Rek . . . He knew what Rek's expression
would be as he saw them arrive.

Terror! Mind-numbing, bowel-loosening terror!

But he was wrong.

Rek had stalked from the hut, furious and trembling. The
scorn on Virae's face was hard to bear. Only anger could
blank it out. And even then, barely. He could not help what
he was, could he? Some men were born to be heroes. Others to be cowards. What right had she to judge him?

"Regnak, my dear! Is it true you have a woman inside?"

Rek's eyes scanned the group. More than twenty men
stood in a half circle behind the tall, broad-shouldered outlaw leader. Beside him stood Grussin the axman, huge and
powerful, his double-headed ax in his hand.

"Morning, Rein," said Rek. "What brings you here?"

"I heard you had a warm bedmate, and I thought, Good
old Rek, he won't mind sharing. And I'd like to invite you
to my camp. Where is she?"

"She's not for you, Rein. But I'll make a trade. There's
a caravan headed—"

"Never mind the caravan!" shouted Reinard. "Just bring
out the woman."

"Spices, jewels, furs. It's a big one," said Rek.

"You can tell us about it as we march. Now I'm losing patience. Bring her out!"

Rek's anger blazed, and his sword snaked from its scabbard.

"Come and get her, then, you bastards!"

Virae stepped from the doorway to stand beside him, blade in hand, as the outlaws drew their weapons and advanced.

"Wait!" ordered Reinard, lifting his hand. He stepped forward, forcing a smile. "Now listen to me, Rek. This is senseless. We've nothing against you. You've been a friend. Now, what's this woman to you? She killed my brother, so you see it's a matter of personal honor. Put up your sword and you can ride away. But I want her alive." And you, too, he thought.

"You want her, you take her!" said Rek. "And me, too. Come on, Rein. You still remember what a sword's for, don't you? Or will you do what you normally do and scuttle back into the trees while other men do your dying for you? Run, you dung worm!" Rek leapt forward, and Reinard backed away at speed and stumbled into Grussin.

"Kill him—but not the woman," he said. "I want that woman."

Grussin walked forward, his ax swinging at his side. Virae advanced to stand beside Rek. The axman stopped ten paces short of the pair, and his eyes met Rek's: there was no give there. He turned his gaze to the woman. Young, spirited—not beautiful but a handsome lass.

"What are you waiting for, you ox!" screamed Reinard. "Take her!"

Grussin turned and walked back to the group. A sense of unreality gripped him. He saw himself again as a young man, saving for his first holding; he had a plow that was his father's, and the neighbors were ready to help him build his home near the elm grove. What had he done with the years?

"You traitor!" shouted Reinard, dragging his sword into the air.

Grussin parried the blow with ease. "Forget it, Rein. Let's go home."

"Kill him!" Reinard ordered. The men looked at one another, some starting forward while others hesitated. "You bastard! You treacherous filth!" Reinard screamed, raising his sword once more. Grussin took a deep breath, gripped his ax in both hands, and smashed the sword into shards, the ax blade glancing from the shattered hilt and hammering into the outlaw leader's side. He fell to his knees, doubled over. Then Grussin stepped forward; the ax lifted and chopped, and Reinard's head rolled to the snow. Grussin let the weapon fall, then walked back to Rek.

"He wasn't always as you knew him," he said.

"Why?" asked Rek, lowering his blade. "Why did you do it?"

"Who knows? It wasn't just for you—or her. Maybe something inside me had just had enough. Where was this caravan?"

"I was lying," lied Rek.

"Good. We will not meet again. I'm leaving Graven. Is she your woman?"

"No."

"You could do worse."

"Yes."

Grussin turned and walked to the body, retrieving his ax. "We were friends for a long time," he said. "Too long."

Without a backward glance he led the group back into the forest.

"I simply don't believe it," said Rek. "That was an absolute miracle."

"Let's finish breakfast now," said Virae. "I'll brew some tea."

Inside the hut Rek began to tremble. He sat down, his sword clattering to the floor.

"What's the matter?" asked Virae.

"It's just the cold," he said, teeth chattering. She knelt beside him, massaging his hands, saying nothing.

"The tea will help," she said. "Did you bring any sugar?"

"It's in my pack, wrapped in red paper. Horeb knows I've a sweet tooth. Cold doesn't usually get to me like this—sorry!"

"It's all right. My father always says sweet tea is wonderful for . . . cold."

"I wonder how they found us," he said. "Last night's snow must have covered our tracks. It's strange."

"I don't know. Here, drink this."

He sipped the tea, holding the leather-covered mug in both hands. Hot liquid splashed over his fingers. Virae busied herself clearing away and repacking his saddlebags. Then she raked the ashes in the hearth and laid a fire ready for the next traveler to use the hut.

"What are you doing at Dros Delnoch?" Rek asked, the warm sweet tea soothing him.

"I am Earl Delnar's daughter," she said. "I live there."

"Did he send you away because of the coming war?"

"No. I brought a message to Abalayn, and now I've got a message for someone else. When I've delivered it, I'm going home. Are you feeling better?"

"Yes," said Rek. "Much better." He hesitated, holding her gaze. "It wasn't just the cold," he said.

"I know: it doesn't matter. Everybody trembles after an action. It's what happens during it that counts. My father told me that after Skeln Pass he couldn't sleep without nightmares for a month."

"You're not shaking," he said.

"That's because I'm keeping busy. Would you like some more tea?"

"Yes. Thanks. I thought we were going to die. And just for a moment I didn't care—it was a wonderful feeling." He wanted to tell her how good it was to have her standing beside him, but he could not. He wanted to walk across the room and hold her—and knew he would not. He merely looked at her while she refilled his mug, stirring in the sugar.

"Where did you serve?" she asked, conscious of his gaze and uncertain of its meaning.

"Dros Corteswain. Under Gan Javi."

"He's dead now," she said.

"Yes, a stroke. He was a fine leader. He predicted the coming war. I'm sure Abalayn wishes he had listened to him."

"It wasn't only Javi who warned him," said Virae. "All

the northern commanders sent reports. My father has had spies among the Nadir for years. It was obvious that they intended to attack us. Abalayn's a fool; even now he's sending messages to Ulric with new treaties. He won't accept that war's inevitable. Do you know we've only ten thousand men at Delnoch?"

"I had heard it was less," said Rek.

"There are six walls and a town to defend. The complement in wartime should be four times as strong. And the discipline is not what it was."

"Why?"

"Because they're all waiting to die," she said, anger in her voice. "Because my father's ill—dying. And because Gan Orrin has the heart of a ripe tomato."

"Orrin? I've not heard of him."

"Abalayn's nephew. He commands the troops, but he's useless. If I'd been a man . . ."

"I'm glad you're not," he said.

"Why?"

"I don't know," he said lamely. "Just something to say . . . I'm glad you're not, that's all."

"Anyway, if I had been a man, I would have commanded the troops. I would have done a damned sight better than Orrin. Why are you staring at me?"

"I'm not staring. I'm listening, dammit! Why do you keep pressing me?"

"Do you want the fire lit?" she asked.

"What? Are we staying that long?"

"If you want to."

"I'll leave it to you," he said.

"Let's stay for today. That's all. It might give us time to . . . get to know each other better. We've made a pretty bad start, after all. And you have saved my life three times."

"Once," he said. "I don't think you would have died of the cold; you're too tough. And Grussin saved us both. But yes, I would like to stay just for today. Mind you, I don't fancy sleeping on the floor again."

"You won't have to," she said.

The abbot smiled at the young albino's embarrassment. He released his hands from the mind hold and walked back to his desk. "Join me, Serbitar," he said aloud. "Do you regret your oath of celibacy?"

"Sometimes," said the young man, rising from his knees. He brushed dust from his white cassock and seated himself opposite the abbot.

"The girl is worthy," Serbitar replied. "The man is an enigma. Will their force be lessened by their lovemaking?"

"Strengthened," said the abbot. "They need each other. Together they are complete, as in the Sacred Book. Tell me of her."

"What can I tell?"

"You entered her mind. Tell me of her."

"She is an earl's daughter. She lacks confidence in herself as a woman, and she is a victim of mixed desires."

"Why?"

"She doesn't know why," he hedged.

"Of that I am aware. Do *you* know why?"

"No."

"What of the man?"

"I did not enter his mind."

"No. But what of the man?"

"He has great fears. He fears to die."

"Is this a weakness?" asked the abbot.

"It will be at Dros Delnoch. Death is almost certain there."

"Yes. Can it be a strength?"

"I do not see how," said Serbitar.

"What does the philosopher say of cowards and heroes?"

"The prophet says, 'By nature of definition only the coward is capable of the highest heroism.' "

"You must convene the Thirty, Serbitar."

"I am to lead?"

"Yes. You shall be the voice of the Thirty."

"But who shall my brothers be?"

The abbot leaned back in his chair. "Arbedark will be the heart. He is strong, fearless, and true; there could be none other. Menahem shall be the eyes, for he is gifted. I shall be the soul."

"No!" said the albino. "It cannot be, master. I cannot lead you."

"But you must. You will decide the other numbers. I shall await your decision."

"Why me? Why must I lead? I should be the eyes. Arbedark should lead."

"Trust me. All will be revealed."

"I was raised at Dros Delnoch," Virae told Rek as they lay before the blazing fire. His head rested on his rolled cloak, her head nestled on his chest. He stroked her hair, saying nothing. "It's a majestic place. Have you ever been there?"

"No. Tell me about it." He did not really want to hear, but neither did he wish to speak.

"It has six outer walls, each of them twenty feet thick. The first three were built by Egel, the Earl of Bronze. But then the town expanded, and gradually they built three more. The whole fortress spans the Delnoch Pass. With the exception of Dros Purdol to the west and Corteswain to the east, it is the only route for an army to pass through the mountains. My father converted the old keep and made it his home. The view is beautiful from the upper turrets. To the south in summer the whole of the Sentran Plain is golden with corn. And to the north you can see forever. Are you listening to me?"

"Yes. Golden views. You can see forever," he said softly.

"Are you sure you want to hear this?"

"Yes. Tell me about the walls again."

"What about them?"

"How thick are they?"

"They are also up to sixty feet high, with jutting towers every fifty paces. Any army attacking the Dros would suffer fearful losses."

"What about the gates?" he asked. "A wall is only as strong as the gate it shields."

"The Earl of Bronze thought of that. Each gate is set behind an iron portcullis and built of layered bronze, iron, and oak. Beyond the gates are tunnels which narrow at the center before opening out onto the level between walls. You could hold the tunnels against an enormous number of men. The whole of the Dros was beautifully designed; it's only the town which spoils it."

"In what way?" he said.

"Originally Egel designed the gap between the walls to be a killing ground with no cover. It was uphill to the next wall, which would slow down the enemy. With enough bowmen you could have a massacre. It was good psychologically, too: By the time they came to take the next wall—if they ever did—they'd know there was more killing ground to come."

"So how did the town spoil it?"

"It just grew. Now we have buildings all the way to Wall Six. The killing ground's gone. Quite the opposite, in fact—now there's cover all the way."

He rolled over and kissed her brow.

"What was that for?" she asked.

"Does it have to be for something?"

"There's a reason for everything," she said.

He kissed her again. "That was for the Earl of Bronze," he said. "Or the coming of spring. Or a vanished snowflake."

"You don't make any sense," she told him.

"Why did you let me make love to you?" he asked.

"What sort of a question is that?"

"Why?"

"None of your damned business!" she said.

He laughed and kissed her again. "Yes, my lady. Quite right. None of my business."

"You're mocking me," she said, struggling to rise.

"Nonsense," he said, holding her down. "You're beautiful."

"I'm not. I never have been. You *are* mocking me."

"I will never mock you. And you *are* beautiful. And the more I look at you, the more beautiful you are."

"You're a fool. Let me up."

He kissed her again, easing his body close to hers. The kiss lingered, and she returned it.

"Tell me about the Dros again," he said at last.

"I don't want to talk about it now. You're teasing me, Rek; I won't have it. I don't want to think about it tonight, not anymore. Do you believe in fate?"

"I do now. Almost."

"I'm serious. Yesterday I didn't mind about going home

and facing the Nadir. I believed in the Drenai cause, and I was willing to die for it. I wasn't scared yesterday."

"And today?" he asked.

"Today, if you asked me, I wouldn't go home." She was lying, but she did not know why. A surge of fear welled in her as Rek closed his eyes and leaned back.

"Yes, you would," he said. "You have to."

"What about you?"

"It doesn't make sense," he said.

"What doesn't?"

"I don't believe in what I'm feeling. I never have. I am almost thirty years old, and I know the world."

"What are you talking about?"

"I'm talking about fate. Destiny. An old man in tattered blue robes without any eyes. I'm talking about love."

"Love?"

He opened his eyes, reached out, and stroked her face.

"I can't tell you what it meant to me when you stood beside me this morning. It was the highest point in my life. Nothing else mattered. I could see the sky—it was more blue than I've ever seen it. Everything was in sharp focus. I was more aware of living than I have ever been. Does that make any sense?"

"No," she said gently. "Not really. Do you truly think I'm beautiful?"

"You are the most beautiful woman who ever wore armor," he said, smiling.

"That's no answer. Why am I beautiful?"

"Because I love you," he said, surprised at the ease with which he could say it.

"Does that mean you're coming with me to Dros Delnoch?"

"Tell me about those lovely high walls again," he said.

◊ 5 ◊

THE MONASTERY GROUNDS were split into training areas, some of stone, some of grass, others of sand or treacherous slime-covered slate. The abbey itself stood at the center of the grounds, a converted keep of gray stone and crenellated battlements. Four walls and a moat surrounded the abbey, the walls a later addition of soft, golden sandstone. By the western wall, sheltered by glass and blooming out of season, were flowers of thirty different shades. All were roses.

The albino Serbitar knelt before his tree, his mind at one with the plant. He had struggled for thirteen years with the rose and understood it. There was empathy. There was harmony.

There was fragrance that pulsed for Serbitar alone. Greenflies upon the rose shriveled and died as Serbitar gazed upon them, and the soft silky beauty of the blooms filled his senses like an opiate.

It was a white rose.

Serbitar sat back, eyes closed, mentally following the surge of new life within the tree. He wore full armor of silver mail shirt, sword, and scabbard, leather leggings worked with silver rings; by his side was a new silver helm bearing the figure "1" in Elder runes. His white hair was braided. His eyes were green, the color of the rose leaves. His slender face, translucent skin over high cheekbones, had the mystic beauty of the consumptive.

He made his farewells, gently easing the gossamer panic of the plant. It had known him since its first leaf had opened.

And now he was to die.

A smiling face grew in his mind, and Serbitar sense-recognized Arbedark. We await you, pulsed the inner message.

I am coming, he answered.

Within the great hall a table had been set, a jug of water and a barley cake before each of thirty places. Thirty men in full armor sat silently as Serbitar entered, taking his place at the head of the table and bowing to the abbot, Vintar, who now sat on his right.

In silence the company ate, each thinking his own thoughts, each analyzing his emotions at this culmination of thirteen years of training.

Finally Serbitar spoke, fulfilling the ritual need of the order.

"Brothers, the search is upon us. We who have sought must obtain that which we seek. A messenger comes from Dros Delnoch to ask us to die. What does the heart of the Thirty feel on this matter?"

All eyes turned to black-bearded Arbedark. He relaxed his mind, allowing their emotions to wash over him, selecting thoughts, analyzing them, forging them into one unifying concept agreed on by all.

Then he spoke, his voice deep and resonant.

"The heart of the matter is that the children of the Drenai face extinction. Ulric has massed the Nadir tribes under his banner. The first attack on the Drenai empire will be at Dros Delnoch, which Earl Delnar has orders to hold until the autumn. Abalayn needs time to raise and train an army.

"We approach a frozen moment in the destiny of the continent. The heart says we should seek our truths at Dros Delnoch."

Serbitar turned to Menahem, a hawk-nosed young man, dark and swarthy, his hair braided in a single ponytail intertwined with silver thread. "And how do the eyes of the Thirty view this thing?"

"Should we go to the Dros, the city will fall," said Menahem. "Should we refuse, the city will still fall. Our presence will merely delay the inevitable. Should the messenger be worthy to ask of us our lives, then we should go."

Serbitar turned to the abbot. "Vintar, how says the soul of the Thirty?"

The older man ran a slender hand through his thinning gray hair, then stood and bowed to Serbitar. He seemed out of place in his armor of silver and bronze.

"We will be asked to kill men of another race," he said, his voice gentle, sad even. "We will be asked to kill them not because they are evil, merely because their leaders wish to do what the Drenai themselves did six centuries ago.

"We stand between the sea and the mountains. The sea will crush us against the mountain, and thus we die. The mountain will hold us against the sea, allowing us to be crushed. Still we die.

"We are all weapon masters here. We seek the perfect death to counterpoint the perfect life. True, the Nadir aggression does not pose a new concept in history. But their action will cause untold horror to the Drenai people. We can say that to defend those people we are upholding the values of our order. That our defense will fail is no reason to avoid the battle. For it is the motive that is pure, not the outcome.

"Sadly, the soul says we must ride for Dros Delnoch."

"So," said Serbitar. "We are agreed. I, too, feel strongly on this matter. We came to this temple as outcasts from the world. Shunned and feared, we came together to create the ultimate contradiction. Our bodies would become living weapons, to polarize our minds to extremes of pacifism. Warrior-priests we are, as the Elders never were. There will be no joy in our hearts as we slay the enemy, for we love all life.

"As we die, our souls will leap forward, transcending the world's chains. All petty jealousies, intrigues, and hatreds will be left behind us as we journey to the Source.

"The voice says we ride."

A three-quarter moon hung in the cloudless night sky, casting pale shadows from the trees around Rek's campfire. A luckless rabbit, gutted and encased in clay, lay on the coals as Virae came back from the stream, wiping her naked upper body with one of Rek's spare shirts.

"If only you knew how much that cost me!" he said as

she sat on a rock by the fire, her body glowing gold as the flames danced.

"It never served a better purpose," she said. "How much longer before that rabbit is ready?"

"Not long. You will catch your death of cold, sitting half-naked in this weather. My blood's chilling to ice just watching you."

"Strange!" she said. "Just this morning you were telling me how your blood ran hot just to look at me."

"That was in a warm cabin with a bed handy. I've never been much for making love in the snow. Here, I've warmed a blanket."

"When I was a child," she said, taking the blanket and wrapping it around her shoulders, "we used to have to run three miles across the downs in the midwinter wearing only a tunic and sandals. That was bracing. And extremely cold."

"If you're so tough, how was it that you turned blue before we found the cabin?" he asked, a broad smile robbing the question of malice.

"The armor," she said. "Too much steel, not enough wool beneath it. Mind you, if I had been riding in front, I wouldn't have gotten so bored and fallen asleep. How long did you say that rabbit would be? I'm starving."

"Soon. I think . . ."

"Have you ever cooked a rabbit this way before?" she asked.

"Not exactly. But it is the right way; I've seen it done. All the fur comes away as you crack the clay. It's easy."

Virae was not convinced. "I stalked that skinny beast for ages," she said, recalling with pleasure the single arrow from forty paces that had downed it. "Not a bad bow, if a little on the light side. It's an old cavalry bow, isn't it? We have several at Delnoch. The modern ones are all silver steel now, better range and a stronger poundage. I'm starving."

"Patience aids the appetite," he told her.

"You'd better not ruin that rabbit. I don't like killing the things at the best of times. But at least there's a purpose if one can eat it."

"I'm not sure how the rabbit would respond to that line of reasoning," said Rek.

"Can they reason?" asked Virae.

"I don't know. I didn't mean it literally."

"Then why say it? You are a strange man."

"It was just an abstract thought. Do you never have an abstract thought? Do you never wonder how a flower knows when it's time to grow? Or how the salmon find their way back to the spawning grounds?"

"No," she said. "Is the rabbit cooked?"

"Well, what *do* you think about when you're not planning how to kill people?"

"Eating," she said. "What about that rabbit?"

Rek tipped the ball of clay from the coals with a stick, watching it sizzle on the snow.

"Well, what do you do now?" she asked. He ignored her and picked up a fist-sized rock, then cracked it hard against the clay, which split to disgorge a half-cooked, half-skinned rabbit.

"Looks good," she said. "What now?"

He poked the steaming meat with a stick.

"Can you face eating that?" he said.

"Of course. Can I borrow your knife? Which bit do you want?"

"I've got some oatcake left in my pack. I think I'll make do with that. Will you put some clothes on!"

They were camped in a shallow depression under a rock face, not deep enough to be a cave but large enough to reflect heat from the fire and cut out the worst of the wind. Rek chewed his oatcake and watched the girl devour the rabbit. It was not an edifying sight. She hurled the remnants of the carcass into the trees. "Badgers should enjoy it," she said. "That's not a bad way to cook rabbit."

"I'm glad you enjoyed it," he said.

"You're not much of a woodsman, are you?" she told him.

"I manage."

"You couldn't even gut the thing. You looked green when the entrails popped out."

Rek hurled the rest of his oatcake in the direction of the

hapless rabbit. "The badgers will probably appreciate dessert," he said. Virae giggled happily.

"You're wonderful, Rek. You're unlike any man I've ever met."

"I don't think I'm going to like what's coming next," he said. "Why don't we just go to sleep."

"No. Listen to me. I'm serious. All my life I have dreamed of finding the right man: tall, kind, strong, understanding. Loving. I never thought he existed. Most of the men I've known have been soldiers—gruff, straight as spears, and as romantic as a bull in heat. And I've met poets, soft of speech and gentle. When I was with soldiers, I longed for poets, and when with poets, I longed for soldiers. I had begun to believe the man I wanted could not exist. Do you understand me?"

"All your life you've been looking for a man who couldn't cook rabbits? Of course I understand you."

"Do you really?" she asked softly.

"Yes. But explain it to me anyway."

"You're what I've always wanted," she said, blushing. "You're my coward-hero—my love."

"I knew there would be something I wouldn't like," he said.

As she placed some logs on the blaze, he held out his hand. "Sit beside me," he said. "You'll be warmer."

"You can share my blanket," she told him, moving around the fire and into his arms, resting her head on his shoulder. "You don't mind if I call you my coward-hero?"

"You can call me what you like," he said, "so long as you're always there to call me."

"Always?"

The wind tilted the flames, and he shivered. "Always isn't such a long time for us, is it? We only have as much time as Dros Delnoch holds. Anyway, you might get tired of me and send me away."

"Never!" she said.

" 'Never' and 'always.' I had not thought about those words much until now. Why didn't I meet you ten years ago? The words might have meant something then."

"I doubt it. I would only have been nine years old."

"I didn't mean it literally. Poetically."

"My father has written to Druss," she said. "That letter and this mission are all that keep him alive."

"Druss? But even if he's alive, he will be ancient by now; it will be obscene. Skeln was fifteen years ago, and he was old then—they will have to carry him into the Dros."

"Perhaps. But my father sets great store by the man. He was awed by him. He feels he's invincible. Immortal. He once described him to me as the greatest warrior of the age. He said that Skeln Pass was Druss's victory and that he and the others just made up the numbers. He used to tell that story to me when I was young. We would sit by a fire like this and toast bread on the flames. Then he'd tell me about Skeln. Marvelous days." She lapsed into silence, staring into the coals.

"Tell me the story," he said, drawing her closer to him, his right hand pushing back the hair that had fallen across her face.

"You must know it. Everyone knows about Skeln."

"True. But I've never heard the story from someone who was there. I've only seen the plays and listened to the saga poets."

"Tell me what you heard and I will fill in the detail."

"All right. There were a few hundred Drenai warriors holding Skeln Pass while the main Drenai army massed elsewhere. It was the Ventrian king, Gorben, they were worried about. They knew he was on the march but not where he would strike. He struck at Skeln. They were outnumbered fifty to one, and they held on until reinforcements arrived. That's all."

"Not quite," said Virae. "Gorben had an inner army of ten thousand men called the Immortals. They had never been beaten, but Druss beat them."

"Oh, come," said Rek. "One man cannot beat an army. That's saga-poet stuff."

"No, listen to me. My father said that on the last day, when the Immortals were finally sent in, the Drenai line had begun to fold. My father has been a warrior all his life. He understands battles and the shift and flow between courage and panic. The Drenai were ready to crack. But then, just as the line was beginning to give, Druss bellowed a battle cry and advanced, cutting and slashing with his ax.

The Ventrians fell back before him. And then suddenly those nearest to him turned to run. The panic spread like brushfire, and the entire Ventrian line crumbled. Druss had turned the tide. My father says he was like a giant that day. Inhuman. Like a god of war."

"That was *then*," said Rek. "I can't see a toothless old man being of much use. No man can resist age."

"I agree. But can you see what a boost to morale it will be just to have Druss there? Men will flock to the banner. To fight a battle alongside Druss the Legend—there's an immortality in it."

"Have you ever met the old man?" asked Rek.

"No. My father would never tell me, but there was something between them. Druss would never come to Dros Delnoch. It was something to do with my mother, I think."

"She didn't like him?"

"No. Something to do with a friend of Druss's. Sieben, I think he was called."

"What happened to him?"

"He was killed at Skeln. He was Druss's oldest friend. That's all I know about it." Rek knew she was lying but let it rest. It was all ancient history, anyway.

Like Druss the Legend . . .

The old man crumpled the letter and let it fall.

It was not age that depressed Druss. He enjoyed the wisdom of his sixty years, the knowledge accrued, and the respect it earned. But the physical ravages of time were another thing altogether. His shoulders were still mighty above a barrel chest, but the muscles had taken on a stretched look—wiry lines that crisscrossed his upper back. His waist, too, had thickened perceptibly over the last winter. And almost overnight, he realized, his black beard streaked with gray had become a gray beard streaked with black. But the piercing eyes that gazed at their reflection in the silver mirror had not dimmed. Their stare had dismayed armies; caused heroic opponents to take a backward step, blushing and shamed; caught the imagination of a people who had needed heroes.

He was Druss the Legend. Invincible Druss, Captain of the Ax. The legends of his life were told to children everywhere, and most of them *were* legends, Druss reflected. Druss the hero, immortal, godlike.

His past victories could have ensured him a palace of riches, concubines by the score. Fifteen years before Abalayn himself had showered him with jewels following his exploits at the Skeln Pass.

By the following morning, however, Druss had gone back to the Skoda mountains, high into the lonely country bordering the clouds. Among the pine and the snow leopards the grizzled old warrior had returned to his lair to taste again of solitude. His wife of thirty years lay buried there. He had a mind to die there, though there would be no one to bury him, he knew.

During the past fifteen years Druss had not been inactive. He had wandered various lands, leading battle companies for minor princelings. Last winter he had retired to his high mountain retreat, there to think and die. He had long known he would die in his sixtieth year, even before the seer's prediction all those decades ago. He had been able to picture himself at sixty—but never beyond. Whenever he tried to consider the prospect of being sixty-one, he would experience only darkness.

His gnarled hands curled around a wooden goblet and raised it to his gray-bearded lips. The wine was strong, brewed himself five years before; it had aged well—better than he. But it was gone, and he remained . . . for a little while.

The heat within his sparse furnished cabin was growing oppressive as the new spring sun warmed the wooden roof. Slowly he removed the sheepskin jacket he had worn all winter and the undervest of horsehair. His massive body, crisscrossed with scars, told of his age. He studied the scars, remembering clearly the men whose blades had caused them: men who would never grow old as he had, men who had died in their prime beneath his singing ax. His blue eyes flicked to the wall by the small wooden door. There it hung, Snaga, which in the old tongue meant "the Sender." Slim haft of black steel, interwoven with eldritch runes in silver thread, and a double-edged blade so shaped that it sang as it slew.

Even now he could hear its sweet song. One last time,

brother of my soul, it called to him. One last bloody day before the sun sets. His mind returned to Delnar's letter. It was written to the memory and not the man.

Druss raised himself from the wooden chair, cursing as his joints creaked. "The sun has set," whispered the old warrior, addressing the ax. "Now only death waits, and he's a patient bastard." He walked from the cabin, gazing out over the distant mountains. His massive frame and gray-black hair mirrored in miniature the mountains he surveyed. Proud, strong, ageless, and snow-topped, they defied the spring sun as it strove to deny them their winter peaks of virgin snow.

Druss soaked in their savage splendor, sucking in the cool breeze and tasting life as if for the last time.

"Where are you, death?" he called. "Where do you hide on this fine day?" The echoes boomed around the valleys ... DEATH, DEATH, Death, Death ... DAY, DAY, Day, Day ...

"I am Druss! And I defy you!"

A shadow fell across Druss's eyes, the sun died in the heavens, and the mountains receded into mist. Pain clamped Druss's mighty chest, soul deep, and he almost fell.

"Proud mortal!" hissed a sibilant voice through the veils of agony. "I never sought you. You have hunted me through these long, lonely years. Stay on this mountain and I guarantee you two score more years. Your muscles will atrophy; your brain will sink into dotage. You will bloat, old man, and I will only come when you beg it.

"Or will the huntsman have one more hunt?

"Seek me if you will, old warrior. I stand on the walls of Dros Delnoch."

The pain lifted from the old man's heart. He staggered once, drew soothing mountain air into his burning lungs, and gazed about him. Birds still sang in the pine, no clouds obscured the sun, and the mountains stood, tall and proud, as they always had.

Druss returned to the cabin and went to a chest of oak, padlocked at the onset of winter. The key lay deep in the valley below. He placed his giant hands about the lock and began to exert pressure. Muscles writhed on his arms, veins bulged on his neck and shoulders, and the metal groaned, changed shape, and—split! Druss threw the padlock aside and opened the chest. Within lay a jerkin of black leather, the shoulders covered in a skin of shining steel, and a black leather skull cap relieved only by a silver ax flanked by silver skulls. Long black leather gauntlets came into view, silver-skinned to the knuckles. Swiftly he dressed, coming finally to the long leather boots, a present from Abalayn himself so many years before.

Lastly he reached for Snaga, which seemed to leap from the wall to his waiting hand.

"One last time, brother," he told it. "Before the sun sets."

◇ 6 ◇

WITH VINTAR STANDING beside him, Serbitar watched from a high balcony as the two riders approached the monastery, cantering their horses toward the northern gate. Grass showed in patches on the snow-covered fields as a warm spring wind eased in from the west.

"Not a time for lovers," said Serbitar aloud.

"It is always a time for lovers, my son. In war most of all," said Vintar. "Have you probed the man's mind?"

"Yes. He is a strange one. A cynic by experience, a romantic by inclination, and now a hero by necessity."

"How will Menahem test the messenger?" asked Vintar.

"With fear," answered the albino.

Rek was feeling well. The air he breathed was crisp and clean, and a warm westerly breeze promised an end to the harshest winter in years. The woman he loved was beside him, and the sky was blue and clear.

"What a great day to be alive!" he said.

"What's so special about today?" asked Virae.

"It's beautiful. Can't you taste it? The sky, the breeze, the melting snow?"

"Someone is coming to meet us. He looks like a warrior," she said.

The rider approached them and dismounted. His face was covered by a black and silver helm crowned with a horsehair plume. Rek and Virae dismounted and approached him.

"Good morning," said Rek. The man ignored him; his dark eyes, seen through the slits in the helm, focused on Virae.

"You are the messenger?" he asked her.

"I am. I wish to see Abbot Vintar."

"First you must pass me," he said, stepping back and drawing a longsword of silver steel.

"Wait a moment," said Rek. "What is this? One does not normally have to fight one's way into a monastery." Once again the man ignored him, and Virae drew her rapier. "Stop it!" ordered Rek. "This is insane."

"Stay out of this, Rek," said Virae. "I will slice this silver beetle into tiny pieces."

"No, you won't," he said, gripping her arm. "That rapier is no good against an armored man. In any case, the whole thing is senseless. You are not here to fight anybody. You simply have a message to deliver, that's all. There must be a mistake here somewhere. Wait a moment."

Rek walked toward the warrior, his mind racing, his eyes checking for weak points in the armored defenses. The man wore a molded breastplate over a mail shirt of silver steel. Protecting his neck was a silver torque. His legs were covered to the thigh in leather trews, cased with silver rings, and upon his shins were leather greaves. Only the man's knees, hands, and chin were open to attack.

"Will you tell me what is happening?" Rek asked him. "I think you may have the wrong messenger. We are here to see the abbot."

"Are you ready, woman?" asked Menahem.

"Yes," said Virae, her rapier cutting a figure eight in the morning air as she loosened her wrist.

Rek's blade flashed into his hand. "Defend yourself," he cried.

"No, Rek, he's mine," shouted Virae. "I don't need you to fight for me. Step aside!"

"You can have him next," said Rek. He turned his attention back to Menahem. "Come on, then. Let's see if you fight as prettily as you look."

Menahem turned his dark eyes on the tall figure before him. Instantly Rek's stomach turned over: this was death! Cold, final worm-in-the-eye-sockets death. There was no hope in this contest. Panic welled in Rek's breast, and his limbs began to tremble. He was a child again, locked in a darkened room, knowing the demons were hiding in the black shadows. Fear in the shape of bile rose in his throat as nausea shook him. He wanted to run ... he needed to run.

Instead Rek screamed and launched an attack, his blade whistling toward the black and silver helm. Startled, Menahem hastily parried and a second blow almost got through. The warrior stepped backward, desperately trying to regain the initiative, but Rek's furious assault had caught him off balance. Menahem parried and moved, trying to circle.

Virae watched in stunned silence as Rek's blistering assault continued. The two men's swords glittered in the morning sunlight, a dazzling web of white light, a stunning display of skill. Virae felt a surge of pride. She wanted to cheer Rek on but resisted the urge, knowing the slightest distraction could sway the contest.

"Help me," pulsed Menahem to Serbitar, "or I may have to kill him." He parried a blow, catching it only inches from his throat. "If I can," he added.

"How can we stop it?" Serbitar asked Vintar. "The man is a baresark. I cannot get through to him. He will kill Menahem before much longer."

"The girl!" said Vintar. "Join with me."

Virae shivered as she watched Rek growing in strength. Baresark! Her father had told her of such men, but never would she have placed Rek in their company. They were mad killers who lost all sense of reason and fear in combat, becoming the most deadly of opponents. All swordsmen gravitated between defense and attack, for despite a desire to win there was an equal desire not to lose. But the baresark lost all fear; his was an all-out attack, and invariably he took his opponent with him even if he fell. A thought struck her powerfully, and suddenly she knew that the warrior was not trying to kill Rek—the contest was but a test.

"Put up your swords," she screamed. "Stop it!"

The two men battled on.

"Rek, listen to me!" she shouted. "It's only a test. He's not trying to kill you."

Her voice came to Rek as from a great distance, piercing the red mist before his eyes. Stepping back, he felt rather than saw the relief in the other man; then he took a deep breath and relaxed, his legs shaky, his hands trembling.

"You entered my mind," he accused the warrior, fixing the man's dark eyes in a cold gaze. "I don't know how. But if you ever do it again, I will kill you. Do you understand me?"

"I understand," Menahem told him softly, his voice muffled within his helm. Rek sheathed his blade at the second attempt and turned to Virae, who was looking at him strangely.

"It wasn't really me," he said. "Don't look at me like that, Virae."

"Oh, Rek, I'm sorry," she said, tears in her eyes. "I'm truly sorry."

A new kind of fear hit him as she turned her face away. "Don't leave me," he said. "It rarely happens, and I would never turn on *you*. Never! Believe me." She turned to face him, throwing her arms about his neck.

"Leave you? What are you talking about? It doesn't matter to me, you fool. I was just sorry for you. Oh, Rek, you're such an idiot. I'm not some tavern girl who squeals at the sight of a rat. I'm a woman who has grown up alongside men. Soldiers. Fighting men. Warriors. You think I would leave you because you are baresark?"

"I can control it," he said, holding her tightly to him.

"Where we are going, Rek, you will not have to," she said.

Serbitar left the monastery balcony and poured a goblet of spring water from a stone jug.

"How did he do it?"

Vintar sat back on a leather chair. "There is a well of courage within him, fueled by many things of which we can only guess. But when Menahem fed him fear, he responded with violence. Because what Menahem could not have understood is that the man fears fear itself. Did you glimpse that memory of his childhood during Menahem's probe?"

"The tunnels, you mean?"

"Yes. What do you make of a child who fears the dark and yet seeks out dark tunnels to travel through?"

"He tried to end his fears by facing them," said Serbitar.

"He still does. And that's why Menahem almost died."

"He will be useful at Dros Delnoch," said Serbitar, smiling.

"More than you know," said Vintar. "More than you know."

"Yes," Serbitar told Rek as they sat within the oak-paneled study overlooking the courtyard. "Yes, we can read minds. But I assure you we will not again attempt to read yours or that of your companion."

"Why did he do that to me?" asked Rek.

"Menahem is the eyes of the Thirty. He had to see that you were worthy to ask of us ... the service. You expect us to fight with your forces, to analyze enemy tactics, and to use our skills in defense of a fortress about which we care nothing. The messenger has to be worthy."

"But I am not the messenger; I am merely a companion."

"We shall see ... How long have you known of your ... affliction?"

Rek turned his gaze to the window and the balcony beyond. A wren landed on the railing, sharpened his beak on the stone, and then flew off. Light clouds were forming, fleece islands in the clear blue of the sky.

"It has happened only twice. Both times in the Sathuli wars. Once when we were surrounded after a dawn raid on a village and the second time when I was part of a guard unit for a spice caravan."

"It is common among warriors," said Serbitar. "It is a gift of fear."

"It saved my life both times, but it scares me," said Rek. "It is as if someone else takes over my mind and body."

"But that is not so, I assure you. It is you alone. Do not fear what you are, Rek—may I call you Rek?"

"Of course."

"I did not wish to be overly familiar. It is a nickname, is it not?"

"A shortened form of Regnak. My foster father, Horeb, shortened it when I was a child. It was a kind of joke. I disliked robust games and never wanted to explore or climb high trees. I wasn't reckless, he said; so he dropped the 'less' and called me Rek. As I said, it's not much of a joke, but the name stuck."

"Do you think," asked Serbitar, "that you will be comfortable at Dros Delnoch?"

Rek smiled. "Are you asking me if I have the nerve?"

"Speaking bluntly? Yes, I suppose I am."

"I don't know. Have you?"

The ghost of a smile hovered on the pale, fleshless face as the albino considered the question. His slender fingers tapped gently at the desk top.

"The question is a good one. Yes, I have the nerve. My fears are unconnected with death."

"You have read my mind," said Rek. "You tell *me* if I have the nerve. I mean it. I don't know if I can stand a drawn-out siege; it is said that men fail under such pressure."

"I cannot tell you," Serbitar answered, "if you will hold or fail. You are capable of both. I cannot analyze all the permutations of a siege. Ask yourself this: What if Virae fell? Would you stay on?"

"No," said Rek instantly. "I would saddle a fast horse and be gone. I don't care about Dros Delnoch. Or the Drenai empire."

"The Drenai are finished," said Serbitar. "Their star has fallen."

"Then you think the Dros will fall?"

"Ultimately it must. But I cannot see that far into the future as yet. The Way of the Mist is strange. Often it will show events still to come, but more often it will show events never to be. It is a perilous path which only the true mystic walks with certainty."

"The Way of the Mist?" asked Rek.

"I'm sorry, why should you know? It is a road on another plane . . . a fourth dimension? A journey of the spirit like a dream. Only you direct the dream and see what you desire to see. It is a concept hard to verbalize to a nonspeaker."

"Are you saying your soul can travel outside the body?" asked Rek.

"Oh, yes, that is the easy part. We saw you in Graven Forest outside the cabin. We helped you then by influencing the axman, Grussin."

"You made him kill Reinard?"

"No. Our powers are not that great. We merely pushed him in a direction he was considering already."

"I'm not sure I am entirely comfortable knowing you have that sort of power," said Rek, avoiding the albino's green eyes.

Serbitar laughed, his eyes sparkling, his pale face mirroring his joy.

"Friend Rek, I am a man of my word. I promised never to use my gift to read your mind, and I shall not. Nor will any of the Thirty. Do you think we would be priests, forsaking the world, if we wished harm to others? I am the son of an earl, but if I wished, I could be a king, an emperor mightier than Ulric. Do not feel threatened. We must be at ease one with the other. More, we must be friends."

"Why?" asked Rek.

"Because we are about to share a moment which comes only once in a lifetime," said Serbitar. "We are going to die."

"Speak for yourself," said Rek. "I do not see that going to Dros Delnoch is just another way of committing suicide. It's a battle, that's all. No more, no less than that. A wall can be defended. A smaller force can hold a larger. History is full of examples: Skeln Pass, for example."

"True," said Serbitar. "But they are remembered because they are exceptions. Let us deal in facts. The Dros is defended by a force less than a third of the full complement. Morale is low; fear is rife. Ulric has a force in excess of half a million warriors, all willing—lusting even—to die for him in battle. I am a weapon master and a student of war. Dros Delnoch will fall. Clear your mind of any other conclusion."

"Then why come with us? What will you gain from it?"

"We die," said Serbitar, "and then live. But I shall say no more of that at this time. I do not wish to depress you, Rek. If it would serve a purpose, I would fill you with hope. But my whole battle strategy will be built around delaying the inevitable. Only then can I function—and serve your cause."

"I hope you will keep that opinion to yourself," said Rek. "Virae believes we can hold. I know enough of warfare and morale to tell you plainly that if your theory were to spread among the men, there would be wholesale desertions; we would lose on the first day."

"I am not a fool, Rek. I say this to *you* because it needs to be said. I shall be your adviser at Delnoch, and you will need me to speak the truth. I shall have no real dealings with the soldiers, neither will the Thirty. Men will avoid us, anyway, once they know what we are."

"Perhaps. Why do you say you will be my adviser? Earl Delnar commands; I shall not even be an officer there."

"Let us say," said Serbitar, "that I will be the adviser to your cause. Time will explain all far better than I. Have I depressed you?"

"Not at all. You have told me everything is hopeless, we are all dead men, and the Drenai are finished. Depressed? Not at all!"

Serbitar laughed and clapped his hands. "I like you, Rek," he said. "I think you will hold firm."

"I will hold firm, all right," said Rek, smiling. "Because I will know that at the last wall I will have two horses waiting ready saddled. By the way, do you not have anything stronger than water to drink?"

"Sadly, no," answered Serbitar. "Alcohol inhibits our strength. If you need spirits, however, there is a village nearby, and I can have someone ride out for you to purchase some."

"You don't drink. There are no women. You eat no meat. What do you do for recreation?"

"We study," said Serbitar. "And we train, and we plant flowers and raise horses. Our time is well occupied, I can assure you."

"No wonder you want to go away and die somewhere," said Rek with feeling.

Virae sat with Vintar in a small sparsely furnished study awash with manuscripts and leather-bound tomes. There was a small desk littered with broken quills and scrawled parchment. She held back a smile as the older man fumbled with his breastplate strap. He could not have looked less like a warrior.

"Can I help you?" she asked, standing up and leaning over the desk.

"Thank you, my dear," he said. "It weighs heavily." He balanced the armor against the desk and poured himself some water, offering the jug to Virae, who shook her head. "I'm sorry the room is such a mess, but I have been hurrying to finish my diary. So much to say, so little time."

"Bring it with you," she said.

"I think not. Too many other problems to wrestle with once we are under way. You have changed since I saw you last, Virae."

"Two years is a long time, Abbot," she said carefully.

"I think it is the young man with you," he said, smiling. "He has a great influence."

"Nonsense. I am the same."

"Your walk is more assured. You are less clumsy than I remember. He has given you something, I think."

"Never mind that. What about the Dros?" she snapped, blushing.

"I am sorry, my dear. I did not wish to embarrass you."

"You have not embarrassed me," she lied. "Now, about Dros Delnoch. How can you help us?"

"As I told your father two years ago, our help will be in organization and planning. We will know the enemy's plans. We can aid you in thwarting them. Tactically we can organize the defenses, and militarily we can fight like a hundred. But our price is high."

"My father has deposited ten thousand gold Raq in Ventria," she said. "With the merchant Asbidare."

"Good. Then that is settled. We ride in the morning."

"May I ask you something?" said Virae. He opened his hands and waited. "Why do you need money?"

"For the next temple of the Thirty. Each temple is financed by the death of the last."

"Oh. What happens if you don't die? I mean, supposing we win?" His eyes searched her face for a matter of moments.

"Then we return the money," he said.

"I see," she said.

"You are unconvinced?"

"It doesn't matter. What do you think of Rek?"

"In what way?" asked Vintar.

"Let's not play games, Father Abbot. I know you can read minds. I want to know what you think of Rek."

"The question is not precise enough—no, let me finish," he said, watching her anger rise. "Do you mean as a man, as a warrior, or as a prospective husband for the daughter of an earl?"

"All three, if you like. I don't know. Just tell me."

"Very well. Do you believe in destiny?"

"Yes," she said, remembering that she had asked the same question of Rek. "Yes, I do."

"Then believe this. You were destined to meet. You are the perfect match. You boost his strengths and counter his weaknesses. What he does for you, you know already. As a man he is not unique or even very special. He has no great talents, is not a poet, a writer, or a philosopher. As a warrior—well, he has a sporadic courage that hides great fears. But he is a man in love. And that will increase his strength and his power to combat his fears. As a husband? In days of peace and plenty, I feel he would be wayward. But for now ... he loves you and is prepared to die for you. You can ask no more of a man than that."

"Why did I meet him now, of all times?" she asked, tears stinging her eyes. "I don't want him to die. I would kill myself, I think."

"No, my dear. I don't think you would, though I agree that you would feel like doing so. Why now? Why not? Live or die, a man and a woman need love. There is a need in the race. We need to share. To belong. Perhaps you will die before the year is out. But remember this: To have may be taken from you; to have had, never. Far better to have tasted love before dying than to die alone."

"I suppose so. But I would have liked children and a settled home. I would like to have taken Rek to Drenan and shown him off a little. I would like some of those bitches at court to see that a man could love me." She bit her lip, straining to hold back the tears.

"They are inconsequential. Whether they see you or not will not alter the fact that they were wrong. And it is a little early for despair. It is spring, and it will be many weeks before we reach the Dros. All things can happen in that time. Ulric may have a heart attack or fall from his horse and crush his skull. Abalayn may make another treaty. The at tack may come at another fortress. Who knows?"

"I know. You are right. I don't know why I'm suddenly so full of self-pity. Meeting Rek was marvelous for me. You should have seen him standing up to Reinard's outlaws. You know of Reinard?"

"Yes."

"Well, you won't have to worry about him anymore. He's dead. Anyway, Rek stood up to twenty of them because they were going to take me. Twenty! He would have fought them all. Damn, I'm going to cry!"

"Why should you not cry? You are in love with a man who adores you, and the future looks bleak and empty of hope." He walked to her, took her hand, and pulled her to her feet. "Virae, it is always harder for the young."

She rested her head on his chest as the tears ran. He put his arms around her and patted her back. "Can Dros Delnoch hold?" she asked him.

"All things can happen. Did you know Druss is on his way there?"

"He agreed? That is good news." She sniffed and wiped her eyes on the sleeve of her shirt. Then Rek's words came back to her. "He's not senile, is he?"

Vintar laughed aloud. "Druss! Senile? Certainly not. What a wonderful thought! That is one old man who will never be senile. It would mean giving in to something. I used to believe that if Druss wanted night to last longer, he would just reach up and drag the sun back down over the horizon."

"You knew him?"

"Yes. And his wife, Rowena. A beautiful child. A speaker of rare talent. Gifted even beyond Serbitar."

"I always thought Rowena was just part of the legend," said Virae. "Did he really cross the world to find her?"

"Yes," said Vintar, releasing Virae and returning to his desk. "She was taken prisoner soon after they wed, when the village was attacked by slavers. He hunted her for years. They were a blissfully happy couple. Like you and Rek, I shouldn't wonder."

"What happened to her?"

"She died. Soon after Skeln Pass. A weak heart."

"Poor Druss," she said. "But he is still strong, you say?"

" 'When he stares, valleys tremble,' " quoted Vintar. " 'Where he walks, beasts are silent; when he speaks, mountains tumble; when he fights, armies crumble.' "

"But can he still fight?" she pressed.

"I think he will manage a skirmish or two," said Vintar, roaring with laughter.

◊ 7 ◊

TWO DAYS AND twenty-seven leagues from Skoda and Druss, with a mile-eating soldier's stride, was nearing the lush valleys at the edge of Skultik forest. He was three days march from Dros Delnoch, and evidence of the coming war met his eyes everywhere. Deserted homes, untended fields, and the people he did meet were wary and mistrustful of strangers. They wore defeat like a cloak, Druss thought. Topping a small rise, he found himself looking down on a village of maybe thirty homes, some crudely built, others showing signs of more careful construction. At the center of the hamlet was a square, an inn, and a stable.

Druss rubbed his thigh, trying to ease the rheumatic pain in his swollen right knee. His right shoulder ached, but this was a dull throbbing he could live with, a reminder of past battles when a Ventrian spear had cut under his shoulder blade. But the knee! This would not bear him many more leagues without rest and an ice pack.

He hawked and spit, wiping a huge hand across his bearded lips. You're an old man, he told himself. There is no point in pretending otherwise. He limped down the hill toward the inn, wondering once more whether he should purchase a mount. His head told him yes; his heart said no. He was Druss the Legend, and he never rode. Tireless, he could walk all night and fight all day. It would be good for morale when Druss walked into Dros Delnoch. Men would say: "Great gods, the old boy's walked from Skoda." And others would answer: "Of course he has. That's Druss. He never rides."

But his head told him to buy a horse and leave it at the forest's edge, a mere ten miles from the Dros. And who would be the wiser?

The inn was crowded, but the innkeeper had rooms to spare. Most of the customers were passing through, heading south or west into neutral Vagria. Druss paid his money, took a canvas sack of ice to his room, and sat on the hard bed, pressing it to his swollen knee. He had not been in the main room for long, but long enough to hear some of the conversations and to recognize many of the men there as soldiers. Deserters.

Always in war, he knew, there were men who would sooner ride than die. But many of the young men downstairs had seemed more demoralized than cowardly.

Were things so bad at Delnoch?

He removed the ice and massaged the fluid away from the joint, his thick fingers pressing and probing, his teeth gritted hard against the pain. Satisfied at last, he opened his small pack and removed a length of sturdy cotton bandage, which he wound tightly about the knee, tucking the end into the fold. Then he rolled down his woolen leggings and pulled his black boot onto his foot, grunting as the injured knee tensed. He stood and walked to the window, pushing it open. His knee felt better—not much, but enough. The sky was cloudless and blue, and a soothing breeze ruffled his beard. High overhead an eagle circled.

Druss returned to his pack, removing the crumpled letter from Delnar. He walked to the window for better light and smoothed the parchment open.

The script was writ large, and Druss chuckled again. He was no reader, and Delnar knew it.

My Dearest Comrade,

Even as I write I receive messages about the Nadir army being gathered at Gulgothir. It is plain that Ulric is ready to expand south. I have written to Abalayn, pleading for more men. There are none to be had. I have sent Virae to Vintar—you remember the Abbot of Swords?—to request the Thirty. I clutch at straws, my friend.

I do not know in what health this letter will find you,

but it is written in desperation. I need a miracle or the Dros will fall. I know you swore never again to enter the gates, but old wounds heal and my wife is dead. As is your friend Sieben. You and I are the only men living to know the truth of the matter. And I have never spoken of it.

Your name alone will stop the desertions and restore morale. I am plagued on all sides by poor officers, politically appointed, but my heaviest load is Gan Orrin, the commander. He is Abalayn's nephew and a martinet. He is despised, and yet I cannot replace him. In truth, I no longer command.

I have a cancer. It consumes me daily.

It is unfair of me to tell you of it, for I know I am using my own impending death to ask of you a favor.

Come and fight with us. We need you, Druss. Without you, we are lost. Just as at Skeln. Come as soon as you can.

Your comrade in arms.

Earl Delnar

Druss folded the letter, pushing it into a deep pocket inside his leather jerkin.

"An old man with a swollen knee and an arthritic back. If you've pinned your hopes on a miracle, my friend, you will need to seek elsewhere."

A silvered mirror stood next to a washbasin on an oak chest, and Druss stared hard at his reflection. The eyes were piercing blue, the beard square-cut, the jaw beneath it firm. He pulled his leather helm from his head and scratched the thick mat of gray hair. His thoughts were somber as he replaced the helm and strode downstairs.

At the long bar he ordered ale and listened to the talk around him.

"They say Ulric has a million men," said one tall youngster. "And you heard what he did at Gulgothir. When the city refused to surrender and he had taken it, he had every second defender hanged and quartered. Six thousand men. They say the air was black with crows. Imagine! Six thousand!"

"Do you know why he did it?" Druss asked, breaking

into the conversation. The men looked at one another, then back at Druss.

"Of course I know. He's a bloodthirsty savage, that's why."

"Not at all," said Druss. "Join me in a drink?" He called the innkeeper and ordered more ale. "He did it so that men like you could spread the word to other cities. Wait! Mistake me not," said Druss as the man's anger flushed his face. "I do not criticize you for telling the story. It is natural for these tales to be passed on. But Ulric is a canny soldier. Assume he took the city and treated the defenders heroically. Other cities would defend just as hard. But this way he sends fear ahead of him. And fear is a great ally."

"You talk like an admirer," said another man, shorter, with a curling blond mustache.

"But I am," said Druss, smiling. "Ulric is one of the greatest generals of the age. Who else in a thousand years has united the Nadir? And with such simplicity. It is the Nadir way to fight anyone not of their tribe. With a thousand tribes thinking this way, they could never become a nation. Ulric took his own tribe, the Wolfshead, and changed the style of Nadir war. To each tribe he conquered, he offered a choice: join him or die. Many chose to die, but many more chose to live. And his army grew. Each tribe keeps its own customs, and they are honored. You cannot take such a man lightly."

"The man is a treacherous cur," offered a man from another group of speakers. "He signed a treaty with us. Now he is to break it."

"I am not defending his morals," said Druss equably. "Merely pointing out that he's a good general. His troops worship him."

"Well, I don't like the way you speak, old man," said the tallest of the listeners.

"No?" said Druss. "Are you a soldier, then?"

The man hesitated, glanced at his companions, then shrugged. "It doesn't matter," he said. "Forget it."

"Are you a deserter, then?"

"I said to forget it, old man," stormed the youngster.

"Are you all deserters?" asked Druss, leaning back

against the bar and scanning the thirty or so men gathered there.

"No, not all," said one young man emerging from the throng. He was tall and slim, dark hair braided beneath a helm of bronze. "But you cannot blame those who are."

"Don't bother with it, Pinar," said one. "We have talked it over."

"I know. Interminably," said Pinar. "But it doesn't change the situation. The gan is a pig. Worse, he is incompetent. But in leaving, you are just making sure your comrades have no chance at all."

"They haven't any chance, anyway," said the short one with the blond mustache. "If they had any sense, they would leave with us."

"Dorian, you are being selfish," said Pinar gently. "When the fighting starts, Gan Orrin will have to forget his idiot rules. We will all be too busy to worry about them."

"Well, I've had enough of it already," said Dorian. "Shining armor. Dawn parades. Forced marches. Midnight inspections. Penalties for sloppy salutes, uncombed crests, talking after lights-out. The man's mad."

"If you're caught, you will be hung," said Pinar.

"He doesn't dare to send anyone after us. They would desert, too. I came to Dros Delnoch to fight the Nadir. I left a farm, a wife, and two daughters. I didn't come here for all that shining armor garbage."

"Then go, my friend," said Pinar. "I hope you do not live to regret it."

"I do regret it already. But my mind is set," said Dorian. "I am heading south to join Woundweaver. Now, there's a soldier!"

"Is Earl Delnar still alive?" asked Druss. The young warrior nodded absently. "How many men still hold their positions?"

"What?" said Pinar, realizing that Druss was speaking to him.

"How many men have you at Delnoch?"

"What concern is it of yours?"

"It's where I am heading."

"Why?"

"Because I have been asked, young laddie," said Druss.

"And in more years than I care to remember, I have never turned down a request from a friend."

"This friend asked you to join us at Dros Delnoch? Is he mad? We need soldiers, archers, pikemen, warriors. I haven't time to be respectful, old man. But you should go home; we have no need of graybeards."

Druss smiled grimly. "You are a blunt speaker, boy. But your brains are in your breeches. I have handled an ax for twice your lifetime. My enemies are all dead, or wished they were." His eyes blazed, and he stepped closer toward the younger man. "When your life has been spent in one war after another for forty-five years, you have to be pretty handy to survive. Now you, laddie—your lips scarcely dry from your mother's milk—are just a beardless boy to me. Your sword looks pretty there at your side. But if I chose, I could kill you without breaking a sweat."

A silence had fallen on the room, and the watchers noted the bright sheen on Pinar's brow.

"Who invited you to Dros Delnoch?" he said at last.

"Earl Delnar."

"I see. Well, the earl has been ill, sir. Now you may or may not be a mighty warrior still. And I most certainly am a beardless boy to you. But let me tell you this: Gan Orrin commands at Dros Delnoch, and he will not allow you to stay, Earl Delnar or no. I am sure your heart is in the right place, and I am sorry if I sounded disrespectful. But you are too old for a war."

"The judgment of youth!" said Druss. "It is seldom of value. All right, much as it goes against the grain, I can see I still have to prove myself. Set me a task, boy!"

"I don't understand you," said Pinar.

"Set me a task. Something no man here can do. And we will see how 'the old man' fares."

"I have no time for these games. I must return to the Dros." He turned to go, but Druss's words hit him like a blow, chilling his blood.

"You don't understand, boy. If you do not set me that task, I will have to kill you. For I will not be shamed."

The young man turned again. "As you say. Very well, shall we adjourn to the marketplace?"

The inn emptied, the crowd forming a circle about the

two men in the deserted village square. The sun beat down, and Druss sucked in a deep breath, glorying in the warmth of spring.

"It will be pointless giving you a test of strength," said Pinar, "for you are built like a bull. But war, as you know, is a test of stamina. Do you wrestle?"

"I have been known to," said Druss, doffing his jerkin.

"Good! Then you may test your skill, one at a time, against three men of my choice. Do you agree?"

"All too simple against these soft, fat runners," said Druss. An angry murmur arose from the crowd, but Pinar silenced them with a raised hand.

"Dorian. Hagir. Somin. Will you give old father here a trial?"

The men were the first three Druss had met at the bar. Dorian removed his cloak and tied his shoulder-length hair behind his neck with a leather thong. Druss, unnoticed, tested his knee: it was not strong.

"Are you ready?" asked Pinar.

Both men nodded, and immediately Dorian rushed the older man. Druss lashed out, grabbing the other's throat, then stooped to push his right hand between the man's legs and lifted. With a grunt and a heave, he hurled him ten feet through the air to land like a sack on the hard-packed earth. Dorian half rose, then sat back, shaking his head. The crowd hooted with laughter.

"Who's next?" asked Druss.

Pinar nodded to another youngster; then, observing the fear on the lad's face, he stepped forward. "You have made your point, graybeard. You are strong, and I am at fault. But Gan Orrin will not allow you to fight."

"Laddie, he will not stop me. If he tries, I will tie him to a fast horse and send him back to his uncle." All eyes turned as a hoarse cry split the air.

"You old bastard!" Dorian had gathered up his long-sword and was advancing toward Druss, who stood with arms folded, waiting.

"No," said Pinar. "Put up your blade, Dorian."

"Back off or draw your sword," Dorian told him. "I have had enough of these games. You think you are a warrior, old man? Then let us see you use that ax. Because if you don't, I will put some air in your belly."

"Boy," said Druss, his eyes cold, "think well about this venture. For make no mistake, you cannot stand before me and live. No man ever has." The words were spoken softly, yet no one disbelieved the old man.

Except Dorian.

"Well, we shall see. Draw your blade!"

Druss slipped Snaga from its sheath, his broad hand curling around its black haft. Dorian attacked!

And died.

He lay on the ground, head half-severed from his neck. Druss hammered Snaga deep into the earth, cleansing the blade of blood, while Pinar stood in stunned silence. Dorian had not been a great swordsman, but he certainly had been skilled. Yet the old man had batted aside the slashing sword and in one flowing motion had returned the attack—all without moving his feet. Pinar looked down at the body of his former companion. You should have stayed at the Dros, he thought.

"I did not want that to happen," said Druss, "but I gave him fair warning. The choice was his."

"Yes," said Pinar. "My apologies for speaking the way I did. You will be a great help to us, I think. Excuse me. I must help them to remove the body. Will you join me for a drink?"

"I will see you in the long bar," said Druss.

The tall dark-haired youngster whom Druss had been scheduled to wrestle approached him as he walked through the crowd.

"Excuse me, sir," he said. "I am sorry about Dorian. He's hot-tempered. Always has been."

"Not anymore," said Druss.

"There will be no blood feud," said the man.

"Good. A man with a wife and daughters has no place losing his temper. The man was a fool. Are you a friend of the family?"

"Yes. My name is Hagir. Our farms are close. We are . . . were . . . neighbors."

"Then, Hagir, when you get home, I hope you will see that his wife is cared for."

"I am not going home. I'm going back to the Dros."

"What changed your mind?"

"With respect, you did, sir. I think I know who you are."

"Make your own decisions; don't place them on my shoulders. I want good soldiers at Dros Delnoch, but also I want men who will stand."

"I didn't leave because I was frightened. I was just fed up with the crazy rules. But if men like you are prepared to be there, I will stick it out."

"Good. Join me for a drink later. Now I am going to have a hot bath."

Druss pushed his way past the men in the doorway and went inside.

"Are you really going back, Hagir?" asked one of the men.

"Yes. Yes, I am."

"But why?" urged another. "Nothing has changed. Except that we shall all be on report and probably flogged."

"It's him—*he*'s going there. The Captain of the Ax."

"Druss! That was Druss?"

"Yes, I am sure of it."

"How sickening!" said the other.

"What do you mean, Somin?" asked Hagir.

"Dorian—Druss was Dorian's hero. Don't you remember him talking about him? Druss this and Druss that. It is one reason he joined up—to be like Druss and maybe even to meet him."

"Well, he met him," said Hagir somberly.

Druss, dark-haired Pinar, tall Hagir, and blunt-featured Somin sat at a corner table in the long room of the inn. Around them a crowd gathered, drawn by the legend of the grizzled old man.

"Just over nine thousand, you say. How many archers?"

Dun Pinar waved a hand. "No more than six hundred, Druss. The rest are remnants of cavalry lancers, infantrymen, pikemen, and engineers. The bulk of the complement is made up of volunteer farmers from the Sentran Plain. They're plucky enough."

"If I remember aright," said Druss, "the first wall is four hundred paces long and twenty wide. You will need a thousand archers on it. And I don't just mean a thousand bows. We need men who can pick a target from a hundred paces."

"We just haven't got them," said Pinar. "On the credit side, we do have almost a thousand legion riders."

"Some good news at least. Who leads them?"

"Gan Hogun."

"The same Hogun who routed the Sathuli at Corte-swain?"

"Yes," said Pinar, pride in his voice. "A skilled soldier, strong on discipline and yet worshiped by his men. He's not very popular with Gan Orrin."

"He wouldn't be," said Druss. "But that's a matter we shall settle at Delnoch. What of supplies?"

"There we have a few problems. There is enough food for a year, and we discovered three more wells, one as far back as the keep. We have close to six hundred thousand arrows, a multitude of javelins, and several hundred spare mail shirts.

"But the biggest problem is the town itself. It has spread from Wall Three down to Wall Six, hundreds of buildings from wall to wall. There is no killing ground, Druss. Once over Wall Six, the enemy has cover all the way to the keep."

"We will tackle that, too, when I arrive. Are there still outlaws in Skultik?"

"Of course. When have there not been?" answered Pinar.

"How many?"

"Impossible to say. Five or six hundred, perhaps."

"Do they have a known leader?"

"Again, hard to say," said Pinar. "According to rumor, there is a young nobleman who heads the largest band. But you know how these rumors grow. Every outlaw leader is an ex-nobleman or a prince. What are you thinking?"

"I'm thinking they are archers," said Druss.

"But you cannot enter Skultik now, Druss. Anything could happen. They could kill you."

"True. All things could happen. My heart could give out, my liver fail. Disease could strike me. A man cannot spend his life worrying about the unexpected. I need archers. In Skultik there are archers. It's that simple, boy."

"But it's not that simple. Send someone else. You are too

valuable to lose like this," Pinar told him, gripping the old man's arm.

"I'm too long in the tooth to change my ways now. Direct action pays off, Pinar. Believe me. And there's more to it, which I will tell you about some other time.

"Now," he said, leaning back and addressing the crowd, "you know who I am and where I am heading. I will speak plainly to you; many of you are runners, some are frightened, others are demoralized. Understand this: When Ulric takes Dros Delnoch, the Drenai lands will become Nadir lands. The farms you are running to will be Nadir farms. Your wives will become Nadir women. There are some things no man can run from. I know.

"At Dros Delnoch you risk death. But all men die.

"Even Druss. Even Karnak the One-Eyed. Even the Earl of Bronze.

"A man needs many things in his life to make it bearable. A good woman. Sons and daughters. Comradeship. Warmth. Food and shelter. But above all these things he needs to be able to know that he is a man.

"And what is a man? He is someone who rises when life has knocked him down. He is someone who raises his fist to heaven when a storm has ruined his crop—and then plants again. And again. A man remains unbroken by the savage twists of fate.

"That man may never win. But when he sees himself reflected, he can be proud of what he sees. For low he may be in the scheme of things: peasant, serf, or dispossessed. But he is unconquerable.

"And what is death? An end to trouble. An end to strife and fear.

"I have fought in many battles. I have seen many men die. And women, too. In the main, they died proud.

"Bear this in mind as you decide your future."

The old man's fierce blue eyes scanned the faces in the crowd, gauging the reaction. He knew he had them. It was time to leave.

He bade his farewells to Pinar and the rest, settled his bill despite the protestations of the innkeeper, and set off for Skultik.

He was angry as he walked, feeling the stares on his

back as the inn emptied to watch him go. He was angry because he knew his speech had been a falsehood, and he was a man who liked the truth. Life, he knew, broke many men. Some as strong as oak withered as their wives died, or left them, as their children suffered or starved. Other strong men broke if they lost a limb or, worse, the use of their legs or their eyesight. Each man had a breaking point, no matter how strong his spirit. Somewhere, deep inside him, there was a flaw that only the fickle cruelty of fate could find. A man's strength was ultimately born of his knowledge of his own weakness, Druss knew.

His own fear was of dotage and senility. The thought of it set him to trembling. Did he really hear a voice at Skoda, or was it merely his own terror booming inside him?

Druss the Legend. Mightiest man of his era. A killing machine, a warrior. And why?

Because I never had the courage to be a farmer, Druss told himself.

Then he laughed, dismissing all somber thoughts and self-doubt. It was a talent he had.

Today had a good feel about it. He felt lucky. If he kept to known trails, he would certainly meet outlaws. One old man alone was a package not to be missed. They would be a sorely inefficient lot if he were to pass through the forest unnoticed and unattended.

The woods were becoming thicker now as he reached the outskirts of Skultik. Huge, gnarled oaks, graceful willows, and slender elm interlinked their branches for as far as the eye could see—and greatly beyond, Druss knew.

The noon sun made shafts of shimmering light through the branches, and the breeze carried the sounds of miniature waterfalls from hidden streams. It was a place of enchantment and beauty.

To his left a squirrel ceased its hunt for food and gazed warily at the old man as he marched past. A fox crouched in the undergrowth, and a snake slithered beneath a fallen trunk as he approached. Overhead birds sang, a chorus full of the sounds of life.

Throughout the long afternoon Druss marched on, occasionally bursting into song, full-bodied and lusty versions of battle hymns from a score of nations.

Toward dusk he became aware that he was being watched.

How he was aware he could never explain. A tightening of the skin on his neck, a growing awareness that his back made a broad target. Whatever it was, he had learned to trust his senses in the matter. He loosened Snaga in its sheath.

Some moments later he entered a small clearing in a grove of beech trees, which were slender and wandlike against a background of oak.

At the center of the clearing, on a fallen trunk, sat a young man, dressed in homespun garments of green tunic and brown leather leggings. Upon his legs lay a longsword, and by his side was a longbow and a quiver of goose-feathered arrows.

"Good day, old man," he said as Druss appeared. Lithe and strong, thought Druss, noting with a warrior's eye the catlike grace of the man as he stood, sword in hand.

"Good day, laddie," said Druss, spotting a movement to his left in the undergrowth. Another whisper of branch on cloth came from his right.

"And what brings you to our charming forest?" asked the young man. Druss casually walked to a nearby beech and sat, leaning his back against the bark.

"A desire for solitude," he said.

"Ah, yes. Solitude! And now you have company. Perhaps this is not a lucky time for you."

"One time is as lucky as another," said Druss, returning the other's smile. "Why don't you ask your friends to join us? It must be damp skulking in the bushes."

"How rude of me, to be sure. Eldred, Ring, come forward and meet our guest." Sheepishly two other young men pushed their way through the greenery to stand beside the first. Both were dressed in identical clothing of green tunic and leather leggings. "Now we are all here," said the first.

"All except the bearded one with the longbow," said Druss.

The young man laughed. "Come out, Jorak. Old father here misses nothing, it seems." The fourth man came into the open. He was large—a head taller than Druss and built like an ox, his massive hands dwarfing the longbow.

"Now, dear sir, we are all here. Be so kind as to divest yourself of all your valuables, for we are in a hurry. There is a stag roasting at camp, and sweet new potatoes garnished with mint. I don't want to be late." He smiled almost apologetically.

Druss bunched his powerful legs beneath him, rising to his feet, his blue eyes glinting with battle joy.

"If you want my purse, you will have to earn it," he said.

"Oh, damn!" said the young man, smiling and reseating himself. "I told you, Jorak, that this old fellow had a warrior look about him."

"And I told you that we should have merely shot him down and then taken his purse," said Jorak.

"Unsporting," said the first. He turned to Druss. "Listen, old man, it would be churlish of us to shoot you down from a distance, and that sets us a pretty problem. We must have your purse, don't you see? No point in being a robber else." He paused, deep in thought, then spoke once more. "You're obviously not a rich man, so whatever we get will not be worth a great deal of effort. How about spinning a coin? You win, you keep your money; we win, we take it. And I'll throw in a free meal. Roast stag! How does that sound?"

"How about if I win, I get your purses *and* a meal?" asked Druss.

"Now, now, old horse! No point in taking liberties when we're trying to be friendly. All right! How about this? Honor needs to be satisfied. How about a little skirmish with Jorak here? You look quite strong, and he's a dab hand at bare-knuckle squabbles."

"Done!" said Druss. "What are the rules?"

"Rules? Whoever is left standing wins. Win or lose, we'll stand you a supper. I rather like you; you remind me of my grandfather."

Druss grinned broadly, reached into his pack, and pulled on his black gauntlets. "You don't mind, do you, Jorak?" he asked. "It's the old skin on my knuckles—it tends to split."

"Let's get it over with," said Jorak, advancing.

Druss stepped in to meet him, taking in the awesome breadth of the man's shoulders. Jorak lunged, hurling a right cross. Druss ducked and crashed his own right fist into the other's belly. A whoosh of air exploded from the giant's mouth. Stepping back, Druss thundered a right hook to the jaw, and Jorak hit the ground face first. He twitched once, then lay still.

"The youth of today," said Druss sadly, "have no stamina!"

The young leader chuckled. "You win, Father Time. But look. For the sake of my fast-diminishing prestige, give me the opportunity of besting you at something. We will have a wager: I wager my purse against yours that I am a better archer."

"Hardly a fair bet, laddie. I will concede that point. But I will make a wager with you: strike the trunk of the tree behind me with one arrow and I'll pay up."

"Come now, dear sir, where is the art in that? Less than fifteen paces, and the bole is three hands wide."

"Try it and see," offered Druss.

The young outlaw shrugged, hefted his bow, and drew a long arrow from his doeskin quiver. With a fluid motion his strong fingers drew back the string and released the shaft. As the outlaw's bow bent, Druss drew Snaga and the ax sang through the air in a glittering arc of white light as he sliced the blade to his right. The outlaw's shaft splintered as the ax struck. The young man blinked and swallowed. "I would have paid to have seen that," he said.

"You did!" said Druss. "Where is your purse?"

"Sadly," said the young man, pulling his pouch from his belt, "it is empty. But the purse is yours, as we agreed. Where did you learn that trick?"

"In Ventria, years ago."

"I've seen some ax work in the past. But that bordered on the incredible. My name is Bowman."

"I am Druss."

"I know that, old horse. Actions speak louder than words."

◇ **8** ◇

HOGUN SWALLOWED BACK despair, his mind working furiously. He and two hundred of his legion riders faced more than a thousand Nadir dog soldiers, the cavalry wing of Ulric's forces.

Sent out to gauge the strength and disposition of the Nadir horde, Hogun was over 150 miles from Delnoch. He had all but pleaded with Orrin to forsake this plan, but the first gan was not to be dissuaded.

"A refusal to obey a direct order is punishable by instant dismissal for any of gan rank. Is that what you wish, Hogun?"

"You know that's not what I'm saying. What I am telling you is that this mission is futile. We know from our spies and countless refugees the strength of Ulric's forces. Sending two hundred men into that wasteland is insane."

Orrin's brown eyes had blazed with anger, his fat chin trembling in a bid to suppress his fury. "Insane, is it? I wonder. Is it just that you don't like the plan, or is the famed Corteswain warrior afraid to meet the Nadir?"

"The black riders are the only seasoned troop of proven worth you have here, Orrin," he said as persuasively as he could. "You could lose all two hundred men with such a scheme and learn from it no more than we already know. Ulric has five hundred thousand men and more than twice that in camp followers, cooks, engineers, and whores. He will be here within six weeks."

"Hearsay," muttered Orrin. "You leave at first light."

Hogun had come close to killing him then, close enough for Orrin to sense danger.

"I am your senior officer," he said, his voice close to a whine. "You will obey me."

And Hogun had. With two hundred of his finest men, mounted on black horses—bred for generations as the finest war mounts on the continent—he had thundered his troop northward as the dawn sun breasted the Delnoch mountains.

Out of sight of the Dros he had slowed the column and signaled the men to ride at ease, free to talk to their riding companions. Dun Elicas cantered alongside him, reining his horse to a walk.

"A bad business, sir."

Hogun smiled but did not answer. He liked young Elicas. The man was a warrior born and a fine lieutenant. He sat a horse as if he had been born on one, a true centaur. And a hellion in battle, with his custom-made silver steel saber, two inches shorter than the standard version.

"What are we supposed to be finding out?" he asked.

"The size and disposition of the Nadir army," answered Hogun.

"We know that already," said Elicas. "What is the fat fool playing at?"

"Enough of that, Elicas," he said sternly. "He wants to be sure the spies were not ... exaggerating."

"He's jealous of you, Hogun; he wants you dead. Face it, man. No one can hear us. You know what he is—a courtier. And he has no guts. The Dros won't last a day; he'll open the gates for sure."

"He's a man under terrible pressure. The whole of the Drenai cause rests on his shoulders," said Hogun. "Give him time."

"We don't have time. Look, Hogun, send me to Woundweaver. Let me explain our situation. He could be replaced."

"No. Believe me, Elicas, it would achieve nothing. He's Abalayn's nephew."

"That old man has a lot to answer for," snarled Elicas. "If we do somehow get out of this business alive, he will fall for sure."

"He has ruled for thirty years. It's too long. But as you say, if we do get out alive, it will be because of Woundweaver. And it's certain he will take control."

"Then let me ride to him now," urged Elicas.

"The time isn't right. Woundweaver cannot act. Now, leave it alone. We will do our job and, with luck, get away without being spotted."

But luck had not been with them. Five days out from Delnoch they had come across three Nadir outriders. They had killed only two, the third ducking down over the neck of his steppe pony and riding like the wind into a nearby wood. Hogun had ordered an immediate withdrawal and might have pulled it off had he enjoyed an ounce of luck. Elicas has been the first to spot the mirror messages flashing from peak to peak.

"What do you think, sir?" he asked as Hogun reined in.

"I think we will need good fortune. It depends on how many dog soldiers they have in the vicinity."

The answer was not long in coming. Toward late afternoon they saw the dust cloud south of them. Hogun glanced over his back trail.

"Lebus!" he called, and a young warrior cantered alongside.

"You have eyes like a hawk. Look back there. What do you see?"

The young soldier shielded his eyes from the sun, then squinted at their back trail.

"Dust, sir. From maybe two thousand horses."

"And ahead?"

"Perhaps a thousand."

"Thank you. Rejoin the troop. Elicas!"

"Sir?"

"Cloaks furled. We will take them with lances and sabers."

"Yes, sir." He cantered back down the column. The black cloaks were unpinned and folded to be strapped to saddles. The black and silver armor glinted in the sunlight as man after man began to prepare for the charge. From saddlebags each rider removed a black and silver forearm guard and slipped it in place. Then small round bucklers were lifted from saddle horns to be fitted to the left arm. Straps were adjusted, and armor tightened. The approaching Nadir could now be seen as individuals, but the sound of their battle cries was muffled by the pounding of horses' hooves.

"Helms down!" yelled Hogun. "Wedge formation!"

Hogun and Elicas formed the point of the wedge, the other riders slipping expertly into position a hundred on either side.

"Advance!" yelled Elicas. The troop broke into a canter; then, at full gallop, the lances tilted. As the distance narrowed, Hogun felt his blood racing and could hear his pounding heart in time with the rolling thunder of the black horses' iron-shod hooves.

Now he could pick out individual Nadir faces and hear their screams.

The wedge smashed into the Nadir ranks, the larger black war-horses cleaving a path through the mass of smaller hill ponies. Hogun's lance speared a Nadir chest and snapped as the man catapulted from his pony. Then his saber slashed into the air; he cut one man from his mount, parried a thrust from the left, and backhanded his blade across the throat of the horseman. Elicas screamed a Drenai war cry from his right, his horse rearing, the front hooves caving in the chest of a piebald pony that ditched his rider beneath the milling mass of black riders.

And then they were through, racing for the distant, fragile safety of Dros Delnoch.

Glancing back, Hogun saw the Nadir re-form and canter to the north. There was no pursuit.

"How many men did we lose?" he asked Elicas as the troop slowed to a walk.

"Eleven."

"It could have been worse. Who were they?"

Elicas recounted the names. All good men, survivors of many battles.

"That bastard Orrin will pay for this," said Elicas bitterly.

"Forget it! He was right. More by luck than any judgment, but he was right."

"What do you mean 'right'? We've learned nothing, and we've lost eleven men," said Elicas.

"We have learned that the Nadir are closer than we believed. Those dog soldiers were Wolfshead tribe. That's Ulric's own; they're his personal guard. He'd never send them that far ahead of his main force. I'd say we now have a month—if we're lucky."

"Damn! I was going to gut the pig and take the consequences."

"Tell the men no fires tonight," said Hogun.

Well, fat man, he thought, this is your first good decision.

May it not be the last.

◊ 9 ◊

THE FOREST HAD an ageless beauty that touched Druss's warrior soul. Enchantment hung in the air. Gnarled oaks became silent sentinels in the silver moonlight, majestic, immortal, unyielding. What cared they for man's wars? A gentle breeze whispered through the interwoven branches above the old man's head. A shaft of moonlight bathed a fallen log, granting it momentarily an ethereal splendor. A lone badger, caught in the light, shuffled into the undergrowth.

A raucous song began among the men crowded around the blazing camp fire, and Druss cursed softly. Once again the forest was merely forest, the oaks outsize plants. Bowman wandered across to him, carrying two leather goblets and a wine sack.

"Finest Ventrian," he said. "It'll turn your hair black."

"I'm all for that," said Druss. The young man filled Druss's goblet, then his own.

"You look melancholy, Druss. I thought the prospect of another glorious battle would lighten your heart."

"Your men are the worst singers I have heard in twenty years. They're butchering that song." Druss replied, leaning his back against the oak, feeling the wine ease his tension.

"Why are you going to Delnoch?" asked Bowman.

"The worst were a bunch of captured Sathuli. They just kept chanting the same bloody verse over and over again. We let them go in the end—we thought that if they sang like that when they got home, they'd break the fighting spirit of their tribe in a week."

"Now look here, old horse," said Bowman. "I am a man

85

not easily thrown. Give me an answer—any answer! Lie if you like. But tell me why you travel to Delnoch."

"Why do you want to know?"

"It fascinates me. A man with half an eye could see that Delnoch will fall, and you're a man with enough experience to know the truth when you see it. So why go?"

"Have you any idea, laddie, how many such lost causes I have been involved in during the past forty or so years?"

"Precious few," said Bowman. "Or you would not be here to tell of them."

"Not so. How do you decide a battle is lost? Numbers, strategic advantage, positioning? It's all worth a sparrow's fart. It comes down to men who are willing. The largest army will founder if its men are less willing to die than to win."

"Rhetoric," snorted Bowman. "Use it at the Dros. The fools there will lap it up."

"One man against five, and the one disabled," said Druss, holding his temper. "Where would your money go?"

"I'm ahead of you, old man. What if the one was Karnak the One-Eyed. Yes? Well, then my money would be on him. But how many Karnaks are there at Dros Delnoch?"

"Who knows? Even Karnak was unknown once. He made his name on a bloody battlefield. There will be many heroes come the last at Dros Delnoch."

"Then you admit it? The Dros is doomed," said Bowman, grinning in triumph. "At the last, you said."

"Damn you, boy! Don't put words in my mouth," snarled Druss, cursing himself. Where are you now, Sieben? he thought. Now that I need you with your glib words and ready wit.

"Then don't try to treat me like a fool. Admit that the Dros is doomed."

"As you say," admitted Druss, "anyone with half an eye could see it. But I don't give a damn, laddie. Until the actual moment when they cut me down, I shall still be looking to win. And the gods of war are fickle at best. Where do you stand on the matter?"

Bowman smiled and refilled both goblets. For a while he was silent, enjoying the wine and the old man's discomfort.

"Well?" said Druss.

"Now we come to it," answered Bowman.

"Come to what?" said Druss, ill at ease under the young archer's cynical gaze.

"The reason for this visit to my woods," said Bowman, spreading his hands, his smile now open and friendly. "Come now, Druss. I've too much respect for you to fence any longer. You want my men for your insane battle. And the answer is no. But enjoy the wine, anyway."

"Am I so transparent?" asked the old warrior.

"When Druss the Legend takes a stroll through Skultik on the eve of the end, he's looking for more than acorns."

"Is this all you want from life?" asked Druss. "You sleep in a wattle hut and eat when you can find game. When you cannot, you starve. In winter you're cold. In summer, the ants crawl into your clothes and the lice prosper. You were not made for a life like this."

"We are not made for life at all, old horse. It is made for us. We live it. We leave it. I'll not throw my life away in your bloody madness. I leave such heroics to men like you. All your years have been spent in one squalid war after another. And what has changed? Have you thought that if you had not defeated the Ventrians fifteen years ago at Skeln, we would now be part of a mighty empire and *they* would have had to worry about the Nadir?"

"Freedom's worth fighting for," said Druss.

"Why? No one can take away the freedom of a man's soul."

"Liberty, then?" offered Druss.

"Liberty is valued only when it is threatened; therefore, it is the threat that highlights the value. We should be grateful to the Nadir, since they heighten the value of our liberty."

"You've lost me, damn you, with your pretty words. You're like those politicians in Drenan, as full of wind as a sick cow. Don't tell me my life has been wasted, I won't have that! I loved a good woman, and I've always been true to my principles. I never did a shameful thing, nor yet a cruel one."

"Ah, but Druss, not all men are you. I will not criticize your principles if you do not try to graft them onto me. I have no time for them. A pretty hypocrite I would be as a robber outlaw with principles."

"Then why did you not let Jorak shoot me down?"

"As I said, it was unsporting. It lacked a sense of style. But on another day, when I was colder or more bad tempered ..."

"You are a nobleman, aren't you?" said Druss. "A rich boy playing at robbers. Why do I sit here and argue with you?"

"Because you need my archers."

"No. I have given up on that thought," said Druss, offering his goblet to the green-garbed outlaw. Bowman filled it, a cynical smile once more upon his mouth.

"Given up? Nonsense. I will tell you what you're thinking. You will argue some more, offer me wages and a pardon for my crimes. If I refuse, you will kill me and take your chances with the same offer to my men."

Druss was shaken, but his face showed nothing.

"Do you also read palms?" he asked, sipping his wine.

"You're too honest, Druss. And I like you. That's why I would like to point out that Jorak is behind the bushes there with an arrow notched."

"Then I have lost," said Druss. "You keep your archers."

"Tut, tut, dear man, I didn't expect such defeatism from Druss the Legend. Put your offer."

"I've no time for your games. I had a friend like you, Sieben the saga master. He could talk all day and convince you the sea was sand. I never won an argument with him. He talked about having no principles—and like you, he lied."

"He was the poet who wrote the legend. He made you immortal," said Bowman softly.

"Yes," said Druss, his mind drifting back over the long years.

"Did you really hunt your woman across the world?"

"That part at least was true. We were wed when we were very young. Then my village was attacked by a slaver called Harib Ka, who sold her to an eastern merchant. I missed the attack, as I was working in the woods. But I followed them. In the end it took me seven years, and when I found her, she was with another man."

"What happened to him?" asked Bowman softly

"He died."

"And she came back with you to Skoda."

"Aye. She loved me. She really did."

"An interesting addendum to your saga," said Bowman. Druss chuckled. "I must be getting melancholy in my old age. I don't usually prattle on about the past."

"What happened to Sieben?" asked the outlaw.

"He died at Skeln."

"You were close?"

"We were like brothers."

"I can't think why I remind you of him," said Bowman.

"Maybe it is because you both hide a dark secret," said Druss.

"Perhaps," admitted the outlaw. "However, make your offer."

"A pardon for every man and five gold Raq a head."

"Not enough."

"It's my best offer, I'll go no further."

"Your offer must be this: A pardon, five gold Raq a head for all 620 men, and an agreement that when Wall Three falls, we leave with our money and our pardons stamped with the earl's seal."

"Why Wall Three?"

"Because that will be the beginning of the end."

"Something of a strategist, are you, boy?"

"You could say that. By the way, how do you feel about women warriors?"

"I have known a few. Why do you ask?"

"I shall be bringing one."

"So? What difference does it make as long as she can aim a bow?"

"I didn't say it made a difference. I just thought I ought to mention it."

"Is there something about this woman that I should know?" asked Druss.

"Only that she's a killer," said Bowman.

"Then she's perfect, and I will welcome her with open arms."

"I wouldn't recommend it," said Bowman softly.

"Be at Delnoch in fourteen days and I'll welcome you all with open arms."

Rek awoke to see the new sun breasting the distant mountains. His body adjusted swiftly from dreamless sleep, and he stretched and slid from the covers, then walked to the tower window of the bedroom. In the courtyard below the Thirty were assembling their mounts, great beasts with short-cropped manes and braided tails. Apart from the sound of steel hooves on cobbles, an eerie silence hung over the scene. None of the men spoke. Rek shivered.

Virae moaned in her sleep, her arm stretching across the wide bed.

Rek watched the men below check their armor and tighten saddle girths. Strange, he thought. Where are the jokes, the laughter, all the sounds soldiers usually make as they prepare for war? Jests to ease the fear, curses to ease the tension?

Serbitar appeared, a white cloak over his silver armor, his braided white hair covered by a silver helm. The Thirty saluted him. Rek shook his head. It was uncanny. Identical timing: like the same salute in thirty mirrors.

Virae opened her eyes and yawned. She rolled over and saw Rek's back silhouetted against the morning sun. She smiled.

"Your belly is receding into memory," she said.

"Mock not," he said, smiling. "Unless you are going to appear in front of thirty warriors in your skin, you need to hurry. They are already in the courtyard."

"It's one way to find out if they're human," she said, sitting up. Rek tore his eyes from her body.

"You have the strangest effect on me," he said, gazing into her eyes. "You always make me think of lovemaking at the wrong times. Now get dressed."

In the courtyard Serbitar led the men in prayer, a silent joining of minds. Vintar watched the young albino fondly, pleased with his swift adjustment to the responsibility of leadership.

Serbitar ended the prayer and returned to the tower. He was uneasy, out of harmony. He mounted the circular stone steps to the tower bedroom, smiling as he remembered his promise to the tall Drenai and his woman. It would have been so much easier to speak than to mount these stairs to check if they were ready.

He knocked on the iron-studded door. Rek opened it, beckoning him in.

"I see you are ready," he said. "We won't be long."

Serbitar nodded. "The Drenai have met the Nadir," he said.

"They are already at Delnoch?" asked Rek, alarmed.

"No, no," answered Serbitar. "The legion met them in the outlands. They did well. Their leader is called Hogun. He, at least, is quality."

"When was this?"

"Yesterday."

"Your powers again?"

"Yes. Does it distress you?"

"It makes me uncomfortable. But only because I do not share the talent."

"A wise observation, Rek. It will come to be more acceptable, believe me." Serbitar bowed as Virae entered from the rear washroom.

"I am sorry to have kept you waiting," she said. Dressed in her armor, silver mail shirt, and bronze shoulder pads, she now also sported a silver helm, raven-winged, and a white cloak—gifts from Vintar. Her fair hair was braided on either side of her face.

"You look like a goddess," Rek told her.

They joined the Thirty in the courtyard, checked their mounts, and rode alongside Serbitar and Menahem, heading for the Drinn estuary.

"Once there," Menahem told them, "we will book passage on a Lentrian ship to Dros Purdol. It will save two weeks of travel. From Purdol we travel by river and road and should reach Delnoch in four weeks at the outside. I fear battle will be joined before we arrive."

As the hours passed, the ride became a personal nightmare for Rek. His back was bruised and his buttocks numb before Serbitar called for a noon break. It was a short one, and the pain had become intense by dusk.

They camped in a small grove of trees near a stream. Virae almost fell from the saddle, fatigue—deep and numbing—showing in her every movement. But she was enough of a horsewoman to tend her mount before slumping to the ground, her back against a tree. Rek took more time wiping the lather from Lancer's back and shoulders. *He* did not need to sit! He covered the horse with a blanket, then walked to the stream. Lancer was bearing up as well as the priests' mounts, Rek thought with pride.

But he was still wary around the gelding. It had a tendency to snap at him even now. Rek smiled, thinking back.

"A fine mount," Serbitar had said that morning, stepping forward to stroke the mane. Lancer had snapped, and Serbitar had leapt backward. "May I speak with him?" Serbitar had asked.

"With a horse?"

"It is more an empathic bond. I shall tell him I mean no harm."

"Go ahead."

After a little while Serbitar smiled. "He is being very friendly, but he is waiting to snap at me again. That, my friend, is a cantankerous animal."

Rek walked back to the campsite to find four fires glowing merrily and the riders eating their oatcakes. Virae was asleep beneath a tree, wrapped in a red blanket, her head resting on her white cloak. He joined Serbitar, Vintar, and Menahem at their fire. Arbedark was talking softly to a nearby group.

"We're pushing hard," said Rek. "The horses won't last."

"We can rest aboard ship," said Serbitar. "And we will be aboard the Lentrian vessel *Wastrel* early tomorrow. It sails with the morning tide, hence the urgency."

"Even my bones are tired," said Rek. "Is there any more news from Delnoch?"

"We will see later," said Menahem, smiling. "I am sorry, friend Rek, for my testing of you. It was a mistake."

"Please forget it—and what I said. The words were spoken in anger."

"That is gracious. Before you joined us, we were talking of the Dros. It is our belief that under existing leadership it cannot last a week. Morale is low, and their leader, Orrin, is overwhelmed by his position and responsibility. We need a fair wind and no delays."

"You mean it could be over before we arrive?" said Rek, his heart leaping.

"I think not," said Vintar. "But the end may be near. Tell me, Regnak, why do you travel to Delnoch?"

"The possibility of stupidity can never be ruled out," Rek told him without humor. "Anyway, we might not lose. Surely there is at least a faint chance."

"Druss will be there soon," said Vintar. "Much will depend on his reception. If it is good and we can arrive while the first wall holds, we should be able to harness the strengths of the defenders and guarantee resistance for about a month. I cannot see a mere ten thousand men holding for longer."

"Woundweaver may send reinforcements," said Menahem.

"Perhaps," said Serbitar. "But unlikely. Already his marshals are scouring the empire. Virtually the entire army is gathered at Delnoch, with three thousand men holding Dros Purdol and another thousand at Corteswain.

"Abalayn has been foolish these last years, running down the army and cultivating trade agreements with Ulric. It was folly. Had it not been the Nadir attacking now, it would have been Vagria before long.

"My father would love to humble the Drenai. He has dreamed about it long enough."

"Your father?" queried Rek.

"Earl Drada of Dros Segril. Did you not know?" said Serbitar.

"No, I didn't. But Segril is only eighty miles west of Delnoch. Surely he will send men when he knows you are there."

"No. My father and I are not friends; my talent unnerves him. However, if I am killed, he will be in blood feud with Ulric. That means he will swing his forces to Woundweaver. It may help the Drenai—but not Dros Delnoch."

Menahem tossed twigs to the fire, holding his dark-skinned hands toward the blaze. "Abalayn has at least got one thing right. This Lentrian Woundweaver is quality. A warrior of the old school, tough, determined, and practical."

"There are times, Menahem," Vintar said, smiling gently, age sitting heavily on him following the hard ride, "when

I doubt you will achieve your aim. Warriors of the old school, indeed!"

Menahem grinned broadly. "I can admire a man for his talents while debating his principles," he said.

"Indeed you can, my boy. But did I not note the merest hint of empathy?" asked Vintar.

"You did, Master Abbot. But only a hint, I assure you."

"I hope so, Menahem. I would not want to lose you before the journey. Your soul must be sure."

Rek shivered. He had no idea what they were talking about. On reflection, he had no wish to know.

Dros Delnoch's first line of defense was the wall Eldibar, spreading snakelike for almost a quarter of a mile across the Delnoch Pass. Forty-eight feet high when viewed from the north, a mere five feet from the south, like a giant step carved from the heart of a mountain in seamed granite.

Cul Gilad sat on the battlements, gazing somberly past the few trees toward the northern plains. His eyes scanned the shimmering distant horizon, searching for the telltale dust clouds that would herald the invasion. There was nothing to see. His dark eyes narrowed as he caught sight of an eagle high in the morning sky. Gilad smiled.

"Fly, you great golden bird. Live!" he shouted. Gilad pushed himself to his feet and stretched his back. His legs were long and slim, his movements fluid, graceful. The new army shoes were half a size too large and packed with paper. His helm, a wondrous thing of bronze and silver, slipped over one eye. Cursing, he hurled it to the floor. One day he would write a battle hymn about army efficiency, he thought. His belly rumbled, and he cast his eyes about for his friend Bregan, gone to fetch their midmorning food. Black bread and cheese—bound to be. Endless wagons of supplies arriving daily at Delnoch, yet the midmorning meal was always black bread and cheese. Shielding his eyes, he could just make out Bregan's tubby form ambling from the mess hall, bearing two platters and a jug. Gilad smiled. Good-natured Bregan. A farmer, a husband, a father. All these things he did well in his own soft, kindly easygoing way. But a soldier?

"Black bread and creamed cheese," said Bregan, smiling. "We've had it only three times, and I'm already tired of it."

"Are the carts still coming in?" asked Gilad.

"By the score. Still, I expect they know best what a warrior needs," said Bregan. "I wonder how Lotis and the boys are bearing up."

"News should be in later. Sybad always gets letters."

"Yes. I've been here only two weeks and yet I miss the family terribly," said Bregan. "I only joined up on the spur of the moment, Gil. That officer's speech just got to me, I suppose."

Gilad had heard it before—almost every day for the two weeks since first they had been issued with armor. Bregan should not be at Delnoch, he knew; he was tough enough, but in a way he lacked the heart. He was a farmer, a man who loved growing things. To destroy was alien to him.

"By the way," said Bregan suddenly, his face echoing his excitement, "you'll never guess who's just arrived!"

"Who?"

"Druss the Legend. Can you believe it?"

"Are you sure, Bregan? I thought he was dead."

"No. He arrived an hour ago. The whole mess hall is buzzing with the news. They say he's bringing five thousand archers and a legion of axmen."

"Don't count on it, my friend," said Gilad. "I've not been here long, but I would like a copper coin for every story I've heard about reinforcements, peace plans, treaties, and leave."

"Well, even if he brings no one, it's still good news, isn't it? I mean, he is a hero, isn't he?"

"He certainly is. Gods, he must be about seventy, though. That's a bit old, isn't it?"

"But he's a *hero*." Bregan stressed the word, his eyes gleaming. "I've heard stories about him all my life. He was a farmer's son. And he's never lost, Gil. Not ever. And he will be with us. Us! The next song about Druss the Legend will have us in it. Oh, I know we won't be named—but we'll know, won't we? I'll be able to tell little Legan that I fought beside Druss the Legend. It makes a difference, doesn't it?"

"Of course it does," said Gilad, dipping his black bread

into the cheese and scanning the horizon. Still no movement. "Does your helmet fit?" he asked.

"No, it's too small. Why?"

"Try mine."

"We've been through that, Gil. Bar Kistrid says it's against the rules to swap."

"A pox on Bar Kistrid and his stupid rules. Try it on."

"They all have numbers stamped inside."

"Who cares? Try it on, for Missael's sake."

Bregan carefully looked around, reached across, and tried on Gilad's helm.

"Well?" asked Gilad.

"It's better. Still a little tight, but much better."

"Give me yours," Gilad placed Bregan's helm over his own head; it was close to perfect. "Wonderful!" he said. "This will do."

"But the rules . . ."

"There is no rule that says a helm must not fit," said Gilad. "How's the swordplay coming along?"

"Not bad," said Bregan. "It's when it's in the scabbard that I feel stupid. It keeps flapping between my legs and tripping me." Gilad burst into laughter, a fine lilting sound that echoed high into the mountains.

"Ah, Breg, what are we doing here?"

"Fighting for our country. It's nothing to laugh at, Gil."

"I'm not laughing at you," he lied. "I'm laughing at the whole stupid business. We face the biggest threat in our history, and they give me a helmet too big, and you a helmet too small, and tell us we can't exchange them. It's too much. Really. Two farmers on a high wall tripping over their swords." He giggled, then laughed aloud again.

"They probably won't notice we've swapped," said Bregan.

"No. All I need now is to find a man with a large chest wearing my breastplate." Gilad leaned forward, the laughter hurting his side.

"It is good news about Druss, isn't it?" said Bregan, mystified by Gilad's sudden good humor.

"What? Oh, yes." Gilad took a deep breath, then smiled at his friend. Yes, it was good news if it could so lift a man like Bregan, he thought. A hero, indeed. Not a hero,

Bregan, you fool. Just a warrior. You are the hero. You have left the family and the farm you love to come here and die in order to protect them. And who will sing your song—or mine? If they remember Dros Delnoch at all in years to come, it will be because a white-maned old man died here. He could hear the psalmists and saga poets chanting their rhymes. And the teachers telling young children—Nadir children and Drenai—the tale of Druss: "And at the end of a long, glorious life Druss the Legend came at last to Dros Delnoch, where he fought mightily and fell."

"They say in the mess hall," said Bregan, "that after a month this bread is riddled with worms."

"Do you believe everything they tell you?" snapped Gilad, suddenly angry. "If I was sure I'd be alive in a month, I would be glad to eat wormy bread."

"Not me," said Bregan. "It can poison you, so they say."

Gilad bit back his anger.

"You know," said Bregan thoughtfully, "I don't know why so many people seem to think we're doomed. Look at the height of this wall. And there are six of them. And at the end of it there's still the Dros itself. Don't you think?"

"Yes."

"What's wrong, Gil? You're acting so strangely. Laughing one minute, angry the next. It's not like you; you've always been so ... cool, I suppose."

"Don't mind me, Breg. I'm just frightened."

"So am I. I wonder if Sybad got a letter. It's not the same, I know—as seeing them, I mean. But it lifts me to hear they're well. I'll bet Legan isn't sleeping too well without me there."

"Don't think about that," said Gilad, sensing the emotional shift in his friend and knowing his tears were not far away. Such a soft man. Not weak. Never weak. But soft, gentle, and caring. Not like himself. He had not come to Delnoch to defend the Drenai and his family; he had come because he was bored. Bored with his life as a farmer, cold to his wife, and uncaring about the land. Up at first light to tend the animals and prepare the fields, tilling and planting until late afternoon. Repairing fences or leather hinge straps or leaking buckets until long after dusk. Then slipping into a rush-mattressed bed beside a fat, carping woman whose complaints would drone on long after sleep had carried him on the all too short journey to a new sunrise.

He had believed nothing could be worse, but he could not have been more wrong.

He thought of Bregan's words about Dros Delnoch's strength. His mind's eye pictured hundreds of thousands of barbarian warriors swarming like ants over a thin line of defenders. It's funny, he thought, how different people view the same event. Bregan can't see how they can take Delnoch.

I can't see how they can fail.

All in all, he thought, smiling, I think I would rather be Bregan.

"I'll bet it's cooler at Dros Purdol," said Bregan. "The sea air blowing in and all that. This pass seems to make even the spring sun burn."

"It blocks the east wind," said Gilad, "and the gray marble reflects the heat down onto us. I expect it's pleasant in winter, though."

"Well, I shall not be here to see that," said Bregan. "I only signed on for the summer, and I'm hoping to be back in time for the harvest supper. That's what I told Lotis."

Gilad laughed, the tension flowing from him. "Never mind Druss," he said. "I'm glad you're with me, Breg, I really am."

Bregan's brown eyes searched Gilad's face for any sign of sarcasm. Satisfied, he smiled. "Thanks for saying that. We never had much to do with one another at the village, and I always felt you thought I was dull."

"I was wrong. Here, take my hand on it. We will stick together, you and I, see off the Nadir, and journey back to the supper with tall tales."

Bregan gripped his hand, grinning, then: "Not like that," he said suddenly. "It has to be the warrior's grip, wrist to wrist."

Both men chuckled.

"Never mind about saga poets," said Gilad. "We will compose our own song. Bregan of the broadsword and Gilad, the demon of Dros Delnoch. How's that?"

"I think you ought to find another name for yourself. My Legan has always been afraid of demons."

The sound of Gilad's laughter reached the eagle high above the pass. It banked sharply and flew to the south.

◊ **10** ◊

DRUSS PACED IMPATIENTLY in the great hall of the keep, gazing absently at the marble statues of past heroes flanking the high walls. No one had questioned him as he had entered the Dros, and everywhere soldiers were sitting in the spring sunshine, some dicing their meager wages, others asleep in the shade. The city folk moved about their business as usual, and a dull, apathetic air hung over the fortress. The old man's eyes had blazed with a cold fury. Officers chatted among the enlisted men; it was almost more than the old warrior could bear. Angry beyond endurance, he had marched to the keep and hailed a young officer in a red cloak who stood in the shade of the portcullis gate.

"You! Where will I find the earl?"

"How should I know?" answered the man, walking past the black-garbed axman. A mighty hand curled around the folds of the red cloak and tugged contemptuously. The officer checked his stride, lost his footing, and crashed back into the old man, who grabbed him by the belt and hoisted him from the floor. His breastplate clanged as his back hit the gateway.

"Maybe you didn't hear me, you son of a slut!" hissed Druss. The young man swallowed hard.

"I think he's in the great hall," he said. "Sir!" he added hurriedly. The officer had never seen battle or any degree of violence, yet he knew instinctively the threat contained in the ice-cold eyes. He's insane, he thought as the old man slowly lowered him to the ground.

"Lead me to him and announce me. The name is Druss. Do you think you can remember it?"

The young man nodded so vigorously that his horsehair-crested helm slipped over his eyes.

Minutes later Druss paced in the great hall, his anger barely held in check. Was this how empires fell?

"Druss, old friend, how you delight my eyes!" If Druss had been surprised by the state of the fortress, he was doubly shocked by the appearance of Earl Delnar, Lord Warden of the North. Supported by the young officer, the man would not pass for the shadow he had cast at Skeln Pass a scant fifteen years before. His skin stretched like parchment over a skull-like countenance, yellow and dry, his eyes burning brightly—feverishly—in dark sockets. The young officer brought him close to the old warrior, and the earl extended a hand like a claw. Gods of Missael, thought Druss. He is five years younger than I!

"I do not find you in good health, my lord," said Druss.

"Still the blunt speaker, I see! No, you do not. I am dying, Druss." He patted the young soldier's arm. "Ease me into that chair by the sunlight, Mendar." The young man pulled the chair into place. Once settled, the earl smiled his thanks and dismissed him to fetch wine. "You frightened the boy, Druss. He was shaking more than I—and I have good reason." He stopped speaking and began to take deep, shuddering breaths. His arms trembled. Druss leaned forward, resting a huge hand on the frail shoulder, wishing he could pour strength into the man. "I will not last another week. But Vintar came to me in a dream yesterday. He rides with the Thirty and my Virae. They will be here within the month."

"So will the Nadir," said Druss, pulling up a high-backed chair to sit opposite the dying earl.

"True. In the interim I would like you to take over the Dros. Prepare the men. Desertions are high. Morale is low. You must . . . take over." Once more the earl paused to breathe.

"I cannot do that—even for you. I am no general, Delnar. A man must know his limitations. I am a warrior—sometimes a champion but never a gan. I understand little of the clerk's work involved in running this city. No, I cannot do that. But I will stay and fight—that will have to be enough."

The earl's fever-sick eyes focused on the ice-blue orbs of the axman. "I know your limitations, Druss, and I understand your fears. But there is no one else. When the Thirty arrive, they will plan and organize. Until then it is as a warrior that you will be needed. Not to fight, although the gods know how well you do that, but to train: to pass on your years of experience. Think of the men here as a rusty weapon which needs a warrior's firm hand. It needs to be sharpened, honed, prepared. It's useless else."

"I may have to kill Gan Orrin," said Druss.

"No! You must understand that he is not evil or even willful. He is a man out of his depth and struggling hard. I don't think he lacks courage. See him and then judge for yourself."

A racking cough burst from the old man's lips, his body shuddering violently. Blood frothed at his mouth as Druss leapt to his side. The earl's hand fluttered toward his sleeve and the cloth held there. Druss pulled it clear and dabbed the earl's mouth, easing him forward and gently tapping his back. At last the fit subsided.

"There is no justice when such as you must die like this," said Druss, hating the feeling of helplessness that overwhelmed him.

"None of us . . . can choose . . . the manner of our passing. No, that is not true . . . For you are here, old war-horse. I see that you at least have chosen wisely."

Druss laughed loudly and heartily. The young officer, Mendar, returned with a flagon of wine and two crystal goblets. He poured for the earl, who produced a small bottle from a pocket in his purple tunic; he uncorked it and poured several drops of dark liquid into his wine. As he drank, a semblance of color returned to his face.

"Darkseed," he said. "It helps me."

"It is habit-forming," said Druss, but the earl chuckled.

"Tell me, Druss," he said, "why did you laugh when I said you had chosen your death?"

"Because I am not ready to give in to the old bastard yet. He wants me, but I will make it damned hard for him."

"You have always seen death as your own personal enemy. Does he exist, do you think?"

"Who knows? I like to think so. I like to think this is all a game. All life is a test between him and me."

"But *is* it?"

"No. But it gives me an edge. I have six hundred archers joining us within fourteen days."

"That is wonderful news. How in heaven did you manage it? Woundweaver sent word he could spare not a man."

"They are outlaws, and I have promised them a pardon—and five gold Raq a head."

"I don't like it, Druss. They are mercenaries and not to be trusted."

"You have asked me to take over," said Druss. "So trust me; I won't let you down. Order the pardons to be drawn up and prepare notes against the treasury in Drenan." He turned to the young officer standing patiently by the window. "You, young Mendar!"

"Sir?"

"Go, and tell . . . ask . . . Gan Orrin if he will see me in an hour. My friend and I have much to talk over, but tell him that I would be grateful for a meeting. Understand?"

"Yes, sir."

"Then get on with it." The officer saluted and left. "Now, before you tire, my friend, let us get down to business. How many fighting men have you?"

"Just over nine thousand. But six thousand of those are recruits, and only a thousand—the legion—are battle-hardened warriors."

"Surgeons?"

"Ten, led by Calvar Syn. You remember him?"

"Aye. A point on the credit side."

For the rest of the hour Druss questioned the earl, and by the end of that time he was visibly weaker. He began to cough blood once more, eyes squeezed shut against the pain that wracked him. Druss lifted him from his chair. "Where is your room?" he asked. But the earl was unconscious.

Druss strode from the hall, bearing the limp form of the Warden of the North. He hailed a passing soldier, gained directions, and ordered Calvar Syn to be summoned.

Druss sat at the foot of the earl's bed as the elderly surgeon ministered to the dying man. Calvar Syn had changed little; his shaven head still gleamed like polished marble, and his black eye patch looked even more tattered than Druss remembered.

"How is he?" asked Druss.

"How do you think he is, you old fool?" answered the surgeon. "He is dying. He cannot last another two days."

"I see you have retained your good humor, Doctor," said Druss, grinning.

"What is there to be good-humored about?" queried the surgeon. "An old friend is dying, and thousands of young men will follow him within the next few weeks."

"Perhaps. It is good to see you, anyway," said Druss, rising.

"Well, it's not good to see you," said Calvar Syn, a gleam in his eye and a faint smile on his lips. "Where you go, the crows gather. Anyway, how is it that you seem so ridiculously healthy?"

"You're the doctor. You tell me."

"Because you are not human! You were carved out of stone on a winter's night and given life by a demon. Now get out! I have work to do."

"Where will I find Gan Orrin?"

"Main barracks. Now *go!*" Druss grinned and left the room.

Dun Mendar took a deep breath. "You don't like him, sir?"

"Like him? Of course I like him!" snapped the surgeon. "He kills men clean, boy. Saves me work. Now you get out, too."

As Druss walked across the parade ground before the main barracks building, he became aware of the stares of the soldiers and the muted whispers as he passed. He smiled inwardly. It had begun! From now on he would be unable to relax for a moment. Never could he show these men a glimpse of Druss the man. He was the Legend. The invincible Captain of the Ax. Indestructible Druss.

He ignored the salutes until he reached the main entrance, where two guards snapped to attention.

"Where will I find Gan Orrin?" he asked the first.

"Third doorway of the fifth corridor on the right," answered the soldier, back straight, eyes staring ahead.

Druss marched inside, located the room, and knocked on the door.

"Come!" said a voice from within, and Druss entered. The desk was immaculately tidy, the office Spartanly furnished but smart. The man behind the desk was tubby, with soft doelike dark eyes. He looked out of place in the gold epaulets of a Drenai gan.

"You are Gan Orrin?" asked Druss.

"I am. You must be Druss. Come in, my dear fellow, and have a seat. You have seen the earl? Yes, of course you have. Of course you have. I expect he has told you about our problems here. Not easy. Not easy at all. Have you eaten?" The man was sweating and ill at ease, and Druss felt sorry for him. He had served under countless commanders in his lifetime. Many were fine, but as many were incompetent, foolish, vain, or cowardly. He did not know as yet into which category Orrin fell, but he sympathized with his problems.

On a shelf by the window stood a wooden platter bearing black bread and cheese. "I will have some of that, if I may," said Druss.

"But of course." Orrin passed it to him. "How is the earl? A bad business. Such a fine man. A friend of his, weren't you? At Skeln together. Wonderful story. Inspiring."

Druss ate slowly, enjoying the gritty bread. The cheese was good, too, mellow and full-flavored. He rethought his original plan to tackle Orrin by pointing out the shambles into which the Dros had fallen, the apathy, and the ramshackle organization. A man must know his limitations, he thought. If he exceeds them, nature has a way of playing cruel tricks. Orrin should never have accepted gan rank, but in peacetime he would be easily absorbed. Now he stood out like a wooden horse in a charge.

"You must be exhausted," Druss said at last.

"What?"

"Exhausted. The work load here is enough to break a

lesser man. Organization of supplies, training, patrols, strategy, planning. You must be completely worn out."

"Yes, it is tiring," said Orrin, wiping the sweat from his brow, his relief evident. "Not many people realize the problems of command. It's a nightmare. Can I offer you a drink?"

"No, thank you. Would it help if I took some of the weight from your shoulders?"

"In what way? You are not asking me to stand down, are you?"

"Great Missael, no," said Druss with feeling. "I would be lost. No, I meant nothing of that kind.

"But time is short, and no one can expect you to bear this burden alone. I would suggest you turn over to me the training and all the responsibility for preparing the defense. We need to block those tunnels behind the gates and set work parties to razing the buildings from Wall Four to Wall Six."

"Block the tunnels? Raze the buildings? I don't understand you, Druss," said Orrin. "They are all privately owned. There would be an uproar."

"Exactly!" said the old warrior gently. "And that is why you must appoint an outsider to take the responsibility. Those tunnels behind the gates were built so that a small rear-guard could hold an enemy force long enough to allow the defenders to move back to the next wall. I propose to destroy the buildings between Walls Four and Six and use the rubble to block the tunnels. Ulric will expend a lot of men in order to breach the gates. And it will avail him nothing."

"But why destroy the buildings?" asked Orrin. "We can bring rubble in from the south of the pass."

"There is no killing ground," said the old warrior. "We must get back to the original plan of the Dros. When Ulric's men breach the first wall, I want every archer in the Dros peppering them. Every yard of open ground will be littered with Nadir dead. We're outnumbered five hundred to one, and we have to level the odds somehow."

Orrin bit his lip and rubbed his chin, his mind working furiously. He glanced at the white-bearded warrior seated calmly before him. As soon as he had heard Druss had arrived, he had prepared for the certainty that he would be replaced, sent back to Drenan in disgrace. Now he was being offered a lifeline. He should have thought of razing the buildings and blocking the tunnels; he knew it, just as he knew he was miscast as a gan. It was a hard fact to accept.

Throughout the last five years, since his elevation, he had avoided self-examination. However, only days before he had sent Hogun and two hundred of his legion lancers into the outlands. At first he had held to the belief that it was a sensible military decision. But as the days had passed and no word came, he had agonized over his orders. It had little to do with strategy but everything to do with jealousy. Hogun, he had realized with sick horror, was the best soldier in the Dros. When he had returned and told Orrin that his decision had proved a wise one, far from bolstering Orrin, it had finally opened his eyes to his own inadequacy. He had considered resigning but could not face the disgrace. He had even contemplated suicide but could not bear the thought of the dishonor it would bring to his uncle, Abalayn. All he could do was die on the first wall. And this he was prepared for. He had feared Druss would rob him even of that.

"I have been a fool, Druss," he said at last.

"Enough of that talk!" snapped the old man. "Listen to me. You are the gan. From this day on no man will speak ill of you. What you fear, keep to yourself, and believe in me. Everyone makes mistakes. Everyone fails at something. The Dros will hold, for I will be damned if I will let it fall. If I had felt you were a coward, Orrin, I would have tied you to a horse and sent you packing. You have never been in a siege or led a troop into battle. Well, now you will do both and do it well, for I will be beside you.

"Get rid of your doubts. Yesterday is dead. Past mistakes are like smoke in the breeze. What counts is tomorrow and every tomorrow until Woundweaver gets here with reinforcements. Make no mistake, Orrin. When we survive and the songs are sung, you will be worth your place in them and no one will sneer. Not a soul. Believe it!

"Now I have talked enough. Give me your seal on parchment and I will start today with my duties."

"Will you want me with you today?"

"Best not," said Druss. "I have a few heads to crack."

Minutes later Druss marched toward the officers' mess flanked by two legion guards, tall men and well disciplined. The old man's eyes blazed with anger, and the guards exchanged a glance as they marched. They could hear the sounds of singing coming from the mess and were set to enjoy the sight of Druss the Legend in action.

He opened the door and stepped into the lavishly furnished interior. A trestle bar had been set up against the far wall, stretching out into the center of the room. Druss pushed his way past the revelers, ignoring the complaints, then placed one hand beneath the trestle and hurled it into the air, scattering bottles, goblets, and food to shower on the officers. Stunned silence was followed by an angry surge of oaths and curses. One young officer pushed his way to the front of the crowd; dark-haired, sullen-eyed, and haughty, he confronted the white-bearded warrior.

"Who the hell do you think you are, old man?" he said.

Druss ignored him, his eyes scanning the thirty or so men in the room. A hand grabbed his jerkin.

"I said who—" Druss backhanded the man across the room to crash into the wall and slither to the floor, half-stunned.

"I am Druss. Sometimes called Captain of the Ax. In Ventria they call me Druss the Sender. In Vagria I am merely the Axman. To the Nadir I am Deathwalker. In Lentria I am the Silver Slayer.

"But who are you? You dung-eating lumps of offal! Who the hell are *you*?" The old man drew Snaga from its sheath at his side. "I have a mind to set an example today. I have a mind to cut the fat from this ill-fated fortress. Where is Dun Pinar?"

The young man pushed himself from the back of the crowd, a half smile on his face, a cool look in his dark eyes. "I am here, Druss."

"Gan Orrin has appointed me to take charge of the training and preparation of the defenses. I want a meeting with all officers on the training ground in an hour. Pinar, you organize it. The rest of you clear up this mess and get yourselves ready. The holiday is over. Any man who fails me will curse the day he was born." Beckoning Pinar to follow him, he walked outside. "Find Hogun," he said, "and bring him to me at once in the main hall of the keep."

"Yes, sir! And sir . . ."

"Out with it, lad."

"Welcome to Dros Delnoch."

The news flashed through the town of Delnoch like a summer storm, from tavern to shop to market stall. Druss was here! Women passed the message to their men; children chanted his name in the alleys. Tales of his exploits were retold, growing by the minute. A large crowd gathered before the barracks, watching the officers milling at the parade ground. Children were lifted high, perched on men's shoulders to catch a glimpse of the greatest Drenai hero of all time.

When he appeared, a huge roar went up from the crowd and the old man paused and waved.

They could not hear what he told the officers, but the men moved with a purpose as he dismissed them. Then, with a final wave, he returned to the keep.

Within the main hall once more, Druss removed his jerkin and relaxed in a high-backed chair. His knee was throbbing, and his back ached like the devil. And still Hogun had not appeared.

He ordered a servant to prepare him a meal and inquired after the earl. The servant told him the earl was sleeping peacefully. He returned with a huge steak, lightly done, which Druss wolfed down, following it with a bottle of finest Lentrian red. He wiped the grease from his beard and rubbed his knee. After seeing Hogun, he would have a hot bath, ready for tomorrow. He knew his first day would tax him to his limits—and he must not fail.

"Gan Hogun, sir," announced the servant. "And Dun Elicas."

The two men who entered lifted Druss's heart. The first—it had to be Hogun—was broad-shouldered and tall, clear-eyed, with a square jaw.

And Elicas, though slimmer and shorter, had the look of eagles about him. Both men wore the black and silver of the legion without badges of rank. It was a long-standing custom, going back to the days when the Earl of Bronze had formed them for the Vagrian Wars.

"Be seated, gentlemen," said Druss.

Hogun pulled up a chair, reversing it in order to lean on the back. Elicas perched himself on the edge of the table, arms folded across his chest.

Elicas watched the two men carefully. He had not known what to expect from Druss, but he had begged Hogun to allow him to be present at the meeting. He worshiped Hogun, but the grim old man seated before him had always been his idol.

"Welcome to Delnoch, Druss," said Hogun. "You have lifted morale already. The men speak of nothing else. I am sorry to have missed you earlier, but I was at the first wall, supervising an archery tourney."

"I understand you have already met the Nadir," said Druss.

"Yes. They will be here in less than a month."

"We shall be ready. But it will need hard work. The men are badly trained—if trained at all. That must change. We have only ten surgeons, no medical orderlies, no stretcher-bearers, and only one hospital—and that is at Wall One, which is no good to us. Comments?"

"An accurate appraisal. All I can add is that, apart from my men, there are only a dozen officers of worth."

"I have not yet decided the worth of any man here. But let us stay positive for the moment. I need a man of mathematical persuasion to take charge of the food stores and to prepare ration rotas. He will need to shift his equations to match our losses. He must also be responsible for liaison and administration with Gan Orrin." Druss watched as the two men exchanged glances but said nothing of it.

"Dun Pinar is your man," said Hogun. "He virtually runs the Dros now."

Druss's eyes were cold as he leaned toward the young general. "There will be no more comments like that, Hogun. It does not become a professional soldier. We start today with a clean slate. Yesterday is gone. I shall make my own judgments, and I do not expect my officers to make sly comments about each other."

"I would have thought you would want the truth," interposed Elicas before Hogun could answer.

"The truth is a strange animal, laddie. It seems to vary from man to man. Now keep silent. Understand me, Hogun, I value you. Your record is a good one. But from now on no one speaks ill of the first gan. It is not good for morale, and what is not good for our morale is good for the Nadir. We have enough problems." Druss stretched out a length of parchment and pushed it to Elicas with a quill and ink. "Make yourself useful, boy, and take notes. Put Pinar at the top; he is our quartermaster. Now, we will need fifty medical orderlies and two hundred stretcher-bearers. The first Calvar Syn can choose from volunteers, but the bearers will need someone to train them. I want them to be able to run all day. Missael knows they will need to when the action gets warm. These men will need stout hearts. It is no easy thing to run about on a battlefield lightly armed. For they will not be able to carry swords and stretchers.

"So who do you suggest to pick and train them?"

Hogun turned to Elicas, who shrugged.

"You must be able to suggest someone," said Druss.

"I don't know the men of Dros Delnoch that well, sir," said Hogun, "and no one from the legion would be appropriate."

"Why not?"

"They are warriors. We shall need them on the wall."

"Who is your best ranker?"

"Bar Britan. But he's a formidable warrior, sir."

"That is why he is the man. Listen well: The stretcher-bearers will be armed with daggers only, and they will risk their lives as much as the men battling on the walls. But it is not a glorious task, so the importance of it must be highlighted. When you name your best ranker as the man to train the bearers and work with them during the battle, this will come home to them. Bar Britan must also be given fifty men of his choice as a moving troop to protect the bearers as best he can."

"I bow to your logic, Druss," said Hogun.

"Bow to nothing, son. I make mistakes as well as any man. If you think me wrong, be so good as to damn well say so."

"Put your mind at rest on that score, Axman!" snapped Hogun.

"Good! Now, as to training. I want the men trained in groups of fifty. Each group is to have a name; choose them from legends, names of heroes, battlefields, whatever, as long as the names stir the blood.

"There will be one officer to each group and five rankers, each commanding ten men. These underleaders will be chosen after the first three days training. By then we should have taken their mark. Understood?"

"Why names?" asked Hogun. "Would it not be simpler if each group had a number? Gods, man, that's 180 names to find!"

"There is more to warfare, Hogun, than tactics and training. I want proud men on those walls. Men who know their comrades and can identify with them. Group Karnak will be representing Karnak the One-Eyed, where Group Six would be merely identified.

"Throughout the next few weeks we will set one group against another in work, play, and mock combat. We will weld them into units—proud units. We will mock and cajole them, sneer at them even. Then, slowly, when they hate us more than they do the Nadir, we will praise them. In as short a time as possible we must make them think of themselves as an elite force. That's half the battle. These are desperate, bloody days, days of death. I want men on those walls, strong men, fit men—but most of all, proud men.

"Tomorrow you will choose the officers and allocate the groups. I want the groups running until they drop and then running again. I want sword practice and wall scaling. I want demolition work done by day and night. After ten days we will move on to unit work. I want the stretcher-bearers running with loads of rock until their arms burn and their muscles tear.

"I want every building from Wall Four to Wall Six razed to the ground and the tunnels blocked.

"I want one thousand men at a time working on the demolition in three-hour shifts. That should straighten backs and strengthen sword arms.

"Any questions?"

Hogun spoke: "No. Everything you wish for will be

done. But I want to know this: Do you believe the Dros can hold until the autumn?"

"Of course I do, laddie," lied Druss easily. "Why else would I bother? The point is, do *you* believe it?"

"Oh, yes," lied Hogun smoothly. "Without a doubt."

The two men grinned.

"Join me in a glass of Lentrian red," said Druss. "Thirsty work, this planning business!"

◊ 11 ◊

IN A WOODEN loft, its window in the shadow of the great keep, a man waited, drumming his fingers on the broad table. Behind him, pigeons ruffled their feathers within a wickerwork coop. The man was nervous. On edge.

Footsteps on the stairs made him reach for a slender dagger. He cursed and wiped his sweating palm on his woolen trousers.

A second man entered, pushed the door shut, and sat opposite the first.

The newcomer spoke: "Well? What orders are there?"

"We wait. But that may change when word reaches them that Druss is here."

"One man can make no difference," said the newcomer.

"Perhaps not. We shall see. The tribes will be here in five weeks."

"Five? I thought . . . "

"I know," said the first man. "But Ulric's firstborn is dead. A horse fell on him. The funeral rites will take five days, and it's a bad omen for Ulric."

"Bad omens can't stop a Nadir horde from taking this decrepit fortress."

"What is Druss planning?"

"He means to seal the tunnels. That's all I know so far."

"Come back in three days," said the first man. He took a small piece of paper and began to write in tiny letters upon it. He shook sand on the ink, blew it, then reread what he had written:

Deathwalker here. Tunnels sealed. Morale higher.

"Perhaps we should kill Druss," said the newcomer, rising.

"If we are told to," said the first man. "Not before."

"I will see you in three days, then."

At the door he adjusted his helm, sweeping his cloak back over his shoulder badge.

He was a Drenai dun.

Cul Gilad lay slumped on the short grass by the wall of the cookhouse at Eldibar, breath heaving from his lungs in convulsive gasps. His dark hair hung in lank rats' tails that dripped sweat to his shoulders. He turned on his side, groaning with the effort. Every muscle in his body seemed to be screaming at him. Three times he and Bregan, with forty-eight others of Group Karnak, had raced against five other groups from Wall One to Wall Two, scaled the knotted ropes, moved to Wall Three, scaled the knotted ropes, moved to Wall Four ... An endless, mindless agony of effort.

Only his fury kept him going, especially after the first wall. The white-bearded old bastard had watched him beat six hundred men to Wall Two, his burning legs and tired arms pumping and pulling in full armor. First man! And what did he say? "A staggering old man followed by staggering old women. Well, don't just lie there, boy. On to Wall Three!"

Then he had laughed. It was the laugh that had done it.

Gilad could have killed him then—slowly. For five miserable endless days the soldiers of Dros Delnoch had run, climbed, fought, torn down buildings in the teeth of hysterical curses from the dispossessed owners, and trundled cart upon cart of rubble into the tunnels at Walls One and Two. Working by day and night, they were bone weary. And still that fat old man urged them on.

Archery tourneys, javelin contests, swordplay, dagger work, and wrestling in between the heavy work made sure that few of the culs bothered to frequent the taverns near the keep.

Damned legion did, though. They glided through the training with grim smiles and hurled scornful jests at the farmers who sought to keep up with them. Let them try working eighteen hours in the fields, thought Gilad. Bastards!

Grunting with pain, he sat up, pushing his back against the wall, and watched others training. He had ten minutes yet before the next shift was required to fill the rubble carts. Stretcher-bearers toiled across the open ground, bearing rocks twice the weight of an injured man. Many had bandaged hands. Alongside them the black-bearded Bar Britan shouted them on.

Bregan tottered toward him and slumped to the grass. His face was cherry red. Silently he handed Gilad an orange half; it was sweet and fresh.

"Thanks, Breg." Gilad's eyes moved over the other eight men in his group. Most were lying silently, though Midras had begun to retch. The idiot had a girl in the town and had visited her the night before, creeping back into barracks for an hour's sleep before daybreak.

He was paying for it now. Bregan was bearing up well: a little faster, a little fitter. And he never complained, which was a wonder.

"Almost time, Gil," he said. Gilad glanced toward the tunnel, where the work was slowing down. Other members of Group Karnak were moving toward the partly demolished homes.

"Come on, lads," said Gilad. "Let's be sitting up. Let's start taking some deep breaths." Groans followed the order, and there was scarcely a movement from the men. "Come on, now. Group Kestrian is already moving. Bastards!" Gilad pushed himself to his feet, pulling Bregan up with him. Then he moved to each of the men. Slowly they rose and began to move toward the tunnel.

"I think I'm dying," said Midras.

"You will if you let us down today," muttered Gilad. "If that old swine laughs at us one more time . . . "

"A pox on him," said Midras. "You don't see him working up a sweat, do you?"

At dusk the weary men trooped away from the tunnels toward the peace and relative sanctuary of the barracks. They hurled themselves onto narrow cots and began to unbuckle breastplates and greaves.

"I don't mind the work," said Baile, a stocky farmer from a village neighboring Gilad's, "but I don't see why we have to do it in full armor."

No one answered him.

Gilad was almost asleep when a voice bellowed: "Group Karnak to the parade ground!"

Druss stood in the parade ground square, hands on hips, his blue eyes scanning the exhausted men who stumbled from the barracks, their eyes squinting against the torchlight. Flanked by Hogun and Orrin, he smiled grimly as the men shambled into ranks.

The fifty men of Group Karnak were joined by Group Kestrian and Group Sword.

Silently they waited for whatever foul idea Druss had now dreamed up.

"You three groups," said Druss, "are to run the length of the wall and back. The last man's group will run again. Go!"

As the men set off for the grueling half mile, someone yelled from the crowd: "What about you, fat man? Coming?"

"Not this time," Druss yelled back. "Don't be last."

"They're exhausted," said Orrin. "Is this wise, Druss?"

"Trust me. When the attacks come, men will be dragged from sleep fast enough. I want them to know their limits."

Three more days passed. Tunnel One was almost filled, and work had begun on Tunnel Two. No one cheered now as Druss walked by, not even among the townsfolk. Many had lost their homes; others were losing business. A deputation had visited Orrin, begging for demolition to cease. Others found that the sight of the clear ground between walls only emphasized that Druss expected the Nadir to take the Dros. Resentment grew, but the old warrior swallowed his anger and pushed on with his plan.

On the ninth day something happened that gave the men a fresh topic of conversation.

As Group Karnak assembled for its run, Gan Orrin approached Dun Mendar, the officer commanding.

"I shall be running with your group today," he said.

"You are taking over, sir?" said Mendar.

"No, no. Just running. A gan must be fit, too, Mendar."

A sullen silence greeted Orrin as he joined the ranks, his bronze and gold armor setting him apart from the waiting soldiers.

Throughout the morning he toiled with the men, scaling

ropes, sprinting between walls. Always he was last. As he ran, some of the men laughed and others jeered. Mendar was furious. The man's making an even greater fool of himself, he thought. And he's making us a laughingstock, too. Gilad ignored the gan, except at one point to pull him over the battlements when it looked as if he might fall.

"Let him drop," yelled a man farther along the wall.

Orrin gritted his teeth and carried on, staying with the troop throughout the day and even working on the demolition. By the afternoon he was working at half the speed of the other soldiers. No one had yet spoken to him. He ate apart from the other men, but not by choice: Where he sat, they did not.

At dusk he made his way to his quarters, body trembling, muscles on fire, and slept in his armor.

At daybreak he stripped, bathed, put on his armor again, and rejoined Group Karnak. Only at sword practice did he excel, but even then he half thought the men were letting him win. And who could blame them?

An hour before dusk Druss arrived with Hogun, ordering four groups to assemble by the gate of Wall Two: Karnak, Sword, Egel, and Fire.

From atop the battlements Druss called down to the two hundred men: "A little race to stretch your muscles, lads. It's a mile from this gate and around the perimeter and back. You will run it twice. Last man's group runs again. Go!"

As they hurtled off, bunching and pushing, Hogun leaned forward.

"Damn!" he said.

"What's wrong?" asked Druss.

"Orrin. He's running with them. I thought he would have had enough yesterday. What's the matter with the man? Is he mad?"

"You run with the men," said Druss. "Why not him?"

"Come on, Druss, what sort of a question is that? I'm a soldier, and I train every day of my life. But him! Look at him—he's last already. You will have to pick the last man apart from Orrin."

"I can't do that, lad. It would shame him. He made his choice, and I expect he has his reasons."

At the first mile Orrin was thirty yards behind the last

man and struggling hard. He fastened his gaze to the back
of the man's breastplate and ran on, ignoring the pain in his
side. Sweat stung his eyes, and his white horsehair-crested
helm fell from his head. It was a relief.

At a mile and a half he was forty yards adrift.

Gilad glanced back from the center of the leading pack,
eased out, and turned, jogging back to the breathless gan.
Once alongside, he joined him stride for stride.

"Listen," he said, breathing easily. "Unclench your fists;
it will help with the breathing. Think of nothing else except
sticking to me. No, don't try to answer me. Count your
breaths. Take a deep breath and blow out as fast as possible. That's it. A deep breath every two strides. And keep
counting. Think of nothing except the number of breaths.
Now stay with me."

He moved in front of the general, keeping to the same
slow pace, then increased it gently.

Druss sat back on the battlements as the race drew near
its end. Orrin was being drawn along by the slim under-
leader. Most of the men had finished the race and were
spread out watching the last few runners. Orrin was still
last but only ten yards adrift of the tiring cul from Group
Fire. Men started yelling for the cul to sprint. Every group
except Karnak was willing him on.

Thirty yards to go. Gilad dropped back alongside Orrin.
"Give it everything," he said. "Run, you fat son of a bitch!"

Gilad increased his pace and sped by the cul. Orrin gritted his teeth and took after him. Anger gave him strength.
Fresh adrenaline flowed to tired muscles.

Ten yards to go and now he was at the man's shoulder.
He could hear the encouragement screamed from the
crowd. The man beside him pulled ahead with a last effort,
his face twisted in agony.

Orrin drew level in the shadow of the gate and lurched
ahead. He hurled himself forward, crashing to the earth and
rolling into the crowd. He could not get up, but hands
grabbed him, hauling him to his feet and pounding his
back. He fought for breath. A voice said: "Keep walking.
It will help. Come on, move your legs." Supported on both
sides, he began to walk. Druss's voice came down from the
battlements.

"That man's group, one more circuit."

Group Fire set off, this time at a slow jog.

Gilad and Bregan helped Orrin to a jutting foundation block and sat him upon it. His legs were shaking, but his breathing was less ragged.

"I am sorry I insulted you," said Gilad. "I wanted to make you angry. My father always said anger helps the strength."

"You don't have to make excuses," said Orrin. "I shall take no action."

"It's not an excuse. I could do that run ten times over; so could most of my men. I just thought it would help."

"It did. Thank you for dropping back."

"I think you did wonderfully well," said Bregan. "I know how you felt. But we've been doing this for nearly two weeks. Today is only your second day."

"Will you join us again tomorrow?" asked Gilad.

"No. I should like to, but I do have other work to do." He smiled suddenly. "On the other hand," he said, "Pinar is very good at paperwork, and I am damned tired of having complaining deputations knocking at my door every five minutes. Yes, I'll be here."

"May I make a suggestion?" said Gilad.

"Of course."

"Get yourself some ordinary armor. You will stand out less."

"I'm supposed to stand out," said Orrin, smiling. "I am the gan."

High above them Druss and Hogun shared a bottle of Lentrian red.

"It took nerve for him to come out today after the jeering yesterday," said Druss.

"Yes, I suppose so," said Hogun. "No, dammit, I'll agree with you and praise the man. But it goes against the grain. You gave him the backbone."

"You can't give a man something that isn't there," said Druss. "He just never looked for it." Druss grinned and took a long swig from the bottle, passing it to Hogun half-drained.

"I like the little man," said Druss. "He's game!"

* * *

Orrin lay back on his narrow bunk, his back cushioned by soft pillows, his hand curled around a clay cup. He tried to tell himself there was no glory in coming second from last. Happily he failed. He had never been athletic, even as a child. But he came from a family of warriors and Drenai leaders, and his father had insisted that he take part in all soldierly pursuits. He had always handled a sword well, which, in his father's eyes, made up for the other, mightier, shortcomings. Like not being able to stand physical pain. Or not being able to understand, even after patient explanation, the great mistake made by Nazredas at the Battle of Plettii. He wondered if his father would have been pleased at his hurling himself to the floor in order to beat a Cul in a footrace. He smiled: he would think him mad.

The sound of knuckles rapping at his door brought him back to the present.

"Come!"

It was Druss, minus his black and silver jerkin. Strange how he looked like an old man, thought Orrin, without his legendary garb. The warrior's beard was combed, and he wore a flowing white shirt-tunic with billowing sleeves gathered in at the wrists. About his middle was a thick black belt with a silver buckle. He was carrying a large bottle of Lentrian red.

"I thought, if you were awake, I might join you for a drink," said Druss, pulling up a chair and reversing it, as Orrin had seen Hogun do on many occasions.

"Why do you do that?" asked Orrin.

"What?" said Druss.

"Turn the chair around."

"Old habits die hard, even among friends. It's a warrior's habit. With your legs astride the chair, it is easier to rise. Also it puts a thick layer of wood between your belly and the man you are talking to or sitting with."

"I see," said Orrin. "I had always meant to ask Hogun, but I never got around to it. What makes men adopt habits like that?"

"The sight of a friend with a knife in his belly!" said Druss.

"I can see that it would. Will you teach me your tricks, Druss, before the Nadir arrive?"

"No. You will have to learn them the hard way. Little things I will help you with at the right time—they may make a difference."

"Little things? You intrigue me, Druss. Tell me something now." Orrin accepted a cup of Lentrian and settled back. Druss drank from the bottle.

"All right," said the axman, half the bottle drained, "answer me this: Why are the men issued with oranges every morning?"

"It keeps them fit and helps prevent dysentery. It's refreshing and cheap. Is that it?" asked Orrin, puzzled.

"Some of it," said Druss. "The Earl of Bronze introduced oranges to the army partly for the reasons you mention but mainly because if you rub the juice into the palm of your hand, your sword will not slip as the hand sweats. Also, if you rub it on your brow, sweat will not drop into your eyes."

"I never knew that. I expect I should have known, but I didn't. How simple! Give me another."

"No," said Druss. "Another time. Tell me, why have you joined in the training with the culs?"

Orrin sat up, his dark eyes fixed on Druss's face. "You don't think it's a good idea?"

"It depends on what you are trying to achieve. Are you seeking respect?"

"Great gods, no!" said Orrin. "I have left it too late for that, Druss. No, it was something you said the other night when the men were turfed out of bed for that night run. I asked you if it was wise, and you said, 'They need to know their limitations.' Well, so do I. I've never been in a battle. I want to know what it's like to be woken from sleep after a full day's training and be expected to fight again.

"I've let down a lot of people here. I may let them down again when the Nadir are scaling the wall, though I hope not. But I need to be fitter and faster. And I shall be.

"Is that such a bad idea?"

Druss tilted the bottle, licked his lips, and smiled.

"No. It's a good idea. But when you are a little fitter, spread yourself around the groups more. It will pay off."

"Pay off?"

"You'll see."

"Have you seen the earl?" asked Orrin suddenly. "Syn says he's bad. Very bad indeed."

"I don't think I have seen worse. He's constantly delirious now. How he hangs on I don't know."

The two men talked on for over an hour, Orrin questioning the old man about his life and the many battles he had taken part in, returning always to the immortal story of Skeln and the fall of King Gorben.

When the keep alarm bell sounded, both men reacted instantly. Druss cursed, threw the bottle aside, and raced for the door. Orrin heaved himself from his bunk and followed. Across the parade ground square and up the short hill to the keep Druss ran, pounding under the portcullis gate and up the long winding stone stairs to the earl's bedchamber. Calvar Syn was at his bedside, with Dun Mendar, Pinar, and Hogun. An old servant stood weeping by the window.

"Is he dead?" asked Druss.

"No. Soon," answered Calvar Syn.

Druss moved to the bedside, sitting beside the frail figure. The earl's eyes opened and blinked twice.

"Druss?" he called, his voice weak. "Are you there?"

"I am here."

"He's coming. I see him. He is hooded and black."

"Spit in his eye for me," said Druss, his huge hand stroking the earl's fevered brow.

"I thought . . . after Skeln . . . I would live forever."

"Be at peace, my friend. One thing I have learned about death is that his bark's worse than his bite."

"I can see them, Druss. The Immortals. They're sending in the Immortals!" The dying man grabbed Druss's arm and tried to haul himself upright. "Here they come! Gods, will you look at them, Druss!"

"They're just men. We will see them off."

"Sit by the fire, child, and I'll tell you of it. But don't tell your mother I told you—you know how she hates the bloodthirsty tales. Ah, Virae, my little love! You will never understand what it has meant to me just being your father . . ." Druss bowed his head as the old earl rambled on, his voice thin and wavering. Hogun gritted his teeth and closed his eyes, Calvar Syn sat slumped in an armchair, and

Orrin stood by the door, remembering his own father's death so many years before.

"We were at the pass for many days, holding out against everything they could throw at us. Tribesmen, chariots, infantry, cavalry. But always the threat of the Immortals hung over us. Never beaten! Old Druss stood at the center of our first line, and as the Immortals marched toward us, we froze. You could feel panic in the air. I wanted to run, and I could see the same feeling reflected on the faces around me. Then old Druss lifted his ax in the air and bellowed at the advancing line. It was wonderful. Magical almost. The spell broke. The fear passed. He raised his ax for them to see, then he shouted. I can hear him now: 'Come on, you fat-bellied whoresons! I am Druss, and this is death!'

"Virae? Virae? I waited for you . . . just one more time. See you. So much . . . So much wanted . . . " The frail body trembled, then lay still. Druss closed the dead man's eyes and wiped a hand across his own.

"He should never have sent her away," said Calvar Syn. "He loved that girl; she was all he lived for."

"Maybe that's why he sent her," said Hogun.

Druss pulled the silk sheet up and over the earl's face and walked to the window. Now he was alone, the last survivor of Skeln. He leaned on the windowsill and sucked in the night air.

Outside the moon bathed the Dros in eldritch light, gray and ghostly, and the old man gazed toward the north. Overhead a fluttering pigeon flew in and circled a loft beneath the keep. It had come out of the north.

He turned from the window.

"Bury him quietly tomorrow," he said. "We will not interrupt training for a full funeral."

"But Druss, this is Earl Delnar!" said Hogun, eyes blazing.

"That," said Druss, pointing at the bed, "is a cancer-ridden corpse. It isn't anyone. Just do as I say."

"You coldhearted bastard," said Dun Mendar.

Druss turned his icy gaze on the officer.

"And just you remember that, laddie, the day you—or any of you—go against me."

◊ **12** ◊

REK LEANED ON the starboard rail with one arm about
Virae's shoulders and stared at the sea. Strange, he
thought, how night changed the mood of the ocean. A vast
semisolid mirror reflecting the stars, while the moon's twin
floated, fragmented and ethereal, a mile or so away. Always
a mile or so away. A gentle breeze billowed the triangular
sail as the *Wastrel* cut a white path through the waves,
gently dipping and rising with the swell. Aft stood the mate
at the spoked wheel, his silver eye patch glinting in the
moonlight. Forward a young seaman cast his lead into the
waves, calling out the changes in depth as they passed over
the hidden reef.

All was tranquility, peace, and harmony. The steady lap-
ping of the waves added to the feeling of isolation that en-
veloped Rek as he stared out to sea. With stars above and
below them they could be floating on the tides of the gal-
axy, far from the all too human struggle that awaited them.

This is contentment, thought Rek.

"What are you thinking?" asked Virae, slipping an arm
around his waist.

"I love you," he said. A dolphin surfaced below them,
calling out a musical welcome before again seeking the
depths. Rek watched his lithe form swimming among the
stars.

"I know you love me," said Virae, "but I was asking you
what you were thinking."

"That's what I was thinking. I am content. At peace."

"Of course you are. We're on a ship, and it's a lovely
night."

"Woman, you have no soul," he said, kissing her brow.

She looked up at him and smiled. "If you think that, you are a fool! I'm just not as practiced as you at telling pretty lies."

"Hard words, my lady. Would I lie to you? You would cut my throat."

"I would, too. How many women have heard you say you love them?"

"Hundreds," said Rek, watching her eyes and seeing the smile fade from them.

"So why should I believe you?"

"Because you do."

"That's no answer."

"Of course it is. You're not some dim-witted milkmaid fooled by an easy smile. You know the truth when you hear it. Why do you suddenly doubt it?"

"I don't doubt you, you oaf! I just wanted to know how many women you've loved."

"Slept with, you mean?"

"If you want to be coarse."

"I don't know," he lied. "It's not my habit to keep count. And if your next question is, 'How do I compare?' you will find yourself alone, because I shall go below."

It was. But he did not.

The mate by the tiller watched them, listened to their easy laughter, and smiled with them, although he could not hear the cause of their good humor. At home he had a wife and seven children, and it made him feel good to watch the young man and his woman. He waved as they went below deck, but they did not see him.

"Nice to be young and in love," said the captain, moving silently from the shadows by his cabin door to stand beside the mate.

"Nice to be old and in love," answered the mate, grinning.

"A calm night, but the breeze is picking up. I don't like the look of the clouds to the west."

"They will pass us by," said the mate. "But we'll have bad weather for sure. It will be behind us, pushing us on. We may pick up a couple of days. Did you know they are headed for Delnoch?"

"Yes," said the captain, scratching his red beard and checking their course by the stars.

"Sad," said the mate with real feeling. "They say Ulric has promised to raze it to the ground. You heard what he did at Gulgothir? Killed every second defender and a third of the women and children. Just lined them up and had his warriors cut them down."

"I heard. It's not my business. We've traded with the Nadir for years; they're all right as people, much the same as anyone else."

"I agree. I had a Nadir woman once. A real hellion—ran off with a tinker. Later I heard she cut his throat and stole his wagon."

"Most likely she only wanted the horse," said the captain. "She could buy herself a real Nadir man for a good horse." Both men chuckled, then stood in silence for a while enjoying the night air.

"Why are they going to Delnoch?" asked the mate.

"She's the earl's daughter. I don't know about him. If she was my daughter, I would have made sure she didn't come back. I'd have sent her to the farthest southern point of the empire."

"The Nadir will reach there—and beyond—before long. It's only a matter of time."

"Well, a lot can happen in that time. The Drenai are sure to surrender long before then. Look! That damned albino and his friend. They make my flesh creep."

The mate glanced along the deck to where Serbitar and Vintar stood at the port rail.

"I know what you mean—they never say anything. I'll be glad to see the back of them," said the mate, making the sign of the claw above his heart.

"That won't ward off their kind of demons," said the captain.

Serbitar smiled as Vintar pulsed: "We are less than popular, my boy."

"Yes. Always it is thus. It is hard to hold back contempt."

"But you must."

"I said hard, not impossible."

"Wordplay. Even to notice that it is hard is an admission of defeat," said Vintar.

"Always the scholar, Father Abbot."

"As long as the world has pupils, Master Priest."

Serbitar grinned, a rare sight. A gull wheeled and circled above the ship; the albino casually mind-touched it as it arced above the mast.

Within its mind was nothing of joy or sorrow or hope. Only hunger and need. And frustration that the ship offered no sustenance.

A feeling of fierce exultation suddenly swept over the young priest in a mind pulse of incredible power, a sense of ecstasy and fulfillment flooding his body. He gripped the rail hard and reached back along the path, shutting off his probe as it neared the door of Rek's cabin.

"Their emotions are very strong," pulsed Vintar.

"It is unseemly to dwell on it," replied Serbitar primly, a blush apparent even in the moonlight.

"Not so, Serbitar, my friend. This world has few redeeming features, and one is the capacity of the people upon it to love one another with great and enduring passion. I rejoice in their lovemaking. It is a beautiful thing for them."

"You are a voyeur, Father Abbot," said Serbitar, smiling now. Vintar laughed aloud.

"It is true. They have such energy, the young."

Suddenly Arbedark's slim, serious face appeared in both men's minds, his features set hard.

"I am sorry," he pulsed. "There is grave news from Dros Delnoch."

"Speak," said Serbitar.

"The earl is dead. And there are traitors within the Dros. Ulric has ordered Druss killed."

"Form a circle around me," shouted Druss as the exhausted men staggered from the wall. "Now sit down before you fall down."

His blue eyes scanned the circle, then he snorted with contempt. "You dregs! Call yourselves soldiers? Finished after a few runs. How the hell do you think you're going to feel after three days fighting, day and night, against a Nadir force that outnumbers you fifty to one? Eh?"

No one answered him. The question was all too obviously rhetorical. Indeed, most of the men were delighted to be berated thus; it meant a further respite from the interminable training.

Druss pointed at Gilad. "You! Which four groups are represented here?"

Gilad swung around checking the faces. "Karnak, Bild, and Gorbadac ... er ... I don't know the other one."

"Well!" bellowed the old man. "Will not one of you beggars own up? Which is the other damned group?"

"Falcon," piped a voice from the back.

"Good! Group officers step forward," said Druss. "The rest of you take a breather." He walked a little distance from the men, beckoning the officers to follow.

"Right, before I tell you what I want, will the officer from Group Falcon make himself known?"

"I am the officer, sir. Dun Hedes," said a young man who was short but well built.

"Then why did *you* not announce your group when I asked. Why was it some spotty farm boy?"

"I am partially deaf, sir, and when I am tired and the blood is pounding, I can hardly hear."

"Then, Dun Hedes, consider yourself relieved of Group Falcon."

"You can't do that to me! I have always served well. You cannot disgrace me!" said the young man, his voice rising.

"Listen to me, you young fool. There is no disgrace in being deaf. And you can feel free to walk with me on the battlements, if you will, when the Nadir arrive. But how well can you serve me as a leader if you can't hear my damned instructions?"

"I will manage," said Dun Hedes.

"And how well will your men manage when they try to ask for advice? What happens if we sound the retreat and you don't hear it? No! The decision's made. Stand down."

"I request the right to see Gan Orrin!"

"As you will. But at the end of today I will have a new dun for Falcon. Now to business. I want each of you—you included, Hedes—to pick your two strongest men. The best you have at hand-to-hand wrestling, bare-knuckle, whatever. They will have their chance to knock me from my feet. That should lighten the mood. Get to it!"

Dun Mendar called Gilad to him as he returned to his group, then squatted down among the men to outline Druss's idea. Chuckles came from various soldiers as men volunteered swiftly. The noise grew as men clamored for the right to down the old warrior, and Druss laughed aloud as he sat apart from the men, peeling an orange. At last the pairs were selected, and he heaved himself to his feet.

"There is an object to this little exercise, but I shall explain that later on. For now, look upon it as light entertainment," said Druss, hands on hips. "However, I find the audience is always more alert if there is something to be won, so I will offer a free afternoon to any group whose champions down me." A cheer greeted this, and he went on. "Mind you, those that don't down me will run an additional two miles." Druss grinned again as the groans erupted.

"Don't be such faint hearts. What do you have before you? Here is one old, fat man. We will start with the Bild pair."

The men could have been twins; both were huge, black-bearded, with massively muscled arms and shoulders. Stripped of their armor, they appeared as formidable a pair of warriors as could be seen among the groups.

"Right, my lads," said Druss, "you can wrestle, or punch, or kick, or gouge. Begin when you're ready." The old man doffed his jerkin as he spoke, and the Bild pair circled slowly, relaxed and smiling. Once on either side of the old man, they lunged. Druss dropped to one knee, ducking under a roundhouse right, then slammed his hand up into the man's groin, grabbing his shirtfront with the other hand and hurling him into his comrade. Both men collapsed to the ground, arms entwined.

Curses exploded from the Bild men seated around the circle, to be drowned by jeers from the other groups.

"Next, Gorbadac!" announced Druss. The two advanced more warily than their predecessors, then the tallest one dived toward Druss's middle with arms outstretched. The axman's knee came up to meet him, and he sagged to the grass. The second attacked almost immediately, only to be backhanded contemptuously across the cheek. He tripped over his fallen comrade and fell heavily. The first man was unconscious and had to be carried to the back of the circle.

"Now Falcon!" said Druss. This time he watched them advance, then bellowed at the top of his voice and charged. The first man's mouth fell open in surprise; the second took a backward step and tripped. Druss hit the first man with a straight left; he went down and lay still.

"Karnak?" said Druss. Gilad and Bregan entered the circle. Druss had seen the dark one before and liked the look of him. A born warrior, the old man had thought. He enjoyed seeing the look of hatred the boy threw at him every time he laughed at him and liked the way he had dropped back to help Orrin. Druss flicked his gaze to the second man. Surely here was an error. The chubby one was no fighter, nor would he ever be—good-natured and tough but never a warrior.

Gilad launched himself forward and checked himself as Druss raised his fists. Druss twisted to keep him in vision; then, hearing a sound from behind, he whirled to see the fat one attack, trip, and fall sprawling at his feet. Chuckling, he swung back to Gilad, turning into a flying kick that hammered into his chest. He took a backward step to brace himself, but the fat one had rolled behind him, and Druss hit the ground with a grunt.

A massive roar rose from two hundred throats. Druss smiled and rolled to his feet smoothly, holding up a hand for silence.

"I want you to think about what you've seen today, my lads," said Druss, "for it wasn't only fun. You have seen what one man can do, and you have also seen what a simple bit of teamwork can achieve.

"Now, when the Nadir are swarming over the walls, you will all be hard pressed to defend yourselves, but you've got to do more than that. You've got to protect your comrades where you can, for no warrior has a defense against a sword in the back. I want each of you to find a sword brother. You don't have to be friends—that will come. But you need understanding, and you need to work at it. You will protect each other's backs when the assault comes, so make your choices well. Those of you who lose a sword brother when the fighting starts, find another. Failing that, do what you can for the men around you.

"I have been a warrior for more than forty years—twice as long as most of you have lived. Bear that in mind. What I say is of value, for I have survived.

"There is only one way to survive in war, and that is by being willing to die. You will find soon that fine swordsmen can be downed by untutored savages who would slice their fingers if asked to carve meat. And how? Because the savage is willing. Worse, he may be baresark.

"The man who takes a backward step against a Nadir warrior is stepping into eternity. Meet them head to head, savage to savage.

"You have heard it said that this is a lost cause, and you will hear it again. I have heard it a thousand times in a hundred lands.

"Mostly you hear it from faint hearts and can ignore it. Often, however, you will hear it from seasoned veterans. Ultimately such prophecies are worthless.

"There are half a million Nadir warriors. An awesome figure! One to numb the mind. But the walls are only so long and so wide. They cannot all come over at once. We will kill them as they do, and we will kill hundreds more as they climb. And day by day we will wear them down.

"You are going to lose friends, comrades, brothers. You are going to lose sleep. You are going to lose blood. Nothing about the next few months will be easy.

"I am not going to talk about patriotism, duty, liberty, and the defense of freedom because that's all dung to a soldier.

"I want you to think about survival. And the best way you can do that is to look down on the Nadir when they arrive and think to yourselves: There are fifty men down there just for me. And one by one, by all the gods, I'll cut them down.

"As for me . . . well, I'm a seasoned campaigner. I'll take a hundred." Druss took a deep breath, allowing time for his words to sink in.

"Now," he said at last, "you can get back to your duties, with the exception of Group Karnak." Turning, he saw

Hogun, and as the men hauled themselves to their feet, he walked back toward the mess hall of Wall One with the young general.

"A nice speech," said Hogun. "It sounded very similar to the one you gave this morning at Wall Three."

"You haven't been very attentive, laddie," said Druss. "I have given that speech six times since yesterday. And I've been knocked down three times. I'm as dry as a sand lizard's belly."

"I will stand you a bottle of Vagrian in the mess hall," said Hogun. "They don't serve Lentrian at this end of the Dros—it's too pricey."

"It will do. I see you have regained your good humor."

"Aye. You were right about the earl's burial. Just too damned quick about being right, that's all," said Hogun.

"What does that mean?"

"Just what it says. You have a way, Druss, of turning your emotions on and off. Most men lack that. It makes you seem what Mendar called you—coldhearted."

"I don't like the phrase, but it fits," said Druss, pushing open the door to the mess hall. "I mourned Delnar as he lay dying. But once dead, he's gone. And I'm still here. And there's a damned long way to go yet."

The two men sat at a window table and ordered drinks from a steward. He returned with a large bottle and two goblets; both men sat silently for a while, watching the training.

Druss was deep in thought. He had lost many friends in his life but none more dear than Sieben and Rowena—the one his sword brother, the other his wife. Thoughts of them both were as tender as open wounds. When I die, he thought, everyone will mourn for Druss the Legend.

But who will mourn for *me*?

◊ **13** ◊

"TELL US WHAT you saw," said Rek as he joined the four leaders of the Thirty in Serbitar's cabin. He had been woken from a deep sleep by Menahem, who had swiftly explained the problems facing the Dros. Now alert, he listened as the blond warrior-priest outlined the threat.

"The Captain of the Ax is training the men. He has demolished all buildings from Wall Three and created a killing ground. He has also blocked the gate tunnels back to Wall Four—he has done well."

"You mentioned traitors," said Rek.

Serbitar lifted a hand. "Patience!" he said. "Go on, Arbedark."

"There is an innkeeper called Musar, originally from the Nadir Wolfshead tribe. He has been at Dros Delnoch for eleven years. He and a Drenai officer are planning to kill Druss. I think there may be others. Ulric has been told of the tunnel blocking."

"How?" asked Rek. "Surely there is no travel to the north?"

"He keeps pigeons," said Arbedark.

"What can you do?" Rek asked Serbitar, who shrugged and looked to Vintar for support. The abbot spread his hands. "We tried to make contact with Druss, but he is not receptive and the distance is still very great. I do not see how we can help."

"What news of my father?" asked Virae. The men looked at one another, ill at ease. Serbitar spoke at last.

"He is dead. I am deeply sorry."

Virae said nothing, her face showing no emotion. Rek

134

put an arm on her shoulder, but she pushed it away and stood. "I'm going on deck," she said softly. "I'll see you later, Rek."

"Shall I come with you?"

"No. It's not for sharing."

As the door closed behind her, Vintar spoke, his voice gentle and sorrowful. "He was a fine man after his fashion. I contacted him before the end; he was at peace and in the past."

"In the past?" said Rek. "What does that mean?"

"His mind had vanished into happier memories. He died well. I think the Source will have him—I shall pray to that effect. But what of Druss?"

"I tried to reach the general, Hogun," said Arbedark, "but the danger was great. I almost lost my bearings. The distance . . ."

"Yes," said Serbitar. "Did you manage to ascertain how the assassination is to be attempted?"

"No. I could not enter the man's mind, but before him was a bottle of Lentrian red that he was resealing. It could be poison or an opiate of some kind."

"There must be something you can do," said Rek, "with all your power."

"All power—but one—has limits," said Vintar. "We can only pray. Druss has been a warrior for many years, a survivor. It means he is not only skillful but lucky. Menahem, you must journey to the Dros and watch for us. Perhaps the attempt will be delayed until we are closer."

"You mentioned a Drenai officer," said Rek to Arbedark. "Who? Why?"

"I know not. As I completed the journey, he was leaving the house of Musar. He acted furtively, and this aroused my suspicions. Musar was in the loft, and upon the table beside him lay a note written in the Nadir tongue. It said, 'Kill Deathwalker.' That is the name by which Druss is known to the tribes."

"You were lucky to see the officer," said Rek. "In a fortress city of that size the chances of seeing a single act of treachery must be amazing."

"Yes," said Arbedark. Rek saw the look that passed between the blond priest and the albino.

"Is there more to it than luck?" he asked.

"Perhaps," said Serbitar. "We will talk of it soon. For now we are helpless. Menahem will watch the situation and keep us informed. If they delay the attempt for two more days, we may be in a position to help."

Rek looked at Menahem, sitting upright at the table, eyes closed and breathing shallowly.

"Has he gone?" he asked.

Serbitar nodded.

Druss managed to look interested as the speeches wore on. Three times since the banquet had ended the old warrior had heard how grateful were the townsfolk, burghers, merchants, and lawyers that he had come among them. How it showed up the faint hearts ever ready to write off the might of the Drenai empire. How, when the battle was won—speedily—Dros Delnoch would attract sightseers from all over the continent. How new verses would be added to Sieben's saga of the Legend. The words droned on, the praise growing more fulsome as the wine flowed.

Some two hundred of Delnoch's richest and most influential families were present at the great hall, seated around the massive round table normally reserved for state occasions. The banquet was the brainchild of Bricklyn, the master burgher, a short self-obsessed businessman who had bent Druss's ear throughout the meal and was now taking the liberty of bending it again in the longest speech so far.

Druss kept his smile firmly fixed, nodding here and there where he felt it appropriate. He had attended many such functions in his life, though they normally followed rather than preceded a battle.

As had been expected, Druss had opened the speeches with a short talk on his life, concluding it with a stirring promise that the Dros would hold if only the soldiers would show the same courage as those families sitting around the table. As had also been expected, he received a tumultuous ovation.

As was his wont on these occasions, Druss drank sparingly, merely sipping the fine Lentrian red placed before him by the stout innkeeper Musar, the banquet's master of ceremonies.

With a start, Druss realized that Bricklyn had finished his speech, and he applauded vigorously. The short gray-haired man sat down at his left, beaming and bowing as the applause continued.

"A fine speech," said Druss. "Very fine."

"Thank you. Yours, I think, was better," said Bricklyn, pouring himself a glass of Vagrian white from a stone jug.

"Nonsense. You are a born speaker."

"It's strange you should say that. I remember when I gave a speech in Drenan for the wedding of Count Maritin—you know the count, of course? Anyway, he said ..." And so it went on, with Druss smiling and nodding and Bricklyn finding more and more stories to outline his qualities.

Toward midnight, as prearranged, Delnar's elderly servant, Arshin, approached Druss and announced—loudly enough for Bricklyn to overhear—that Druss was needed on Wall Three to supervise a new detachment of archers and their placement. It was not before time. Throughout the evening Druss had drunk no more than a single goblet, yet his head swam and his legs shook as he pushed himself upright. He made his apologies to the stout burgher, bowed to the assembly, and marched from the room. In the corridor outside he stopped and leaned against a pillar.

"Are you all right, sir?" asked Arshin.

"The wine was bad," muttered Druss. "It's hit my stomach worse than a Ventrian breakfast."

"You'd better get to bed, sir. I will take a message to Dun Mendar to attend you in your room."

"Mendar? Why the hell should he attend me?"

"I'm sorry, sir. I couldn't mention it in the hall as you had told me what to say when I approached you, but Dun Mendar asked if you could spare him a moment. He has a serious problem, he said."

Druss rubbed his eyes and took several deep breaths. His belly felt weak, disconnected, and fragile. He toyed with the idea of sending Arshin to explain to the young Karnak officer but then realized word would get around that Druss was sick. Or worse, that he could not hold his wine.

"Maybe the air will do me good. Where is he?"

"He said he would meet you at the inn by Unicorn Alley.

Turn right outside the keep until you reach the first market square, then turn left by the miller's. Walk on through Baker's Row until you reach the armory repair shop, then turn right. That's Unicorn Alley, and the inn is at the far end."

Druss asked the man to repeat the directions, then pushed himself from the wall and staggered out into the night. The stars were bright, the sky cloudless. He sucked in the crisp air and felt his stomach turn.

"Damn this," he said angrily, and found a secluded spot by the keep, away from the sentries, where he made himself vomit. Cold sweat covered his brow and his head ached as he pushed himself upright, but at least his stomach seemed more settled. He headed toward the first square, located the miller's store, and turned left. Already the smell of baking bread was coming from the ovens in Baker's Row.

The smell made him retch again. Angry now at his condition, he hammered on the first door he came to. A short, fat baker in a white cotton apron opened the door and peered nervously at him.

"Yes?" he said.

"I am Druss. Do you have a loaf ready?"

"It's only just past midnight. I have some bread from yesterday, but if you wait for a while I will have fresh. What's the matter? You look green."

"Just get me a loaf—and hurry!" Druss clamped a hand to the door frame, pulling himself upright. What the hell was wrong with that wine? Or maybe it was the food. He hated rich food. Too many years on dried beef and raw vegetables. His body could not take it, but it had never reacted like this before.

The man trotted back down the short hallway bearing a hefty chunk of black bread and a small phial.

"Drink this," he said. "I have an ulcer, and Calvar Syn says it settles the stomach faster than anything else." Gratefully Druss downed the contents of the phial. It tasted like charcoal. Then he tore a great bite from the bread, sliding gratefully to the floor with his back against the door. His stomach rebeled, but he gritted his teeth and finished the loaf; within a few minutes he was feeling better. His head ached like the devil and his vision was a little blurred, but his legs felt fine and he had strength enough to bluff his way through a short chat with Mendar.

"My thanks, baker. What do I owe you?"

The baker was about to ask for two copper coins but realized in time that the old man had no pockets visible and no money sack. He sighed and said what was expected.

"No money necessary from you, Druss. Naturally."

"Decent of you," said Druss.

"You should get back to your quarters," said the baker. "And get a good night's sleep." He was about to add that Druss was no youngster any more but thought better of it.

"Not yet. Got to see one of my officers."

"Ah, Mendar," said the baker, smiling.

"How did you know?"

"I saw him not twenty minutes since with three or four others heading down toward the Unicorn. We don't see many officers here at this time of night. The Unicorn's a soldier's drinking house."

"Yes. Well, thanks again. I'll be on my way."

Druss stood in the doorway for a few moments after the baker had returned to his oven. If Mendar was with three or four others, they might expect him to join them for a drink, and he racked his brains to think of a reason for refusing. Unable to come up with a convincing excuse, he cursed and started down Baker's Row.

All was darkness now and silence. The silence jarred him, but his head ached too hard to consider it.

Ahead he could see the anvil sign of the armory repairer gleaming in the moonlight. He stopped again, blinking as the sign shimmered and distorted, and shook his head.

Silence . . . What was it about the damned silence?

He walked on, ill at ease, loosening Snaga in her sheath more as a reflex habit than as a conscious awareness of danger. He turned right . . .

Something swished through the air. Light exploded in his eyes as the club hit him; he went down hard and rolled in the dirt as a dark figure sprang forward. Snaga sang through the air, slicing through the man's thigh, crunching on bone that splintered and broke, tearing a scream from the assassin. Druss lurched to his feet as more shapes came from the shadows. His vision blurred, he could still make out the gleam of steel in the moonlight. Bellowing a war cry, he lunged forward. A sword arced toward him, but he batted it aside and drove his ax through the skull of the swordsman, simultaneously kicking out at a second man. A sword blade cut through his shirt, nicking his chest. He hurled Snaga and turned to meet the third man.

It was Mendar!

Druss moved sideways with arms outstretched like a wrestler. The young officer, sword in hand, advanced confidently. Druss glanced at the second man; he was lying groaning on the ground, his weakening fingers desperately trying to pull the ax from his belly. Druss was angry with himself. He should never have hurled the ax—he blamed it on the headache and sickness. Now Mendar leapt and swung his sword, and Druss jumped backward as the silver steel swished by him, an inch from his neck.

"You can't back away much longer, old man!" said Mendar, grinning.

"Why are you doing this?" asked Druss.

"Playing for time? Sorry? You wouldn't understand."

Once more he leapt and slashed, and once more Druss jumped clear. But now his back was against a building, and there was nowhere to run.

Mendar laughed. "I didn't realize it would be so easy to kill you, Druss," he said, and lunged. Druss twisted, slammed his hand against the flat of the sword, then leapt forward as the weapon sliced the skin over his ribs and hammered a fist into Mendar's face. The tall officer staggered back with blood pouring from his mouth. A second blow crashed under his heart, snapping a rib. He went down, losing his grip on his sword, but huge fingers gripped his throat and hauled him upright. He blinked. The grip relaxed just enough for him to squeeze air through his windpipe.

"Easy, boy? Nothing in life is easy."

A whisper of sound came from behind him.

Druss grabbed Mendar and swung him around. A double-headed ax cleaved the officer's shoulder, lodging against the breastbone. Druss hurdled the body and shoulder-charged the assassin as he struggled to free his weapon. The man was hurled backward. As Druss clamhered to his feet, the killer turned and sprinted out into Baker's Row.

Druss cursed and returned to the dying officer. Blood poured from the ghastly wound, soaking into the hard-packed earth.

"Help me," said Mendar. "Please!"

"Think yourself lucky, you whoreson. I would have killed you much more slowly. Who was he?"

But Mendar was dead. Druss retrieved Snaga from the other dead assassin, then searched for the man whose leg he had wounded. Following a trail of blood into a narrow alley, he found the man lying back against a wall, a dagger rammed to the hilt in his heart, his fingers still curled about the handle.

Druss rubbed his eyes, and his hand came away sticky. He ran his fingers over his temple. A lump the size of an egg, tender and broken, made him curse once more.

Was nothing simple in the world anymore?

In his day a battle was a battle, army against army.

Pull yourself together, he told himself. There have always been traitors and assassins.

It was just that he had never been a target before.

Suddenly he laughed as he remembered the silence. The inn was empty. As he turned into Unicorn Alley, he should have realized the danger. Why would five men be waiting for him after midnight in a deserted alley?

You old fool, he told himself. You must be getting senile.

Musar sat alone in his loft, listening to the pigeons as they ruffled their feathers to greet the new dawn. He was calm now, tranquil almost, and his large hands no longer trembled. He walked to the window, leaning far out over the sill to gaze north. His one all-consuming ambition had been to see Ulric ride into Dros Delnoch and on to the rich southlands, to see the rise, at long last, of the Nadir empire.

Now his Drenai wife and his eight-year-old son lay below, their sleep deepening toward death as he savored his last dawn.

It had been hard watching them sip their poisoned drinks, listening to his wife's amiable chatter about her plans for tomorrow. When his son had asked him if he could go riding with Brentar's boy, he had said that he could.

He should have followed his first instincts and poisoned the old warrior, but Dun Mendar had convinced him otherwise. Suspicion would then have fallen instantly on the master of ceremonies. This way was surer, Mendar had promised: drug him and kill him in a dark alleyway. So simple!

How could one so old move so swiftly?

Musar had felt he could bluff it out. He knew Druss would never recognize him as the fifth assassin, for his face had been half-covered by a dark scarf. But the risks were too great, maintained his Nadir lord, Surip. The last message had congratulated him on his work over these last twelve years and had concluded "Peace on you, brother, and your family."

Musar filled a deep bucket with warm water from a large copper kettle.

Then he took a dagger from a shelf at the rear of the loft and sharpened it on a small whetstone. The risks were too great? Indeed they were. Musar knew the Nadir had another man at Delnoch, more highly placed than he. On no account would he be compromised.

He plunged his left arm into the bucket, then, holding the dagger firmly with his right, he severed the arteries of the wrist. The water changed color.

He had been a fool to marry, he thought, tears shining in his eyes.

But she had been so lovely . . .

Hogun and Elicas watched as men from the legion cleared away the bodies of the assassins. Spectators looked on from nearby windows, calling down questions, but the legion ignored them.

Elicas tugged at his small gold earring as Lebus the tracker outlined the skirmish. Elicas had never lost his fascination for the tracker's skill. On a trail Lebus could tell one the sex of the horses, the age of the riders, and damned near the conversations around the camp fires. It was a science beyond his understanding.

"The old man entered the alley over there. The first man

was hidden in the shadows. He struck him, and Druss fell. He rose fast. See the blood there? An ax cut across the thigh. Then he charged the other three, but he must have thrown his ax because he backed away to the wall there."

"How did he manage to kill Mendar?" asked Hogun, who already knew from Druss. But he, too, appreciated Lebus' skill.

"That had me puzzled, sir," said the tracker. "But I think I have it. There was a fifth attacker who stayed back during the struggle. There is some indication that Druss and Mendar had ceased to fight and were standing close. The fifth man must have moved in then. See the heel mark there? That belongs to Druss. See the deep round imprint? I would say he swung Mendar around to block the fifth man."

"Good work, Lebus," said Hogun. "The men say you could track a bird in flight, and I believe them."

Lebus bowed and moved away.

"I begin to believe Druss is everything they say he is," said Elicas. "Astonishing!"

"True," said Hogun, "but worrying. To have an army the size of Ulric's opposing us is one thing; traitors at the Dros is quite another. And as for Mendar . . . it is almost beyond belief."

"From a good family, I understand. I have put it around that Mendar aided Druss against Nadir infiltrators. It may work. Not everyone has Lebus' talent, and anyway, the ground will be well trodden over by full daylight."

"The Mendar story is a good one," said Hogun. "But word will get out."

"How is the old man?" asked Elicas.

"Ten stitches in his side and four in his head. He was asleep when I left. Calvar Syn says it's a miracle the skull didn't crack."

"Will he still judge the open swords?" asked the younger man. Hogun merely raised an eyebrow. "Yes, I thought he would. That's a shame."

"Why?" asked Hogun.

"Well, if he hadn't judged it, you would have done so. And then I would have missed the pleasure of beating you."

"You conceited pup!" said Hogun, laughing. "The day

has not yet come when you could breach my guard, even with a wooden sword."

"There's a first time for everything. And you're not getting any younger, Hogun. Why, you must be over thirty. One foot in the grave!"

"We shall see. A side bet, perhaps?"

"A flagon of red?" said Elicas.

"Done, my lad! Nothing tastes sweeter than wine another man has paid for."

"As I shall no doubt find out this evening," retorted Elicas.

◊ **14** ◊

THE MARRIAGE WAS a simple one, performed by the Abbot of Swords, Vintar, and witnessed by the captain and mate of the *Wastrel*. The sea was calm, the night sky cloudless. Overhead gulls wheeled and dived, a sure sign of approaching land.

Antaheim, one of the Thirty, tall and slender, his dark features showing his Vagrian descent, supplied the ring: an unadorned band of gold.

Now, as the dawn neared and the others slept, Rek stood alone at the prow, starlight glinting on his silver headband, wind streaming his hair like a dark banner.

The die was cast now. He was chained by his own hand to the Delnoch cause. Sea spray stung his eyes, and he stepped back, sitting down with his back to the rail and hugging his cloak tightly about him. All his life he had sought direction and an escape from fear, an end to trembling hands and an unsteady heart. Now his fears had vanished like candle wax before a flame.

Earl Regnak of Dros Delnoch, Warden of the North.

At first Virae had refused his offer, but ultimately, he knew, she would be forced to accept. If she had not married him, Abalayn would have sent a husband posthaste. It was inconceivable that Delnoch should lack a leader and equally inconceivable for a woman to take on the duties.

The captain had sprinkled their heads with seawater in the ritual blessing, but Vintar, a lover of truth, had omitted the blessing of fertility and replaced it with the more simple "Be happy, my children, now and until the end of your lives."

Druss had escaped the attempt on his life, Gan Orrin had found his strength, and the Thirty were only two days from Dros Purdol and the last stage of their journey. The winds had been kind, and *Wastrel* was two, maybe three days ahead of schedule.

Rek studied the stars and remembered the sightless seer and his prophetic verse.

"The earl and the legend will be together at the wall, and men shall dream, and men shall die, but shall the fortress fall?"

In his mind's eye Rek pictured Virae as she had been when he had left her almost an hour ago, her light hair tangled upon the pillow, her eyes closed, and her face peaceful in rest. He had wanted to touch her, to pull her close and feel her arms about him. Instead he had covered her gently with a blanket, dressed, and quietly climbed to the deck. Away to starboard he could hear the dolphins' ghostly music.

Now he pulled himself upright and returned to his cabin. Once more Virae had kicked away the blanket. Rek undressed slowly and eased himself down beside her.

And this time he touched her.

Amidships, the leaders of the Thirty finished their prayers and broke bread together, which Vintar blessed. They ate in silence, breaking the bond of unity to enjoy their own thoughts. At last Serbitar leaned back and signaled the opening. Their minds blended together.

"The old man is a fearsome warrior," said Menahem.

"But he is no strategist," said Serbitar. "His method of holding the Dros will be to man the walls and do battle until a conclusion is reached."

"There is little choice," said Menahem. "We will offer no other option."

"That is true. What I am saying is that Druss will merely pack the walls with men, which is not a serviceable idea. He has ten thousand men, and to defend efficiently he will be able to use only seven thousand at any given time. The other walls must be manned, essential services run, messengers assigned. There must also be a floating force ready to offer instant aid to any weak spot.

"Our strength must be to achieve maximum efficiency

with total economy of effort. Withdrawals must be meticulously timed. Every officer must be not only aware but totally sure of his role."

"And we must," said Arbedark, "develop an aggressive attitude to defense. We have seen ourselves that Ulric is stripping whole forests in order to build his ballistae and siege towers. We must have inflammables, also containers for them."

For over an hour, as the dawn breasted the eastern horizon, the leaders set about their plans: eliminating some ideas, refining and expanding others.

Finally Serbitar called on them to join hands. Arbedark, Menahem, and Vintar relaxed their control, drifting down into the darkness, as Serbitar drew their power to him.

"Druss! Druss!" he pulsed, his mind soaring across the ocean, past Dros Purdol, the port fortress, on along the Delnoch range past the Sathuli settlements, over the vast Sentran Plain—faster and faster he flew.

Druss awoke with a start, blue eyes scanning the room, nostrils flared to scent danger in the air. He shook his head. Someone was saying his name, but there was no sound. Swiftly he made the sign of the claw over his heart. Still someone called him.

Cold sweat appeared on his brow.

He reached across the bed, snatching Snaga from the chair by the wall.

"Listen to me, Druss," pleaded the voice.

"Get out of my head, you whoreson!" bellowed the old man, rolling from the bed.

"I am of the Thirty. We are traveling to Dros Delnoch to aid you. Listen to me!"

"Get *out* of my head!"

Serbitar had no choice, for the pain was incredible. He released the old warrior and returned to the ship.

Druss staggered to his feet, fell, and rose again. The door opened, and Calvar Syn moved swiftly to him.

"I told you not to get up before noon," he snapped.

"Voices," said Druss. "Voices . . . inside my head!"

"Lie down. Now listen. You are the captain, and you expect men to obey you. That's what discipline is about. I am the surgeon, and I expect to be obeyed by my patients. Now tell me about the voices."

Druss laid his head on the pillow and closed his eyes. His head ached abominably, and his stomach was still queasy. "There was only one voice. It said my name. Then it said it was from the Thirty and that they were coming to aid us."

"Is that all?"

"Yes. What is happening to me, Calvar? I've never had this before from a blow on the head."

"It could be the blow; concussion can cause some very strange effects, including seeing visions and hearing voices. But they rarely last. Take my advice, Druss. The worst thing you can do at the moment is get overexcited. You could black out . . . or worse. Blows to the head can be fatal, even after a period of several days. I want you to rest and relax, and if the voice comes again, listen to it, even reply to it. But do not become alarmed. Understand?"

"Of course I understand," said Druss. "I don't normally panic, Doctor, but some things I do *not* like."

"I know that, Druss. Do you need something to help you sleep now?"

"No. Wake me at noon. I have to judge a contest of swordsmanship. And don't fret," he said, seeing the gleam of annoyance in the surgeon's one good eye. "I shall not get excited, and I will come straight back to bed afterward."

Outside the room Hogun and Orrin waited. Calvar Syn joined them, signaled for silence, and beckoned them to a nearby office.

"I'm not happy," he told them. "He's hearing voices, and believe me, that is not a good sign. But he's strong as a bull."

"Is he in any danger?" asked Hogun.

"It's hard to say. This morning I didn't think so. But he has been under a lot of strain recently, and that may not help his condition. And although it is easy to forget, he is no longer a young man."

"What about the voices?" said Orrin. "Could he go mad?"

"I think I would bet against that," replied Calvar. "He said it was a message from the Thirty. Earl Delnar told me he had sent Virae to them with a message, and it could be that they have a speaker among them. Or it could be someone of Ulric's; he also has speakers among his shamans. I have told Druss to relax and listen to any future voices and report them to me."

"That one old man is vital to us," said Orrin softly. "Do everything you can, Calvar. It would be a hammer blow to morale if anything happened to him."

"Do you think I don't know that?" snapped the surgeon.

The banquet to celebrate the open swords was a raucous affair. All who had reached the last hundred were invited; officers and enlisted men were seated side by side, swapping jests, tales, and tall, tall stories.

Gilad was seated between Bar Britan, who had beaten him soundly, and Dun Pinar, who had in turn vanquished Britan. The black-bearded Bar was cursing Pinar good-humoredly and complaining that the latter's wooden sword lacked the balance of his own cavalry saber.

"I'm surprised you didn't ask to be allowed to fight on horseback," said Pinar.

"But I did," protested Britan, "and they offered me the target pony." The three men burst into laughter, which others joined as the joke spread around the table. The target pony was a saddle tied to a moving rail and pulled by ropes. It was used for archery practice and jousting.

As the wine flowed, Gilad relaxed. He had seriously considered missing the banquet, fearing that his background would leave him ill at ease with the officer class. He had agreed to come only when the men of his group had lobbied him, pointing out that he was the only member of Karnak who had reached the last hundred. Now he was glad he had been persuaded. Bar Britan was a dry, witty companion, while Pinar, despite his breeding—or perhaps because of it—made Gilad feel among friends.

At the far end of the table sat Druss, flanked by Hogun and Orrin, while beside them sat the archer leader from Skultik. Gilad knew nothing about the man, save that he had brought six hundred bowmen to the Dros.

Hogun, in full legion dress armor of silver breastplate

edged with ebony and black and silver mail shirt, stared at the silver sword lying on the table before Druss.

The final had been watched by more than five thousand soldiers as Hogun and Orrin had taken their places. The first strike had been Hogun's, a neat parry and riposte after a four-minute duel. The second had been Orrin's, following a feint to the head. Hogun had blocked swiftly, but a subtle twist of the wrist had sent his opponent's wooden blade down to touch Hogun's side. After some twenty minutes Hogun led by two strikes to one, one strike from victory.

During the first break Druss strolled to where Hogun and his seconds sat drinking watered wine in the shade of Wall One.

"Nice work," said Druss. "He's good, though."

"Yes," said Hogun, wiping the sweat from his brow with a white towel. "But he is not as strong on the right."

"True. But you are slow against the leg cut."

"A lancer's main fault. It comes from too much work in the saddle," said Hogun. "He is shorter than I, which gives him an advantage in that respect."

"True. It has done Orrin good to reach the final. His cheers outnumber yours, I think."

"Yes, but that will not disturb me," said Hogun.

"I hope it does not," said Druss. "Still, nothing could be better for morale than seeing the fortress gan perform so well." Hogun glanced up, holding Druss's gaze, then the old warrior smiled and moved back to his judge's seat.

"What was that about?" asked Elicas, walking behind Hogun and kneading the muscles of his neck and shoulder. "Encouraging words?"

"Yes," said Hogun. "Do some work on the forearm, will you. The muscles are knotted there."

The young general grunted as Elicas probed the flesh with his powerful thumbs. Was Druss asking him to lose? Surely not. And yet . . .

It would do no harm for Orrin to win the silver sword and would certainly increase his growing standing with the troops.

"What are you thinking?" asked Elicas.

"I'm thinking that he's weak on the right."

"You will take him, Hogun," said the young officer. "Try that vicious parry-riposte you used on me."

At two strikes even Hogun's wooden blade snapped. Orrin stepped back, allowing a replacement, and offered his opponent a swift practice with the new weapon. Hogun was unhappy with the balance and changed the sword again. He needed time to think. *Had* Druss suggested that he lose?

"You're not concentrating," said Elicas sternly. "What's the matter with you? The legion has a lot of wages tied up in this tourney."

"I know."

His mind cleared. No matter what the reason, he could not fight to lose.

He threw everything he could into the last attack, blocked a backhand sweep, and lunged. Just before his blade thudded against Orrin's belly, however, the gan's sword tapped his neck. Orrin had read the move and lured him in. In real combat both men would have died, but this was not real combat and Orrin had won. The two men shook hands as the cheering soldiers swarmed forward.

"That's my money gone," said Elicas. "Still, there is a bright side."

"What's that?" said Hogun, rubbing at his burning forearm.

"I cannot afford to settle our own bet. You will have to stand for the wine. It's the least you can do, Hogun, after letting down the legion!"

The banquet lifted Hogun's spirits, and the speeches from Bar Britan on behalf of the soldiers and Dun Pinar for the officers were witty and short; the food was good, the wine and ale plentiful, and the camaraderie reassuring. It is hardly the same Dros, thought Hogun.

Outside at the portcullis gates Bregan stood sentry duty with a tall young cul from Group Fire. Bregan did not know his name and could not ask, since sentries were forbidden to talk on duty. A strange rule, thought Bregan, but there to be obeyed.

The night was chilly, but he barely noticed it. His thoughts were back in the village with Lotis and the children. Sybad had received a letter that day, and all was well. Legan, Bregan's five-year-old son, was mentioned. It

seemed that when he had climbed a tall elm and could not
get down, he had cried and called for his father. Bregan had
asked Sybad to write a few words for him in his next letter
home. He had wanted him to say how much he loved and
missed them all, but he could not bring himself to ask
Sybad to pen such endearments. Instead, he asked him to
tell Legan to be a good boy and obey his mother. Sybad
took notes from all the villagers and spent the early evening
composing the letter, which was sealed in wax and delivered to the mail room. A rider would carry it south with
other letters and army dispatches for Drenan.

Lotis would have banked the fire by now and doused the
lamps, Bregan thought. She would be lying in their rush-
filled bed, probably asleep. Legan would be asleep beside
her, he knew, for Lotis always found it difficult to sleep
alone when Bregan was away.

"You will stop the savages, Daddy, won't you?"

"Yes," Bregan had told him. "But they probably won't
come. The politicians will sort it out, just like they have always done before."

"Will you be home soon?"

"I'll be back for harvest supper."

"Promise?"

"I promise."

The banquet over, Druss invited Orrin, Hogun, Elicas, and
Bowman to the earl's study above the great hall. The servant Arshin brought them wine, and Druss introduced the
outlaw to the fortress leaders. Orrin shook hands coolly, his
eyes showing his distaste. For two years he had sent patrols
into Skultik with orders to catch and hang the outlaw
leader. Hogun was less concerned with Bowman's pedigree
and more interested in the skills the outlaws could bring.
Elicas had no preconceived opinion but instinctively liked
the blond archer.

Once seated, Bowman cleared his throat and told them
the size of the Nadir horde gathered at Gulgothir.

"How do you come by this intelligence?" asked Orrin.

"Three days ago we . . . met . . . some travelers in
Skultik. They were journeying from Dros Purdol to Segril
and had come across the northern desert. They were way-

laid near Gulgothir and taken into the city, where they stayed for four days. Because they were Vagrian merchants, they were treated civilly but questioned by a Nadir officer called Surip. One of them is a former Vagrian officer, and he made the estimate of their strength."

"But half a million?" said Orrin. "I thought the figure was exaggerated."

"Underplayed if anything," said Bowman. "Outlying tribes were still coming in when he left. I'd say you will have quite a battle on your hands."

"I don't wish to be pedantic," said Hogun, "but do you not mean *we* have a battle on our hands?"

Bowman glanced at Druss. "Have you not told them, old horse? No? Ah, what a deliciously embarrassing moment, to be sure."

"Told us what?" asked Orrin.

"That they are mercenaries," said Druss uneasily. "They stay only until the fall of Wall Three. It has been agreed."

"And for this ... this pitiful aid they expect pardons!" shouted Orrin, rising to his feet. "I will see them swing first."

"After Wall Three we will have less need of archers," said Hogun calmly. "There is no killing ground."

"We need archers, Orrin," said Druss. "We need them badly. And this man has six hundred of the finest. We know walls will fall, and we will need every shaft. The postern gates will be sealed by then. I don't like this situation, either, but needs must ... Better to have cover for the first three walls than to have none at all. Do you agree?"

"And if I don't?" said the gan, still angry.

"Then I shall send them away," said Druss. Hogun began an angry outburst but was silenced by a wave of Druss's hand. "You are the gan, Orrin. It is your decision."

Orrin sat down, breathing deeply. He had made many mistakes before Druss arrived; he knew that now. This situation angered him deeply, but he had no choice but to back the axman, and Druss knew it, too. The two men exchanged glances and smiled.

"They shall stay," said Orrin.

"A wise decision," said Bowman. "How soon will the Nadir arrive, do you think?"

"Too damned soon," muttered Druss. "Sometime within the next three weeks, according to our scouts. Ulric lost a son, which has given us a few more days. But it's still not enough."

For some time the men discussed the many problems facing the defenders. Finally Bowman spoke, this time hesitantly.

"Look here, Druss, there is something I feel I should mention, but I don't want to be thought ... strange. I've been toying with the idea of not mentioning it, but ..."

"Speak on, laddie. You're among friends ... mostly."

"I had a strange dream last night, and you appeared in it. I would have dismissed it, but seeing you today made me think again. I dreamed I was woken from a deep sleep by a warrior in silver armor. I could see right through him, as if he were a ghost. He told me that he had been trying to contact you, but without success. When he spoke, it was like a voice in my mind. He said that his name was Serbitar and that he was traveling with his friends and a woman called Virae.

"He said it was important for me to tell you to collect inflammables and containers, since Ulric has built great siege towers. He also suggested fire gullies across the spaces between walls. In my mind he showed me a vision of you being attacked. He told me a name: Musar.

"Does any of it make any sense?"

For a moment no one spoke, although Druss seemed hugely relieved.

"Indeed it does, laddie. Indeed it does!"

Hogun poured a fresh glass of Lentrian and passed it to Bowman.

"What did this warrior look like?" he asked.

"Tall, slender. I think his hair was white, though he was young."

"It is Serbitar," said Hogun. "The vision is a true one."

"You know him?" asked Druss.

"Of him only. He is the son of Earl Drada of Dros Segril. It is said that the boy was fey and had a demon; he could read men's thoughts. He is an albino, and as you know, the Vagrians consider this an ill omen. He was sent to the temple of the Thirty, south of Drenan, when he was about thirteen. It is also said that his father tried to smother him when he was a babe but that the child sensed him coming and hid outside his bedroom window. These, of course, are but stories."

"Well, his talents have grown, it seems," said Druss. "But I don't give a damn. He'll be useful here, especially if he can read Ulric's mind."

◊ 15 ◊

FOR TEN DAYS work progressed. Fire gullies ten yards wide were dug four feet deep across the open ground between Walls One and Two and again between Walls Three and Four. These were filled with brushwood and small timber, while vats were placed along each gully, ready to pour oil onto the dry wood.

Bowman's archers hammered white stakes in the open ground at various points between walls and also out on the plain before the fortress. Each line of stakes represented sixty paces, and his men practiced for several hours each day, black clouds of shafts slicing the air above each row as the commands were shouted.

Target dummies were set up on the plain, only to be splintered by scores of arrows, even at 120 paces. The skills of the Skultik archers were formidable.

Hogun rehearsed withdrawals, timing the men by drumbeats as they dashed from the battlements, across the plank bridges of the fire gullies to scale the ropes to the next wall. Each day they became more swift.

Minor points began to occupy more time as the overall fitness and readiness of the troops increased.

"When do we add the oil?" Hogun asked Druss as the men took an afternoon break.

"Between Walls One and Two, it will have to be filled on the day of the first attack. Until the first day we will have no real idea of how well the men will stand up to the assault."

"There remains the problem," added Orrin, "of who lights the gullies and when. For example, if the wall is breached, we could have Nadir tribesmen racing side by side with our own men. No easy decision to throw in a lighted torch."

"And if we give men the duty," said Hogun, "what happens if they are killed on the wall?"

"We will have to have a torch duty," said Druss. "And the decision will be relayed by a bugler from Wall Two. An officer of cool nerve will be needed to judge the issue. When the bugle sounds, the gully goes up no matter who is left behind."

Matters such as these occupied Druss more and more, until his head swam with plans, ideas, stratagems, and ploys. Several times during such discussions the old man's temper flared and his huge fists hammered the table, or else he strode around the room like a caged bear.

"I'm a soldier, not a damned planner," he would announce, and the meeting would be adjourned for an hour.

Combustibles were carted in from outlying villages, a seemingly endless number of dispatches arrived from Drenan and Abalayn's panicked government, and a multitude of small problems—concerning delayed mail, new recruits, personal worries, and squabbles between groups—threatened to overwhelm the three men.

One officer complained that the latrine area of Wall One was in danger of causing a health hazard, since it was not of regulation depth and lacked an adequate cesspit.

Druss set a working party to enlarge the area.

Abalayn himself demanded a complete strategic appraisal of all Dros Delnoch's defenses, which Druss refused since the information could be leaked to Nadir sympathizers. This in turn brought a swift rebuke from Drenan and a firm request for an apology. Orrin penned this, claiming it would keep the politicians off their backs.

Then Woundweaver sent a requisition for the legion's mounts, claiming that since the order was to hold to the last man, the horses would be of little use at Delnoch. He allowed that twenty should be retained for dispatch purposes. This so enraged Hogun that he was unapproachable for days.

Added to this, the burghers had begun to complain about the rowdy behavior of the troops in civilian areas. All in all

Druss was beginning to feel at the end of his tether and had begun to voice openly his desire that the Nadir would arrive and the devil with the consequences!

Three days later his wish was partly answered.

A Nadir troop, under a flag of truce, galloped in from the north. Word spread like wildfire, and by the time it reached Druss in the main hall of the keep, an air of panic was abroad in the town.

The Nadir dismounted in the shadow of the great gates and waited. They did not speak. From their pack saddles they took dried meat and water sacks and sat together, eating and waiting.

By the time Druss arrived with Orrin and Hogun, they had completed their meal. Druss bellowed down from the battlements.

"What is your message?"

"Open the gates!" called back the Nadir officer, a short barrel-chested man, bowlegged and powerful.

"Are you the Deathwalker?" called the man.

"Yes."

"You are old and fat. It pleases me."

"Good! Remember that when next we meet, for I have marked you, loudmouth, and my ax knows the name of your spirit. Now, what is your message?"

"The Lord Ulric, Prince of the North, bids me to tell you that he will be riding to Drenan to discuss an alliance with Abalayn, Lord of the Drenai. He wishes it known that he expects the gates of Dros Delnoch to be open to him; that being so, he guarantees there will be no harm to any man, woman, or child, soldier or otherwise, within the city. It is the Lord Ulric's wish that the Drenai and the Nadir become as one nation. He offers the gift of friendship."

"Tell the Lord Ulric," said Druss, "that he is welcome to ride to Drenan at any time. We will even allow an escort of a hundred warriors, as befits a prince of the north."

"The Lord Ulric allows no conditions," said the officer.

"These are *my* conditions—they shall not change," said Druss.

"Then I have a second message. Should the walls be contested and the gates closed, the Lord Ulric wishes it known that every second defender taken alive will be slain, that all the women will be sold into slavery, and that one in three of all citizens will lose his right hand."

"Before that can happen, laddie, the Lord Ulric has to take the Dros. Now you give him this message from Druss the Deathwalker: In the north the mountains may tremble as he breaks wind, but this is Drenai land, and as far as I am concerned he is a potbellied savage who couldn't pick his own nose without a Drenai map.

"Do you think you can remember that, laddie. Or shall I carve it on your ass in large letters?"

"Inspiring as your words were, Druss," said Orrin, "I must tell you that my stomach turned over as you spoke them. Ulric will be furious."

"Would that he were," said Druss bitterly as the Nadir troop galloped back to the north. "If that were the case, he would truly be just a potbellied savage. No! He will laugh . . . loud and long."

"Why should he?" asked Hogun.

"Because he has no choice. He has been insulted and should lose face. When he laughs, the men will laugh with him."

"It was a pretty offer he made," said Orrin as the three men made the long walk back to the keep. "Word will spread. Talks with Abalayn . . . One empire of Drenai and Nadir . . . Clever!"

"Clever and true," said Hogun. "We know from his record that he means it. If we surrender, he will march through and harm no one. Threats of death can be taken and resisted; offers of life are horses of a different color. I wonder how long it will be before the burghers demand another audience."

"Before dusk," predicted Druss.

Back on the walls Gilad and Bregan watched the dust from the Nadir horsemen dwindle into the distance.

"What did he mean, Gil, about riding to Drenan for discussions with Abalayn?"

"He meant he wants us to let his army through."

"Oh. They didn't look terribly fierce, did they? I mean, they seem quite ordinary, really, save that they wear furs."

"Yes, they are ordinary," said Gilad, removing his helm

and combing his hair with his fingers, allowing the cool breeze to get to his head. "Very ordinary. Except that they live for war. Fighting comes as naturally to them as farming does to you. Or me," he added as an afterthought, knowing this to be untrue.

"I wonder why," said Bregan. "It has never made much sense to me. I mean, I understand why some men become soldiers: to protect the nation and all that. But a whole race of people living to be soldiers seems . . . unhealthy. Does that sound right?"

Gilad laughed. "Indeed it sounds right. But the northern steppes make poor farmland. Mainly they breed goats and ponies. Any luxuries they desire, they must steal. Now to the Nadir, so Dun Pinar told me at the banquet, the word for 'stranger' is the same as the word for 'enemy.' Anyone not of the tribe is simply there to be killed and stripped of goods. It is a way of life. Smaller tribes are wiped out by larger tribes. Ulric changed the pattern; by amalgamating beaten tribes into his own, he grew more and more powerful. He controls all the northern kingdoms now and many to the east. Two years ago he took Manea, the sea kingdom."

"I heard about that," said Bregan. "But I thought he had withdrawn after making a treaty with the king."

"Dun Pinar says the king agreed to be Ulric's vassal and Ulric holds the king's son hostage. The nation is his."

"He must be a pretty clever man," said Bregan. "But what would he do if he ever conquered the whole world? I mean, what good is it? I would like a bigger farm and a house with several floors. That I can understand. But what would I do with ten farms? Or a hundred?"

"You would be rich and powerful. Then you could tell your tenant farmers what to do, and they would all bow as you rode past in your fine carriage."

"That doesn't appeal to me, not at all," said Bregan.

"Well, it does to me," said Gilad. "I've always hated it when I had to tug the forelock for some passing nobleman on a tall horse. The way they look at you, despising you because you work a smallholding; paying more money for their handmade boots than I can earn in a year of slaving.

No, I wouldn't mind being rich, so pig-awful rich that no man could ever look down on me again."

Gilad turned his face away to stare out over the plains, his anger fierce, almost tangible.

"Would you look down on people, then, Gil? Would you despise me because I wanted to remain a farmer?"

"Of course not. A man should be free to do what he wants to do as long as it doesn't hurt others."

"Maybe that's why Ulric wants to control everything. Maybe he is sick of everyone looking down on the Nadir."

Gilad turned back to Bregan, and his anger died within him.

"Do you know, Breg, that's just what Pinar said when I asked him if he hated Ulric for wanting to smash the Drenai. He said, 'Ulric isn't trying to smash the Drenai but to raise the Nadir.' I think Pinar admires him."

"The man I admire is Orrin," said Bregan. "It must have taken great courage to come out and train with the men as he has done. Especially being as unpopular as he was. I was so pleased when he won back the swords."

"Only because you won five silver pieces on him," Gilad pointed out.

"That's not fair, Gil! I backed him because he was Karnak; I backed you, too."

"You backed me for a quarter copper and him for a half silver, according to Drebus, who took your bet."

Bregan tapped his nose, smiling. "Ah, but then you don't pay the same price for a goat as for a horse. But the thought was there. After all, I knew you couldn't win."

"I damn near had that Bar Britan. It was a judge's decision at the last."

"True," said Bregan. "But you would never have beaten Pinar or that fellow with the earring from the legion. But what's even more to the point, you never could have beaten Orrin. I've seen you both fence."

"Such judgment!" said Gilad. "It's small wonder to me that you didn't enter yourself, so great is your knowledge."

"I don't have to fly in order to know that the sky is blue," said Bregan. "Anyway, who did you back?"

"Gan Hogun."

"Who else? Drebus said you had placed two bets," said Bregan innocently.

"You know very well. Drebus would have told you."

"I didn't think to ask."

"Liar! Well, I don't care. I backed myself to reach the last fifty."

"And you were so close," said Bregan. "Only one strike in it."

"One lucky blow and I could have won a month's wages."

"Such is life," said Bregan. "Maybe next year you can come back and have another try."

"And maybe corn will grow on the backs of camels!" said Gilad.

Back at the keep Druss was struggling to keep his temper as the city elders argued back and forth about the Nadir offer. Word had spread to them with bewildering speed, and Druss had barely managed to eat a chunk of bread and cheese before a messenger from Orrin informed him that the elders had called a meeting.

It was a Drenai rule, long established, that except in time of battle the elders had a democratic right to see the city lord and debate matters of importance. Neither Orrin nor Druss could refuse. No one could argue that Ulric's ultimatum was unimportant.

Six men constituted the city elders, an elected body that effectively ruled all trade within the city. The master burgher and chief elder was Bricklyn, who had entertained Druss so royally on the night of the assassination attempt. Malphar, Backda, Shinell, and Alphus were all merchants, while Beric was a nobleman, a distant cousin of Earl Delnar and highly placed in city life. Only lack of a real fortune kept him at Delnoch and away from Drenan, which he loved.

Shinell, a fat, oily silk merchant, was the main cause of Druss's anger. "But surely we have a right to discuss Ulric's terms and must be allowed a say in whether they are accepted or rejected," he said again. "It is of vital interest to the city, after all, and by right of law our vote must carry."

"You know full well, my dear Shinell," said Orrin

smoothly, "that the city elders have full rights to discuss all civil matters. This situation hardly falls within that category. Nevertheless, your point of view is noted."

Malphar, a red-faced wine dealer of Lentrian stock, interrupted Shinell as he began his protest. "We are getting nowhere with this talk of rules and precedent. The fact remains that we are virtually at war. Is it a war we can win?" His green eyes scanned the faces around him, and Druss tapped his fingers on the tabletop, the only outward sign of his tensions. "Is it a war we can carry long enough to force an honorable peace? I don't think it is," continued Malphar. "It is all nonsense. Abalayn has run the army down until it is only a tenth of the size it was a few years ago. The navy has been halved. This Dros was last under siege two centuries ago, when it almost fell. Yet our records tell us that we had forty thousand warriors in the field."

"Get on with it, man! Make your point," said Druss.

"I shall, but spare me your harsh looks, Druss. I am no coward. What I am saying is this: If we cannot hold and cannot win, what is the point of this defense?"

Orrin glanced at Druss, and the old warrior leaned forward. "The point is," he said, "that you don't know whether you've lost until you've lost. Anything can happen: Ulric could suffer a stroke; plague could hit the Nadir forces. We have to try to hold."

"What about the women and children?" asked Backda, a skull-faced lawyer and property owner.

"What about them?" said Druss. "They can leave at any time."

"To go where, pray? And with what monies?"

"Ye gods!" thundered Druss, surging to his feet. "What will you be wanting me to do next? Where they go—if they do—how they go—is their concern and yours. I am a soldier, and my job is to fight and kill. And believe me, I do that very well. We have been ordered to fight to the last, and that we will do.

"Now, I may not know very much about law and all the little niceties of city politics, but I do know this: Any man who speaks of surrender during the coming siege is a traitor.

"And I will see him hang."

"Well said, Druss," offered Beric, a tall middle-aged man with shoulder-length gray hair. "I couldn't have put it better myself. Very stirring." He smiled as Druss sank back to his seat. "There is one point, though. You say you have been asked to fight to the end. That order can always be changed; politics being what it is, the question of expediency comes into it. At the moment it is expedient for Abalayn to ask us to prepare for war. He may feel it gives him greater bargaining power with Ulric. Ultimately, though, he must consider surrender. Facts are facts: The tribes have conquered every nation they have attacked, and Ulric is a general above comparison.

"I suggest we write to Abalayn and urge him to reconsider this war."

Orrin shot Druss a warning glance.

"Very well put, Beric," he said. "Obviously Druss and I, as loyal military men, must vote against it; however, feel free to write and I will see the petition is forwarded with the first available rider."

"Thank you, Orrin. That is very civilized of you," said Beric. "Now can we move on to the subject of the demolished homes?"

Ulric sat before the brazier, a sheepskin cloak draped over his naked torso. Before him squatted the skeletal figure of his shaman, Nosta Khan.

"What do you mean?" Ulric asked him.

"As I said, I can no longer travel over the fortress. There is a barrier to my power. Last night, as I floated above Deathwalker, I felt a force like a storm wind. It pushed me back beyond the outer wall."

"And you saw nothing?"

"No. But I sensed . . . felt . . ."

"Speak!"

"It is difficult. In my mind I could feel the sea and a slender ship. It was a fragment only. Also there was a mystic with white hair. I have puzzled long over this. I believe Deathwalker has called upon a white temple."

"And their power is greater than yours?" said Ulric.

"Merely different," hedged the shaman.

"If they are coming by sea, then they will make for Dros

Purdol," said Ulric, staring into the glimmering coals. "Seek them out."

The shaman closed his eyes, freed the chains of his spirit, and soared free of his body. Formless, he raced high above the plain, over hills and rivers, mountains and streams, skirting the Delnoch range until at last the sea lay below him, shimmering beneath the stars. Far he roved before sighting *Wastrel*, picking out the tiny glint of her aft lantern.

Swiftly he dropped from the sky to hover by the mast. By the port rail stood a man and a woman. Gently he probed their minds, then drifted down through the wooden deck, beyond the hold, and onto the cabins. These he could not enter, however. As lightly as the whisper of a sea breeze, he touched the edge of the invisible barrier. It hardened before him, and he recoiled. He floated to the deck, closing on the mariner at the stern, smiled, then raced back toward the waiting Nadir warlord.

Nosta Khan's body trembled, and his eyes opened.

"Well?" asked Ulric.

"I found them."

"Can you destroy them?"

"I believe so. I must gather my acolytes."

On *Wastrel* Vintar rose from his bed, his eyes troubled, his mind uneasy. He stretched.

"You felt it, too," pulsed Serbitar, swinging his long legs clear of the second bed.

"Yes. We must be wary."

"He did not try to breach the shield," said Serbitar. "Was that a sign of weakness or confidence?"

"I don't know," answered the abbot.

Above them at the stern the second mate rubbed his tired eyes, slipped a looped rope over the wheel, and transferred his gaze to the stars. He had always been fascinated by these flickering, far-off candles. Tonight they were brighter than usual, like gems strewn on a velvet cloak. A priest had once told him they were holes in the universe through which the bright eyes of the gods gazed down on the peoples of the earth. It was pretty nonsense, but he had enjoyed listening.

Suddenly he shivered. Turning, he lifted his cloak from

the aft rail and slung it about his shoulders. He rubbed his hands.

Floating behind him, the spirit of Nosta Khan lifted its hands, focusing power upon the long fingers. Talons grew, glinting like steel, serrated and sharp. Satisfied, he closed in on the mariner, plunging his hands into the man's head.

Searing agony blanketed the brain within as the man staggered and fell, blood pouring from his mouth and ears and seeping from his eyes. Without a sound he died. Nosta Khan loosened his grip. Drawing on the power of his acolytes, he willed the body to rise, whispering words of obscenity in a language long erased from the minds of ordinary men. Darkness swelled around the corpse, shifting like black smoke to be drawn in through the bloody mouth. The body shuddered.

And rose.

Unable to sleep, Virae dressed silently, climbed to the deck, and wandered to the port rail. The night was cool, the soft breeze soothing. She gazed out over the waves to the distant line of land silhouetted against the bright, moonlit sky.

The view always calmed her, the blending of land and sea. As a child at school in Dros Purdol she had delighted in sailing, especially at night, when the land mass appeared to float like a sleeping monster of the deep, dark and mysterious and wonderfully compelling.

Suddenly she narrowed her eyes. Was the land moving? To her left the mountains seemed to be receding, while on the right the shoreline seemed closer. No, not *seemed*. *Was*. She glanced at the stars. The ship had veered northwest, yet they were days from Purdol.

Puzzled, she walked aft toward the second mate as he stood with hands on the wheel.

"Where are we heading?" she asked him, mounting the four steps to the stern and leaning on the rail.

His head turned toward her. Blank, blood-red eyes locked on hers as his hands left the wheel and reached for her.

Fear entered her soul like a lance, only to be quelled by rising anger. She was not some Drenai milkmaid to be terrified thus; she was Virae, and she carried the blood of warriors in her veins.

Dropping her shoulder, she threw a light hand punch to his jaw. His head snapped back, but still he came on. Stepping inside the groping arms, she grabbed his hair and smashed a head butt into his face. He took it without a sound, his hands curling around her throat. Twisting desperately before the grip tightened, she threw him with a rolling hip lock, and he hit the deck hard on his back. Virae staggered. He rose slowly and came for her again.

Running forward, she leapt into the air and twisted, hammering both feet into his face. He fell once more.

And rose.

Panicked now, Virae searched for a weapon, but there was nothing. Smoothly she vaulted the wheel rail to land on the deck. He followed her.

"Move away from him!" screamed Serbitar, racing forward with sword drawn. Virae ran to him.

"Give me that!" she said, tearing the sword from his hand. Confidence surged in her as her hand gripped the ebony hilt. "Now, you son of a slut!" she shouted, striding toward the mariner.

He made no effort to avoid her, and the sword flashed in the moonlight, slicing into his exposed neck. Twice more she struck, and the grinning head toppled from the body. But the corpse did not fall.

Oily smoke oozed from the severed neck to create a second head, formless and vague. Coal-red eyes glittered within the smoke.

"Get back!" shouted Serbitar. "Get away from him!"

This time she obeyed, backing toward the albino.

"Give me the sword."

Vintar and Rek had joined them.

"What on earth is it?" whispered Rek.

"Nothing on earth," replied Vintar.

The thing stood its ground, arms folded across its chest.

"The ship is heading for the rocks," said Virae, and Serbitar nodded.

"It is keeping us from the wheel. What do you think, Father Abbot?"

"The spell was planted in the head, which must be thrown overboard. The beast will follow it," replied Vintar. "Attack it."

Serbitar moved forward, supported by Rek. The corpse bent its body, right hand closing on the hair of the severed head. Holding the head to its chest, it waited for the attack.

Rek leapt forward, slashing a cut at the arm. The corpse staggered. Serbitar ran in, slicing the tendons behind the knee. As it fell, Rek hammered the blade two-handed across its arm. The arm fell clear, the fingers releasing the head, which rolled across the deck. Dropping his sword, Rek dived at it. Swallowing his revulsion, he lifted it by the hair and hurled it over the side. As it hit the waves, the corpse on the deck shuddered. As if torn by a great wind, the smoke flowed from the neck to vanish beneath the rail and into the darkness of the deep.

The captain came forward from the shadows by the mast.

"What was it?" he asked.

Vintar joined him, placing a hand gently on the man's shoulder.

"We have many enemies," he said. "They have great powers. But fear not. We are not powerless, and no harm will befall the ship again. I promise you."

"And what of his soul?" asked the captain, wandering to the rail. "Have they taken it?"

"It is free," said Vintar. "Believe me."

"We will all be free," said Rek, "if someone doesn't turn the ship away from those rocks."

In the darkened tent of Nosta Khan the acolytes silently backed out, leaving him sitting in the center of the circle chalked on the dirt floor. Lost in thought, Nosta Khan ignored them. He was drained and angry.

For they had bested him, and he was a man unused to defeat. It tasted bitter in his mouth.

He smiled.

There would be another time . . .

◊ 16 ◊

Blessed by a following wind, *Wastrel* sped north until at last the silver gray towers of Dros Purdol broke the line of the horizon. The ship entered the harbor a little before noon, piloting past the Drenai war triremes and the merchant vessels anchored in the bay.

On the milling docks street traders sold charms, ornaments, weapons, and blankets to mariners, while burly dockers carried provisions up swaying gangplanks, stacking cargo and checking loads. All was noise and apparent confusion.

The harborside was rich in color and the hectic pace of city life, and Rek felt a pang of regret to be leaving the ship. As Serbitar led the Thirty ashore, Rek and Virae said their good-byes to the captain.

"With one exception, it has been a more than pleasant voyage," Virae told him. "I thank you for your courtesy."

"I was glad to be of service, my lady. I will forward the marriage papers to Drenan on my return. It was a first for me. I have never taken part in the wedding of an earl's daughter, much less conducted one. I wish you well." Bending forward, he kissed her hand.

He wanted to add "Long life and happiness," but he knew their destination.

Virae strode down the gangplank as Rek gripped the captain's hand. He was surprised when the man embraced him.

"May your sword arm be strong, your spirit lucky, and your horse swift when the time comes," he said.

Rek grinned. "The first two I will need. As to the horse, do you believe *that* lady will consider flight?"

"No, she's a wonderful lass. Be lucky."

"I will try hard," said Rek.

At the quayside a young red-caped officer eased his way through the crowd to confront Serbitar.

"Your business in Dros Purdol?" he asked.

"We are traveling to Delnoch as soon as we can obtain horses," answered the albino.

"The fortress will soon be under siege, sir. Are you aware of the coming war?"

"We are. We travel with the Lady Virae, daughter of Earl Delnar, and her husband, Regnak."

Seeing Virae, the officer bowed. "A pleasure, my lady. We met at your eighteenth birthday celebration last year. You probably won't remember me."

"On the contrary, Dun Degas! We danced, and I trod on your foot. You were most kind and took the blame."

Degas smiled and bowed again. How she has changed! he thought. Where was the clumsy girl who had contrived to trip on the hem of her skirt? Who had blushed as red as the wine when, during a heated conversation, she had crushed a crystal goblet, drenching the woman to her right. What had changed? She was the same woman-girl he remembered—her hair mousy blond, her mouth too wide, her brows thunder-dark over deep-set eyes. He saw her smile as Rek stepped forward, and his question was answered. She had become desirable.

"What are you thinking, Degas?" she asked. "You look far away."

"My apologies, my lady. I was thinking Earl Pindak will be delighted to receive you."

"You will have to convey my regrets," said Virae, "for we must leave as soon as possible. Where can we purchase mounts?"

"I am sure we can find you good horses," said Degas. "It is a shame you did not arrive sooner, since four days ago we sent three hundred men to Delnoch to aid the defense. You could have traveled with them; it would have been safer. The Sathuli have grown bold since the Nadir threat."

"We shall get there," said the tall man with Virae. Degas's eyes measured him. A soldier, he thought, or has been at some time. Carries himself well. Degas directed the party to a large inn, promising to supply the horses within two hours.

True to his word, he returned with a troop of Drenai cavalrymen riding thirty-two horses. They were not of the pedigree of the mounts left behind in Lentria, being mustangs bred for mountain work, but they were sturdy animals. When the horses had been allocated and the provisions packed, Degas approached Rek.

"There is no charge for these mounts, but I would be obliged if you could deliver these dispatches to the earl. They came by sea from Drenan yesterday and missed our force. The one with the red seal is from Abalayn."

"The earl will receive them," said Rek. "Thank you for your help."

"It is nothing. Good luck!" The officer moved on to make his farewells to Virae. Pushing the letters into the saddlebag of his roan mare, Rek mounted and led the party west from Purdol along the line of the Delnoch mountains. Serbitar cantered alongside him as they entered the first of the deep woods beyond the town.

"You look troubled," said Rek.

"Yes. There will be outlaws, renegades, perhaps deserters, and certainly Sathuli tribesmen along our route."

"But that is not what troubles you."

"You are perceptive," said Serbitar.

"How true. But then, I saw the corpse walk."

"Indeed you did," said Serbitar.

"You have hedged about that night for long enough," said Rek. "Now give me the truth of it. Do you know what it was?"

"Vintar believes it to be a demon summoned by Nosta Khan. He is the head shaman to Ulric's Wolfshead tribe and therefore lord of all Nadir shamans. He is old, and it is said he first served Ulric's great-grandfather. He is a man steeped in evil."

"And his powers are greater than yours?"

"Individually, yes. Collectively? I don't think so. We are currently stopping him from entering Delnoch, but he in turn has cast a veil over the fortress and we cannot enter."

"Will he attack us again?" asked Rek.

"Assuredly. The question is what method he will choose."

"I think I will leave you to worry about that," said Rek. "I can take in only so much gloom in one day."

Serbitar did not answer him. Rek reined his mount and waited for Virae.

That night they camped by a mountain stream but lit no fires. In the early evening Vintar recited poetry, his voice soft and melodious, his words evocative.

"They are his own work," Serbitar whispered to Virae, "though he will not own to them. I know not why. He is a fine poet."

"But they are so sad," she said.

"All beauty is sad," replied the albino. "For it fades."

He left her and retreated to a nearby willow, sitting with his back to the tree, a silver ghost in the moonlight.

Arbedark joined Rek and Virae, handing them honey cakes he had purchased at the port. Rek glanced over at the lonely figure of the albino.

"He travels," said Arbedark. "Alone."

As the dawn bird song began, Rek groaned and eased his aching body away from the probing tree roots that were denting his side. His eyes opened. Most of the Thirty were still asleep, though tall Antaheim stood sentry by the stream. At the willow Serbitar remained where he had been during the recital.

Rek sat up and stretched, his mouth dry. Pushing back his blanket, he walked to the horses, removed his pack, rinsed his mouth with water from his canteen, and went to the stream. Taking out a bar of soap, he stripped the shirt from his chest and knelt by the swiftly rushing water.

"Please don't do that," said Antaheim.

"What?"

The tall warrior walked across to him, squatting by his side. "The soap bubbles will carry downstream. It is not wise thus to announce our movements."

Rek cursed himself for a fool and apologized swiftly.

"That is not necessary. I am sorry to have intruded. Do you see that plant there, by the lichen rock?" Rek twisted, then nodded. "It is a lemon mint. Wash in the water, then

crush some of the leaves and clean your body. It will re-
fresh you and create . . . a more pleasant aroma."

"Thank you. Is Serbitar still traveling?"

"He should not be. I will seek him." Antaheim closed his
eyes for several seconds. When they opened again, Rek recognized panic, and the warrior ran from the stream. In that
moment all the members of the Thirty surged from their
blankets and raced to Serbitar by the willow.

Rek dropped his shirt and soap on the bank and moved
to join them. Vintar was bending over the albino's still
form; he closed his eyes and placed his hands on the young
leader's slender face. For long moments he remained thus.
Sweat broke out upon his forehead, and he began to sway.
When he lifted a hand, Menahem joined him instantly, raising Serbitar's head. The swarthy warrior lifted the albino's
right eyelid: the iris was red as blood.

Virae dropped to her knees beside Rek. "His eyes are
green normally," she said. "What is happening?"

"I don't know," said Rek.

Antaheim rose from the group and sprinted for the undergrowth, returning minutes later with what appeared to be an
armful of vine leaves, which he tipped to the ground. Gathering dried twigs, he fashioned a small fire; then, setting up
a tripod of branches, he hung a pot above the flames, filled
it with water, and crushed the leaves between his palms,
dropping them into the pot. Soon the water began to bubble, and a sweet aroma filled the air. Antaheim lifted the
pan from the flames, adding cold water from his canteen,
then transferred the green liquid to a leather-covered pottery
mug, which he passed to Menahem. Slowly they opened
Serbitar's mouth, and while Vintar held the albino's nostrils, they poured in the liquid. Serbitar gagged and swallowed, and Vintar released his nose. Menahem laid his head
back on the grass, and Antaheim swiftly killed the fire.
There had been little smoke.

"What's going on?" asked Rek as Vintar approached
him.

"We will talk later," said Vintar. "Now I must rest." He
stumbled to his blankets and lay down, slipping instantly
into a deep, dreamless sleep.

"I feel like a one-legged man in a footrace," said Rek.

Menahem joined them, his dark face gray with exhaustion as he sipped water from a leather canteen. He stretched his long legs out on the grass and lay on his side, supporting himself on his elbow. He turned toward Rek.

"I didn't mean to eavesdrop," he said, "but I did overhear you. You must forgive Vintar. He is older than the rest of us, and the strain of the hunt proved too much for him."

"The hunt? What hunt?" asked Virae.

"We sought Serbitar. He had journeyed far, and the path was sundered. He could not return, and we had to find him. Vintar guessed rightly that he had retreated into the mists and taken his chances. He had to seek him."

"I'm sorry, Menahem. You look worn out," said Rek, "but try to remember that we do not know what you are talking about. Into the mists? What the devil does that mean?"

Menahem sighed. "How can one explain colors to a blind man?"

"One says," snapped Rek, "that red is like silk, blue is like cool water, and yellow is like sunshine on the face."

"Forgive me, Rek. I am tired, I did not mean to be rude," said Menahem. "I cannot explain the mists to you as I understand them. But I will try to give you some idea.

"There are many futures but only one past. When we travel beyond ourselves, we walk a straight path, journeying much as we are doing now. We direct ourselves over vast distances. But the path back remains solid, for it is locked in our memories. Do you understand?"

"So far," said Rek. "Virae?"

"I'm not an idiot, Rek."

"Sorry. Go on, Menahem."

"Now try to imagine that there are other paths. Not just from, say, Drenan to Delnoch but from today into tomorrow. Tomorrow has not yet happened, and the possibilities for it are endless. Each one of us makes a decision that will affect tomorrow. But let us say we do travel into tomorrow. Then we are faced with a multitude of paths, gossamer-thin and shifting. In one tomorrow Dros Delnoch has already fallen; in another it has been saved or is about to fall or about to be saved. Already we have four paths. Which is true? And when we tread the path, how do we return to today, which from where we are standing is a multitude of yesterdays? To which do we return? Serbitar journeyed far beyond tomorrow. And Vintar found him as we held the path in sight."

"You used the wrong analogy," said Rek. "It is nothing like explaining colors to a blind man. Rather, it is more like teaching archery to a rock. I haven't the remotest idea what you are talking about. Will Serbitar be all right?"

"We don't know yet. If he lives, he will have information of great value."

"What happened to his eyes? How did they change color?" asked Virae.

"Serbitar is an albino—a true albino. He needs certain herbs in order to maintain his strength. Last night he journeyed too far and lost his way. It was foolhardy. But his heartbeat is strong, and he is now resting."

"Then he won't die?" said Rek.

"That we cannot say. He traveled a path which stretched his mind. It could be he will suffer the pull; this happens sometimes to travelers. They move so far from themselves that they just drift, like smoke. If his spirit is broken, it will pass from him and return to the mist."

"Can't you do anything?"

"We have done all we can. We cannot hold him forever."

"When will we know?" asked Rek.

"When he awakes. If he awakes."

The long morning wore on, and Serbitar still lay unmoving. The Thirty volunteered no conversation, and Virae had walked upstream to bathe. Bored and tired, Rek took the dispatches from his pouch. The bulky scroll sealed in red wax was addressed to Earl Delnar. Rek broke the seal and spread the letter wide. In flowing script the message read:

My dear friend,

Even as you read this, our intelligence is that the Nadir will be upon you. We have tried repeatedly to secure peace, having offered all that we have save the right to govern ourselves as a free people. Ulric will have none of this—he wishes to secure for himself a kingdom stretching between the northern and southern seas.

I know the Dros cannot hold, and I therefore rescind my order that you fight to the last. It will be a battle without profit and without hope.

Woundweaver is—needless to say—against this policy and has made it clear that he will take his army into the hills as a raiding force should the Nadir be allowed to pass to the Sentran Plain.

You are an old soldier, and the decision must be yours.

Pin the blame for surrender upon me. It is mine by right, since I have brought the Drenai people to this parlous state.

Do not think of me unkindly. I have always tried to do that which was best for my people.

But perhaps the years have told more heavily upon me than I realized, for my wisdom has been lacking in my dealings with Ulric.

It was signed simply "Abalayn," and below the signature was the red seal of the Drenai dragon.

Rek refolded the scroll and returned it to his saddlebag.

Surrender . . . A helping hand at the brink of the abyss.

Virae returned from the stream, her hair dripping and her features flushed.

"Ye gods, that was good!" she said, sitting beside him. "Why the long face? Serbitar not awake yet?"

"No. Tell me, what would your father have done if Abalayn had told him to surrender the Dros?"

"He would never have given that order to my father."

"But if he had?" insisted Rek.

"The point does not arise. Why do you always ask questions that have no relevance?"

He put a hand on her shoulder. "Listen to me. What would he have done?"

"He would have refused. Abalayn would know that my father is the lord of Dros Delnoch, the High Warden of the North. He can be relieved of command but not ordered to give up the fortress."

"Suppose Abalayn had then left the choice to Delnar. What then?"

"He would have fought to the last; it was his way. Now will you tell me what all this is about?"

"The dispatch Degas gave me for your father. It is a letter from Abalayn withdrawing his 'fight to the last' order."

"How dare you open that?" stormed Virae. "It was addressed to my father and should have been given to me. How *dare* you!" Her face red with fury, she suddenly struck out at him. When he parried the blow, she launched another, and without thinking he struck her flat-handed, sending her sprawling to the grass.

She lay there, eyes blazing.

"I'll tell you how I dare," he said, suppressing his anger with great effort. "Because *I* am the carl. And if Delnar is dead, then it was addressed to me. Which means that the decision to fight is mine. As is the decision to open the gates to the Nadir."

"That's what you want, isn't it? A way out?" She rose to her feet, snatching up her leather jerkin.

"Think what you like," he said. "It doesn't matter to me. Anyway, I should have known better than to talk to you about the letter. I'd forgotten how much this war means to you. You can't wait to see the crows feast, can you? Can't wait for the bodies to start swelling and rotting! You hear me?" he shouted at her back as she walked away.

"Trouble, my friend?" asked Vintar as he sat down opposite the angry Rek.

"Nothing whatsoever to do with you," snapped the new earl.

"Of that I don't doubt," said Vintar calmly. "But I might be able to help. After all, I've known Virae for many years."

"I'm sorry, Vintar. That was unforgivable of me."

"I have found in my life, Rek, that there are a few actions which are unforgivable. And certainly there are no words said that carry such a penalty. It is a man's lot, I fear, to strike out when he has suffered hurt. Now, can I help?"

Rek told him about the dispatch and Virae's reaction.

"A thorny problem, my boy. What will you do?"

"I have not yet made up my mind."

"That is as well. No one should make a hasty decision over such a weighty matter. Do not be too hard on Virae; she is now sitting by the stream and feeling very miserable. She is desperately sorry for what she said and is merely waiting for you to apologize so that she can tell you it was all her own fault."

"I'll be damned if I will apologize," said Rek.

"It will be a frosty ride if you do not," said the abbot.

A soft moan came from the sleeping Serbitar. Instantly Vintar, Menahem, Arbedark, and Rek moved over to him. The albino's eyes fluttered and opened . . . Once more they were the green of rose leaves. He smiled at Vintar.

"Thank you, Lord Abbot," he whispered. Vintar patted his face gently.

"Are you all right?" asked Rek.

Serbitar smiled. "I am well. Weak but well."

"What happened?" asked Rek.

"Nosta Khan. I tried to force entry at the fortress and was flung into the outer mists. I was lost . . . broken. I saw futures that were terrible and chaos beyond all imagining. I fled." He lowered his eyes. "I fled in panic, I know not where or when."

"Speak no more, Serbitar," said Vintar. "Rest now."

"I cannot rest," said the albino, struggling to rise. "Help me, Rek."

"Maybe you should rest, as Vintar says," Rek told him.

"No. Listen to me. I did enter Delnoch, and I saw death there. Terrible death!"

"The Nadir are there already?" asked Rek.

"No. Be silent. I could not see the man clearly, but I saw the Musif well being poisoned behind Wall Two. Anyone who drinks from that well will die."

"But we should arrive before the fall of Wall One," said Rek. "And surely they will not need the Musif well until then."

"That is not the point. Eldibar, or Wall One as you call it, is indefensible. It is too wide; any capable commander will give it up. Don't you understand? That's why the traitor poisoned the other well. Druss is bound to fight his first battle there, and the men will be fed that day at dawn. By midday the deaths will begin, and by dusk you will have an army of ghosts."

"We must ride," said Rek. "Now! Get him on a horse."

Rek ran to find Virae as the Thirty saddled their mounts. Vintar and Arbedark helped Serbitar to his feet.

"There was more, was there not?" said Vintar.

"Aye, but some tragedies are best left unspoken."

For three days they rode in the shadow of the Delnoch range into deep glens and over wooded hills. They rode swiftly but with caution, Menahem scouting ahead and pulsing messages to Serbitar. Virae had said little since the argument and avoided Rek studiously. He in turn gave no ground and made no attempt to breach the silence, though it hurt him deeply.

On the morning of the fourth day, as they breasted a small hill above thick woods, Serbitar held up a hand to halt the column.

"What's wrong?" asked Rek, drawing alongside.

"I have lost contact with Menahem."

"Trouble?"

"I don't know. He could have been thrown from his horse."

"Let us go and find out," said Rek, spurring the mare.

"No!" called Serbitar, but the horse was already on the move downhill and gathering speed. Rek tugged at the reins to bring the animal's head up, then leaned back in the saddle as the beast slithered to the foot of the hill. Once more on firm ground, Rek glanced about him. Among the trees he could see Menahem's gray standing with head down, and beyond the warrior himself lying facedown on the grass. Rek cantered the mare toward him, but as he passed under the first tree, a whisper of movement alerted him and he flung himself from his saddle as a man leapt from the branches. Rek landed on his side, rolled, and regained his feet, dragging his sword free of its scabbard. His attacker was joined by two others; all wore the flowing white robes of the Sathuli.

Rek backed toward the fallen Menahem and glanced down. The warrior's head was bleeding at the temple. Slingshot, Rek realized, but had no chance to check if the priest was still alive. Other Sathuli now crept from the undergrowth, their broad tulwars and long knives in hand.

Slowly they advanced, grins splitting their dark, bearded features. Rek grinned back.

"This is a good day to die," he said. "Why don't you join me?"

He slid his right hand farther up the hilt of his sword, making room for his left. This was no time for fancy swordplay; it would be hack and stand, two-handed. Once again he felt the strange sense of departure that heralded the baresark rage. This time he welcomed it.

With an ear-piercing scream he attacked them all, slashing through the throat of the first man as his mouth opened in astonishment. Then he was among them, his blade a whistling arc of bright light and crimson death. Momentarily stunned by his assault, they fell back, then leapt forward again, screaming their own war cries. More tribesmen burst from the undergrowth behind him as the thunder of hooves was heard.

Rek was not aware of the arrival of the Thirty. He parried a blow and backhanded his blade across the face of his assailant, stepping over the corpse to engage yet another tribesman.

Serbitar fought in vain to establish a defensive ring that could include Rek. His slender blade swept out, kissing and killing with surgical precision. Even Vintar, the oldest and least capable swordsman, found little difficulty in slaying the Sathuli warriors. Savage as they were, they were untutored in fencing skills, relying on ferocity, fearlessness, and weight of numbers to wear down a foe. And this tactic would work again, Vintar knew, for they were outnumbered perhaps four to one with no avenue of retreat open to them.

The clash of steel on steel and the cries of the wounded echoed in the small clearing. Virae, cut across the upper arm, disemboweled one man and ducked beneath a slashing tulwar as a new attacker stormed in. Tall Antaheim stepped forward to block a second slash. Arbedark moved through the battle like a dancer; a short sword in each hand, he choreographed death and destruction like a silver ghost of Elder legends.

Rek's anger grew. Was it all for this? Meeting Virae, coming to terms with his fears, taking the mantle of earl? All so that he could die on a tribesman's tulwar in an unnamed wood? He hammered his blade through the clumsy guard of the Sathuli before him, then kicked the falling corpse into the path of a new attacker.

"Enough!" he yelled suddenly, his voice ringing through the trees. "Put up your swords, all of you!" The Thirty obeyed instantly, stepping back and forming a ring of steel about the fallen Menahem, leaving Rek standing alone. The Sathuli slowly lowered their swords, glancing nervously one to another.

All battles, as they knew, followed the same pattern: fight and win, fight and die, or fight and run. There was no other way. But the tall one's words were spoken with power, and his voice held them momentarily.

"Let your leader step forth," ordered Rek, plunging his sword blade into the ground at his feet and folding his arms, though the Sathuli blades still ringed him.

The men before him stepped aside as a tall, broad-shouldered man in robes of blue and white moved forward. He was as tall as Rek, though hawk-nosed and swarthy. A trident beard gave him a sardonic look, and the saber scar from brow to chin completed the impression.

"I am Regnak, Earl of Dros Delnoch," said Rek.

"I am Sathuli—Joachim Sathuli—and I shall kill you," replied the man grimly.

"Matters like this should be settled by men such as you and I," said Rek. "Look about you—everywhere are Sathuli corpses. How many of my men are among them?"

"They will join them soon," said Joachim.

"Why do we not settle this like princes?" said Rek. "You and I alone."

The man's scarred eyebrow lifted. "That would only equal the odds against you. You have no bargaining power; wherefore should I grant you this?"

"Because it will save Sathuli lives. Oh, I know they give their lives gladly, but for what? We carry no provisions, no gold. We have only horses, and the Delnoch ranges are full of them. This is now a matter of pride, not of booty. Such matters are for you and I to decide."

"Like all Drenai, you talk a good fight," said the Sathuli, turning away.

"Has fear turned your bowels to water?" asked Rek softly.

The man turned back, smiling. "Ah, now you seek to anger me. Very well! We will fight. When you die, your men will lay down their swords?"

"Yes."

"And if I die, we allow you to pass?"

"Yes."

"So be it. I swear this on the soul of Mehmet, blessed be his name."

Joachim drew a slender scimitar, and the Sathulis around Rek moved back to form a circle about the two men. Rek drew his blade from the earth, and the battle began.

The Sathuli was an accomplished swordsman, and Rek was forced back as soon as the fight started. Serbitar, Virae, and the others watched calmly as blade met blade time and again. Parry, riposte, thrust and parry, slash and check. Rek defended frantically at first, then slowly began to counter. The battle wore on, with both men sweating freely. It was obvious to all that they were evenly matched in skill and virtually identical in strength and reach. Rek's blade sliced the skin above Joachim's shoulder. The scimitar licked out to open a wound on the back of Rek's hand. Both men circled warily, breathing deeply.

Joachim attacked; Rek parried, launching a riposte. Joachim jumped back, and they circled again. Arbedark, the finest swordsman of the Thirty, was lost in wonder at their technique.

Not that he could not match it, for he could, rather that his skill was honed by mental powers that the two combatants would never comprehend on a conscious level. Yet both were using the same skills subconsciously. It was as much a battle of minds as of blades, yet even here the men were well matched.

Serbitar pulsed a question to Arbedark. "It is too close for me to judge. Who will win?"

"I know not," replied Arbedark. "It is fascinating."

Both men were tiring fast. Rek had established a two-handed grip on his longsword, his right arm no longer able to bear the full weight of the blade. He launched an attack that Joachim parried desperately; then his sword caught the scimitar an inch above the hilt, and the curved blade snapped. Rek stepped forward, touching the point of his sword to Joachim's jugular. The swarthy Sathuli did not move but merely gazed back defiantly, his brown eyes meeting Rek's gaze.

"And what is your life worth, Joachim Sathuli?"

"A broken sword," answered Joachim. Rek held out his hand and received the useless hilt.

"What is the meaning of this?" asked the surprised Sathuli leader.

"It is simple," answered Rek. "All of us here are as dead men. We ride for Dros Delnoch to face an army the like of which has not been seen before in this world. We shall not survive the summer. You are a warrior, Joachim, and a worthy one. Your life is worth more than a broken blade. We proved nothing by this contest, save that we are men. Before me I have nothing but enemies and war.

"Since we will meet no more in this life, I would like to believe that I have left at least a few friends behind me. Will you take my hand?" Rek sheathed his sword and held out his hand.

The tall Sathuli smiled. "There is a strangeness in this meeting," he said, "for as my blade broke, I wondered, in that moment when death faced me, what I would have done had your sword snapped. Tell me, why do you ride to your death?"

"Because I must," said Rek simply.

"So be it, then. You ask me for friendship, and I give it, though I have sworn mighty oaths that no Drenai would feel safe on Sathuli land. I give you this friendship because you are a warrior and because you are to die."

"Tell me, Joachim, as one friend to another, what would you have done if *my* blade had broken?"

"I would have killed you," said the Sathuli.

◊ 17 ◊

THE FIRST OF the spring storms burst over the Delnoch mountains as Gilad relieved the watch sentry on Wall One. Thunder rumbled angrily overhead while crooked spears of jagged lightning tore the night sky, momentarily lighting the fortress. Fierce winds whistled along the walls, shrieking sibilantly.

Gilad hunched himself under the overhang of the gate tower, tugging the small brazier of hot coals into the lee of the wall. His cape was wet through, and water dripped steadily from his drenched hair onto his shoulders to trickle inside his breastplate, soaking the leather of his mail shirt. But the wall reflected the heat from the brazier, and Gilad had spent worse nights on the Sentran Plain, digging out buried sheep in the winter blizzards. He regularly raised himself to peer over the wall to the north, waiting for a flash of lightning to illuminate the plain. Nothing moved there.

Farther down the wall an iron brazier exploded as lightning struck it, and showers of hot coals fell close to him. What a place to be wearing armor, he thought. He shuddered and hunched closer to the wall. Slowly the storm moved on, swept over the Sentran Plain by the fierce wind from the north. For a while the rain remained, sheeting against the gray stone battlements and running down the tower walls, hissing and spitting as random drops vaporized on the coals.

Gilad opened his small pack and removed a strip of dried meat. He tore off a chunk and began to chew. Three more hours, then a warm bunk for three more.

From the darkness behind the battlements came the sound of movement. Gilad spun around, scrabbling for his sword, phantom childhood fears flooding his mind. A large figure loomed into the light from the brazier.

"Stay calm, laddie! It's only me," said Druss, seating himself on the other side of the brazier. He held out his huge hands to the flames.

His white beard was wet through, his black leather jerkin gleaming as if polished by the storm. The rain had petered to a fine drizzle, and the wind had ceased its eerie howling. Druss hummed an old battle hymn for a few moments as the heat warmed him. Gilad, tense and expectant, waited for the sarcastic comments to follow. "Cold, are we? Need a little fire to keep away the phantoms, do we?" Why pick my watch, you old bastard? he thought. After a while, the silence seemed oppressive and Gilad could bear it no longer.

"A cold night to be out walking, sir," he said, cursing himself for the respectful tone.

"I have seen worse. And I like the cold. It's like pain—it tells you you're alive."

The firelight cast deep shadows on the old warrior's weather-beaten face, and for the first time Gilad saw the fatigue etched there. The man is bone-tired, he thought. Beyond the legendary armor and the eyes of icy fire, he was just another old man. Tough and strong as a bull, maybe, but old. Worn out by time, the enemy that never tired.

"You may not believe it," said Druss, "but this is the worst time for a soldier—the waiting before the battle. I've seen it all before. You ever been in a battle, lad?"

"No, never."

"It's never as bad as you fear it will be once you realize that dying is nothing special."

"Why do you say that? It's special to me. I have a wife and a farm which I'd like to see again. I've a lot of living to do yet," said Gilad.

"Of course you have. But you could survive this battle and come down with the plague, or be killed by a lion, or develop a cancer. You could be robbed and killed or fall from a horse. Ultimately you will die anyway. Everyone dies. I'm not saying you should give up and just open your arms to welcome it. You must fight it all the way. An old soldier—a good friend of mine—told me early in my life that he who fears to lose will never win. And it's true. You know what a baresark is, boy?"

"A strong warrior," said Gilad.

"Yes, he is. But he's more than that: he's a killing machine who cannot be stopped. Do you know why?"

"Because he's insane?"

"Yes, there is that to him. But more. He doesn't defend, because when he's fighting he doesn't care. He just attacks, and lesser men—who do care—die."

"What do you mean by lesser men? A man doesn't have to be a killer to be great."

"That's not what I meant . . . but I suppose it could have been. If I tried to farm—as your neighbor—men would say that I was not as good as you. They would look down on me as a bad farmer. On these battlements men will be judged by how long they stay alive. Lesser men, or lesser soldiers if you will, either charge or fall."

"Why did you come here, Druss?" asked Gilad, meaning to ask why the axman had chosen to interrupt his watch. But the warrior misunderstood.

"I came to die," he said softly, warming his hands and staring into the coals. "To find some spot on the battlements to make a stand and then to die. I didn't expect to have to take over the damned defense. A pox on it! I'm a soldier, not a general."

As Druss talked on, Gilad realized the axman was not talking to him—not to Cul Gilad, the former farmer. He was chatting to just another soldier at just another fire at just another fortress. In microcosm this scene was Druss's life, the wait before the war.

"I always promised her that I would stop and tend the farm, but always someone, somewhere, had a battle to fight. I thought for years that I was representing something— liberty, freedom, I don't know. The truth was always much more simple. I love to fight. She knew but had the good grace never to point it out. Can you imagine what it's like to be a legend—*the* damned legend? Can you, boy?"

"No, but it must make you feel proud," said Gilad, uncertain.

"It makes you tired. It saps your strength when it should raise it. Because you can't afford to be tired. You're Druss the Legend, and you're invulnerable, invincible. You laugh at pain. You can march forever. With one blow you can topple mountains. Do I look as if I can topple mountains?"

"Yes," said Gilad.

"Well, I damned well can't. I'm an old man with a weak knee and an arthritic back. My eyes are not so good as they were, either.

"When I was young and strong, the bruises always healed quickly. I was tireless then. I could fight all damned day. As I grew older, I learned to fake it and snatch rest where I could. To use my experience in battle where before I had just powered my way through. In my fifties I was careful, and anyway by that time the legend made men tremble. Three times since I have fought men who could have beaten me, but they beat themselves because they knew who I was and were afraid.

"Do you think I'm a good leader?"

"I don't know. I'm a farmer, not a soldier," said Gilad.

"Don't hedge with me, boy. I asked for an opinion."

"No, you're probably not. But you *are* a great warrior. I suppose in years gone by you would have been a war chief. I can't tell. You've done wonders with the training; there's a new spirit at the Dros."

"There were always leaders in my day," said Druss. "Strong men with quick minds. I have tried to remember all their lessons. But it's hard, boy. Do you see? It's hard. I've never been afraid of enemies I can face with an ax or my hands, if need be. But the enemies at this fortress are not the same. Morale, preparation, fire gullies, supplies, liaison, organization. It saps the soul."

"We'll not fail you, Druss," said Gilad, his heart reaching out to the older man. "We will stand firm beside you. You have given us that, though I hated you for most of the training."

"Hate breeds strength, laddie. Of course you will hold. You're men. Did you hear about Dun Mendar?"

"Yes, it was tragic. A good job that he was there to aid you," said Gilad.

"He was there to kill me, boy. And he almost did."

"What?" said Gilad, shocked.

"You heard me. And I don't expect you to repeat it. He was in the pay of the Nadir, and he led the assassins."

"But . . . that means you stood alone against them all," said Gilad. "Five of them and you survived?"

"Aye, but they were a motley crew and ill trained. Do you know why I told you that . . . about Mendar?"

"Because you wanted to talk?"

"No. I've never been much of a talker, and I have little need for sharing my fears. No, I wanted you to know that I trust you. I want you to take over Mendar's role. I'm promoting you to dun."

"I don't want it," said Gilad fiercely.

"Do you think I want this responsibility? Why do you think I've spent this time here? I am trying to make you understand that often—more often than not—we are forced into doing what we fear. You will take over as of tomorrow."

"Why? Why me?"

"Because I have watched you, and I think you have a talent for leadership. You've impressed me in leading your ten. And you helped Orrin in that race. That was pride. Also, I need you and others like you."

"I've no experience," said Gilad, knowing it sounded lame.

"That will come. Think on this: Your friend Bregan is no soldier, and some of your men will die at the first attack. Having a good officer will save some of them."

"All right. But I can't afford to dine in the officers' mess or run up an armorer's bill. You will have to supply me with the uniform."

"Mendar's gear should fit you, and you will put it to more noble use."

"Thank you. You said earlier on that you came here to die. Does that mean you think we cannot win?"

"No, it doesn't. Forget what I said."

"Damn you, Druss, don't patronize me! You just talked about trust. Well, I'm an officer now, and I asked you a straight question. I won't repeat the answer. So trust me."

Druss smiled, and his eyes met the fierce gaze of the young sentry.

"Very well. We have no chance in the long term. Every day brings us closer to a Nadir victory. But we will make them pay dearly. And you can believe that, laddie, for that's Druss the Legend talking."

"Never mind the legend," said Gilad, returning the other's smile. "That's the man who took on five assassins in a darkened alley."

"Don't build me up too high because of that, Gilad. All men have talents. Some build, some paint, some write, some fight. For me it is different. I have always had a way with death."

The girl moved along the battlements, ignoring the comments of the soldiers, her auburn hair glinting in the morning sun, her long legs, slender and bronzed, the object of many friendly though intimate comments from the troops. She smiled once when one of the men she passed murmured to a companion, "I think I'm in love." She blew him a kiss and winked.

Bowman smiled, gently shaking his head. He knew Caessa was making a meal of her entrance, but with a body like hers, who would blame her? She was as tall as most men, willowy and graceful, and her every movement combined to promise pleasure to any man watching. Physically, Bowman thought, she is the perfect woman. The ultimate female.

He watched her string her longbow. Jorak looked at him questioningly, but he shook his head. The rest of the archers stood back. This was Caessa's moment, and after an entrance like that she deserved a little applause.

Straw dummies had been set up one hundred paces from the wall. The heads were painted yellow, the torsos red. It was a standard distance for a fine archer, but shooting down from a battlement added several degrees to the difficulty.

Caessa reached over her shoulder to the doeskin quiver and drew a black feathered shaft. She checked it for line, then notched it to the string.

"Head," she said.

With one flowing movement she drew back the string, and as it touched her cheek, she loosed the shaft. It flashed through the morning air and hammered into the neck of the nearest dummy. The watching men burst into rapturous applause, and Caessa glanced at Bowman. He raised an eyebrow.

Five more arrows lanced into the straw target before Bowman raised a hand to signal the other archers forward. Then he called Caessa to him and walked from the battlements.

"You took your time getting here, lady," he said, smiling.

She linked her arm in his and blew him a kiss. As always he felt arousal stirring. As always he suppressed it.

"Did you miss me?" Her voice was deep and throaty, a sound as full of sexual promise as her body was a vision.

"I always miss you," he said. "You raise my spirits."

"Only your spirits?"

"Only my spirits."

"You lie. I can see it in your eyes," she said.

"You see nothing that I do not want you to see—or anyone else. You are safe with me, Caessa. Have I not told you? But allow me to say that for a woman who does not seek the company of men, you make a very spectacular entrance. Where are your trousers?"

"It was hot. The tunic is decorous enough," she said, absently tugging at the hem.

"I wonder if you really know what you want," he said.

"I want to be left alone."

"Then why do you seek my friendship?"

"You know what I mean."

"Yes, *I* do," he told her, "but I'm not sure that you do."

"You are very serious today, O Lord of the Forest. I can't think why. We are all being paid. We have our pardons, and the quarters are a sight better than Skultik."

"Where have they placed you?" he asked.

"The young officer—Pinar?—insisted that I have a room in the main barracks. He wouldn't hear of me sharing with the rest of the men. It was quite touching, really. He even kissed my hand!"

"He's all right," said Bowman. "Let's have a drink." He led her into the Eldibar mess hall and on through the officers' section at the rear, ordering a bottle of white wine.

Seated by the window, he drank in silence for a while, watching the men train.

"Why did you agree to this?" she asked him suddenly. "And don't give me any of that rubbish about pardons. You don't give a damn about that or about the money."

"Still trying to read me? It can't be done," he said, sipping his wine. Then he turned and called out for bread and cheese. She waited until the serving soldier had left.

"Come on, tell me!"

"Sometimes, my dear, as you will no doubt find when you are a little older, there are no simple reasons for a man's actions. Impulse. An act spurred by the moment. Who knows why I agreed to come here? I certainly do not!"

"You're lying again. You just won't say. Is it that old man, Druss?"

"Why are you so interested? In fact, why are you here?"

"Why not? It should be exciting and not terribly dangerous. We are leaving, aren't we, when the third wall goes?"

"Of course. That was the agreement," he said.

"You don't trust me, do you?" she said, smiling.

"I don't trust anybody. You know, sometimes you do act just like every other woman I have known."

"Is that a compliment, O Master of the Green Wood?"

"I think not."

"Then what does it mean? After all, I am a woman. How do you expect me to act?"

"There you go again. Let's get back to trust. What made you ask?"

"You won't say why you came, and then you lie about leaving. Do you think I'm a complete fool? You have no intention of quitting this doomed pile of rock. You will stay to the end."

"And where do you come by this remarkable intelligence?" he asked.

"It's written all over your face. But don't worry; I won't let on to Jorak or any of the others. But don't count on me to stay. I have no intention of dying here."

"Caessa, my little dove, you only prove how little you know me. Anyway, for what it's worth—"

Bowman ceased his explanation as the tall figure of

Hogun entered the doorway and the gan threaded his way through the tables toward them. It was Caessa's first sight of the legion general, and she was impressed. He moved with grace, one hand resting on his sword hilt. His eyes were clear, his jaw strong, and his features fair—handsome almost. She disliked him instantly. Her view was strengthened when he pulled up a chair, reversed it, and sat facing Bowman, ignoring her totally.

"Bowman, we must talk," he said.

"Go ahead. First, let me introduce Caessa. Caessa, my dear, this is Gan Hogun of the legion." He turned and nodded once in her direction.

"Do you mind if we talk alone?" he asked Bowman. Caessa's green eyes blazed with anger, but she kept silent and stood, desperate for a parting remark that would sting the man.

"I will see you later," said Bowman as she opened her mouth. "Get yourself some food now." As she turned on her heel and left the room, Bowman watched her, delighting in the feline grace of her walk.

"You've upset her," he said.

"Me? I didn't even speak to her," said Hogun, removing his black and silver helm and placing it on the table. "Anyway, that's immaterial. I want you to speak to your men."

"What about?"

"They spend a lot of their time loafing around and jeering at the soldiers as they train. It's not good for morale."

"Why shouldn't they? They are civilian volunteers. It will all stop when the fighting starts."

"The point is, Bowman, that the fighting may start before the Nadir arrive. I have just stopped one of my men from gutting that black-bearded giant, Jorak. Much more of this and we will have murder on our hands."

"I'll talk to them," said Bowman. "Calm yourself and have a drink. What did you think of my lady archer?"

"I really didn't look too closely. She seemed pretty."

"I think it must be true what they say about the cavalry," said Bowman. "You are all in love with your horses! Great gods, man, she's more than merely pretty!"

"Talk to your men now. I will feel a lot better then. Tensions are rising pretty badly, and the Nadir are only two days away."

"I said I would. Now, have a drink and relax. You're getting as edgy as your men, and that can't be good for morale."

Hogun grinned suddenly. "You're right. It's always like this before a fight. Druss is like a bear with a sore head."

"I hear you lost the open swords to the fat one," said Bowman, grinning. "Tut, tut, old horse! This is no time to be currying favor with the hierarchy."

"I didn't let him win; he's a fine swordsman. Don't judge him too harshly, my friend; he may yet surprise you. He certainly surprised me. What did you mean when you said I upset the girl?"

Bowman smiled, then laughed loudly. He shook his head and poured another glass of wine.

"My dear Hogun, when a woman is beautiful, she comes to expect a certain—how shall I say?—a certain reverence from men. You should have had the good grace to be thunderstruck by her beauty. Stunned into silence or, better still, into a babbling fool. Then she would have merely ignored you and answered your devotion with arrogant disdain. Now you have slighted her, and she will hate you. Worse than this, she will do all in her power to win your heart."

"I don't think that makes a great deal of sense. Why should she try to win my heart if she hates me?"

"So that she can be in a position to treat you with disdain. Do you know nothing about women?"

"I know enough," said Hogun. "I also know that I don't have time for this foolishness. Should I apologize to her, do you think?"

"And let her know you know how slighted she was? My dear boy, your education has been sadly lacking!"

◊ **18** ◊

DRUSS WELCOMED THE arrival of the Dros Purdol riders, not so much for their numbers, more for the fact that their arrival proved that the Dros had not been forgotten by the outside world.

Yet still, Druss knew, the defenders would be badly stretched. The first battle on Eldibar, Wall One, would either raise the men or destroy them. The Delnoch fighting edge was sharp enough, but spirit was a different thing. One could fashion the finest steel into a sword blade of passing excellence, but occasionally the move from fire to water would cause it to crack where blades of lesser metal survived. An army was like that, Druss knew. He had seen highly trained men panic and run, and farmers stand their ground, armed with picks and hoes.

Bowman and his archers practiced daily now on Kania, Wall Three, which had the longest stretch of ground between the mountains. They were superb. The six hundred archers could send three thousand arrows arching through the air every ten heartbeats. The first charge would bring the Nadir into range for nearly two minutes before the siege ladders could reach the walls. The attacking warriors would suffer terrible losses over the open ground. It would be bloody carnage. But would it be enough?

They were about to see the greatest army ever assembled, a horde that within twenty years had built an empire stretching across a dozen lands and five score cities. Ulric was on the verge of creating the largest empire in known history, a mighty achievement for a man not yet out of his forties.

Druss walked the Eldibar battlements, chatting to individual soldiers, joking with them, laughing with them. Their hatred of him had vanished like dawn mist during these last days. They saw him now for what he was: an iron old man, a warrior from the past, a living echo of ancient glories.

They remembered then that he had chosen to stand with them. And they knew why. This was the only place in all the world for the last of the old heroes: Druss the Legend, standing with the last hopes of the Drenai on the battlements of the greatest fortress ever built, waiting for the largest army in the world. Where else would he be?

Slowly the crowds gathered about him as more men made their way to Eldibar. Before long Druss was threading his way through massed ranks on the battlements, while even more soldiers gathered on the open ground behind them. He climbed to the crenellated battlement wall and turned to face them. His voice boomed out, silencing the chatter.

"Look about you!" he called, the sun glinting from the silver shoulder guards on his black leather jerkin, his white beard glistening. "Look about you now. The men you see are your comrades—your brothers. They will live with you and die for you. They will protect you and bleed for you. Never in your lives will you know such comradeship again. And if you live to be as old as I am, you will always remember this day and the days to follow. You will remember them with a clearness you would never have believed. Each day will be like crystal, shining in your minds.

"Yes, there will be blood and havoc, torture and pain, and you will remember that, too. But above all will be the sweet taste of life. And there is nothing like it, my lads.

"You can believe this old man when he says it. You may think life is sweet now, but when death is a heartbeat away, then life becomes unbearably desirable. And when you survive, everything you do will be enhanced and filled with greater joy: the sunlight, the breeze, a good wine, a woman's lips, a child's laughter.

"Life is nothing unless death has been faced down.

"In times to come, men will say, 'I wish I had been there with them.' By then the cause won't matter.

"You are standing at a frozen moment in history. The world will be changed when this battle is over. Either the Drenai will rise again or a new empire will dawn.

"You are now men of history." Druss was sweating now and strangely tired, but he knew he had to go on. He was desperate to remember Sieben's saga of the Elder days and the stirring words of an Elder general. But he could not. He breathed in deeply, tasting the sweet mountain air.

"Some of you are probably thinking that you may panic and run. You won't! Others are worried about dying. Some of you will. But all men die. No one ever gets out of this life alive.

"I fought at Skeln Pass when everyone said we were finished. They said the odds were too great, but I said be damned to them! For I am Druss, and I have never been beaten, not by Nadir, Sathuli, Ventrian, Vagrian, or Drenai.

"By all the gods and demons of this world, I will tell you now—I do not intend to be beaten here, either!" Druss was bellowing at the top of his voice as he dragged Snaga into the air. The ax blade caught the sun and the chant began.

"Druss the Legend! Druss the Legend!" The men on other battlements could not hear Druss's words, but they heard the chant and took it up. Dros Delnoch echoed to the sound, a vast cacophony of noise that crashed and reverberated through the peaks, scattering flocks of birds, which took to the skies in fluttering panic. At last Druss raised his arms for silence and gradually the chant subsided, though more men were running from Wall Two to hear his words. By then almost five thousand men were gathered about him.

"We are the knights of Dros Delnoch, the siege city. We will build a new legend here to dwarf Skeln Pass. And we will bring death to the Nadir in their thousands. Aye, in their hundreds of thousands. *Who are we?*"

"Knights of Dros Delnoch!" thundered the men.

"And what do we bring?"

"Death to the Nadir!"

Druss was about to continue when he saw men's heads turn to face down into the valley. Columns of dust in the distance created clouds that rose to challenge the sky like a gathering storm. Like the father of all storms. And then, through the dust could be seen the glinting spears of the Nadir, filling the valley from all sides, sweeping forward, a vast dark blanket of fighting men with more following. Wave after wave of them came into sight. Vast siege towers pulled by hundreds of horses, giant catapults, leather-covered battering rams, thousands of carts and hundreds of thousands of horses, vast herds of cattle, and more men than the mind could total.

Not one heart among the watchers failed to miss a beat at the sight. Despair was tangible, and Druss cursed softly. He had nothing more to say. And he felt he had lost them. He turned to face the Nadir horsemen bearing the horsehair banners of their tribes. By now their faces could be seen, grim and terrible. Druss raised Snaga into the air and stood, legs spread, a picture of defiance. Angry now, he stared at the Nadir outriders.

As they saw him, they pulled up their horses and stared back. Suddenly the riders parted to allow a herald through. Galloping his steppe pony forward, he rode toward the gates, swerving as he came beneath the wall where Druss stood. He dragged on the reins, and the horse skidded to a stop, rearing and snorting.

"I bring this command from the Lord Ulric," he shouted. "Let the gates be opened and he will spare all within save the white-bearded one who insulted him."

"Oh, it's you again, lardbelly," said Druss. "Did you give him my message as I said it?"

"I gave it, Deathwalker. As you said it."

"And he laughed, did he not?"

"He laughed. And swore to have your head. And my Lord Ulric is a man who always fulfills his desires."

"Then we are two of a kind. And it is my desire that he should dance a jig on the end of a chain, like a performing bear. And I will have it so, even if I have to walk into your camp and chain him myself."

"Your words are like ice on the fire, old man—noisy and without worth," said the herald. "We know your strength. You have maybe eleven thousand men. Mostly farmers. We know all there is to know. Look at the Nadir army! How can you hold? What is the point? Surrender yourself. Throw yourself on the mercy of my lord."

"Laddie, I have seen the size of your army, and it does not impress me. I have a mind to send half my men back to their farms. What are you? A bunch of potbellied, bow-legged northerners. I hear what you say. But don't tell me what you can do. Show me! And that's enough of talk. From now on *this* will talk for me." He shook Snaga before him, sunlight flashing from the blade.

Along the line of defenders Gilad nudged Bregan. "Druss the Legend!" he chanted, and Bregan joined him with a dozen others. Once more the sound began to swell as the herald wheeled his mount and raced away. The noise thundered after him:

"Druss the Legend! Druss the Legend!"

Druss watched silently as the massive siege engines inched toward the wall, vast wooden towers sixty feet high and twenty feet wide, ballistae by the hundred, ungainly cata-pults on huge wooden wheels. Countless numbers of men heaved and strained at thousands of ropes, dragging into place the machines that had conquered Gulgothir.

The old warrior studied the scene below, seeking out the legendary warmaster Khitan. It did not take long to find him. He was the still center of the whirlpool of activity be-low, the calm amid the storm. Where he moved, work ceased as his instructions were given, then began again with renewed intensity.

Khitan glanced up at the towering battlements. He could not see Deathwalker but felt his presence and grinned.

"You cannot stop my work with one ax," he whispered.

Idly he scratched the scarred stump at the end of his arm. Strange how after all these years he could still feel his fin-gers. The gods had been kind that day when the Gulgothir tax gatherers had sacked his village. He had been barely twelve years old, and they had slain his family. In an effort to protect his mother, he had run forward with his father's dagger. A slashing sword had sent his hand flying through the air to land beside the body of his brother. The same sword had lanced into his chest.

To this day he could not explain why he had not died

along with the other villagers, or indeed why Ulric had spent so long trying to save him. Ulric's raiders had surprised the killers and routed them, taking two prisoners. Then a warrior checking the bodies had found Khitan, barely alive. They had taken him into the steppes, laying him in Ulric's tent. There they had sealed the weeping stump with boiling tar and dressed the wound in his side with tree moss. For almost a month he had remained semiconscious, delirious with fever. He had one memory of that terrible time, a memory he would carry to the day he died.

His eyes had opened to see above him a face, strong and compelling. The eyes were violet, and he felt their power. "You will not die, little one. Hear me?" The voice was gentle, but as he sank once more into the nightmares and delirium, he knew that the words were not a promise. They were a command.

And Ulric's commands were to be obeyed.

Since that day Khitan had spent every conscious moment serving the Nadir lord. Useless in combat, he had learned to use his mind, creating the means by which his lord could build an empire.

Twenty years of warfare and plunder. Twenty years of savage joy.

With his small entourage of assistants Khitan threaded his way through the milling warriors and entered the first of the twenty siege towers. They were his special pride. In concept they had been startlingly simple. Create a wooden box, three-sided and twelve feet high. Place wooden steps inside against the walls leading to the roof. Now take a second box and place it atop the first. Secure it with iron pins. Add a third and you have a tower. It was relatively easy to assemble and dismantle, and the component parts could be stacked on wagons and carried wherever the general needed them.

But if the concept was simple, the practicalities had been plagued by complexities. Ceilings collapsed under the weight of armed men, walls gave way, wheels splintered, and worst of all, once it was over thirty feet high the structure was unstable and prone to tip.

Khitan recalled how for more than a year he had worked harder than his slaves, sleeping less than three hours a night. He had strengthened the ceilings, but this had merely made the entire structure more heavy and less stable. In despair he had reported to Ulric. The Nadir warlord had sent him to Ventria to study at the University of Tertullus. He felt that he had been disgraced, humiliated. Nevertheless he had obeyed; he would suffer anything to please Ulric.

But he had been wrong, and the year he had spent studying under Rebow, the Ventrian lecturer, had proved to be the most glorious time of his life.

He learned of mass centers, parallel vectors, and the need for equilibrium between external and internal forces. His appetite for knowledge was voracious, and Rebow found himself warming to the ugly Nadir tribesman. Before long the slender Ventrian invited Khitan to share his home, where studies could be carried on long into the night. The Nadir was tireless. Often Rebow would fall asleep in his chair, only to wake several hours later and find the small, one-armed Khitan still studying the exercises he had set him. Rebow was delighted. Rarely had a student showed such aptitude, and never had he found a man with such a capacity for work.

Every force, learned Khitan, had an equal and opposite reaction, so that, for example, a jib exerting a push at its top end also had to exert an equal and opposite push at the foot of its supporting post. This was his introduction to the world of creating stability through understanding the nature of stress.

For him the University of Tertullus was a kind of paradise.

On the day he had left for home, the little tribesman had wept as he embraced the stricken Ventrian. Rebow had begged him to reconsider, to take a post at the university, but Khitan had not the heart to tell him he was not in the least tempted. He owed his life to one man and dreamed of nothing but serving him.

At home once more, he set to work. Under construction the towers would be tiered, creating an artificial base five times the size of the structure. While a tower was being moved into position, only the first two levels would be manned, creating a mass weight low to the ground. Once it was positioned by a wall, ropes would be hurled from the center of the tower and iron pins hammered into the ground, creating stability. The wheels would be iron-spoked and rimmed, and there would be eight to a tower to distribute the weight.

Using his new knowledge, he designed catapults and ballistae. Ulric was well pleased, and Khitan was ecstatic.

Now, bringing his mind back to the present, Khitan climbed to the top of the tower, ordering the men to lower the hinged platform at the front. He gazed at the walls three hundred paces distant and saw the black-garbed Deathwalker leaning on the battlements.

The walls were higher than at Gulgothir, and Khitan had added a section to each tower. Ordering the platform to be raised once more, he tested the tension in the support ropes and climbed down through the five levels, stopping here and there to check struts or ties.

Tonight his four hundred slaves would go to work beneath the walls, chipping away at the rocky floor of the pass and placing the giant pulleys every forty paces. The pulleys, six feet high and cast around greased bearings, had taken months to design and years to construct to his satisfaction, finally being completed at the ironworks of Lentria's capital a thousand miles to the south. They had cost a fortune, and even Ulric had blanched when the final figure was estimated. But they had proved their worth over the years.

Thousands of men would pull a tower to within sixty feet of a wall. Thereafter the line would shrink as the gap closed; the three-inch-diameter ropes could be curled around the pulleys, passed under the towers, and hauled from behind.

The slaves who dug and toiled to create the pulley beds were protected from archers by movable screens of stretched oxhide, but many were slain by rocks hurled from the walls above. This was of no concern to Khitan. What did concern him was possible damage to the pulleys, which were not protected by iron casing.

With one last lingering look at the walls, he made his way back to his quarters in order to brief the engineers. Druss watched him until he entered the city of tents that now filled the valley for over two miles.

So many tents. So many warriors. Druss ordered the defenders to stand down and relax while they could, seeing in their faces the pinched edge of fear, the wide eyes of barely controlled panic. The sheer scale of the enemy had cut into morale. He cursed softly, stripped off his black leather jerkin, stepped back from the battlements, and lowered his huge frame to the welcoming grass beyond. Within moments he was asleep. Men nudged one another and pointed; those closest to him chuckled as the snoring began. They were not to know that was his first sleep for two days or that he lay there for fear that his legs would not carry him back to his quarters. They knew only that he was Druss: The Captain of the Ax.

And that he held the Nadir in contempt.

Bowman, Hogun, Orrin, and Caessa also left the walls for the shade of the mess hall, the green-clad archer pointing at the sleeping giant.

"Was there ever such a one?" he said.

"He just looks old and tired to me," said Caessa. "I can't see why you regard him with such reverence."

"Oh, yes, you can," said Bowman. "You are just being provocative as usual, my dear. But then, that's the nature of your gender."

"Not so," said Caessa, smiling. "What is he, after all? He is a warrior. Nothing more, nothing less. What has he ever done to make him such a hero? Waved his ax? Killed men? I have killed men. It is no great thing. No one has written a saga about me."

"They will, my lovely, they will," said Bowman. "Just give them time."

"Druss is more than just a warrior," said Hogun softly. "I think he always has been. He is a standard, an example if you like . . . "

"Of how to kill people?" offered Caessa.

"No, that's not what I meant. Druss is every man who has refused to quit, to surrender when life offered no hope, to stand aside when the alternative was to die. He is a man who has shown other men there is no such thing as guaranteed defeat. He lifts the spirit merely by being Druss and being seen to be Druss."

"Just words!" said Caessa. "You men are all the same.

Always lofty words. Would you sing the praises of a farmer who fought for years against failed crops and floods?"

"No," admitted Hogun. "But then, it is the life of a man like Druss which inspires the farmers to battle on."

"Garbage!" Caessa sneered. "Arrogant garbage! The farmer cares nothing for warriors or war."

"You will never win, Hogun," said Bowman, holding open the mess hall door. "Give up now, while you can."

"There is a fundamental error in your thinking, Caessa," said Orrin suddenly as the members of the group seated themselves around a trestle table. "You are ignoring the simple fact that the vast majority of our troops here *are* farmers. They have signed on for the duration of this war." He smiled gently and waved his hand for the mess servant.

"Then the more fool them," said Caessa.

"We are all fools," agreed Orrin. "War is a ridiculous folly, and you are right: men love to prove themselves in combat. I don't know why, for I have never desired it myself. But I have seen it too often in others. But even for me Druss is, as Hogun describes him, an example."

"Why?" she asked.

"I cannot put it into words, I'm afraid."

"Of course you can."

Orrin smiled and shook his head. He filled their goblets with white wine, then broke the bread and passed it around. For a while they ate in silence, then Orrin spoke again.

"There is a green leaf called Neptis. When chewed, it will relieve toothache or head pain. No one knows why; it just does. I suppose Druss is like that. When he is around, fear seems to fade. That's the best I can do to explain."

"He doesn't have that effect on me," said Caessa.

On the tower battlements Bregan and Gilad watched the Nadir preparations. Along the wall Dun Pinar supervised the setting of notched poles to repel siege ladders, while Bar Britan oversaw the plugging of scores of pottery jugs containing oil. Once filled and plugged, the jugs were placed in wicker baskets at various points along the walls. The mood was grim. Few words were exchanged as men checked their weapons, sharpened already-sharp swords, oiled armor, or checked each shaft in their quivers.

* * *

Hogun and Bowman left the mess hall together, leaving
Orrin and Caessa deep in conversation. They sat on the
grass some twenty paces from the axman, Bowman lying
on his side and resting on his elbow.

"I once read some fragments from the Book of Elders,"
said the archer. "One line in particular strikes me now.
'Come the moment, come the man.' Never did a moment
call for a man more desperately than this. And Druss has
arrived. Providence, do you think?"

"Great gods, Bowman! You're not turning superstitious,
are you?" asked Hogun, grinning.

"I should say not. I merely wonder whether there is such
a thing as fate that such a man should be supplied at such
a time."

Hogun plucked a stem of couch grass and placed it between his teeth. "All right, let us examine the argument.
Can we hold for three months until Woundweaver gathers
and trains his army?"

"No. Not with these few."

"Then it matters not whether Druss's arrival was a coin-
cidence or otherwise. We may hold for a few more days
because of his training, but that is not enough."

"Morale is high, old horse, so best not repeat those sen-
timents."

"Do you think me a fool? I will stand and die with Druss
when the time comes, as will the other men. I share my
thoughts with you because you will understand them. You
are a realist, and moreover, you remain only until the third
wall falls. With you I can be frank, surely."

"Druss held Skeln Pass when all others said it would
fall," said Bowman.

"For eleven days—not three months. And he was fifteen
years younger then. I don't belittle what he did; he is worthy of his legends. Knights of Dros Delnoch! Have you
ever seen such knights? Farmers, peasants, and raw recruits.
Only the legion has seen real action, and they are trained
for hit-and-run charges from horseback. We could fold on
the first attack."

"But we won't, will we!" said Bowman, laughing. "We
are Druss's knights and the ingredients of a new legend."

His laughter sang out, rich and full of good humor. "Knights of Dros Delnoch! You and me, Hogun. They will sing about us in days to come. Good old Bowman, he came to the aid of an ailing fortress for love of liberty, freedom, and chivalry—"

"And gold. Don't forget the gold," said Hogun.

"A minor point, old horse. Let us not ruin the spirit of the thing."

"Of course not. I do apologize. However, surely you have to die heroically before you can be immortalized in song and saga."

"A moot point," admitted Bowman. "But I'm sure I will find a way around it."

Above them on Musif, Wall Two, several young culs were ordered to help fetch buckets for the tower well. Grumbling, they left the battlements to join the line of soldiers waiting by the stores.

Each armed with four wooden buckets, the men filed from the building toward the shallow cave beyond where the Musif well nestled in the cold shadows. Attaching the buckets to a complicated system of pulleys, they lowered them slowly toward the dark water below.

"How long is it since this has been used?" asked one soldier as the first bucket reappeared, covered in cobwebs.

"Probably about ten years," answered the officer, Dun Garta. "The people who had homes here used the center well. A child died in here once, and the well was polluted for over three months. That and the rats kept most people away."

"Did they ever get the body out?" asked the cul.

"Not as I heard. But don't worry, lad. It's only bones by now and won't affect the taste. Go on, try some."

"Funnily enough, I don't feel very thirsty."

Garta laughed and dipped his hands into the bucket, lifting the water to his mouth.

"Spiced with rat droppings and garnished with dead spiders!" he said. "Are you sure you won't have some?"

The men grinned, but none stepped forward.

"All right, the fun's over," said Garta. "The pulleys are working, the buckets are ready, and I should say the job's done. So let's lock the gate and get back to work."

Garta awoke in the night, pain ripping at him like an angry rat trapped in his belly. As he rolled from the bed and struggled to rise, his groaning woke the other three men sharing the room. One of them rushed to his side.

"What is it, Garta?" he said, turning the writhing man onto his back. Garta drew up his knees, his face purple. His hand snaked out, grabbing the other's shirt.

"The . . . water! Water!" He started to choke.

"He wants water!" yelled the man supporting him.

Garta shook his head. Suddenly his back arched as pain seared him.

"Great gods! He's dead," said his companion as Garta slumped in his arms.

◊ 19 ◊

Rek, Serbitar, Virae, and Vintar sat around a small campfire an hour before dawn. The camp had been made late the night before in a secluded hollow on the south side of a wooded hill.

"Time is short," said Vintar. "The horses are exhausted, and it is at least a five-hour ride to the fortress. We might get there before the water is issued and we might not. Indeed, it may already be too late. But we do have one other choice."

"Well, what is it?" said Rek.

"It must be your decision, Rek. None other can make it."

"Just tell me, Abbot. I am too tired to think."

Vintar exchanged glances with the albino.

"We can—the Thirty can—join forces and seek to pierce the barrier around the fortress."

"Then try it," said Rek. "Where is the problem?"

"It will take all our powers and may not succeed. If it does not, we will not have the strength to ride on. Indeed, even if we do succeed, we will need to rest for most of the day."

"Do you think you can pierce the barrier?" said Virae.

"I do not know. We can only try."

"Think what happened when Serbitar tried," said Rek.

"You could all be hurled into the . . . whatever. What then?"

"We die," answered Serbitar softly.

"And you say it is *my* choice?"

"Yes," answered Vintar, "for the rule of the Thirty is a

207

simple one. We have pledged our service to the master of Delnoch; you are that master."

Rek was silent for several minutes, his weary brain numbed by the weight of the decision. He found himself thinking of so many other worries in his life that at the time had seemed momentous. There had never been a choice like this. His mind clouded with fatigue, and he could not concentrate.

"Do it!" he said. "Break the barrier." Pushing himself to his feet, he walked away from the fire, ashamed that such an order should be forced from him at a time when he could not think clearly.

Virae joined him, her arm circling his waist.

"I'm sorry," she said.

"For what?"

"For what I said when you told me about the letter."

"It doesn't matter. Why should you think well of me?"

"Because you are a man and you act like one," she said. "Now it's your turn."

"My turn?"

"To apologize, you dolt! You struck me."

He pulled her to him, lifting her from her feet, and kissed her.

"That wasn't an apology," she said. "And you scratched my face with your stubble."

"If I apologize, will you let me do it again?"

"Strike me, you mean?"

"No, kiss you!"

Back at the hollow the Thirty formed a circle around the fire, removing their swords and plunging them into the ground at their feet.

The communion began, their minds flowing, streaming into Vintar. He welcomed each by name in the halls of his subconscious.

And merged. The combined power rocked him, and he struggled to retain the memory of himself. He soared like a ghostly giant, a new being of incredible power. The tiny thing that was Vintar clung on inside the new colossus, forcing down the combined essence of twenty-nine personalities.

Now there was only one.

It called itself Temple and was born under the Delnoch stars.

Temple reared high under the clouds, stretching ethereal arms across the Delnoch crags.

He soared exultantly, new eyes drinking in the sights of the universe. Laughter welled within him. Vintar reeled at the center, driving himself deeper into the core.

At last Temple became aware of the abbot, more as a tiny thought niggling at the edge of his new reality.

"Dros Delnoch. West."

Temple flew west, high over the crags. Beneath him the fortress lay silent, gray, and ghostly in the moonlight. He sank toward it and sensed the barrier.

Barrier?

To him?

He struck at it—and was hurled into the night, angry and hurt. His eyes blazed, and he knew fury: The barrier had touched him with pain.

Again and again Temple launched himself toward the Dros, striking blows of fearful power. The barrier trembled and changed.

Temple drew back, confused, watching.

The barrier drew in on itself like swirling mist, reforming. Then it darkened into a thick plume, blacker than the night. Arms emerged, legs formed, and a horned head grew with seven slanted red eyes.

Temple had learned much during his few minutes of life.

Joy, freedom, and knowledge of life had come first. Then pain and fury.

Now he knew fear and gained the knowledge of evil.

His enemy flew at him, curving black talons slashing the sky. Temple met him head on, curling his arms around its back. Sharp teeth tore at his face, talons ripping his shoulders. His own huge fists locked together at the creature's spine, drawing it in upon itself.

Below on Musif, Wall Two, three thousand men took up their positions. Despite all arguments, Druss had refused to surrender Wall One without a fight and waited there with six thousand men. Orrin had raged at him that such action was stupidity; the width of the wall made for an impossible task. Druss was obstinate even when Hogun backed Orrin.

"Trust me," Druss urged them. But he lacked the words to convince them. He tried to explain that the men needed a small victory on the first day in order to hone that final edge to their morale.

"But the risk, Druss!" said Orrin. "We could *lose* on the first day. Can't you see that?"

"You are the gan," snarled Druss then. "You can overrule me if you wish."

"But I will not, Druss. I will stand beside you on Eldibar."

"And I," said Hogun.

"You will see that I am right," said Druss. "I promise you."

Both men nodded, smiling to mask their despair.

Now the duty culs were queuing by the wells, gathering the water buckets and making their way along the battlements, stepping over the legs and bodies of men still sleeping.

On Wall One Druss dipped a copper dish into a bucket and drank deeply. He was not sure that the Nadir would attack that day. His instincts told him Ulric would allow another full day of murderous tension, the sight of his army preparing for battle draining the defenders of courage and sapping them of hope. Even so Druss had little choice. The move was Ulric's: The Drenai would have to wait.

Above them Temple suffered the fury of the beast, his shoulders and back shredded, his strength fading. The horned creature was also weakening. Death faced them both.

Temple did not want to die, not after such a short bittersweet taste of life. He wanted to see at close hand all those things he had glimpsed from afar, the colored lights of expanding stars, the silence at the center of distant suns.

His grip tightened. There would be no joy in the lights, no thrill amid the silence if this thing was left alive behind him. Suddenly the creature screamed, a high terrible sound, eerie and chilling. Its back snapped, and it faded like mist.

Semiconscious within Temple's soul, Vintar cried out.

Temple looked down, watching the men, tiny frail creatures, preparing to break their fast with dark bread and water. Vintar cried out again, and Temple's brow furrowed.

He pointed his finger at the wall.

Men began to scream, hurling water cups and buckets from the Musif battlements. In each vessel black worms wriggled and swam. Now more men surged to their feet, milling and shouting.

"What the devil's happening up there?" said Druss as the noise flowed down to him. He glanced down at the Nadir and saw that men were streaming back from the siege engines toward the tent city. "I don't know what's going on," said Druss. "But even the Nadir are leaving. I'm going back to Musif."

In the city of tents Ulric was no less angry as he shouldered his way through to the wide tent of Nosta Khan. His mind was icy calm as he confronted the sentry outside.

The news was spreading through the army like a steppe gorse fire: As dawn had broken, the tents of Nosta Khan's sixty acolytes had been filled with soul-searing screams. Guards had rushed in to find men writhing broken-backed on the dirt floors, their bodies bent like overstrung bows.

Ulric knew that Nosta Khan had marshaled his followers, drawing on their combined power to thwart the white templars, but he had never truly understood the appalling dangers.

"Well?" he asked the sentry.

"Nosta Khan is alive," the man told him.

Ulric lifted the flap and stepped into the stench of Nosta Khan's home. The old man lay on a narrow pallet bed, his face gray with exhaustion, his skin bathed in sweat. Ulric pulled up a stool and sat beside him.

"My acolytes?" whispered Nosta Khan.

"All dead."

"They were too strong, Ulric," said the old man. "I have failed you."

"Men have failed me before," said Ulric. "It matters not."

"It matters to me!" shouted the shaman, wincing as the effort stretched his back.

"Pride," said Ulric. "You have lost nothing; you have merely been beaten by a stronger enemy. It will avail them little, for my army will still take the Dros. They cannot hold. Rest yourself—and take no risks, shaman. I order it!"

"I will obey."

"I know that. I do not wish you to die. Will they come for you?"

"No. The white templars are filled with notions of honor. If I rest, they will leave me be."

"Then rest. And when you are strong, we will make them pay for your hurt."

Nosta Khan grinned. "Aye."

Far to the south Temple soared toward the stars. Vintar could not stop him and fought to stay calm as Temple's panic washed over him, seeking to dislodge him. With the death of the enemy, Vintar had tried to summon the Thirty from within the new mind of the colossus. In that moment Temple looked inside himself and discovered Vintar.

Vintar had tried to explain his presence and the need for Temple to relinquish his individuality. Temple absorbed the truth and fled from it like a comet, seeking the heavens.

The abbot again tried to summon Serbitar, seeking the niche in which he had placed him in the halls of his subconscious. The spark of life that was the albino blossomed under the abbot's probing, and Temple shuddered, feeling as if part of himself had been cut free. He slowed in his flight.

"Why are you doing this to me?" he asked Vintar.

"Because I must."

"I will die!"

"No. You will live in all of us."

"Why must you kill me?"

"I am truly sorry," said Vintar gently. With Serbitar's aid he sought Arbedark and Menahem. Temple shrank, and Vintar closed his heart with grief to the overwhelming despair. The four warriors summoned the other members of the Thirty and with heavy hearts returned to the hollows.

Rek hurried across to Vintar as the abbot opened his eyes and moved.

"Were you in time?" he asked.

"Yes," muttered Vintar wearily. "Let me rest now."

* * *

It was an hour short of dusk when Rek, Virae, and the Thirty rode under the great portcullis gate set beneath the Delnoch keep. Their horses were weary, lather-covered, and wet-flanked. Men rushed to greet Virae, soldiers doffing helms and citizens asking for news from Drenan. Rek stayed in the background until they were inside the keep. A young officer escorted the Thirty to the barracks while Rek and Virae made their way to the topmost rooms. Rek was exhausted.

Stripping off his clothes, he bathed himself with cold water and then shaved, removing the four-day stubble and cursing as the keen razor—a gift from Horeb—nicked his skin. He shook most of the dust from his garments and dressed once more. Virae had gone to her own rooms, and he had no idea where they were. Strapping on his sword belt, he made his way back to the main hall, stopping twice to ask servants the way. Once there, he sat alone, gazing at the marble statues of ancient heroes. He felt lost: insignificant and overpowered.

As soon as they had arrived, they had heard the news that the Nadir horde was before the walls. There was a tangible air of panic among the townsfolk, and they had seen refugees leaving by the score with carts piled high, a long, sorrowful convoy heading south.

Rek was unsure whether tiredness or hunger was predominant in him at that moment. He heaved himself to his feet, swayed slightly, then cursed loudly. Near the door was a full-length oval mirror. As he stood before it, the man who stared back at him appeared tall, broad-shouldered, and powerful. His gray-blue eyes were purposeful, his chin strong, his body lean. The blue cape, though travel-worn, still hung well, and the thigh-length doeskin boots gave him the look of a cavalry officer.

As Rek gazed at the Earl of Dros Delnoch, he saw himself as others would see him. They were not to know of his inner doubts and would see only the image he had created.

So be it.

He left the hall and stopped the first soldier he met to ask him where Druss was to be found. Wall One, the soldier said, and described the location of the postern gates. The tall young earl set out for Eldibar as the sun sank; going through the town, he stopped to buy a small loaf of honey cake, which he ate as he walked. It was growing darker as he reached the postern gate of Wall Two, but a sentry showed him the way through and at last he entered the killing ground behind Wall One. Clouds obscured the moon, and he almost fell into the fire pit that stretched across the pass. A young soldier hailed him and showed him the first wooden bridge across it.

"One of Bowman's archers, are you?" asked the soldier, not recognizing the tall stranger.

"No. Where is Druss?"

"I have no idea. He could be on the battlements, or you might try the mess hall. Messenger, are you?"

"No. Which is the mess hall?"

"See the lights over there? That's the hospital. Past there is the storeroom; keep walking until you hit the smell of the latrines, then turn right. You can't miss it."

"Thank you."

"It's no trouble. Recruit, are you?"

"Yes," said Rek. "Something like that."

"Well, I'd better come with you."

"There is no need."

"Yes, there is," said the man, and Rek felt something sharp in the small of his back. "This is a Ventrian dagger, and I suggest you just walk along with me for a short way."

"What's the point of all this?"

"First, someone tried to kill Druss the other day, and second, I don't know you," said the man. "So walk on and we will find him together."

The two men moved on toward the mess hall. Now that they were closer, they could hear the sounds from the buildings ahead. A sentry hailed them from the battlements; the soldier answered, then asked for Druss.

"He's on the wall near the gate tower," came the answer.

"This way," said the soldier, and Rek climbed the short steps to the battlement walls. Then he stopped dead. On the plain thousands of torches and small fires illuminated the Nadir army. Siege towers straddled the pass like wooden giants from mountain wall to mountain wall. The whole valley was lit as far as the eye could see; it was like a view of the second level of hell itself.

"Not a pretty sight, is it?" said the soldier.

"I don't think it will look any better by daylight," said Rek.

"You are not wrong," agreed the other. "Let's move."

Ahead of them Druss was seated on the battlements, talking to a small group of soldiers. He was telling a wonderfully embroidered tall story that Rek had heard before. The punch line evoked the desired effect, and the night silence was broken by the sound of laughter.

Druss laughed heartily with the men, then noticed the newcomers. He turned and studied the tall man in the blue cape.

"Well?" he asked the soldier.

"He was looking for you, Captain, so I brought him along."

"To be more precise," said Rek, "he thought I might be an assassin. Hence the dagger behind me."

Druss raised an eyebrow. "Well, are you an assassin?"

"Not recently. Can we talk?"

"We appear to be doing just that."

"Privately."

"You start talking and I will decide how private it is to be," said Druss.

"My name is Regnak. I have just arrived with warriors from the temple of the Thirty and Virae, the daughter of Delnar."

"We will talk privately," decided Druss. The men wandered away out of earshot.

"So speak," said Druss, his cold gray eyes fixed on Rek's face.

Rek seated himself on the battlement wall and stared out over the glowing valley.

"A little on the large side, isn't it?"

"Scare you, does it?"

"To the soles of my boots. However, you're obviously in no mood to make this an easy meeting, so I will simply spell out my position. For better or worse, I am the earl. I'm not a fool, nor yet a general, though often the two are synonymous. As yet I will make no changes. But bear this in mind . . . I will take a backseat to no man when decisions are needed."

"You think that bedding an earl's daughter gives you that right?" asked Druss.

"You know it does! But that's not the point. I have fought before, and my understanding of strategy is as sound as that of any man here. Added to that, I have the Thirty, and their knowledge is second to none. But even more important, if I have to die at this forsaken place, it will not be as a bystander. I shall control my own fate."

"You seek to take a lot on yourself, laddie."

"No more than I can handle."

"Do you really believe that?"

"No," said Rek frankly.

"I didn't think you did," said Druss with a grin. "What the hell made you come here?"

"I think fate has a sense of humor."

"She always had in my day. But you look like a sensible young fellow. You should have taken the girl to Lentria and set up home there."

"Druss, nobody takes Virae anywhere she does not want to go. She has been reared on war and talk of war; she can cite all your legends and the facts behind every campaign you ever fought. She's an Amazon, and this is where she wants to be."

"How did you meet?"

Rek told him about the ride from Drenan, through Skultik, the death of Reinard, the temple of the Thirty, the shipboard wedding, and the battle with the Sathuli. The old man listened to the straightforward story without comment.

"And here we are," concluded Rek.

"So you're baresark," said Druss.

"I didn't say that!" retorted Rek.

"But you did, laddie—by not saying it. It doesn't matter. I have fought beside many such. I am only surprised the Sathuli let you go; they're not known for being an honorable race."

"I think their leader—Joachim—is an exception. Listen, Druss, I would be obliged if you could keep quiet about the baresark side."

Druss laughed. "Don't be a fool, boy! How long do you think it will stay a secret once the Nadir are on the walls?

You stick by me and I will see that you don't swat anyone from our side."

"That's good of you, but I think you could be a little more hospitable. I'm as dry as a vulture's armpit."

"There is no doubt," said Druss, "that talking works up more of a thirst than fighting. Come on, we will find Hogun and Orrin. This is the last night before the battle, so it calls for a party."

◇ 20 ◇

As the dawn sky lightened on the morning of the third day, the first realities of apocalypse hammered home on the walls of Dros Delnoch. Hundreds of ballistae arms were pulled back by thousands of sweating warriors. Muscles bunching and knotting, the Nadir drew back the giant arms until the wicker baskets at their heads were almost horizontal. Each basket was loaded with a block of jagged granite.

The defenders watched in frozen horror as a Nadir captain raised his arm. The arm swept down, and the air became filled with a deadly rain that crashed and thundered amid and around the defenders. The battlements shook as the boulders fell. By the gate tower, three men were smashed to oblivion as a section of crenellated battlement exploded under the impact of one huge rock. Along the wall men cowered, hurling themselves flat, hands over their heads. The noise was frightening; the silence that followed was terrifying. For as the first thunderous assault ceased and soldiers raised their heads to gaze below, it was only to see the same process being casually repeated. Back and farther back went the massive wooden arms. Up went the captain's hand. Down it went.

And the rain of death bore down.

Rek, Druss, and Serbitar stood above the gate tower, enduring the first horror of war along with the men. Rek had refused to allow the old warrior to stand alone, though Orrin had warned that for both leaders to stand together was lunacy. Druss had laughed. "You and the lady Virae

218

shall watch from the second wall, my friend. And you will see that no Nadir pebble can lay me low."

Virae, furious, had insisted that she be allowed to wait on the first wall with the others, but Rek had summarily refused. An argument was swiftly ended by Druss: "Obey your husband, woman!" he thundered. Rek had winced at that, closing his eyes against the expected outburst. Strangely, Virae had merely nodded and retired to Musif, Wall Two, to stand beside Hogun and Orrin.

Now Rek crouched by Druss and gazed left and right along the wall. Swords and spears in hand, the men of Dros Delnoch waited grimly for the deadly storm to cease.

During the second reloading Druss ordered half the men back to stand beneath the second wall, out of range of the catapults. There they joined Bowman's archers.

For three hours the assault continued, pulverizing sections of the wall, butchering men, and obliterating one overhanging tower, which collapsed under the titanic impact and crumbled slowly into the valley below. Most of the men leapt to safety, and only four were carried screaming over the edge to be broken on the rocks below.

Stretcher-bearers braved the barrage to carry wounded men back to the Eldibar field hospital. Several rocks had hit the building, but it was solidly built and so far none had broken through. Bar Britan, black-bearded and powerful, raced alongside the bearers with sword in hand, urging them on.

"Gods, that's bravery!" said Rek, nudging Druss and pointing. Druss nodded, noting Rek's obvious pride at the man's courage. Rek's heart went out to Britan as the man ignored the lethal storm.

At least fifty men had been stretchered away. Fewer than Druss had feared. He raised himself to stare over the battlements.

"Soon," he said. "They are massing behind the siege towers."

A boulder crashed through the wall ten paces away from him, scattering men like sand in the wind. Miraculously, only one failed to rise, the rest rejoining their comrades. Druss raised his arm to signal Orrin. A trumpet sounded, and Bowman and the rest of the men surged forward. Each archer carried five quivers of twenty arrows as they raced across the open ground, over the fire-gully bridges, and on toward the battlements.

With a roar of hate almost tangible to the defenders, the Nadir swept toward the wall in a vast black mass, a dark tide set to sweep the Dros before it. Thousands of the barbarians began to haul the huge siege towers forward, while others ran with ladders and ropes. The plain before the walls seemed alive as the Nadir poured forward, screaming their battle cries.

Breathless and panting, Bowman arrived to stand beside Druss, Rek, and Serbitar. The outlaws spread out along the wall.

"Shoot when you're ready," said Druss. The green-clad outlaw swept a slender hand through his blond hair and grinned.

"We can hardly miss," he said. "But it will be like spitting into a storm."

"Every little bit helps," said the axman.

Bowman strung his yew bow and notched an arrow. To the left and right of him the move was repeated a thousand times. Bowman sighted on a leading warrior and released the string, the shaft slashing the air to slice and hammer through the man's leather jerkin. As he stumbled and fell, a ragged cheer went up along the wall. A thousand arrows followed, then another thousand and another. Many Nadir warriors carried shields, but many did not. Hundreds fell as the arrows struck, tripping the men behind. But still the black mass kept coming, trampling the wounded and dead beneath them.

Armed with his Vagrian bow, Rek loosed shaft after shaft into the horde, his lack of skill an irrelevant factor since, as Bowman had said, one could hardly miss. The arrows were a barbed mockery of the clumsy ballistae attack so recently used against them. But they were taking a heavier toll.

The Nadir were close enough now for individual faces to be clearly seen. Rough-looking men, thought Rek, but tough and hardy, raised to war and blood. Many of them lacked armor, others wore mail shirts, but most were clad in black breastplates of lacquered leather and wood. Their screaming battle cries were almost bestial. No words could be heard; only their hate could be felt. Like the angry scream of some vast, inchoate monster, thought Rek as the familiar sensation of fear gripped his belly.

Serbitar raised his helm visor and leaned over the battlements, ignoring the few arrows that flashed up and by him.

"The ladder men have reached the walls," he said softly.

Druss turned to Rek. "The last time I stood beside an Earl of Dros Delnoch in battle, we carved a legend," he said.

"The odd thing about sagas," offered Rek, "is that they very rarely mention dry mouths and full bladders."

A grappling hook whistled over the wall.

"Any last words of advice?" asked Rek, dragging his sword free from its scabbard.

Druss grinned, drawing Snaga. "Live!" he said.

More grappling irons rattled over the walls, jerking taut instantly and biting into the stone as hundreds of hands applied pressure below. Frantically the defenders lashed razor-edged blades at the vine ropes until Druss bellowed at the men to stop.

"Wait until they're climbing!" he shouted. "Don't kill ropes—kill *men*!"

Serbitar, a student of war since he was thirteen, watched the progress of the siege towers with detached fascination. The obvious idea was to get as many men on the walls as possible by using ropes and ladders and then to pull in the towers. The carnage below among the men pulling the tower ropes was horrific as Bowman and his archers peppered them with shafts. But more always rushed in to fill the places of the dead and dying.

On the walls, despite the frenzied slashing of ropes, the sheer numbers of hooks and throwers had enabled the first Nadir warriors to gain the battlements.

Hogun, with five thousand men on Musif, Wall Two, was sorely tempted to forget his orders and race to the aid of Wall One. But he was a professional soldier, reared on obedience, and he stood his ground.

Tsubodai waited at the bottom of the rope as the tribesmen slowly climbed above him. A body hurtled by him to splinter on the jagged rocks, and blood splashed his lacquered leather breastplate. He grinned, recognizing the twisted features of Nestzan, the race runner.

"He had it coming to him," he said to the man beside him. "Now, if he'd been able to run as fast as he fell, I wouldn't have lost so much money!"

Above them the climbing men had stopped now as the Drenai defenders forced the attackers back toward the ramparts. Tsubodai looked up at the man ahead of him.

"How long are you going to hang there, Nakrash?" he called. The man twisted his body and looked down.

"It's these Green Steppe dung eaters," he shouted. "They couldn't gain a foothold on a cowpat."

Tsubodai laughed happily, stepping away from the rope to see how the other climbers were moving. All along the wall it was the same: the climbing had stopped, the sounds of battle echoing down from above. As bodies crashed to the rocks around him, he dived back into the lee of the wall.

"We'll be down here all day," he said. "The Khan should have sent the Wolfshead in first. These Greens were useless at Gulgothir, and they're even worse here."

His companion grinned and shrugged. "Line's moving again," he said.

Tsubodai grasped the knotted rope and pulled himself up beneath Nakrash. He had a good feeling about today. Maybe he could win the horses Ulric had promised to the warrior who would cut down the old graybeard everyone was talking about.

"Deathwalker." A potbellied old man without a shield.

"Tsubodai," called Nakrash. "You don't die today, hey? Not while you still owe me on that footrace."

"Did you see Nestzan fall?" Tsubodai shouted back. "Like an arrow. You should have seen him swinging his arms. As if he wanted to push the ground away from him."

"I'll be watching you. Don't die, do you hear me?"

"You watch yourself. I'll pay you with Deathwalker's horses."

As the men climbed higher, more tribesmen filled the rope beneath him. Tsubodai glanced down.

"Hey, you!" he called. "Not a lice-ridden Green, are you?"

"From the smell you must be Wolfshead," replied the climber, grinning.

Nakrash scaled the battlements, dragging his sword clear and then turning to pull Tsubodai alongside him. The attackers had forced a wedge through the Drenai line, and still neither Tsubodai nor Nakrash could join the action.

"Move away! Make room!" called the man behind them.

"You wait there goat breath," said Tsubodai. "I'll just ask the round eyes to help you over. Hey, Nakrash, stretch those long legs of yours and tell me where Deathwalker is."

Nakrash pointed to the right. "I think you will soon get a chance at those horses. He looks closer than before." Tsubodai leapt lightly to the ramparts, straining to see the old man in action.

"Those Greens are just stepping up and asking for his ax, the fools." But no one heard him above the clamor.

The thick wedge of men ahead of them was thinning fast, and Nakrash leapt into a gap and slashed open the throat of a Drenai soldier who was trying desperately to free his sword from a Nadir belly. Tsubodai was soon beside him, hacking and cutting at the tall round-eyed southerners.

Battle lust swept over him, as it had during ten years of warfare under Ulric's banner. He had been a youngster when the first battle had begun, tending his father's goats on the granite steppes far to the north. Ulric had been a war leader for only a few years at that time. He had subdued the Long Monkey tribe and offered its men the chance to ride with his forces under their own banner. They had refused and died to a man. Tsubodai remembered that day: Ulric had personally tied their chieftain to two horses and ordered him torn apart. Eight hundred men had been beheaded, and their armor handed over to youngsters like Tsubodai.

On the next raid he had taken part in the first charge. Ulric's brother, Gat-sun, had praised him highly and given him a shield of stretched cowhide edged with brass. He had lost it in a knucklebone game the same night, but he still remembered the gift with affection. Poor Gat-sun! Ulric had had him executed the following year for trying to lead a rebellion. Tsubodai had ridden against him and had been among the loudest to cheer as his head fell. Now, with seven wives and forty horses Tsubodai was, by any reckoning, a rich man. And still to see thirty.

Surely the gods loved him.

A spear grazed his shoulder. His sword snaked out, half severing the arm. Oh, how the gods loved him! He blocked a slashing cut with his shield.

Nakrash came to his rescue, disemboweling the attacker, who fell screaming to the ground to vanish beneath the feet of the warriors pushing from behind.

To his right the Nadir line gave way, and he was pushed back as Nakrash took a spear in the side. Tsubodai's blade slashed the air, taking the lancer high in the neck; blood spurted, and the man fell back. Tsubodai glanced at Nakrash, lying at his feet writhing, his hands grasping the slippery lance shaft.

Leaning down, he pulled his friend clear of the action. There was nothing more he could do, for Nakrash was dying. It was a shame and put a pall on the day for the little tribesman. Nakrash had been a good companion for the last two years. Looking up, he saw a black-garbed figure with a white beard cleaving his way forward, a terrible ax of silver steel in his blood-splashed hands.

Tsubodai forgot about Nakrash in an instant. All he could see were Ulric's horses. He pushed forward to meet the axman, watching his movements, his technique. He moved well for one so old, thought Tsubodai as the old man blocked a murderous cut and backhanded his ax across the face of a tribesman, who was hurled screaming over the battlements.

Tsubodai leapt forward, aiming a straight thrust for the old man's belly. From then on it seemed to him that the scene was taking place under water. The white-bearded warrior turned his blue eyes on Tsubodai, and a chill of terror seeped into his blood. The ax seemed to float against his sword blade, sweeping the thrust aside, then the blade reversed and with an agonizing lack of speed cleaved Tsubodai's chest.

His body slammed back into the ramparts and slid down to rest beside Nakrash. Looking down, he saw bright blood replaced by dark arterial gore. He pushed his hand into the gash, wincing as a broken rib twisted under his fist.

"Tsubodai?" said Nakrash softly. Somehow the sound carried to him.

He hunched his body over his friend, resting his head on his chest.

"I hear you, Nakrash."

"You almost had the horses. Very close."

"Damn good, that old man, hey?" said Tsubodai.

The noise of the battle receded. Tsubodai realized it had been replaced by a roaring in his ears, like the sea gathering shingle.

He remembered the gift Gat-sun had given him and the way he had spit in Ulric's eye on the day of his execution.

Tsubodai grinned. He had liked Gat-sun.

He wished he had not cheered so loudly.

He wished . . .

Druss hacked at a rope and turned to face a Nadir warrior who was scrambling over the wall. Batting aside a sword thrust, he split the man's skull, then stepped over the body and tackled a second warrior, gutting him with a backhand slash. Age vanished from him now. He was where he was always meant to be—at the heart of a savage battle. Behind him Rek and Serbitar fought as a pair, the slim albino's slender rapier and Rek's heavy longsword cutting and slashing.

Druss was joined now by several Drenai warriors, and they cleared their section of the wall. Along the wall on both sides similar moves were being repeated as the five thousand warriors held. The Nadir could feel it, too, as slowly the Drenai inched them back. The tribesmen fought with renewed determination, cutting and killing with savage skill. They had only to hold on until the siege tower ledges touched the walls, then thousands more of their comrades could swarm in to reinforce them. And they were but a few yards away.

Druss glanced behind. Bowman and his archers were fifty paces back, sheltering behind small fires that had been hastily lit. Druss raised his arm and waved at Hogun, who ordered a trumpet sounded.

Along the wall several hundred men pulled back from the fighting to gather up wax-sealed clay pots and hurl them at the advancing towers. Pottery smashed against wooden frames, splashing dark liquid to stain the wood.

Gilad, with sword in one hand and clay pot in the other, parried a thrust from a swarthy axman, crashed his sword into the other's face, and threw his globe. He just had time to see it shatter in the open doorway at the top of the tower, where Nadir warriors massed, before two more invaders pressed forward to tackle him. The first he gutted with a stabbing thrust, only to find his sword trapped in the depths of the dying man's belly. The second attacker screamed and slashed at Gilad, who released his grip on his sword hilt and leapt backward. Instantly another Drenai warrior intercepted the Nadir, blocked his attack, and all but beheaded him with a reverse stroke. Gilad tore his sword free of the Nadir corpse and smiled his thanks to Bregan.

"Not bad for a farmer!" yelled Gilad, forcing his way back into the battle and slicing through the guard of a bearded warrior carrying an iron-pitted club.

"Now, Bowman!" shouted Druss.

The outlaws notched arrows whose tips were partially covered by oil-soaked cloth and held them over the flames of the fires. Once the arrows were burning, they fired them over the battlements to thud into the siege tower walls. Flames sprang up instantly, and black smoke, dense and suffocating, was whipped upward by the morning breeze. One flaming arrow flashed through the open doorway of the tower where Gilad's globe of oil had struck to pierce the leg of a Nadir warrior whose clothes were oil-drenched. Within seconds the man was a writhing, screaming human torch, blundering into his comrades and setting them ablaze.

More clay pots sailed through the air to feed the flames on the twenty towers, and the terrible stench of burning flesh was swept over the walls by the breeze.

With the smoke burning his eyes, Serbitar moved among the Nadir, his sword weaving an eldritch spell. Effortlessly he slew, a killing machine of deadly, awesome power. A tribesman reared up behind him, knife raised, but Serbitar twisted and opened the man's throat in one smooth motion.

"Thank you, Brother," he pulsed to Arbedark on Wall Two.

Rek, while lacking Serbitar's grace and lethal speed, used

his sword to no less effect, gripping it two-handed to bludgeon his way to victory beside Druss. A hurled knife glanced from his breastplate, slicing the skin over his bicep. He cursed and ignored the pain as he ignored other minor injuries received that day: the gashed thigh and the ribs bruised by a Nadir javelin that had been turned aside by his breastplate and mail shirt.

Five Nadir burst through the defenses and raced on toward the defenseless stretcher-bearers. Bowman skewered the first from forty paces, and Caessa the second, then Bar Britan raced to intercept them with two of his men. The battle was brief and fierce, the blood from Nadir corpses staining the earth.

Slowly, almost imperceptibly, a change was coming over the battle. Fewer tribesmen were gaining the walls, for their comrades had been forced back to the battlements and there was little room to gain purchase. The Nadir now fought not to conquer but to survive. The tide of war—fickle at best—had turned, and they had become the defenders.

But the Nadir were grim men and brave. For they neither cried out nor sought to surrender but stood their ground and died fighting.

One by one they fell, until the last of the warriors was swept from the battlements to lie broken on the rocks below.

Silently now the Nadir army retired from the field, stopping out of bowshot range to slump to the ground and stare back at the Dros with dull, unremitting hatred. Black plumes of smoke rose from the smoldering towers, and the stink of death filled their nostrils.

Rek leaned on the battlements and rubbed his face with a bloodied hand. Druss walked forward, wiping Snaga clean with a piece of torn cloth. Blood flecked the iron gray of the old man's beard, and he smiled at the new earl.

"You took my advice then, laddie?"

"Only just," said Rek. "Still, we didn't do too badly today."

"This was just a sortie. The real test will come tomorrow."

* * *

Druss was wrong. Three times more the Nadir attacked that day before dusk sent them back to their campfires, dejected and temporarily defeated. On the battlements weary men slumped to the bloody ground, tossing aside helmets and shields. Stretcher-bearers carried wounded men from the scene, while the corpses were left to lie for the time being, their needs no longer being urgent. Three teams were detailed to check the bodies of Nadir warriors. The dead were hurled from the battlements, and the living were dispatched with speed, their bodies pitched to the plain below.

Druss rubbed his tired eyes. His shoulder burned with fatigue, his knee was swollen, and his limbs felt leaden. But he had come through the day better than he had hoped. He glanced around. Some men lay sprawled asleep on the stone. Others merely sat with their backs to the walls, eyes glazed and minds wandering. There was little conversation. Farther along the wall the young earl was talking to the albino. They had both fought well, and the albino seemed fresh; only the blood that spattered his white cloak and breastplate gave evidence of his day's work. Regnak, though, seemed tired enough for both. His face, gray with exhaustion, looked older, the lines more deeply carved. Dust, blood, and sweat merged together on his features, and a rough bandage on his forearm was beginning to drip blood to the stones.

"You'll do, laddie," said Druss softly.

"Druss, old horse, how are you feeling?" Bowman asked.

"I have had better days," snarled the old man, lurching upright and gritting his teeth against the pain from his knee. The young archer almost made the mistake of offering Druss an arm to lean on but checked himself in time. "Come and see Caessa," he said.

"About the last thing I need now is a woman. I'll get some sleep," answered Druss. "Just here will be fine." With his back to the wall, he slid gently to the ground, keeping his injured knee straight. Bowman turned and walked back to the mess hall, where he found Caessa and explained the problem. After a short argument she gathered some linen while Bowman sought a jug of water, and in the gathering twilight they walked back to the battlements. Druss was asleep, but he awoke as they approached him.

The girl was a beauty, no doubt about that. Her hair was auburn but gold-tinted in the moonlight, matching the tawny flecks in her eyes. She stirred his blood as few women had the power to do now. But there was something else about her, something unattainable. She crouched down by him, her slender fingers probing gently at the swollen knee. Druss grunted as she dug more deeply. Then she removed his boot and rolled up the trouser leg. The knee was discolored and puffy, the veins in the calf below swollen and tender.

"Lie back," she told him. Moving alongside him, left hand curled around his thigh, she lifted the leg and held his ankle in her right hand. Slowly she flexed the joint.

"There is water on the knee," she said as she set down his leg and began to massage the joint. Druss closed his eyes. The sharpness of the pain receded to a dull ache. The minutes passed, and he dozed. She woke him with a light slap on the calf, and he found his knee was tightly bandaged.

"What other problems do you have?" she asked coolly.

"None," he said.

"Don't lie to me, old man. Your life depends on it."

"My shoulder burns," he admitted.

"You can walk now. Come with me to the hospital, and I will ease the pain." She gestured to Bowman, who leaned forward and helped the axman to his feet. The knee felt good, better than it had in weeks.

"You have real skill, woman," he said. "Real skill."

"I know. Walk slowly—it will feel a little sore by the time we get there."

In a side room at the hospital she told him to remove his clothes. Bowman smiled and leaned back against the door with arms folded across his chest.

"All of them?" asked Druss.

"Yes. Are you shy?"

"Not if you're not," said Druss, slipping from his jerkin and shirt, then sitting on the bed to remove his trousers and boots.

"Now what?" he asked.

Caessa stood before him, examining him critically, running her hands over his broad shoulders and probing his muscles.

"Stand up," she told him, "and turn around." He did so, and she scrutinized his back. "Move your right arm above your head—slowly." As the examination continued, Bowman watched the old warrior, marveling at the number of scars he carried. Everywhere: front and back; some long and straight, others jagged; some stitched, others blotchy and overlapped. His legs, too, showed evidence of many light wounds. But by far the greatest number was in the front. Bowman smiled. You have always faced your enemies, Druss, he thought.

Caessa told the warrior to lie on the bed facedown and began to manipulate the muscles of his back, easing out knots and pummeling crystals under the shoulder blades.

"Get me some oil," she asked Bowman without looking around. He fetched liniment from the stores, then left the girl to her work. For over an hour she massaged the old man, until at last her arms burned with fatigue. Druss had fallen asleep long since, and she covered him with a blanket and silently left the room. In the corridor outside she stood for a moment, listening to the cries of the wounded in the makeshift wards and watching the orderlies assisting the surgeons. The smell of death was strong here, and she made her way out into the night.

The stars were bright, like frozen snowflakes on a velvet blanket, the moon a bright silver coin at the center. She shivered. Ahead of her a tall man in black and silver armor strode toward the mess hall. It was Hogun. He saw her and waved, changed direction, and came toward her. She cursed under her breath; she was tired and in no mood for male company.

"How is he?" asked Hogun.

"Tough!" she said.

"I know that, Caessa. The whole world knows it. But how is he?"

"He's old, and he's tired—exhausted. And that's after only one day. Don't pin too many hopes on him. He has a knee which could collapse under him at any time, a bad back which will grow worse, and too many crystals in too many joints."

"You paint a pessimistic picture," said the general.

"I tell it as it is. It is a miracle that he's alive tonight. I cannot see how a man of his age, with the physical injuries he's carrying, could fight all day and survive."

"And he went where the fighting was thickest," said Hogun. "As he will do tomorrow."

"If you want him to survive, make sure he rests the day after."

"He will never stand for it," said Hogun.

"Yes, he will. He *may* get through tomorrow—and that I doubt. But by tomorrow night he will hardly be able to move his arm. I will help him, but he will need to rest one day in three. And an hour before dawn tomorrow I want a hot tub set up in his room here. I will massage him again before the battle begins."

"You're spending a lot of time over a man whom you described as old and tired and whose deeds you mocked only a short time since."

"Don't be a fool, Hogun. I am spending this time with him because he *is* old and tired, and though I do not hold him in the same reverence as you, I can see that the men need him. Hundreds of little boys playing at soldiers to impress an old man who thrives on war."

"I will see that he rests after tomorrow," said Hogun.

"If he survives," Caessa added grimly.

◊ 21 ◊

BY MIDNIGHT THE final toll for the first day's battle was known. Four hundred seven men were dead. One hundred sixty-eight were wounded, and half of those would not fight again.

The surgeons were still working, and the head count was being double-checked. Many Drenai warriors had fallen from the battlements during the fighting, and only a complete roll call would supply their numbers.

Rek was horrified, though he tried not to show it during the meeting with Hogun and Orrin in the study above the great hall. There were seven present at the meeting: Hogun and Orrin representing the warriors, Bricklyn for the townsfolk, and Serbitar, Vintar, and Virae. Rek had managed to snatch four hours sleep and felt fresher for it; the albino had slept not at all and seemed no different.

"These are grievous losses for one day's fighting," said Bricklyn. "At that rate we could not hold out for more than two weeks." His graying hair was styled after the fashion of the Drenai court, swept back over his ears and tightly curled at the nape of the neck. His face, though fleshy, was handsome, and he had a highly practiced charm. The man was a politician and therefore not to be relied upon, thought Rek.

Serbitar answered Bricklyn. "Statistics mean nothing on the first day," he said. "The wheat is being separated from the chaff."

"What does that mean, Prince of Dros Segril?" asked the burgher, the question more sharp in the absence of his usual smile.

"No disrespect was intended to the dead," replied Serbitar. "It is merely a reality in war that the men with the least skill are those first to fall. Losses are always greater at the outset. The men fought well, but many of the dead lacked skill—that is why they are dead. The losses will diminish, but they will still be high."

"Should we not concern ourselves with what is tolerable?" asked the burgher, turning to Rek. "After all, if we should believe that the Nadir will breach the walls eventually, what is the point of continued resistance? Are lives worth nothing?"

"Are you suggesting surrender?" asked Virae.

"No, my lady," replied Bricklyn smoothly. "That is for the warriors to decide, and I will back any decision they make. But I believe we must examine alternatives. Four hundred men died today, and they should be honored for their sacrifice. But what of tomorrow? And the day after. We must be careful that we do not put pride before reality."

"What is he talking about?" Virae asked Rek. "I cannot understand any of it."

"What are these alternatives you speak of?" said Rek. "As I see it, there are only two. We fight and win, or we fight and lose."

"These are the plans uppermost at this time," said Bricklyn. "But we must think of the future. Do we believe we can hold out here? If so, we must fight on by all means. But if not, then we must pursue an honorable peace, as other nations have done."

"What is an honorable peace?" asked Hogun softly.

"It is where enemies become friends and quarrels are forgotten. It is where we receive the Lord Ulric into the city as an ally to Drenan, having first obtained from him the promise that no harm will come to the inhabitants. Ultimately all wars are so concluded, as evidenced by the presence here of Serbitar, a Vagrian price. Thirty years ago we were at war with Vagria. Now we are friends. In thirty years time we may have meetings like this with Nadir princes. We must establish perspectives here."

"I take your point," said Rek, "and it is a good one."

"You may think so. Others may not!" snapped Virae.

"It is a good one," continued Rek smoothly. "These

meetings are no place for saber-rattling speeches. We must, as you say, examine realities. The first reality is this: We are well trained, well supplied, and we hold the mightiest fortress ever built. The second reality is that Magnus Woundweaver needs time to train and build an army to resist the Nadir even if Delnoch falls. There is no point in discussing surrender at this time, but we will bear it in mind for future meetings.

"Now, is there any other town business to discuss, for the hour is late and we have kept you overly long, my dear Bricklyn?"

"No, my lord. I think we have concluded our business," answered the burgher.

"Then may I thank you for your help—and your sage counsel—and bid you good night."

The burgher stood, bowed to Rek and Virae, and left the room. For several seconds they listened to his departing footsteps. Virae, flushed and angry, was about to speak when Serbitar broke the silence.

"That was well said, my lord Earl. He will be a thorn in our side."

"He is a political animal," said Rek. "He cares nothing for morality, honor, or pride. But he has his place and his uses. What of tomorrow, Serbitar?"

"The Nadir will begin with at least three hours of ballistae bombardment. Since they cannot advance their army while such an assault is in progress, I would suggest we retire all but fifty men to Musif an hour before dawn. When the barrage ceases, we will move forward."

"And what," said Orrin, "if they launch their second assault at dawn? They will be over the walls before our force can reach the battlements."

"They do not plan such a move," said the albino simply.

Orrin was unconvinced but felt uncomfortable in the presence of Serbitar. Rek noted his concern.

"Believe me, my friend, the Thirty have powers beyond the ken of normal men. If he says it, then it is so."

"We shall see, my lord," said Orrin doubtfully.

"How is Druss?" asked Virae. "He looked quite exhausted when I saw him at dusk."

"The woman Caessa tended to him," said Hogun, "and she says he will be well. He is resting at the hospital."

Rek wandered to the window, opened it, and breathed in the crisp night air. From there he could see far down into the valley, where the Nadir camp fires blazed. His eyes rested on the Eldibar hospital, where lamps still burned.

"Who would be a surgeon?" he said.

At Eldibar Calvar Syn, waist wrapped in a bloody leather apron, moved like a sleepwalker. Fatigue bit deep into his bones as he moved from bed to bed, administering potions.

The day had been a nightmare—more than a nightmare—for the bald, one-eyed surgeon. In thirty years he had seen death many times. He had watched men die who should have lived and seen men survive wounds that should have slain them outright. And often his own very special skills had thwarted death where others could not even staunch the wound. But today had been the worst day of his life. Four hundred strong young men, this morning fit and in their prime, were now rotting meat. Scores of others had lost limbs or fingers. Those with major wounds had been transferred to Musif. The dead had been carted back behind Wall Six for burial beyond the gates.

Around the weary surgeon orderlies flung buckets of salted water to the bloody floor, brushing away the debris of pain.

Calvar Syn walked silently into Druss's room and gazed down on the sleeping figure. By the bedside hung Snaga, the silver slayer. "How many more, you butcher?" said Calvar. The old man stirred but did not wake.

The surgeon stumbled into the corridor and made his way to his own room. There he hurled the apron across a chair and slumped to his bed, lacking even the energy to pull a blanket across his body. Sleep would not come. Nightmare images of agony and horror flitted across his mind, and he began to sob. A face entered his mind, elderly and gentle. The face grew, absorbing his anguish and radiating harmony. Larger and larger it became, until like a warm blanket it covered his pain. And he slept deeply and dreamlessly.

"He rests now," said Vintar as Rek turned away from the window in the keep.

"Good," said Rek. "He won't rest much tomorrow. Serbitar, have you had any more thoughts about our traitor?"

The albino shook his head. "I don't know what we can do. We are watching the food and the wells. There is no other way he can affect us. You are guarded, as is Druss and Virae."

"We must find him," said Rek. "Can you not enter the mind of every man in the fortress?"

"Of course! We would surely have an answer for you within three months."

"I take the point," Rek said, smiling ruefully.

Khitan stood silently, watching the smoke billow up from his towers. His face was expressionless, his eyes dark and shrouded. Ulric approached him, placing a hand on his shoulder.

"They were just wood, my friend."

"Yes, my lord. I was thinking that in future we need a false-fronted screen of soaking hides. It should not be too difficult, though the increased weight could prove a problem in terms of stability."

Ulric laughed. "I thought to find you broken with grief. And yet already you plan."

"I feel stupid, yes," answered Khitan. "I should have foreseen the use of the oil. I knew the timbers would never burn merely from fire arrows and gave no thought to other combustibles. No one will beat us like that again."

"Most assuredly, my learned architect," said Ulric, bowing.

Khitan chuckled. "The years are making me pompous, my lord. Deathwalker did well today. He is a worthy opponent."

"Indeed he is, but I don't think today's plan was his. They have white templars among them, who destroyed Nosta Khan's acolytes."

"I thought there was some devilry in that," muttered Khitan. "What will you do with the defenders when we take the fortress?"

"I have said that I will slay them."

"I know. I wondered if you had changed your mind. They are valiant."

"And I respect them. But the Drenai must learn what happens to those who oppose me."

"So, my lord, what will you do?"

"I shall burn them all on one great funeral pyre—all save one, who shall live to carry the tale."

An hour before dawn Caessa slipped silently into Druss's room and approached the bedside. The warrior was sleeping deeply, lying on his belly with his massive forearms cradling his head. As she watched him, Druss stirred. He opened his eyes, focusing on her slender legs clad in thigh-length doeskin boots. Then his gaze traveled upward. She wore a body-hugging green tunic with a thick silver-studded leather belt that accentuated her small waist. By her side hung a short sword with an ebony handle. He rolled over and met her gaze; there was anger in her tawny eyes.

"Finished your inspection?" she snapped.

"What ails you, girl?"

All emotion left her face, withdrawing like a cat into shadows.

"Nothing. Turn over. I want to check your back."

Skillfully she began to knead at the muscles of his shoulder blade, her fingers like steel pins, causing him to grunt occasionally through gritted teeth.

"Turn over again."

With Druss once more on his back, she lifted his right arm, locked her own arms around it, and gave a sharp pull and twist. A violent cracking sound followed, and for a fraction of a second Druss thought she had broken his shoulder. Releasing his arm, she rested it on his left shoulder, then crossed his left arm to sit on the right shoulder. Leaning forward to pull him onto his side, she placed her clenched fist under his spine between the shoulder blades, then rolled him back. Suddenly she threw her weight across his chest, forcing his spine into her fist. Twice more he grunted as alarming sounds filled the air, which he identified as a kind of crunching snap. Sweat beaded his forehead.

"You're stronger than you look, girl."

"Be quiet and sit up, facing the wall."

This time she seemed almost to break his neck, placing her hands under his chin and over his ear, wrenching first to the left and then to the right. The sound was like a dry branch snapping.

"Tomorrow you rest," she said as she turned to leave.

He stretched and moved his injured shoulder. He felt good, better than he had in weeks.

"What were those cracking sounds?" he asked, halting her at the door.

"You have arthritis. The first three dorsals were locked solid; therefore, blood could not flow properly. Also, the muscle under the shoulder blade had knotted, causing spasms which reduced the strength of your right arm. But heed me, old man, tomorrow you must rest. That or die."

"We all die," he said.

"True. But you are needed."

"Do you dislike me—or all men?" he asked as her hand touched the door handle.

She turned to look at him, smiled, pushed the door shut, and came back into the room, stopping within inches of his burly naked frame.

"Would you like to sleep with me, Druss?" she asked sweetly, laying her left arm across his shoulder.

"No," he said softly, gazing into her eyes. The pupils were small, unnaturally so.

"Most men do," she whispered, moving closer.

"I am not most men."

"Are you dried up, then?" she asked.

"Perhaps."

"Or is it boys you lust after? We have some like that in our band."

"No, I can't say I have ever lusted after a man. But I had a real woman once, and since then I have never needed another."

She stepped away from him. "I have ordered a hot bath for you, and I want you to stay in it until the water cools. It will help the blood flow through those tired muscles." With that she turned and was gone. For a few moments Druss stared at the door, then he sat down on the bed and scratched his beard.

The girl disturbed him. There was something in her eyes. Druss had never been good with women, not intuitive as some men were. Women were another race to him, alien and forbidding. But this child was something else again; in her eyes was madness, madness and fear. He shrugged and did what he always had done when a problem eluded him: forgot about it.

After the bath he dressed swiftly, combed his hair and beard, then snatched a hasty breakfast in the Eldibar mess hall and joined the fifty volunteers on the battlements as the dawn sunlight pierced the early morning mist. It was a crisp morning, fresh with the promise of rain. Below him the Nadir were gathering, carts piled with boulders making their slow way to the catapults. Around him there was little conversation; on days such as this a man's thoughts turned inward. Will I die today? What is my wife doing now? Why am I here?

Farther along the battlements Orrin and Hogun walked among the men. Orrin said little, leaving the legion general to make jokes and ask questions. He resented Hogun's easy style with the enlisted men, but not too deeply; it was probably more regret than resentment.

A young cul—Bregan, was it?—made him feel better as they passed the small group of men near the gate tower.

"Will you be fighting with Karnak today, sir?" he asked.

"Yes."

"Thank you, sir. It is a great honor—for all of us."

"It is nice of you to say so," said Orrin.

"No, I mean it," said Bregan. "We were talking about it last night."

Embarrassed and pleased, Orrin smiled and walked on.

"Now that," offered Hogun, "is a greater responsibility than checking supply lines."

"In what way?"

"They respect you. And that man hero-worships you. It is not an easy thing to live up to. They will stand beside you when all have fled. Or they will flee with you when all else stand."

"I won't run away, Hogun," said Orrin.

"I know you won't; that's not what I meant. As a man, there are times when you want to lie down, or give in, or walk away. It's usually left to the individual, but in this case you are no longer one man. You are fifty. You are Karnak. It is a great responsibility."

"And what of you?" asked Orrin.

"I am the legion," he answered simply.

"Yes, I suppose you are. Are you frightened today?"

"Of course."

"I'm glad of that," said Orrin, smiling. "I wouldn't like to be the only one."

As Druss had promised, the day brought fresh horror: stone missiles obliterating sections of battlements, then the terrible battle cries and the surging attack with ladders to the wall, and a snarling horde breasting the granite defense to meet the silver steel of the Drenai. Today it was the turn of three thousand men from Musif, Wall Two, to relieve warriors who had fought long and hard the day before. Swords rang, men screamed and fell, and chaos descended for long hours. Druss strode the walls like a fell giant, blood-spattered and grim, his ax cleaving the Nadir ranks, his oaths and coarse insults causing the Nadir to center on him. Rek fought with Serbitar beside him, as on the previous day, but with them now were Menahem and Antaheim, Virae and Arbedark.

By afternoon the twenty-foot-wide battlements were slippery with blood and cluttered by bodies, yet still the battle raged. Orrin, by the gate towers, fought like a man possessed, side by side with the warriors from Group Karnak. Bregan, his sword broken, had gathered a Nadir ax, two-headed and long-handled, which he wielded with astonishing skill.

"A real farmer's weapon!" yelled Gilad during a brief lull.

"Tell that to Druss!" shouted Orrin, slapping Bregan on the back.

At dusk the Nadir fell back once more, sent on their way by jeers and catcalls. But the toll had been heavy. Druss, bathed in crimson, stepped across the bodies and limped to where Rek and Serbitar stood cleaning their weapons.

"The wall's too damned wide to hold for long," he muttorod, leaning forward to clean Snaga on the jerkin of a dead Nadir.

"Too true," said Rek, wiping the sweat from his face with the edge of his cloak. "But you are right; we cannot just give it to them yet."

"At present," said Serbitar, "we are killing them at a rate of three to one. It is not enough. They will wear us down."

"We need more men," said Druss, sitting back on the battlements and scratching his beard.

"I sent a messenger last night to my father at Dros Segril," said Serbitar. "We should have reinforcements in about ten days."

"Drada hates the Drenai," said Druss. "Why should he send men?"

"He must send my personal bodyguard. It is the law of Vagria, and though my father and I have not spoken for twelve years, I am still his firstborn son. It is my right. Three hundred swords will join me here—no more than that, but it will help."

"What was the quarrel?" asked Rek.

"Quarrel?" queried the albino.

"Between you and your father."

"There was no quarrel. He saw my talents as 'gifts of darkness' and tried to kill me. I would not allow it. Vintar rescued me." Serbitar removed his helm, untied the knot that bound his white hair, and shook his head. The evening breeze ruffled his hair. Rek exchanged glances with Druss and changed the subject.

"Ulric must realize by now that he has a battle on his hands."

"He knew that anyway," answered Druss. "It won't worry him yet."

"I don't see why not; it worries me," said Rek, rising as Virae joined them with Menahem and Antaheim. The three members of the Thirty left without a word, and Virae sat beside Rek, hugging his waist and resting her head on his shoulder.

"Not an easy day," said Rek, gently stroking her hair.

"They looked after me," she whispered. "Just like you told them to, I suppose."

"Are you angry?"

"No."

"Good. We have only just met, and I don't want to lose you yet."

"You two ought to eat," said Druss. "I know you don't feel like it, but take the advice of an old warrior." The old man stood, glanced back once at the Nadir camp, and walked slowly toward the mess hall. He was tired. Almighty tired.

Ignoring his own advice, he skirted the mess hall and made for his room at the hospital. Inside the long building he paused to listen to the moans from the wards. The stench of death was everywhere. Stretcher-bearers pushed past him bearing bloodied corpses, orderlies hurled buckets of water to the floor, others with mops or buckets of sand prepared the ground for the next day. He spoke to none of them.

Pushing open the door of his room, he stopped. Caessa sat within. "I have food for you," she said, avoiding his eyes. Silently he took the platter of beef, red beans, and thick black bread and began to eat.

"There is a bath for you in the next room," she said as he finished. He nodded and stripped off his clothing.

He sat in the hip bath and cleaned the blood from his hair and beard. When cold air touched his wet back, he knew she had entered. She knelt by the bath and poured an aromatic liquid into her hands, then began washing his hair. He closed his eyes, enjoying the sensation of her fingers on his scalp. After rinsing his hair with warm fresh water, she rubbed it dry with a clean towel.

Back in his room, Druss found that she had laid out a clean undervest and black woolen trousers and had sponged his leather jerkin and boots. She poured him a goblet of Lentrian wine before leaving. Druss finished the wine and lay back on the bed, resting his head on his hand. Not since Rowena had a woman tended to him in this fashion, and his thoughts were mellow.

Rowena, his child bride, taken by slavers soon after the wedding at the great oak. Druss had followed them, not even stopping to bury his parents. For months he had traveled the land until at last, in the company of Sieben the poet, he had discovered the slavers' camp. Having found out from them that Rowena had been sold to a merchant who was heading east, he slew the leader in his tent and set out once more. For five years he wandered across the continent, a mercenary, building a reputation as the most fearsome warrior of his time, becoming at last the champion of Ventria's god-king, Gorben.

Finally he had found his wife in an eastern palace and had wept. For without her he had always been only half a man. She alone made him human, stilling for a while the dark side of his nature, making him whole, showing him the beauty in a field of flowers, where he looked for perfection in a blade of steel.

She used to wash his hair and stroke the tension from his neck and the anger from his heart.

Now she was gone, and the world was empty, a shifting blur of shimmering gray where once there had been colors of dazzling brightness.

Outside a gentle rain began to fall. For a while Druss listened to it pattering on the roof. Then he slept.

Caessa sat in the open air, hugging her knees. Had anyone approached her, he could not have seen where the rain ended and the tears began.

◊ 22 ◊

FOR THE FIRST time all the members of the Thirty manned Eldibar as the Nadir massed for the charge. Serbitar had warned Rek and Druss that today would be different: no ballistae bombardment, merely an endless series of charges to wear down the defenders. Druss had refused all advice to rest for the day and stood at the center of the wall. Around him were the Thirty in their silver steel armor and white cloaks. With them was Hogun, while Rek and Virae stood with the men of Group Fire forty paces to the left. Orrin remained with Karnak on the right. Five thousand men waited, swords in hands, shields buckled, helms lowered.

The sky was dark and angry, huge clouds bunching to the north. Above the walls a patch of blue waited for the storm. Rek smiled suddenly as the poetry of the moment struck him.

The Nadir began to move forward in a seething furious mass, their pounding feet sounding like thunder.

Druss leapt to stand on the crenellated battlements above them.

"Come on, you whoresons!" he bellowed. "Deathwalker waits!" His voice boomed out over the valley, echoed by the towering granite walls. At that moment lightning split the sky, a jagged spear above the Dros. Thunder followed.

And the bloodletting began.

As Serbitar had predicted, the center of the line suffered the most ferocious attacks, wave upon wave of tribesmen breasting the walls to die under the steel defense of the Thirty. Their skill was consummate. A wooden club knocked Druss from his feet, and a burly Nadir warrior aimed an ax blow for his skull. Serbitar leapt forward to block the blow, while Menahem dispatched the man with a throat slash. Druss, exhausted, stumbled over a fallen body and pitched to the feet of three attackers. Arbedark and Hogun came to the rescue as he scrabbled for his ax.

The Nadir burst through the line on the right, forcing Orrin and Group Karnak away from the battlements and back onto the grass of the killing ground. As Nadir reinforcements swept over the wall unopposed, Druss saw the danger first and bellowed a warning. He cut two men from his path and raced alone to fill the breach. Hogun desperately tried to follow him, but his way was blocked.

Three young culs from Karnak joined the old man as he hammered and cut his way to the walls, but they were soon surrounded. Orrin—his helm lost, his shield splintered—stood his ground with the remnants of his group. He blocked a wide, slashing cut from a bearded tribesman and lanced a return thrust through the man's belly. Then he saw Druss and knew that save for a miracle he was doomed.

"With me, Karnak!" he yelled, hurling himself into the advancing mass. Behind him Bregan, Gilad, and twenty others surged forward, joined by Bar Britan and a squad of stretcher guards. Serbitar, with fifteen of the Thirty, cleaved a path along the walls.

The last of Druss's young companions fell with a broken skull, and the old warrior stood alone as the Nadir circle closed about him. He ducked beneath a swinging sword, grabbed the man's jerkin, and smashed a head butt to his nose. A sword blade cut his upper arm, and another sliced his leather jerkin above the hip. Using the stunned Nadir as a shield, Druss backed to the battlements, but an ax blade thudded into the trapped tribesman and tore him from Druss's grasp. With nowhere to go, Druss braced his foot against the battlements and dived forward into the mass; his great weight carried them back, and several tumbled to the earth with him. He lost hold of Snaga, grabbed at the neck of the warrior above him and crushed his windpipe, then, hugging the body to him, waited for the inevitable killing thrust. As the body was kicked away, Druss lashed out at the leg beside him, sweeping the man from his feet.

"Whoa, Druss! It's me—Hogun."

The old man rolled over and saw Snaga lying several yards away. He stood and snatched up the ax.

"That was close," said the legion gan.

"Yes," said Druss. "Thank you! That was good work!"

"I would like to take the credit, but it was Orrin and the men from Karnak. They fought their way to you, though I don't know how."

It had begun to rain, and Druss welcomed it, turning his face to the sky with mouth open, eyes closed.

"They're coming again!" someone yelled. Druss and Hogun walked to the battlements and watched the Nadir charge. It was hard to see them through the rain.

To the left Serbitar was leading the Thirty from the wall, marching silently back toward Musif.

"Where in hell's name are *they* going?" muttered Hogun.

"There's no time to worry about that," snarled Druss, cursing silently as his shoulder flamed with fresh agonies.

The Nadir horde swept forward. Then thunder rumbled, and a huge explosion erupted at the center of the Nadir ranks. Everything was confusion as the charge faltered.

"What happened?" asked Druss.

"Lightning struck them," said Hogun, removing his helm and unbuckling his breastplate. "It could happen here next—it's all this damned metal."

A distant trumpet sounded, and the Nadir marched back to their tents. At the center of the plain was a vast crater surrounded by blackened bodies. Smoke rose from the hole.

Druss turned and watched the Thirty enter the postern gate at Musif.

"They *knew*," he said softly. "What manner of men are they?"

"I don't know," answered Hogun. "But they fight like devils, and at the moment that's all I care about."

"They knew," Druss said again, shaking his head.

"So?"

"How much more do they know?"

"Do you tell fortunes?" the man asked Antaheim as they crouched together beneath the makeshift canvas roof with five others from Group Fire. Rain pattered on the canvas and dripped steadily to the stones below. The roof, hastily constructed, was pinned to the battlements behind them and supported by spears at the two front corners. Within, the men huddled together. They had seen Antaheim walking alone in the rain, and one of the men, Cul Rabil, had called him over despite the warnings of his comrades. Now an uncomfortable atmosphere existed within the canvas shelter.

"Well, do you?" asked Rabil.

"No," said Antaheim, removing his helm and untying the battle knot in his long hair. He smiled. "I am not a magician. Merely a man as you—all of you—are. My training is different, that is all."

"But you can speak without talking," said another man. "That's not natural."

"It is to me."

"Can you see into the future?" asked a thin warrior, making the sign of the protective horn beneath his cloak.

"There are many futures. I can see some of them, but I do not know which will come to pass."

"How can there be many futures?" asked Rabil.

"It is not an easy concept to explain, but I will try. Tomorrow an archer will shoot an arrow. If the wind drops, it will hit one man; if the wind rises, it will hit another. Each man's future therefore depends on the wind. I cannot predict which way the wind will blow, for that, too, depends on many things. I can look into tomorrow and see both men die, whereas only one may actually fall."

"Then what is the point of it all? Your talent, I mean," asked Rabil.

"Now, that is an excellent question and one which I have pondered for many years."

"Will we die tomorrow?" asked another.

"How can I tell?" answered Antaheim. "But all men must die eventually. The gift of life is not permanent."

"You say 'gift,' " said Rabil. "This implies a giver?"

"Indeed it does."

"Which, then, of the gods do you follow?"

"We follow the Source of all things. How do you feel after today's battle?"

"In what way?" asked Rabil, pulling his cloak closer about him.

"What emotions did you feel as the Nadir fell back?"

"It's hard to describe. Strong." He shrugged. "Filled with power. Glad to be alive." The other men nodded at this.

"Exultant?" offered Antaheim.

"I suppose so. Why do you ask?"

Antaheim smiled. "This is Eldibar, Wall One. Do you know the meaning of the word 'Eldibar'?"

"Is it not just a word?"

"No, it is far more. Egel, who built this fortress, had names carved on every wall. 'Eldibar' means 'exultation.' It is there that the enemy is first met. It is there he is seen to be a man. Power flows in the veins of the defenders. The enemy falls back against the weight of our swords and the strength of our arms. We feel, as heroes should, the thrill of battle and the call of our heritage. We are exultant! Egel knew the hearts of men. I wonder, Did he know the future?"

"What do the other names mean?"

Antaheim shrugged. "That is for another day. It is not good luck to talk of Musif while we shelter under the protection of Eldibar." Antaheim leaned back into the wall and closed his eyes, listening to the rain and the howling wind.

Musif. The wall of despair! Where strength has not been great enough to hold Eldibar, how can Musif be held? If we could not hold Eldibar, we cannot hold Musif. Fear will gnaw at our vitals. Many of our friends will have died at Eldibar, and once more we will see in our minds the laughing faces. We will not want to join them. Musif is the test.

And we will not hold. We will fall back to Kania, the wall of renewed hope. We did not die on Musif, and Kania is a narrower fighting place. And anyway, are there not three more walls? The Nadir can no longer use their ballistae here, so that is something, is it not? In any case, did we not always know we would lose a few walls?

Sumitos, the wall of desperation, will follow. We are tired, mortally weary. We fight now by instinct, mechanically and well. Only the very best will be left to stem the savage tide.

Valteri, Wall Five, is the wall of serenity. Now we have come to terms with mortality. We accept the inevitability of our deaths and find in ourselves depths of courage we

would not have believed possible. The humor will begin
again, and each will be a brother to each other man. We
will have stood together against the common enemy, shield
to shield, and we will have made him suffer. Time will pass
on this wall more slowly. We will savor our senses as if we
have discovered them anew. The stars will become jewels
of beauty we never saw before, and friendship will have a
sweetness never previously tasted.

And finally Geddon, the wall of death . . .

I shall not see Geddon, thought Antaheim.

And he slept.

"Tests! All we keep hearing about is that the real test will
come tomorrow. How many damn tests are there?" stormed
Elicas. Rek raised a hand as the young warrior interrupted
Serbitar.

"Calm down!" he said. "Let him finish. We have only a
few moments before the city elders arrive."

Elicas glared at Rek but was silent after looking at
Hogun for support and seeing his almost imperceptible
shake of the head. Druss rubbed his eyes and accepted a
goblet of wine from Orrin.

"I am sorry," said Serbitar gently. "I know how irksome
such talk is. For eight days now we have held the Nadir
back, and it is true I continue to speak of fresh tests. But
you see, Ulric is a master strategist. Look at his army—it
is twenty thousand tribesmen. This first week has seen
them bloodied on our walls. They are not his finest troops.
Even as we have trained our recruits, so does he. He is in
no hurry; he has spent these days culling the weak from his
ranks, for he knows there are more battles to come when,
and if, he takes the Dros. We have done well, exceedingly
well. But we have paid dearly. Fourteen hundred men have
died, and four hundred more will not fight again.

"I tell you this: Tomorrow his veterans will come."

"And where do you gain this intelligence?" snapped
Elicas.

"Enough, boy!" roared Druss. "It is sufficient that he has
been right till now. When he is wrong, you may have your
say."

"What do you suggest, Serbitar?" asked Rek.

"Give them the wall," answered the albino.

"What?" said Virae. "After all the fighting and dying? That is madness."

"Not so, my lady," said Bowman, speaking for the first time. All eyes turned to the young archer, who had forsaken his usual uniform of green tunic and hose. Now he wore a splendid buckskin topcoat, heavy with fringed thongs, sporting an eagle crafted from small beads across the back. His long blond hair was held in place by a buckskin headband, and by his side hung a silver dagger with an ebony haft shaped like a falcon whose spread wings made up the knuckle guard.

He stood. "It is sound good sense. We knew that walls would fall. Eldibar is the longest and therefore the most difficult to hold. We are stretched there. On Musif we would need fewer men and therefore would lose fewer. And we have the killing ground between the walls. My archers could create an unholy massacre among Ulric's veterans before even a blow is struck."

"There is another point," said Rek, "and one equally important. Sooner or later we will be pushed back from the wall, and despite the fire gullies, our losses will be enormous. If we retire during the night, we will save lives."

"And let us not forget morale," Hogun pointed out. "The loss of the wall will hit the Dros badly. If we give it up as a strategic withdrawal, however, we will turn the situation to our advantage."

"What of you, Orrin? How do you feel about this?" asked Rek.

"We have about five hours. Let's get it started," answered the gan.

Rek turned to Druss. "And you?"

The old man shrugged. "Sounds good," he said.

"It's settled, then," said Rek. "I leave you to begin the withdrawal. Now I must meet the council."

Throughout the long night the silent retreat continued. Wounded men were carried on stretchers, medical supplies loaded on to handcarts, and personal belongings packed hastily into kit bags. The more seriously injured had long since been removed to the Musif field hospital, and Eldibar barracks had been little used since the siege had begun.

By dawn's first ghostly light the last of the men entered the postern gates at Musif and climbed the long winding stairways to the battlements. Then began the work of rolling boulders and rubble onto the stairs to block the entrances. Men heaved and toiled as the light grew stronger. Finally, sacks of mortar powder were poured onto the rubble and then packed solid into the gaps. Other men with buckets of water doused the mixtures.

"Given a day," said Maric the builder, "that mass will be almost immovable."

"Nothing is immovable," said his companion. "But it will take them weeks to make it passable, and even then the stairways were designed to be defensible."

"One way or the other, I shall not see it," said Maric. "I leave today."

"You are early, surely," said his friend. "Marrissa and I also plan to leave. But not until the fourth wall falls."

"First wall, fourth wall, what is the difference? All the more time to put distance between myself and this war. Ventria has need of builders. And their army is strong enough to hold the Nadir for years."

"Perhaps. But I will wait."

"Don't wait too long, my friend," said Maric.

Back at the keep Rek lay staring at the ornate ceiling. The bed was comfortable, and Virae's naked form nestled into him, her head resting on his shoulder. The meeting had finished two hours since, and he could not sleep. His mind was alive with plans, counterplans, and all the myriad problems of a city under siege. The debate had been acrimonious, and pinning down any of those politicians was like threading a needle under water. The consensus opinion was that Delnoch should surrender.

Only the red-faced Lentrian, Malphar, had backed Rek. That oily serpent, Shinell, had offered to lead a delegation to Ulric personally. And what of Beric, who felt himself tricked by fate in that his bloodline had included rulers of Delnoch for centuries, yet he had lost out by being a second son? Bitterness was deep within him. The lawyer, Backda, had said little, but his words were acid when they came.

"You seek to stop the sea with a leaking bucket."

Rek had struggled to hold his temper. He had not seen any of them standing on the battlements with sword in hand. Nor would they. Horeb had a saying that matched these men:

"In any broth, the scum always rises to the top."

He had thanked them for their counsel and agreed to meet in five days time to answer their proposals.

Virae stirred beside him. Her arm moved the coverlet, exposing a rounded breast. Rek smiled and for the first time in days thought about something other than war.

Bowman and a thousand archers stood on the ramparts of Eldibar, watching the Nadir mass for the charge. Arrows were loosely notched to the string, and hats were tilted at a jaunty angle to keep the right eye in shadow against the rising sun.

The horde screamed its hatred and surged forward.

Bowman waited. He licked his dry lips.

"Now!" he yelled, smoothly drawing back the string to touch his right cheek. The arrow leapt free with a thousand others, to be lost within the surging mass below. Again and again they fired until their quivers were empty. Finally Caessa leapt to the battlements and fired her last arrow straight down at a man pushing a ladder against the wall. The shaft entered at the top of the shoulder and sheared through his leather jerkin, lancing through his lung and lodging in his belly. He dropped without a sound.

Grappling irons clattered to the ramparts.

"Back!" yelled Bowman, and began to run across the open ground, across the fire-gully bridges and the trench of oil-soaked brush. Ropes were lowered, and the archers swiftly scaled them. Back at Eldibar the first of the Nadir had gained the wall. For long moments they milled in confusion before they spotted the archers clambering to safety. Within minutes the tribesmen had gathered several thousand strong. They hauled their ladders over Eldibar and advanced on Musif. Then arrows of fire arced over the open ground to vanish within the oil-soaked brush. Instantly thick smoke welled from the gully, closely followed by roaring flames twice the height of a man.

The Nadir fell back. The Drenai cheered.

The brush blazed for over an hour, and the four thousand warriors manning Musif stood down. Some lay in groups on the grass; others wandered to the three mess halls for a second breakfast. Many sat in the shade of the rampart towers.

Druss strolled among the men, swapping jests here and there, accepting a chunk of black bread from one man, an orange from another. He saw Rek and Virae sitting alone near the eastern cliff and wandered across to join them.

"So far, so good!" he said, easing his huge frame to the grass. "They're not sure what to do now. Their orders were to take the wall, and they've accomplished that."

"What next, do you think?" asked Rek.

"The old boy himself," answered Druss. "He will come. And he'll want to talk."

"Should I go down?" asked Rek.

"Better if I do. The Nadir know me. Deathwalker. I'm part of their legends. They think I'm an ancient god of death stalking the world."

"Are they wrong? I wonder," said Rek, smiling.

"Maybe not. I never wanted it, you know. All I wanted was to get my wife back. Had slavers not taken her, I would have been a farmer. Of that I am sure, though Rowena doubted it. There are times when I do not much like what I am."

"I'm sorry, Druss. It was a jest," said Rek. "I do not see you as a death god. You are a man and a warrior. But most of all a man."

"It's not you, boy; your words only echo what I already feel. I shall die soon . . . Here at this Dros. And what will I have achieved in my life? I have no sons or daughters. No living kin . . . few friends. They will say, 'Here lies Druss. He killed many and birthed none.' "

"They will say more than that," said Virae, suddenly. "They'll say, 'Here lies Druss the Legend, who was never mean, petty, or needlessly cruel. Here was a man who never gave in, never compromised his ideals, never betrayed a friend, never despoiled a woman, and never used his strength against the weak.' They'll say, 'He had no sons, but many a woman asleep with her babes slept more soundly for knowing Druss stood with the Drenai.' They'll say many things, whitebeard. Through many generations they will say them, and men with no strength will find strength when they hear them."

"That would be pleasant," said the old man, smiling.

The morning drifted by, and the Dros shone in the warm sunlight. One of the soldiers produced a flute and began to play a lilting springtime melody that echoed down the valley, a song of joy in a time of death.

At midday Rek and Druss were summoned to the ramparts. The Nadir had fallen back to Eldibar, but at the center of the killing ground was a man seated on a huge purple rug. He was eating a meal of dates and cheese and sipping wine from a golden goblet. Thrust into the ground behind him was a standard sporting a wolf's head.

"He's certainly got style," said Rek, admiring the man instantly.

"I ought to go down before he finishes the food," said Druss. "We lose face as we wait."

"Be careful!" urged Rek.

"There are only a couple of thousand of them," answered Druss with a broad wink.

Hand over hand, he lowered himself to the Eldibar ground below and strolled toward the diner.

"I am a stranger in your camp," he said.

The man looked up. His face was broad and clean-cut, the jaw firm. The eyes were violet and slanted beneath dark brows; they were eyes of power.

"Welcome, stranger, and eat," said the man. Druss sat cross-legged opposite him. Slowly the man unbuckled his lacquered black breastplate and removed it, laying it carefully at his side. Then he removed his black greaves and forearm straps. Druss noted the powerful muscles of the man's arms and the smooth, catlike movements. A warrior born, thought the old man.

"I am Ulric of the Wolfshead."

"I am Druss of the Ax."

"Well met! Eat."

Druss took a handful of dates from the silver platter before him and ate slowly. He followed this with goat's milk cheese and washed it down with a mouthful of red wine. His eyebrows rose.

"Lentrian red," said Ulric. "Without poison."

Druss grinned. "I'm a hard man to kill. It's a talent."

"You did well. I am glad for you."

"I was grieved to hear of your son. I have no sons, but I know how hard it is for a man to lose a loved one."

"It was a cruel blow," said Ulric. "He was a good boy. But then, all life is cruel, is it not? A man must rise above grief."

Druss was silent, helping himself to more dates.

"You are a great man, Druss. I am sorry you are to die here."

"Yes. It would be nice to live forever. On the other hand, I am beginning to slow down. Some of your men have been getting damn close to marking me—it's an embarrassment."

"There is a prize for the man who kills you. One hundred horses, picked from my own stable."

"How does the man prove to you that he slew me?"

"He brings me your head and two witnesses to the blow."

"Don't allow that information to reach my men. They will do it for fifty horses."

"I think not! You have done well. How is the new earl settling in?"

"He would have preferred a less noisy welcome, but I think he is enjoying himself. He fights well."

"As do you all. It will not be enough, however."

"We shall see," said Druss. "These dates are very good."

"Do you believe you can stop me? Tell me truly, Deathwalker."

"I would like to have served under you," said Druss. "I have admired you for years. I have served many kings. Some were weak, others willful. Many were fine men, but you . . . you have the mark of greatness. I think you will get what you want eventually. But not while I live."

"You will not live long, Druss," said Ulric gently. "We have a shaman who knows these things. He told me that he saw you standing at the gates of Wall Four—Sumitos, I believe it is called—and the grinning skull of death floated above your shoulders."

Druss laughed aloud. "Death always floats where I stand, Ulric! I am he who walks with death. Does your shaman not know your own legends? I may choose to die at Sumitos. I may choose to die at Musif. But wherever I choose to die, know this: As I walk into the Valley of Shadows, I will take with me more than a few Nadir for company on the road."

"They will be proud to walk with you. Go in peace."

◊ 23 ◊

BLOODY DAY FOLLOWED bloody day, an endless succession of hacking, slaying, and dying, skirmishes carrying groups of Nadir warriors out onto the killing ground before Musif and threatening to trap the Drenai army on the walls. But always they were beaten back and the line held. Slowly, as Serbitar had predicted, the strong were separated from the weak. It was easy to tell the difference. By the sixth week only the strong survived. Three thousand Drenai warriors either were dead or had been removed from the battle with horrifying injuries.

Druss strode like a giant along the ramparts day after day, defying all advice to rest, daring his weary body to betray him, drawing on hidden reserves of strength from his warrior's soul. Rek also was building a name, though he cared not. Twice his baresark attacks had dismayed the Nadir and shattered their line. Orrin still fought with the remnants of Karnak, now only eighteen strong. Gilad fought beside him on the right, and on his left was Bregan, still using the captured ax. Hogun had gathered fifty of the legion about him and stood back from the rampart line, ready to fill in any gap that developed.

The days were full of agony and the screams of the dying. And the list in the hall of the dead grew longer at every sunrise. Dun Pinar fell, his throat torn apart by a jagged dagger. Bar Britan was found under a mound of Nadir bodies, a broken lance jutting from his chest. Tall Antaheim of the Thirty was struck by a javelin in the back. Elicas of the legion was trapped by the rampart towers as he hurled himself at the Nadir, screaming defiance, and fell beneath a

score of blades. Jorak, the huge outlaw, had his brains
dashed out by a club and, dying, grabbed two Nadir warriors and threw himself from the battlements, dragging
them screaming to their deaths on the rocks below.

Amid the chaos of slashing swords many deeds of individual heroism passed unseen. One young soldier battling
back to back with Druss saw an enemy lancer bearing
down on the old man. Unthinking, he threw himself in the
way of the flashing steel point, to die writhing among the
other broken bodies on the ramparts. Another soldier, an officer named Portitac, leapt into the breach near the gate
tower and stepped onto the ramparts, where he seized the
top of a ladder and flung himself forward, pulling the ladder out from the wall. Twenty Nadir near the top died with
him on the rocks, and five others broke limbs. Many were
such tales of bravery.

And still the battles raged. Rek now sported a slanting
scar from eyebrow to chin, gleaming red as he battled on.
Orrin had lost three fingers from his left hand but after only
two days behind the lines had joined his men once more on
the wall.

From the capital at Drenan the messages came endlessly:

Hold on.
Give Woundweaver time.
Just one more month.

And the defenders knew they could not hold.
But still they fought on.

Twice the Nadir tried night attacks, but on both occasions
Serbitar warned the defenders and the assailants paid dearly
for their efforts. At night, handholds were difficult to find
and the long climb to the battlements was fraught with
peril. Hundreds of tribesmen died without need for the
touch of Drenai steel or a black-shafted arrow.

Now the nights were silent and in some ways as bad as
the days. For the peace and tranquillity of the moon darkness acted as a weird counterpoint to the crimson agonies
of the sunlight. Men had time to think: to dream of wives,

children, farms, and even more potently of a future that might have been.

Hogun and Bowman had taken to walking together on the battlements at night, the grim legion general and the bright witty outlaw. Hogun found that in Bowman's company he could forget the loss of Elicas; he could even laugh again. For his part, Bowman felt a kinship with the gan, for he, too, had a serious side, although he kept it well hidden.

But on this particular night Bowman was in a more melancholy mood, and his eyes were distant.

"What ails you, man?" asked Hogun.

"Memories," answered the archer, leaning over the ramparts to stare at the Nadir camp fires below.

"They must be either very bad or very good to touch you so."

"These are very bad, my friend. Do you believe in gods?"

"Sometimes. Usually when my back is against a wall and the enemy surrounds me," said Hogun.

"I believe in the twin powers of growth and malevolence. I believe that on rare occasions each of these powers chooses a man and in different ways destroys him."

"And these powers have touched you, Bowman?" asked Hogun gently.

"Perhaps. Think back on recent history—you will find examples."

"I do not need to. I know where this tale is leading," said Hogun.

"What do you know?" asked the archer, turning to face the dark-cloaked officer. Hogun smiled gently, though he noted that Bowman's fingers were curled around the hilt of his dagger.

"I know that you are a man whose life has been marred by some secret tragedy: a wife dead, a father slain ... something. There may even be some dark deed which you perpetrated and cannot forget. But even if that were the case, the very fact that you remember it with such pain means that you acted out of character. Put it behind you, man! Who among us can change the past?"

"I wish I could tell you," said Bowman. "But I cannot.

I am sorry, I am not fit company this evening. You go on.
I will stay here a while."

Hogun wanted to clap his hand on the other's shoulder
and say something witty to break the mood, as Bowman
had so often done for him. But he could not. There were
times when a grim-faced warrior was needed, even loved,
but this was not one of them, and he cursed himself and left
silently.

For over an hour Bowman stood on the ramparts, staring
out over the valley, listening to the faint songs of the Nadir
women drifting out from the far camp below.

"You are troubled?" said a voice.

Bowman swung around to face Rek. The young earl was
dressed in the clothes in which he had arrived: thigh-length
doeskin boots, a high-collared tunic with a gold-embroid-
ered collar, and a reversed sheepskin jerkin. By his side
was his longsword.

"I am merely tired," said Bowman.

"I, too. Is my scar fading?"

Bowman peered closely at the jagged red line from brow
to chin. "You were lucky not to lose an eye," he commented.

"Useless Nadir steel," said Rek. "I made a perfect block,
and his blasted sword snapped and lashed across my face.
Good gods, man, have you any idea how long I've protected my face?"

"It's too late to worry about that now," said Bowman,
grinning.

"Some people are born ugly," said Rek. "It's not their
fault, and I for one have never held it against a man that he
is ugly. But others—and I count myself among them—are
born with handsome features. That is a gift which should
not be lightly taken away."

"I take it you made the perpetrator pay for his deed."

"Naturally! And you know, I think he was smiling even
as I slew him. But then, he was an ugly man. I mean really
ugly. It's not right."

"Life can be so unfair," agreed Bowman. "But you must
look on the bright side, my lord Earl. You see, unlike me,
you were never stupendously handsome. Merely well fea-
tured. The brows were too thick, the mouth a shade too

wide. And your hair is now growing a little thinner. Now, had you been blessed with the nearly miraculous good looks possessed by such as I, you would have truly had something to grieve over."

"There is something in what you say," said Rek. "You have indeed been greatly blessed. It was probably nature's way of making it up to you for being short."

"Short? I am almost as tall as you."

"Ah, but what a large word 'almost' is. Can a man be almost alive? Almost right? In the question of height, my friend, we do not deal in subtle shades of gray. I am taller; you are shorter. But I would concur there is not a more handsome short man at the fortress."

"Women have always found me the perfect height," said Bowman. "At least when I dance with them, I can whisper love words in their ears. With your long shanks, their heads would nestle near your armpit."

"Get a lot of time for dancing in the forest, do you?" asked Rek amiably.

"I didn't always live in the forest. My family . . ." Bowman stuttered to silence.

"I know your family background," said Rek. "But it's about time you talked about it. You've carried it too long."

"How could you know?"

"Serbitar told me. As you know, he has been inside your mind . . . when you carried his messages to Druss."

"I suppose the entire damned fortress knows," said Bowman. "I will leave at dawn."

"Only Serbitar and I know the story—and the truth of it. But leave if you will."

"The truth of it is that I killed my father and brother." Bowman was white-faced and tense.

"Twin accidents—you know it well!" said Rek. "Why must you torture yourself?"

"Why? Because I wonder at accidents in life. I wonder how many are caused by our own secret desires. There was a footracer once, the finest I ever saw. He was preparing for the great games, to run for the first time against the fastest men from many nations. On the day before the race he fell and twisted his ankle. Was it really an accident, or was he frightened to face the great test?"

"Only he will ever know," said Rek. "But therein lies the secret. He knows, and so should you. Serbitar tells me that you were hunting with your father and brother. Your father was to the left, your brother to the right, when you followed a deer into the thicket. A bush before you rustled, and you aimed and let the arrow fly. But it was your father, who had come unannounced. How could you know he would do such a thing?"

"The point is that he taught us never to shoot until we saw the target."

"So you made a mistake. What else is new on the face of the world?"

"And my brother?"

"He saw what you had done, misunderstood, and ran at you in a rage. You pushed him away, and he fell, striking his head on a rock. No one could wish such a burden on himself. But you have nursed it, and it is now time for you to release it."

"I never loved my father or my brother," said Bowman. "My father killed my mother. He left her alone for months and had many mistresses. When my mother took one lover, he had him blinded and her slain ... horribly."

"I know. Don't dwell on it."

"And my brother was made in his image."

"This also I know."

"And do you know what I felt when they were both lying dead at my feet?"

"Yes. You were exultant."

"And is that not terrible?"

"I don't know if you have considered this, Bowman, but think on it. You blame the gods for bringing a curse upon you, but the curse really fell on the two men who deserved it.

"I don't know yet whether I fully believe in fate, but certain things do happen in a man's life which he cannot explain. My being here, for instance. Druss's conviction that he will die here, for he has made a pact with death. And you ... But I do believe that you were merely the instrument of ... who knows? ... a law of natural justice, perhaps.

"Whatever you believe about yourself, know this: Serbitar

searched your heart, and he found no malice there. And he *knows*."

"Perhaps," said Bowman. Then he grinned suddenly. "Have you noticed that when Serbitar removes that horse-hair helm, he is shorter than I am?"

The room was Spartanly furnished: a rug, a pillow, and a chair, all bunched beneath the small window by which the albino stood naked and alone. Moonlight bathed his pale skin, and the night breeze ruffled his hair. His shoulders were bowed, his eyes closed. Weariness was upon him like no other weariness he had felt in all his young life. For it was born of the spirit and the truth.

The philosophers often talked of lies sitting under the tongue like salted honey. This, Serbitar knew, was true enough. But more often the hidden truth was worse. Far worse. For it settled in the belly and grew to engulf the spirit.

Below him were the Vagrian quarters that housed Suboden and the three hundred men who had come from Dros Segril. For several days he had fought alongside his personal bodyguard and become again the Prince of Dros Segril, son of Earl Drada. But the experience had been painful, for his own men had made the sign of the protective horn as he approached. They rarely spoke to him, and then only to answer a direct question speedily. Suboden, blunt-speaking as always, had asked the albino to return to his comrades.

"We are here, Prince Serbitar, because it is our duty. This we will accomplish best without you beside us."

More painful than this, however, was the long discussion he had had with the Abbot of Swords, the man he revered, loved as a father, mentor, and friend.

Serbitar closed his eyes and opened his mind, soaring free of the body prison and sweeping aside the curtains of time.

Back he traveled, back and farther back. Thirteen long, wearisome, joy-filled years flowed past him, and he saw again the caravan that had brought him to the Abbot of Swords. Riding at the head of ten warriors was the giant red-bearded Drada, the young Earl of Segril—battle-hardened, volatile, a pitiless enemy but a true friend. Behind him ten of his most trusted warriors, men who would die for him without a moment's hesitation, for they loved him above life. At the rear is a cart upon which, on a straw pallet covered with silken sheets, lies the young prince, a canvas screen shielding his ghost-white face from the sun.

Drada wheels the black horse round and gallops back to the cart. He leans on his saddle horn and glances down at the boy. The boy looks up; framed against the bright sky, he can see only the flaring wings of his father's battle helmet.

The cart is moving again, into the shade of the ornate black gates. They swing open, and a man appears.

"I bid you welcome, Drada," he says, the voice at variance with the silver armor he wears, for it is a gentle sound, the voice of a poet.

"I bring you my son," answers the earl, his voice gruff, soldierly.

Vintar moves to the cart and looks down on the boy. He places a hand on the pale forehead, smiles, and pats the boy's head.

"Come walk with me, boy," he says.

"He cannot walk," says Drada.

"But he can," says Vintar.

The boy turns his red eyes toward Vintar questioningly and for the first time in his lonely life feels a touching of minds. There are no words. Vintar's gentle poet's face enters with a promise of strength and friendship. The fragile muscles on Serbitar's skeletal body begin to shake as an infusion of power regenerates wasted cells.

"What is the matter with the boy?" Drada's voice fills with alarm.

"Nothing. Say farewell to your son."

The red-bearded warrior turns his horse's head to the north and gazes down at the white-haired child. "Do as you are told. Be good." He hesitates, pretends his horse is skittish. He is trying to find words for a final farewell, but he cannot. Always he has found difficulty with this red-eyed child. "Be good," he says again, then raises an arm and leads his men northward on the long journey home.

As the wagon pulls away, bright sunlight streams onto

the pallet and the boy reacts as if lanced. His face mirrors pain; his eyes squeeze shut. Vintar gently seeks his mind and pulses: "Stand now and follow the pictures I will place on your eyelids."

At once the pain eases, and the boy can see more clearly than ever before. And his muscles lift him at last, a sensation he thought he had forgotten since a year ago, when he collapsed in the snow of the Delnoch mountains. From that moment to this he has lain paralyzed, unspeaking.

Now he stands, and with eyes tightly shut he sees more clearly. Without guilt he realizes he has forgotten his father and is happy for it.

The spirit of the older Serbitar tastes again the total joy that flooded the youth that day as, arm in arm with Vintar the soul, he walked across the courtyard until at last, in a brightly lit corner, they came to a tiny rose cutting nestling by a high stone wall.

"This is your rose, Serbitar. Love it. Cherish it and grow with it. One day a flower will form on that tiny plant. And its fragrance will be for you alone."

"Is it a white rose?"

"It is whatever you will it to be."

And through the years that followed Serbitar found peace and joy in comradeship, but never more than in the experience of true contentment with Vintar the soul on that first day.

Vintar had taught him to recognize the herb Lorassium and eat of its leaves. At first they had made him drowsy and filled his mind with colors. But as the days had passed, his powerful young mind had mastered the visions and the green juices had strengthened his weak blood. Even his eyes had changed color to reflect the power of the plant.

And he had learned to run again, savoring the joy of the wind in his face, to climb and wrestle, to laugh and live.

And he had learned to speak without speaking, move without moving, and see without seeing.

Through all these blissful years Serbitar's rose had blossomed and grown.

A white rose . . .

* * *

And now it had all come to this! One glimpse into the future had destroyed thirteen years of training and belief. One speeding shaft, viewed through the mists of time, had changed his destiny.

Serbitar had stared horror-struck at the scene below him on the battle-scarred walls of the Dros. His mind had recoiled from the violence he saw there, and he had fled, comet-swift, to a far corner of a distant universe, losing himself and his sanity among exploding stars and new suns' birthing.

And still Vintar had found him.

"You must return."

"I cannot. I have seen."

"As have I."

"Then you know that I would rather die than see it again."

"But you must, for it is your destiny."

"Then I refuse my destiny."

"And your friends? Do you refuse them also?"

"I cannot watch you die again, Vintar."

"Why not? I myself have seen the scene a hundred times. I have even written a poem about it."

"As we are now—shall we be again, after death? Free souls?"

"I do not know, but I would have it so. Now return to your duty. I have pulsed the Thirty. They will keep your body alive for as long as they can."

"They always have. Why should I be the last to die?"

"Because we would have it so. We love you, Serbitar. And always have. A shy child you were, who had never tasted friendship. Suspicious you were of the slightest touch or embrace—a soul crying alone in a cosmic wilderness. Even now you are alone."

"But I love you all."

"Because you need our love."

"Not so, Vintar!"

"Do you love Rek and Virae?"

"They are not of the Thirty."

"Neither were you until we made it so."

* * *

And Serbitar had returned to the fortress and felt ashamed. But the shame he had felt earlier was as nothing compared with the feeling he now experienced.

Was it but an hour since that he had walked the ramparts with Vintar, and complained of many things, and confessed to many sins?

"You are wrong, Serbitar. So wrong. I also feel blood lust in battle. Who does not? Ask Arbedark or Menahem. While we are still men, we will feel as other men do."

"Then is it for nothing that we are priests?" cried Serbitar. "We have spent years of our lives studying the insanity of war, of man's lust for power, his need for bloodshed. We raise ourselves above the common man with powers that are almost godlike. Yet in the final analysis we come to this, lusting after battle and death. It *is* for nothing!"

"Your conceit is colossal, Serbitar," said Vintar, an edge to his voice and the suggestion of anger showing in his eyes. "You speak of 'godlike.' You speak of the 'common man.' Where in your words is the humility we strive for?

"When you first came to the temple, you were weak and lonely and several years the youngest. But you learned the more swiftly. And you were chosen as the voice. Did you only acquire the disciplines and forgo the philosophy?"

"It would appear so," answered Serbitar.

"You are wrong again. For in wisdom there is suffering. You are pained not because you disbelieve but because you believe. Let us return to basics. Why do we travel to a distant war?"

"To die."

"Why do we choose this method? Why not simply allow ourselves to starve?"

"Because in war a man's will to live is strongest. He will fight hard to stay alive. He will learn again to love life."

"And what will that force *us* to face?"

"Our doubts," whispered Serbitar.

"But you never thought that such doubt would come to you, so sure were you of your godlike powers?"

"Yes, I was sure. Now I am not. Is this such a great sin?"

"You know it is not. Why am I alive, my boy? Why did I not die with Magnar's Thirty two decades ago?"

"You were the one chosen to found the new temple."

"Why was I chosen?"

"You were the most perfect. It has to be so."

"Then why was I not the leader?"

"I do not understand you."

"How is the leader chosen?"

"I know not. You have never said.'

"Then guess, Serbitar."

"Because he is the best choice. The most . . ."

"Perfect?"

"I would have said so, but I see where you are leading. If you were the most perfect, why did Magnar lead? Well, why did he?"

"You have seen the future; you should have seen and heard this conversation. You tell me."

"You know that I did not," said Serbitar. "There was no time for study of the minutiae."

"Oh, Serbitar, still you will not understand! What you saw and chose to examine *was* the minutiae, the meaningless and the trivial. What does it mean to the history of this planet that this Dros falls? How many other castles have fallen throughout the ages? Of what cosmic importance was their failure? How vital are our deaths?"

"Tell me then, my lord abbot, how is the leader chosen?"

"Have you not guessed it, my son?"

"I believe so,"

"Then speak."

"He is the least perfect of the acolytes," said Serbitar softly, his green eyes scarching Vintar's face and begging denial.

"He is the least perfect," echoed Vintar sadly.

"But why?" asked Serbitar.

"So that his task will be the more difficult, the more demanding. To give him the chance to rise and match the position he holds."

"And I have failed?"

"Not yet, Serbitar. Not yet."

◊ 24 ◊

Day by day more people left the siege city, piling their possessions onto carts, wagons, or the backs of mules and forming convoys that snaked their way inland toward the relative security of the Skoda mountains and the capital beyond.

With each departure fresh problems faced the defenders. Fighting men had to be seconded to other duties, such as latrine clearance, stores supply, and food preparation. Now the drain on resources came on two fronts.

Druss was furious and insisted that the gates be closed, the evacuation stopped. Rek pointed out that even more soldiers would then be needed to police the south road.

Then the first disaster of the campaign struck the defenders.

On the high day of summer—ten weeks after the battle began—Musif fell and chaos reigned. The Nadir breached the wall at the center, driving a wedge into the killing ground beyond. The men, threatened with encirclement, fell back and raced for the fire gullies. Running skirmishes began as discipline fled, and two gully bridges collapsed as warriors milled upon them.

On Kania, Wall Three, Rek waited as long as he dared before ordering the gullies lit with flame arrows. Druss, Orrin, and Hogun scrambled to safety just as the blaze took. But beyond the gully more than eight hundred Drenai warriors battled on hopelessly in tight shield rings that grew smaller moment by moment. Many on Kania turned away, unable to bear the sight of their friends' futile battles. Rek stood with fists clenched and watched in despair. The fight-

269

ing did not last long. Hopelessly outnumbered, the Drenai were engulfed, and the battle song of victory was sung by thousands of tribesmen.

They gathered before the flames chanting, waving blood-stained swords and axes in the air. Few on the walls under-stood the words, but understanding was unnecessary. The message was primal, the meaning clear. It struck the heart and soul with blistering clarity.

"What do they sing?" Rek asked Druss as the old man recovered his breath following the long rope climb to the ramparts.

"It's their glory chant:

> Nadir we,
> Youth-born,
> bloodletters
> ax wielders,
> victors still."

Beyond the fire tribesmen burst into the field hospital, slaying men in their beds and dragging others out into the sunlight, where they could be seen by their comrades on the wall. Then they were peppered with arrows or slowly dis-membered. One was even nailed to the window shutters of the barracks, to hang screaming for two hours before being disemboweled and beheaded.

The Drenai dead, stripped of their weapons and armor, were hurled into the fire gullies, and the stench of burning flesh filled the air and stung the eyes.

The evacuation at the south gates became a flood as the city emptied. Soldiers joined in, discarding their weapons and mingling with the crowds. No effort was made to stop them, on Rek's direct order.

In a little house near the Street of Millers Maerie tried to comfort the small child sobbing in her arms. The noise in the street outside frightened her as families loaded their possessions onto carts and wagons tethered with oxen or milk cows. It was pandemonium.

Maerie cuddled the child, crooning a lullaby tune and kissing the tight curls on his head.

"I must go back to the wall," said her husband, a tall young man with dark hair and wide, gentle blue eyes. How tired he looked, hollow-eyed and gaunt.

"Don't go, Carin," she said as he strapped his sword belt about his waist.

"Don't go? I must."

"Let us leave Delnoch. We have friends in Purdol, and you could find work there."

He was not an intuitive man, and he missed the note of desperation in her voice, failed to sense the rising panic behind her eyes.

"Don't let these fools frighten you, Maerie. Druss is still with us, and we will hold Kania. I promise you."

The sobbing child clutched his mother's dress, soothed by the gentle strength of his father's voice. Too young to understand the words yet, he was comforted by the pitch and tone. The noise outside receded from him, and he slept on his mother's shoulder. But Maerie was older and wiser than the child, and to her the words were just words.

"Listen to me, Carin. I want to leave. Today!"

"I can't talk now. I must go back. I will see you later. It will be all right." Leaning forward, he kissed her, then stepped into the chaos of the street.

She looked around her, remembering: the chest by the door, a gift from Carin's parents. The chairs made by her uncle, Damus, fashioned with care like all his work. They had brought the chairs and chest with them two years before.

Good years?

Carin was kind, thoughtful, loving. There was so much goodness to him. Easing the child into his cot, she wandered to the small bedroom, shutting the window against the noise. Soon the Nadir would come. The door would be smashed in, and filthy tribesmen would come for her, tearing at her clothing . . .

She shut her eyes.

Druss was still here, he had said.

Stupid Carin! Kind, loving, thoughtful, stupid Carin! Carin the miller.

She had never been truly happy with him, though without this war she might never have realized it. She had been so close to contentment. Then he had joined the defenders, coming home so proudly in that ludicrous breastplate and oversized helm.

Stupid Carin. Kind Carin.

The door opened, and she turned to see her friend Delis, her blond hair covered in a travel shawl and a heavy cloak over her shoulders.

"Are you coming?" she asked.

"Yes."

"Is Carin coming with you?"

"No."

Swiftly she gathered her belongings, pushing them into a canvas bag issued to Carin. Delis carried the bag to the wagon outside while Maerie lifted her son from his cot, wrapping him in a second blanket. Stooping, she pulled open the small chest, pushing aside the linen and pulling clear the small bag of silver that Carin had hidden there.

She did not bother to close the door.

In the keep Druss raged at Rek, swearing to kill any deserter he recognized.

"It's too late for that," said Rek.

"Damn you, boy!" muttered Druss. "We have fewer than three thousand men. How long do you think we will hold if we allow desertions?"

"How long if we don't?" snapped Rek. "We are finished, anyway! Serbitar says Kania can be held for maybe two days, Sumitos for perhaps three, Valteri the same, and Geddon less. Ten days in all. Ten miserable days!" The young earl leaned on the balcony rail above the gates and watched the convoys start south. "Look at them, Druss! Farmers, bakers, tradesmen. What right have we to ask them to die? What will it matter to them if we fail? The Nadir will not kill every baker in Drenan; it will just mean a change of masters."

"You give up too easily," snarled Druss.

"I'm a realist. And don't give me any Skeln Pass lectures. I'm not going anywhere."

"You might as well," said Druss, slumping into a leather chair. "You have already lost hope."

Rek turned from the window, eyes blazing. "What is it

with you warriors? It is understandable that you talk in clichés but unforgivable if you think in them. Lost hope, indeed! I never *had* any hope. This enterprise was doomed from the start, but we do what we can and what we must. So a young farmer with a wife and children decides to go home. Good! He shows a sense which men like you and I will never understand. They will sing songs about us, but he will ensure that there are people to sing them. He plants. We destroy.

"Anyway, he has played his part and fought like a man. It is criminal that he should feel the need to flee in shame."

"Why not give them all the chance to go home?" asked Druss. "Then you and I could stand on the walls and invite the Nadir to come at us one at a time like sportsmen."

Suddenly Rek smiled, tension and anger flowing from him. "I won't argue with you, Druss," he said softly. "You are a man I admire above all others. But in this I think you are wrong. Help yourself to wine. I shall be back soon."

Less than an hour later the earl's message was being read to all sections.

Bregan brought the news to Gilad as he ate in the shade offered by the field hospital under the towering cliff face of West Kania.

"We can go home," said Bregan, his face flushed. "We can be there by harvest supper!"

"I don't understand," said Gilad. "Have we surrendered?"

"No. The earl says that any who wish to leave can now do so. He says that we can leave with pride, that we have fought like men—and as men, we must be given the right to go home."

"Are we going to surrender?" asked Gilad, puzzled.

"I don't think so," said Bregan.

"Then I shall not go."

"But the earl says it's all right!"

"I don't care what he says."

"I don't understand this, Gil. Lots of the others are going. And it is true that we've played our part. Haven't we? I mean, we've done our best."

"I suppose so." Gilad rubbed his tired eyes and turned to

watch the smoke from the fire gully drift lazily skyward.
"They did their best, too," he whispered.

"Who did?"

"Those who died. Those who are still going to die."

"But the earl says it's all right. He says that we can leave
with our heads held high. Proud."

"Is that what he says?"

"Yes."

"Well, my head wouldn't be high."

"I don't understand you, I really don't. You have said all
along that we can't hold this fortress. Now we have a
chance to leave. Why can't you just accept it and come
with us?"

"Because I'm a fool. Give my love to everyone back
there."

"You know I won't go unless you come, too."

"Don't you start being a fool, Breg! You've got everything to live for. Just picture little Legan toddling toward
you and all the stories you will be able to tell. Go on. *Go!*"

"No. I don't know why you're staying, but I shall stay,
too."

"That you must not do," said Gilad gently. "I want you
to go back, I really do. After all, if you don't, there will be
no one to tell them what a hero I am. Seriously, Breg, I
would feel so much better if I knew that you were away
from all this. The earl's right. Men like you have played
their part. Magnificently.

"And as for me . . . well, I just want to stay here. I've
learned so much about myself and about other men. I'm not
needed anywhere but here. I'm not necessary. I will never
be a farmer, and I have neither the money to be a businessman nor the breeding to be a prince. I'm a misfit. This is
where I belong, with all the other misfits. Please, Bregan.
Please go!"

There were tears in Bregan's eyes, and the two men embraced. Then the curly-haired young farmer rose. "I hope
everything works out for you, Gil. I'll tell them all—I
promise I will. Good luck!"

"And to you, farmer. Take your ax. They can hang it in
the village hall."

Gilad watched him walk back toward the postern gates

and the keep beyond. Bregan turned once and waved. Then he was gone.

Altogether 650 men chose to leave.

Two thousand forty remained. Added to these were Bowman, Caessa, and fifty archers. The other outlaws, having fulfilled their promise, returned to Skultik.

"Too damned few now," muttered Druss as the meeting ended.

"I never liked crowds, anyway," said Bowman lightly.

Hogun, Orrin, Rek, and Serbitar remained in their seats as Druss and Bowman wandered out into the night.

"Don't despair, old horse," said Bowman, slapping Druss on the back. "Things could be worse, you know."

"Really? How?"

"Well, we could be out of wine."

"We *are* out of wine."

"We are? That's terrible. I would never have stayed had I known. Luckily, however, I do just happen to have a couple of flagons of Lentrian red stored in my new quarters. So at least we can enjoy tonight. We might even be able to save some for tomorrow."

"That's a good idea," said Druss. "Maybe we could bottle it and lay it down for a couple of months to age a little. Lentrian red, my foot! That stuff of yours is brewed in Skultik from soap, potatoes, and rats' entrails. You would get more taste from a Nadir slop bucket."

"You have the advantage of me there, old horse, since I have never tasted a Nadir slop bucket. But my brew does hit the spot rather."

"I think I'd rather suck a Nadir's armpit," muttered Druss.

"Fine, I'll drink it all myself," snapped Bowman.

"No need to get touchy, boy. I'm with you. I have always believed that friends should suffer together."

The artery writhed under Virae's fingers like a snake, spewing blood into the cavity of the stomach.

"Tighter!" ordered Calvar Syn, his own hands deep in the wound, pushing aside blue slimy entrails as he sought frantically to stem the bleeding within. It was useless; he knew it was useless, but he owed it to the man beneath him to use every ounce of his skill. Despite all his efforts he could feel the life oozing between his fingers. Another stitch, another small Pyrrhic victory.

The man died as the eleventh stitch sealed the stomach wall.

"He's dead?" asked Virae. Calvar nodded, straightening his back. "But the blood is still flowing," she said.

"It will do so for a few moments."

"I really thought he would live," she whispered. Calvar wiped his bloody hands on a linen cloth and walked around beside her. He put his hands on her shoulders, turning her toward him.

"His chances were one in a thousand even if I had stopped the bleeding. The lance cut his spleen, and gangrene was almost certain."

Her eyes were red, her face gray. She blinked and her body shook, but there were no tears as she looked down at the dead face.

"I thought he had a beard," she said, confused.

"That was the one before."

"Oh, yes. He died, too."

"You should rest." Putting his arms around her, he led her from the room and out into the ward, past the stacked rows of triple-tiered bunk beds. Orderlies moved quietly among the rows. Everywhere the smell of death and the sweet, nauseous odor of putrefaction were mixed with the antiseptic bitterness of Lorassium juice and hot water scented with lemon mint.

Perhaps it was the unwelcome perfume, but she was surprised to find that the well was not dry and tears could still flow.

He led her to a back room, filled a basin with warm water, and washed the blood from her hands and face, dabbing her gently as if she were a child.

"He told me that I love war," she said. "But it's not true. Maybe it was then. I don't know anymore."

"Only a fool loves war," said Calvar, "or a man who has never seen it. The trouble is that the survivors forget about the horrors and remember only the battle lust. They pass on that memory, and other men hunger for it. Put on your cloak and get some air. Then you will feel better."

"I don't think I can come back tomorrow, Calvar. I will stay with Rek at the wall."

"I understand."

"I feel so helpless watching men die in here." She smiled, "I don't like feeling helpless, I'm not used to it."

He watched her from the doorway, her tall figure draped in a white cloak, the night breeze billowing her hair.

"I feel helpless, too," he said softly.

The last death had touched him more deeply than it should have, but then, he had known the man, whereas others were but nameless strangers.

Carin, the former miller. Calvar remembered that the man had a wife and son living at Delnoch.

"Well, at least someone will mourn for you, Carin," he whispered to the stars.

◊ 25 ◊

REK SAT AND watched the stars shining high above the keep tower and the passage of an occasional cloud, black against the moonlit sky. The clouds were like cliffs in the sky, jagged and threatening, inexorable and sentient. Rek pulled his gaze from the window and rubbed his eyes. He had known fatigue before but never this soul-numbing weariness, this depression of the spirit. The room was dark now. He had forgotten to light the candles, so intent had he been on the darkening sky. He glanced about him. So open and welcoming during the hours of daylight, the room was now shadow-haunted and empty of life. He was an interloper. He drew his cloak about him.

He missed Virae, but she was working at the field hospital with the exhausted Calvar Syn. Nevertheless the need in him was great, and he rose to go to her. Instead he just stood there. Cursing, he lit the candles. Logs lay ready in the fireplace, so he lit the fire—though it was not cold—and sat in the firm leather chair watching the small flames grow through the kindling and eat into the thicker logs above. The breeze fanned the flame, causing the shadows to dance, and Rek began to relax.

"You fool," he said to himself as the flames roared and he began to sweat. He removed his cloak and boots and pulled the chair back from the blaze.

A soft tap at the door roused Rek from his thoughts. He called out, and Serbitar entered the room. For a moment Rek did not recognize him; he was without his armor, dressed in a tunic of green, his long white hair tied at the nape of the neck.

"Am I disturbing you, Rek?" he said.

"Not at all. Sit down and join me."

"Thank you. Are you cold?"

"No. I just like to watch fires burn."

"I do, too. It helps me think. A primal memory, perhaps, of a warm cave and safety from predatory animals," said Serbitar.

"I wasn't alive then—despite my haggard appearance."

"But you were. The atoms that make up your body are as old as the universe."

"I have not the faintest idea what you're talking about, though I don't doubt that it is all true," said Rek.

An uneasy silence developed, then both men spoke at once, and Rek laughed. Serbitar smiled and shrugged.

"I am unused to casual conversation. Unskilled."

"Most people are when it comes down to it. It's an art," said Rek. "The thing to do is relax and enjoy the silences. That's what friends are all about; they are people with whom you can be silent."

"Truly?"

"My word of honor as an earl."

"I am glad to see you retain your humor. I would have thought it impossible to do so under the circumstances."

"Adaptability, my dear Serbitar. You can only spend so long thinking about death—then it becomes boring. I have discovered that my great fear is not of dying but of being a bore."

"You are seldom boring, my friend."

"Seldom? 'Never' is the word I was looking for."

"I beg your pardon. 'Never' is the word I was, of course, seeking."

"How will tomorrow be?"

"I cannot say," answered Serbitar swiftly. "Where is the lady Virae?"

"With Calvar Syn. Half the civilian nurses have fled south."

"You cannot blame them," said Serbitar. He stood and walked to the window. "The stars are bright tonight," he said. "Though I suppose it would be more accurate to say that the angle of the earth makes visibility stronger."

"I think I prefer 'the stars are bright tonight,' " said Rek, who had joined Serbitar at the window.

Below them Virae was walking slowly, a white cloak wrapped about her shoulders and her long hair flowing in the night breeze.

"I think I will join her, if you'll excuse me," said Rek.

Serbitar smiled. "Of course. I will sit by the fire and think, if I may!"

"Make yourself at home," said Rek, pulling on his boots.

Moments after Rek had left, Vintar entered. He, too, had forsaken armor for a simple tunic of white wool, hooded and thick.

"That was painful for you, Serbitar. You should have allowed me to come," he said, patting the younger man's shoulder.

"I could not tell him the truth."

"But you did not lie," whispered Vintar.

"When does evasion of the truth become a lie?"

"I do not know. But you brought them together, and that was your purpose. They have this night."

"Should I have told him?"

"No. He would have sought to alter that which cannot be altered."

"Cannot or must not?" asked Serbitar.

"Cannot. He could order her not to fight tomorrow, and she would refuse. He cannot lock her away; she is an earl's daughter."

"If we told her?"

"She would refuse to accept it or else defy fate."

"Then she is doomed."

"No. She is merely going to die."

"I will do everything in my power to protect her, Vintar. You know that."

"As will I. But we will fail. Tomorrow night you must show the earl Egel's secret."

"He will be in no mood to see it."

Rek put his arm about her shoulders, leaned forward, and kissed her cheek.

"I love you," he whispered.

She smiled and leaned into him, saying nothing.

"I simply can't say it," said Virae, her large eyes turned full upon him.

"That's all right. Do you feel it?"

"You know that I do. I just find it hard to say. Romantic words sound ... strange ... clumsy when I use them. It's as if my throat wasn't made to form the sounds. I feel foolish. Do you understand what I'm saying?" He nodded and kissed her again. "And anyway, I haven't had your practice."

"True," he said.

"What does that mean?" she snapped.

"I was just agreeing with you."

"Well, don't. I'm in no mood for humor. It's easy for you—you're a talker, a storyteller. Your conceit carries you on. I want to say all the things I feel, but I cannot. And then, when you say them first, my throat just seizes up and I know I should say something, but I still can't."

"Listen, lovely lady, it doesn't matter! They are just words, as you say. I'm good with words; you're good with actions. I know that you love me; I don't expect you to echo me every time I tell you how I feel. I was just thinking earlier about something Horeb told me years ago. He said that for every man there is the one woman and that I would know mine when I saw her. And I do."

"When I saw you," she said, turning in to him and hugging his waist, "I thought you were a popinjay." She laughed.

"You should have seen your face as that outlaw charged toward you!"

"I was concentrating. I've told you before that marksmanship was never my strong point."

"You were petrified."

"True."

"But you still rescued me."

"True. I'm a natural hero."

"No, you're not, and that's why I love you. You're just a man who does his best and tries to be honorable. That is rare."

"Despite my conceit—and you may find this hard to believe—I get very uncomfortable when faced with compliments."

"But I want to say what I feel; it's important to me. You are the first man I ever really felt comfortable with as a woman. You brought me to life. I may die during this siege, but I want you to know that it has been worth it."

"Don't talk about dying. Look at the stars. Feel the night. It's beautiful, isn't it?"

"Yes, it is. Why don't you take me back to the keep and then I can show you how actions speak louder than words."

"Why don't I just do that!"

They made love without passion but gently, lovingly, and fell asleep watching the stars through the bedroom window.

The Nadir captain Ogasi urged his men on, baying the war chant of Ulric's Wolfshead tribe and smashing his ax into the face of a tall defender. The man's hands scrabbled at the wound as he fell back. The hideous battle song carried them forward, cleaving the ranks and gaining them a foothold on the grass beyond.

But as always Deathwalker and the white templars rallied the defenders.

Ogasi's hatred gave him power as he cut left and right, trying to force his way toward the old man. A sword cut his brow, and he staggered momentarily, recovering to disembowel the swordsman. On the left the line was being pushed back, but on the right it was sweeping out like the horn of a bull.

The powerful Nadir wanted to scream his triumph to the skies.

At last they had them!

But again the Drenai rallied. Pushing himself back into the throng in order to wipe away the blood from his eyes, Ogasi watched the tall Drenai and his sword maiden block the horn as it swung. Leading maybe twenty warriors, the tall man in the silver breastplate and blue cape seemed to have gone mad. His laughter sang out over the Nadir chant, and men fell back before him.

His baresark rage carried him deep among the tribesmen, and he used no defense. His red-drenched sword blade sliced, hammered, and cut into their ranks. Beside him the woman ducked and parried, protecting his left, her own slender blade every bit as deadly.

Slowly the horn collapsed in upon itself, and Ogasi found himself being drawn back to the battlements. He tripped over the body of a Drenai archer who was still clutching his bow. Kneeling, Ogasi dragged it from the dead hand and pulled a black-shafted arrow from the quiver. Leaping lightly to the battlements, he strained for sight of Deathwalker, but the old man was at the center, obscured by Nadir bodies. Not so the tall baresarker—men were scattering before him. Ogasi notched the arrow to the string, drew, aimed, and with a whispered curse let fly.

The shaft skinned Rek's forearm—and flew on.

Virae turned, seeking Rek, and the shaft punched through her mail shirt to bury itself below her right breast. She grunted at the impact, staggered, and half fell. A Nadir warrior broke through the line, racing toward her.

Gritting her teeth, she drew herself upright, blocked his wild attack, and opened his jugular with a backhand cut.

"Rek!" she called, panic welling within her as her lungs began to bubble, absorbing the arterial blood. But he could not hear her. Pain erupted, and she fell, twisting her body away from the arrow so as not to drive it deeper.

Serbitar ran to her side, lifting her head.

"Damn!" she said. "I'm dying!"

He touched her hand, and immediately the pain vanished. "Thank you, friend! Where's Rek?"

"He is baresark, Virae. I could not reach him now."

"Oh, gods! Listen to me—don't let him be alone for a while after . . . you know. He is a great romantic fool, and I think he might do something silly. You understand?"

"I understand. I will stay with him."

"No, not you. Send Druss. He is older, and Rek worships him." She turned her eyes to the sky. A solitary storm cloud floated there, lost and angry. "He warned me to wear a breastplate, but it's so damned heavy." The cloud seemed larger now. She tried to mention it to Serbitar, but the cloud loomed and the darkness engulfed her.

Rek stood at the balcony window, gripping the rail, tears streaming from his eyes and uncontrollable sobs bursting through gritted teeth. Behind him lay Virae, still, cold, and at peace. Her face was white, her breast red from the arrow wound that had pierced a lung. The blood had stopped flowing now.

Shuddering breaths filled Rek's lungs as he fought to control his grief. Blood dripped from a forgotten wound in his forearm. He rubbed his eyes and turned back to the bed; sitting beside her, he lifted her arm and felt for a pulse, but there was nothing.

"Virae!" he said softly. "Come back. Come back. Listen. I love you! You're the one." He leaned over her, watching her face. A tear appeared there, then another . . . But they were his own. He lifted her head and cradled it in his arms. "Wait for me," he whispered. "I'm coming." He fumbled at his belt, pulling the Lentrian dagger from its sheath, and held it to his wrist.

"Put it down, boy," said Druss from the doorway. "It would be meaningless."

"Get out!" shouted Rek. "Leave me."

"She's gone, lad. Cover her."

"Cover her? Cover my Virae! No! No, I can't. Oh, gods in Missael, I can't just cover her face."

"I had to once," said the old man as Rek slumped forward, tears stinging his eyes and silent sobs racking his frame. "My woman died. You are not the only one to face death."

For a long while Druss stood silently in the doorway, his heart aching. Then he pushed the door shut and walked into the room.

"Leave her for a while and talk to me, boy," he said, taking Rek by the arm. "Here by the window. Tell me again how you met."

And Rek told him of the attack in the forest, the killing of Reinard, the ride to the temple, and the journey to Delnoch.

"Druss!"

"Yes."

"I don't think I can live with this."

"I have known men who couldn't. But there is no need to cut your wrists. There's a horde of tribesmen out there who will do it for you gladly."

"I don't care about them anymore; they can have the damned place. I wish I had never come here."

"I know," said Druss gently. "I spoke to Virae yesterday in the hospital. She told me she loved you. She said—"

"I don't want to hear it."

"Yes, you do, because it's a memory you can hold. And it keeps her alive in your mind. She said that if she died, it would be worth it just to have met you. She worshiped you, Rek. She told me of the day you stood by her against Reinard and all his men—she was so proud of you. I was, too, when I heard about it. You had something, boy, that few men ever possess."

"And now I've lost it."

"But you *had* it! That can never be taken away from you. Her only regret was she was never really able to tell you how she felt."

"Oh, she told me—it didn't need words. What happened to you when your wife died? How did it feel?"

"I don't think I need to tell you. You know how I felt. And don't think it's any easier after thirty years. If anything, it becomes harder. Now, Serbitar is waiting to see you in the hall. He says it's important."

"Nothing is important anymore. Druss, will you cover her face? I couldn't bear to do it."

"Yes. Then you must see the albino. He has something for you."

Serbitar was waiting at the bottom of the stairs as Rek slowly descended to the main hall. The albino wore full armor and a helm topped with white horsehair. The visor was down, shielding his eyes. He looked, Rek thought, like a silver statue. Only his hands were bare, and they were white as polished ivory.

"You wanted me?" said Rek.

"Follow me," said Serbitar. Turning on his heel, he strode from the hall toward the spiral stone stairwell leading to the dungeons below the keep. Rek had been ready to refuse any request, but now he was forced to follow, and his anger grew. The albino stopped at the top of the stairs and removed a flaming torch from a copper wall bracket.

"Where are we going?" asked Rek.

"Follow me," repeated Serbitar.

Slowly and carefully the two men descended the cracked,

worn steps until at last they reached the first level of dungeons. Long disused, the hallway glittered with watersodden cobwebs and wet moss-covered arches. Serbitar moved on until they reached an oak door, a rusty bolt holding it fast. He struggled with the bolt for some moments, finally working it free, then both men had to haul on the door before it creaked and groaned and opened. Another stairwell beyond yawned dark before them.

Once again Serbitar started down. The steps ended in a long corridor, ankle-deep in water. They waded through to a final door shaped like an oak leaf and bearing a gold plaque with inscribed lettering in the Elder tongue.

"What does it say?" asked Rek.

"It says, 'To the worthy—welcome. Herein lies Egel's secret and the soul of the Earl of Bronze.' "

"What does it mean?"

Serbitar tried the door handle, but the door was locked, seemingly from within, since no bolt, chain, or keyhole could be seen.

"Do we break it down?" said Rek.

"No. You open it."

"It is locked. Is this a game?"

"Try it."

Rek turned the handle gently, and the door swung open without a sound. Soft lights sprang up within the room, glowing globes of glass set in the recesses of the walls. The room was dry, though now the water from the corridor outside flowed in and spread across the richly carpeted floor.

At the center of the room, on a wooden stand, was a suit of armor unlike anything Rek had ever seen. It was wonderfully crafted in bronze, the overlapping scales of metal glittering in the light. The breastplate carried a bronze eagle with wings flaring out over the chest and up to the shoulders. Atop this was a helmet, winged and crested with an eagle's head. Gauntlets there were, scaled and hinged, and greaves. Upon the table before the armor lay a bronze-ringed mail shirt lined with softest leather and mail leggings with bronze-hinged kneecaps. But above all Rek was drawn to the sword encased in a block of solid crystal. The blade was golden and over two feet in length; the hilt was double-handed, the guard a pair of flaring wings.

"It is the armor of Egel, the first Earl of Bronze," said Serbitar.

"Why was it allowed to lie here?"

"No one could open the door," answered the albino.

"It was not locked," said Rek.

"Not to you."

"What does that mean?"

"The meaning is clear: You and no other were meant to open the door."

"I can't believe that."

"Shall I fetch you the sword?" asked Serbitar.

"If you wish."

Serbitar walked to the crystal cube, drew his sword, and hammered at the block. Nothing happened. His blade clanged back into the air, leaving no mark upon the crystal.

"You try," said Serbitar.

"May I borrow your sword?"

"Just reach for the hilt."

Rek moved forward and lowered his hand to the crystal, waiting for the cold touch of glass, which never came. His hand sank into the block, his fingers curling around the hilt. Effortlessly he drew the blade forth.

"Is it a trick?" he asked.

"Probably. But it is none of mine. Look!" The albino put his hands on the now-empty crystal and heaved himself up upon it. "Pass your hands below me," he said.

Rek obeyed; for him the crystal did not exist.

"What does it mean?"

"I do not know, my friend. Truly I do not."

"Then how did you know it was here?"

"That is even more difficult to explain. Do you remember that day in the grove when I could not be awakened?"

"Yes."

"Well, I traveled far across the planet and even beyond, but in my travels I breasted the currents of time and I visited Delnoch. It was night, and I saw myself leading you through the hall and down to this room. I saw you take the sword, and I heard you ask the question you have just asked. And then I heard my answer."

"So, at this moment you are hovering above us listening?"

"Yes."

"I know you well enough to believe you, but answer me this: That may explain how you are here now with me, but how did the first Serbitar know the armor was here?"

"I genuinely cannot explain it, Rek. It is like looking into the reflection of a mirror and watching it go on and on into infinity. But I have found in my studies that often there is more to this life than we reckon with."

"Meaning?"

"There is the power of the Source."

"I am in no mood for religion."

"Then let us instead say that all those centuries ago Egel looked into the future and saw this invasion, so he left his armor here, guarded by magic which only you—as the earl—could break."

"Is your spirit image still observing us?"

"Yes."

"Does it know of my loss?"

"Yes."

"Then you knew she would die?"

"Yes."

"Why did you not tell me?"

"It would have been a waste of joy."

"What does that mean?" said Rek, anger building inside him and pushing away the grief.

"It means that were you a farmer anticipating a long life, I might have warned you, to prepare you. But you are not; you are fighting a savage horde, and your life is at risk every day. As was Virae's. You knew that she might die. Had I told you this was certain, not only would it have gained you nothing, it also would have robbed you of the joy you had."

"I could have saved her."

"No, you could not."

"I don't believe that."

"Why would I lie? Why would I wish her dead?"

Rek did not answer. The word "dead" entered his heart and crushed his soul. Tears welled in him again, and he fought them back, concentrating on the armor.

"I will wear that tomorrow," he said through gritted teeth. "I will wear it and die."

"Perhaps," answered the albino.

◇ 26 ◇

THE DAWN WAS clear, the air fresh and sweet as two thousand Drenai warriors prepared for the assault on Kania. Below them the Nadir shamans were moving through the ranks of tribesmen, sprinkling the blood of chickens and sheep on the bared blades that the warriors held before them.

Then the Nadir massed, and a great swelling chant came from thousands of throats as the horde moved forward, bearing ladders, knotted ropes, and grappling irons. Rek watched from the center of the line. He lifted the bronze helm and placed it over his head, buckling the chin strap. To his left was Serbitar, to his right Menahem. Others of the Thirty were spread along the wall.

And the carnage began.

Three assaults were turned back before the Nadir gained a foothold on the battlements. And that was short-lived. Some two score tribesmen breached the defense, only to find themselves faced with a madman in bronze and two silver ghosts who strode among them dealing death. There was no defense against these men, and the bronze devil's sword could cut through any shield or armor; men died under that terrible blade screaming as if their souls were ablaze. That night the Nadir captains carried their reports to the tent of Ulric, and the talk was all of the new force upon the battlements. Even the legendary Druss seemed more human—laughing as he did in the face of Nadir swords—than this golden machine of destruction.

"We felt like dogs being beaten from his path with a stick," muttered one man. "Or weaponless children being thrust aside by an elder."

Ulric was troubled, and though he lifted their spirits at last by pointing out again and again that it was merely a man in bronze armor, after the captains had left, he summoned the ancient shaman, Nosta Khan, to his tent. Squatting before a blazing brazier of coals, the old man listened to his warlord, nodding the while. At last he bowed and closed his eyes.

Rek was asleep, exhausted by battle and sorrow. The nightmare came slowly, enveloping him like black smoke. His dream eyes opened, and before him was a cave mouth, black and terrible. Fear emanated from it like a tangible force. Behind him was a pit, stretching down into the fiery bowels of the earth, from which came strange sounds, whimpers, and screams. In his hand was no sword, upon his body no armor. A slithering sound came from the pit, and Rek turned to see oozing up from it a gigantic worm, slime-covered and putrescent. The stench made him reel back. The mouth of the worm was huge and could swallow a man with ease; around it were triple rows of pointed fangs, and lodged between one set was the arm of a man, bloody and broken. Rek backed toward the cave mouth, but a hissing made him spin around. From the blackness of the cave came a spider, its giant maw dripping poison. Within its mouth was a face, green and shimmering, and from the mouth of the face flowed words of power. As each word sounded, Rek grew weaker, until he could hardly stand.

"Are you just going to stand there all day?" said a voice.

Rek turned to see Virae by his side, dressed in a flowing gown of white. She smiled at him.

"You're back!" he said, reaching out for her.

"No time for that, you fool! Here! Take your sword." Her arms reached toward him, and the bronze sword of Egel appeared in her hands. A shadow fell across them as Rek snatched the sword, spinning around to face the worm that was towering above them. The blade swept through three feet of the creature's neck as the mouth descended, and green gore spouted from the wound. Rek struck again and again until the creature, almost cut in two, flopped backward into the pit.

"The spider!" yelled Virae, and he spun once more. The

beast was upon him, its huge mouth mere paces away. Rek
hurled his sword into the gaping maw, and it flew like an
arrow to split the green face within like a melon. The spider
reared into the air and toppled backward. A breeze blew up,
and the beast became black smoke that drifted into the air
and then was gone.

"I suppose you would have gone on standing there if I
hadn't come along," said Virae.

"I think so," answered Rek.

"You fool," she said, smiling, and he moved forward ten-
tatively, holding out his arms.

"Can I touch you?" he asked.

"An odd request for a husband to make."

"You won't disappear?"

Her smile faded. "Not yet, my love."

His arms crushed her to him, tears spilling from his eyes.
"I thought you were gone forever. I thought I would never
see you again."

For a while they said nothing but merely stood together
embracing.

Finally she gently pushed him away. "You must go
back," she said.

"Back?"

"To Delnoch. You are needed there."

"I need you more than I need Delnoch. Can we not stay
here? Together?"

"No. There is no 'here.' It doesn't exist. Only you and I
are real. Now you must return."

"I will see you again, won't I?"

"I love you, Rek. I will always love you."

He awoke with a start, eyes focusing on the stars outside
his window. Her face could still be seen, fading against the
midnight sky.

"Virae!" he shouted. "Virae!" The door opened, and
Serbitar ran to the bedside.

"Rek, you're dreaming. Wake up!"

"I am awake. I saw her. She came to me in a dream and
rescued me."

"All right, but she's gone now. Look at me."

Rek gazed into Serbitar's green eyes. He saw concern
there, but this soon faded and the albino smiled.

"You are all right," said Serbitar. "Tell me of the dream."

Afterward Serbitar questioned him about the face. He wanted every detail that could be remembered. Finally he smiled.

"I think you were the victim of Nosta Khan," he said. "But you held him off—a rare feat, Rek."

"Virae came to me. It was not a dream?"

"I think not. The Source released her for a time."

"I would like to believe that, I truly would."

"I think you should. Have you looked for your sword?"

Rek swung out of the bed and padded over to the table where his armor lay. The sword was gone.

"How?" whispered Rek. Serbitar shrugged.

"It will return. Never fear!"

Serbitar lit the candles and stoked the fire to life in the hearth. As he finished, a gentle tapping came at the door.

"Come in," called Rek.

A young officer entered, bearing the sword of Egel.

"I am sorry to disturb you, sir, but I saw the light. One of the sentries found your sword upon the Kania battlements, so I brought it here. I wiped the blood from it first, sir."

"Blood?"

"Yes, sir. It was covered in blood. Strange how wet it still was."

"Thank you again." Rek turned to Serbitar. "I don't understand."

In the tent of Ulric the candles flickered. The warlord sat transfixed, staring at the headless body on the floor before him. The sight was one that would haunt him for the rest of his days. One moment the shaman had been sitting in trance before the coals, the next a red line had been drawn across his neck and his head had toppled into the fire.

Finally Ulric called his guards to remove the corpse, having first wiped his own sword blade across the bloody neck.

"He angered me," he told the guards.

The Nadir chieftain left his tent and walked out under the stars. First the legendary axman, then the warriors in silver. Now a bronze devil whose magic was greater than Nosta Khan's. Why did he feel this chill in his soul? Dros Delnoch was just another fortress. Had he not conquered a hundred such? Once he passed the gates of Delnoch, the Drenai empire was his. How could they hold against him? The answer was simple: They could not! One man—or devil—in bronze could not stem the Nadir tribes.

But what new surprises does this Dros hold? he asked himself.

He glanced up at the towering walls of Kania.

"You will fall!" he shouted. His voice echoed through the valley. "I shall bring you down!"

In the ghostly light of the predawn Gilad made his way from the mess canteen with a bowl of hot broth and a chunk of crusty black bread. Slowly he threaded his way through the ranks of men lining the walls until he came to his own position above the blocked postern tunnel. Togi was already there, sitting hunched and round-shouldered with his back to the wall. He nodded as Gilad squatted beside him, then spit on the whetstone in his callused hand and continued to sharpen his long cavalry saber.

"Feels like rain," said Gilad.

"Aye. It'll slow their climbing."

Togi never initiated a conversation yet always found a point others would miss. Theirs was a strange friendship: Togi, a taciturn black rider of fifteen years' standing, and Gilad, a volunteer farmer from the Sentran Plain. Gilad could not remember quite how they had come into contact, for Togi's face was scarcely memorable. He had just grown aware of the man. Men of the legion had now been spread along the wall, joining other groups. No one had said why, but it was obvious to Gilad: These were the warrior elite, and they added steel to the defense wherever they were placed. Togi was a vicious warrior who fought silently. No screams or war cries, merely a ruthless economy of movement and rare skill that left Nadir warriors dead or dismembered.

Togi did not know his own age, only that as a youth he had joined the riders as a stable boy and later had won his black cloak in the Sathuli wars. He had had a wife years back, but she had left him, taking their son with her. He had no idea where they had gone and professed not to care much. He had no friends that he spoke of and cared little for authority. Gilad had asked him once what he thought of the legion officers.

"They fight as well as the rest of us," he said. "But it is the only thing we will ever do together."

"What do you mean?" asked Gilad.

"Nobility. You can fight or die for them, but you will never be one of them. To them we don't exist as people."

"Druss is accepted," Gilad pointed out.

"Aye. By me also," answered Togi, a fierce gleam in his dark eyes. "That's a man, that one. But it alters nothing. Look at the silver men who fight under the albino—not one of them is from a lowly village. An earl's son leads them; nobles all of them."

"Then why do you fight for them if you hate them so much?"

"Hate them? I don't hate them. It's just the way life is. I don't hate anybody, and they don't hate me. We understand each other, that's all. To me the officers are no different from the Nadir; they're both different races. And I fight because that's what I do—I'm a soldier."

"Did you always want to be a soldier?"

"What else was there?"

Gilad spread his hands. "Anything you choose."

"I'd like to have been a king."

"What kind of king?"

"A bloody tyrant!" answered Togi. He winked but did not smile. He rarely smiled, and when he did, it was the merest flicker of movement around the eyes.

The day before, as the Earl of Bronze had made his dramatic entrance on to the walls, Gilad had nudged Togi and pointed.

"New armor—it suits him," said the rider.

"It looks old," said Gilad.

Togi merely shrugged. "So long as it does the job . . ."

That day Togi's saber had snapped six inches above the hilt. He had hurled himself on the leading Nadir and rammed the broken blade into his neck, snatching the man's short sword and laying about him ferociously. His speed of thought and quicksilver movements amazed Gilad. Later, during a lull between assaults, he had retrieved a second saber from a dead soldier.

"You fight well," Gilad had said.

"I'm alive," Togi had answered.

"Is that the same thing?"

"It is on these walls, though good men have fallen. But that is a matter of luck. The bad or the clumsy do not need bad luck to kill them, and even good luck wouldn't save them for long."

Now Togi stowed the whetstone in his pouch and wiped the curving blade with an oiled cloth. The steel shone blue-white in the gathering light.

Farther along the line Druss was chatting to the warriors, lifting their spirits with jests. He made his way toward them, and Gilad pushed himself to his feet, but Togi remained where he was. Druss, white beard ruffled by the breeze, stopped and spoke quietly to Gilad.

"I'm glad you stayed," he said.

"I had nowhere to go," answered Gilad.

"No. Not many men appreciate that," said the old warrior. He glanced down at the crouching rider. "I see you there, Togi, you young pup. Still alive, then?"

"So far," he said, looking up.

"Stay that way," said Druss, and walked on along the line.

"That is a great man," said Togi. "A man to die for."

"You knew him before this?"

"Yes." Togi would say no more, and Gilad was about to press him, when the blood-chilling sound of the Nadir war chant signaled the dawn of one more red day.

Below the walls, among the Nadir, was a giant called Nogusha. Ulric's champion for ten years, he had been sent forward with the first wave, and with him as personal bodyguards were twenty Wolfshead tribesmen. Their duty was to protect him until he could meet and kill Deathwalker. Strapped to his back was a three-foot sword, the blade six inches wide; by his side were two daggers in twin sheaths. An inch over six feet, Nogusha was the tallest warrior in the Nadir ranks and the most deadly, a veteran of three hundred hand-to-hand contests.

The horde reached the walls. Ropes swirled over the battlements, and ladders rattled on the gray stone. Nogusha barked commands to the men around him, and three tribesmen climbed above him, the others swarming alongside. The bodies of the first two above him plummeted down to the rocks below, but the third created a space for Nogusha before being hacked to death. As Nogusha gripped the battlements with one huge hand, his sword flashed into the air, while on either side of him the bodyguards closed in. The massive sword cleaved a passage as the group formed a wedge driving toward Druss some twenty paces distant. Although the Drenai closed in behind Nogusha's band, blocking the wall, none could approach the giant tribesman. Men died beneath his flashing broadsword. On either side of him his bodyguards were faring less well: one by one they fell until at last only Nogusha still stood. By now he was only paces away from Druss, who turned and saw him, battling alone and soon to fall. Their eyes met, and understanding was there instantly. This was a man Druss would be hard put not to recognize: Nogusha the swordsman, Ulric's executioner, a man whose deeds were the fabric of fresh Nadir legends, a living, younger counterpart to Druss himself.

The old man leapt lightly from the ramparts to the grass beyond, where he waited. He made no move to halt the attack on the Nadir warrior. Nogusha saw Druss waiting, slashed a path, and jumped clear. Several Drenai warriors made to follow him, but Druss waved them back.

"Well met, Nogusha," said the old man.

"Well met, Deathwalker."

"You will not live to collect Ulric's reward," said Druss. "There is no way back."

"All men must die. And this moment for me is as close to paradise as I could wish for. All my life you have been there before me, making my deeds seem shadows."

Druss nodded solemnly. "I, too, have thought of you."

Nogusha attacked with stunning speed. Druss hammered the sword aside, stepped in, and struck a blow of awesome power with his left fist. Nogusha staggered but recovered swiftly, blocking the downward sweep of Druss's ax. The battle that followed was brief and viciously fought. No matter how high the skill, a contest between an axman and a swordsman could never last long. Nogusha feinted to the left, then swept his sword up under Druss's guard. With no time for thought, Druss hurled himself under the arcing blade, slamming his shoulder into Nogusha's midriff. As the tribesman was hurled backward, the sword's blade sliced the back of Druss's jerkin, gashing the skin and flesh of his upper back. The old man ignored the sudden pain and threw himself across the body of the fallen swordsman. His left hand clamped over the right wrist of his opponent, and Nogusha did likewise.

The struggle was now titanic as each man strained to break the other's grip. Their strength was nearly identical, and while Druss had the advantage of being above the fallen warrior and thus in a position to use his weight to bear down, Nogusha was younger and Druss had been cut deeply. Blood welled down his back, pooling above the thick leather belt around his jerkin.

"You . . . cannot hold . . . against me," hissed Nogusha through clenched teeth.

Druss, face purple with effort, did not answer. The man was right; he could feel his strength ebbing. Nogusha's right arm began to lift, the sword blade glinting in the morning sun. Druss's left arm was beginning to shake with the effort and would give out at any moment. Suddenly the old man lifted his head and rammed his forehead down onto Nogusha's helpless face. The man's nose splintered as the edge of his adversary's silver-rimmed helm crashed upon it. Thrice more Druss butted the tribesman, and Nogusha began to panic. Already his nose and one cheekbone were smashed. He twisted, released Druss's arm, and exploded a mighty punch to his chin, but Druss rode it and hammered Snaga into the man's neck. Blood burst from the wound, and Nogusha ceased to struggle. His eyes met the old man's, but no word was said: Druss had no breath, and Nogusha had no vocal chords. The tribesman transferred his gaze to the sky and died. Druss slowly pulled himself upright; then, taking Nogusha by the feet, he dragged him up the short steps to the battlements. Meanwhile the Nadir had fallen back, ready for another charge. Druss called two men and ordered them to pass up Nogusha's body, then he climbed onto the ramparts.

"Hold on to my legs but do not let yourselves be seen,"

Druss whispered to the soldiers behind him. In full view of the Nadir massed below, he pulled the body of Nogusha upright in a tight bear hug, took hold of his neck and groin, and with a mighty effort raised the huge body above his head. With a heave and a scream he hurled the body out over the walls. But for the men holding him, he would have fallen. They helped him down, their faces anxious.

"Get me to the hospital before I bleed to death," he whispered.

◊ 27 ◊

CAESSA SAT BESIDE the bed, silent but watchful, her eyes never leaving the sleeping Druss. Thirty stitches laced the wound on the axman's broad back, the line curving alongside the shoulder blade and over the shoulder itself, where the cut was deepest. The old man was asleep, drugged with poppy wine. The blood loss from the wound had been prodigious, and he had collapsed on the way to the hospital. Caessa had stood by Calvar Syn as the stitches were inserted. She had said nothing. Now she merely sat.

She could not understand her fascination for the warrior. Certainly she did not desire him—men had never raised desire in her. Love? Was it love? She had no way of knowing, no terms of reference to gauge her feelings by. Her parents had died horribly when she was seven. Her father, a peaceful placid farmer, had tried to stop raiders from robbing his barn, and they had cut him down without a moment's thought. Caessa's mother had seized her by the hand and raced for the woods above the cliff. But they had been seen, and the chase was short. The woman could not carry the child, for she was pregnant. And she would not abandon her. She had fought like a wildcat but had been overpowered, abused, and slain. All the while the child had sat beneath an oak tree, frozen with terror, unable even to scream. A bearded man with foul breath had finally come to her, lifted her brutally by the hair, carried her to the cliff edge, and hurled her out over the sea.

She had missed the rocks, though her head was gashed in the fall and her right leg was broken. A fisherman saw her plunge and pulled her clear. From that day on she changed.

The laughing child laughed no more, or danced, or sang. Sullen she was, and vicious she became. Other children would not play with her, and as she grew older, she found herself more and more alone. At the age of fifteen she killed her first man, a traveler who had chattered to her by a river's edge, asking directions. She crept into his camp and cut his throat while he slept, sitting beside him to watch him die.

He was the first of many.

The death of men made her cry. In her tears she became alive. For Caessa, to live was the most important single objective of her life. And so men died.

In later years, after her twentieth birthday, Caessa devised a new method of selecting victims: those who were attracted to her. They would be allowed to sleep with her, but later, as they dreamed—perhaps of the pleasures they had enjoyed—she would draw a sharpened blade gently across their throats. She had killed no one since joining Bowman some six months before, for Skultik had become her last refuge.

Yet now she sat beside the bed of an injured man and wished for him to live. Why?

She drew her dagger and pictured its blade drawing across the old man's throat. Usually this death fantasy made her warm with desire, but now it created a sense of panic. In her mind's eye she saw Druss sitting beside her in a darkened room, a log fire burning in the hearth. His arm was over her shoulder, and she was nestling into his chest. She had pictured the scene many times, but now she saw it afresh, for Druss was so large, a giant in her fantasy. And she knew why.

She was seeing him through the eyes of a seven-year-old.

Orrin slipped quietly into the room. He was thinner now, drawn and haggard, yet stronger. An indefinable quality marked his features. Lines of fatigue had aged him, but the change was more subtle; it emanated from the eyes. He had been a soldier longing to be a warrior; now he was a warrior longing to be anything else. He had seen war and cruelty, death and dismemberment. He had watched the sharp beaks of crows at work on dead men's eyes and the growth of worms in pus-filled sockets. And he had found himself and wondered no longer.

"How is he?" he asked Caessa.

"He will recover. But he will not fight for weeks."

"Then he will not fight again, for we have only days. Prepare him to be moved."

"He cannot be moved," she said, turning to look at him for the first time.

"He must be. We are giving up the wall, and we draw back tonight. We lost over four hundred men today. Wall Four is only a hundred yards long; we can hold that for days. Get him ready."

She nodded and rose. "You are tired, too, General," she said. "You should rest."

"I will soon," he answered, and smiled. The smile sent a shiver down her back. "We will all rest soon, I think."

Bearers transferred Druss to a stretcher, lifting him gently and covering him with white blankets against the night cold. With other wounded men they made a convoy to Wall Four, where ropes were lowered and the stretchers were silently raised. No torches were lit, and only the light of the stars bathed the scene. Orrin climbed the last rope and hauled himself over the battlements. A helping hand reached out and pulled him upright; it was Gilad.

"You always seem on hand to help me, Gilad. Not that I'm complaining."

Gilad smiled. "With the weight you've lost, General, you would win that race now."

"Ah, the race! It seems like a different age. What happened to your friend. The one with the ax?"

"He went home."

"A wise man. Why did you stay?"

Gilad shrugged. He had grown tired of the question.

"It's a nice night, the best yet," said Orrin. "Strange, I used to lie in bed at night and watch the stars. They always made me sleepy. Now I have no need of sleep. I feel I'm throwing away life. Do you feel that?"

"No, sir. I sleep like a baby."

"Good. Well, I'll say good night, then."

"Good night, sir."

Orrin walked away slowly, then turned. "We didn't do too badly, did we?" he said.

"No, sir," replied Gilad. "I think the Nadir will remember us without affection."

"Yes. Good night." He had begun the walk down the short rampart steps when Gilad stepped forward.

"Sir!"

"Yes?"

"I ... I wanted to say ... Well, just that I have been proud to serve under you. That's all, sir."

"Thank you, Gilad. But I am the one who should be proud. Good night."

Togi said nothing as Gilad returned to the wall, but the young officer could feel the rider's eyes upon him.

"Well, say it," said Gilad. "Get it over with."

"Say what?"

Gilad looked at his friend's blank face and searched his eyes for signs of humor or contempt. Nothing showed. "I thought you would think ... I don't know," he said lamely.

"The man has shown quality and courage, and you told him so. There is no harm in that, although it wasn't your place. In peacetime I'd think you were crawling, currying favor with a comment like that. Not here. There is nothing to gain, and he knew that. So it was well said."

"Thank you," said Gilad.

"For what?"

"For understanding. You know, I believe he is a great man, greater than Druss, perhaps. For he has neither Druss's courage nor Hogun's skill, yet he is still here. Still trying."

"He'll not last long."

"None of us will," said Gilad.

"No, but he won't see the last day. He's too tired—up here he's too tired." Togi tapped his temple.

"I think you're wrong."

"No, you don't. That's why you spoke to him as you did. You sensed it, too."

Druss floated on an ocean of pain, burning, searing his body. His jaw clamped shut, teeth grinding against the insistent agony creeping like slow acid through his back.

Words were almost impossible, hissed through gritted teeth, and the faces of those around his bed shivered and swam, blurring beyond recognition.

He became unconscious, but the pain followed him down into the depths of dreams where gaunt, shadow-haunted landscapes surrounded him and jagged mountains reared black against a gray, brooding sky. Druss lay on the mountain, unable to move against the pain, his eyes focused on a small grove of lightning-blasted trees some twenty paces from where he lay. Standing before them was a man dressed in black. He was lean, and his eyes were dark. He moved forward and sat on a boulder, gazing down at the axman.

"So, it comes to this," he said. The voice had a hollow ring like wind whistling through a cavern.

"I shall recover," hissed Druss, blinking away the sweat dripping into his eyes.

"Not from this," said the man. "You should be dead now."

"I have been cut before."

"Ah, but the blade was poisoned—green sap from the northern marshes. Now you are riddled with gangrene."

"No! I will die with my ax in my hand."

"Think you so? I have waited for you, Druss, through these many years. I have watched the legions of travelers cross the dark river at your hands. And I have watched you. Your pride is colossal, your conceit immense. You have tasted glory and prized your strength above all else. Now you will die. No ax. No glory. Never to cross the dark river to the Forever Halls. There is satisfaction for me in this; can you understand that? Can you comprehend it?"

"No. Why do you hate me?"

"Why? Because you conquer fear. And because your life mocks me. It is not enough that you die. All men die, peasants and kings—all are mine, come the end. But you, Druss, you are special. Were you to die as you desire, you would mock me still. So for you I have devised this exquisite torture.

"You should by now be dead from your wound. But I have not yet claimed you. And now the pain will grow more intense. You will writhe . . . You will scream . . . Finally your mind will snap and you will beg. *Beg* for me. And I shall come and take you by the hand, and you will be mine. Men's last memories of you will be of a mewling, weeping wreck. They will despise you, and your legend will be tainted at the last."

Druss forced his massive arms beneath him and struggled to rise. But the pain drove him down once more, forcing a groan through clenched teeth.

"That's it, axman. Struggle on. Try harder. You should have stayed on your mountain and enjoyed your dotage. Vain man! You could not resist the call of blood. Suffer— and bring me joy."

In the makeshift hospital Calvar Syn lifted the hot towels from Druss's bare back, replacing them swiftly as the stench filled the room. Serbitar stepped forward and also examined the wound.

"It is hopeless," said Calvar Syn, rubbing his hand over the polished dome of his skull. "Why is he still alive?"

"I don't know," said the albino softly. "Caessa, has he spoken?"

The girl glanced up from her bedside chair, her eyes dull with fatigue. She shook her head. The door opened, and Rek moved inside silently. He lifted his eyebrows in a question to the surgeon, but Calvar Syn shook his head.

"Why?" asked Rek. "The wound was no worse than he has had before."

"Gangrene. The wound will not close, and the poison has spread through his body. He cannot be saved. All the experience I have gained in forty years says he should now be dead. His body is putrefying at an amazing rate."

"He is a tough old man. How long can he last?"

"He will not live to see tomorrow," answered the surgeon.

"How goes it on the wall?" asked Serbitar. Rek shrugged. His armor was bloody, and his eyes tired.

"We are holding for the moment, but they are in the tunnel beneath us, and the gate will not stand. It's a damned shame we had no time to fill the gate tunnel. I think they will be through before dusk. They have already burst a postern gate, but Hogun and a few others are holding the stairwell.

"That's why I came, Doctor. I'm afraid you will have to prepare once more for evacuation. From now on the hospital will be at the keep. How soon can you move?"

"How can I say? Men are being brought in all the time."

"Begin your preparations, anyway. Those who are too badly hurt to be moved must be dispatched."

"What?" shouted the surgeon. "Murdered, you mean?"

"Exactly so. Move those who can move. The others . . . how do you think the Nadir will treat them?"

"I will move everyone, regardless. If they die during the evacuation, it will still be better than knifing them in their beds."

"Then begin now. We are wasting time," said Rek.

On the wall Gilad and Togi joined Hogun at the postern stairwell. The stairs were littered with corpses, but more Nadir warriors rounded the bend in the spiral and scrambled over the bodies. Hogun stepped forward, blocking a thrust, and disemboweled the leading man. He fell, tripping the warrior behind him. Togi slashed a two-handed stroke through the second man's neck as he fell in turn. Two more warriors advanced, holding round oxhide shields before them. Behind, others pushed forward.

"It's like holding back the sea with a bucket," yelled Togi.

Above them the Nadir gained a foothold on the ramparts, driving a wedge into the Drenai formation. Orrin saw the danger and raced forward with fifty men of the new Group Karnak. Below them to the right the battering ram thundered against the giant gates of oak and bronze. So far the gates held, but ominous cracks had appeared beneath the crossed center beams, and the wood groaned under the impact.

Orrin battled his way to the Nadir wedge, using his sword two-handed, cutting and slashing with no attempt at defense. Beside him a Drenai warrior fell, his throat gashed. Orrin backhanded a cut to the attacker's face, then blocked a blow from his left.

It was three hours to dusk.

Bowman knelt on the grass behind the battlements, three quivers of arrows before him on the ground. Coolly he notched shaft to his bow, drew, and let fly. A man to the left of Orrin fell, the arrow piercing his temple. Then a second Nadir fell to Orrin's sword before another arrow downed a third. The wedge was falling apart as the Drenai hacked their way forward.

At the stairwell Togi was bandaging a long gash in his forearm while a fresh squad of legion warriors held the entrance. Gilad leaned against a boulder, wiping sweat from his brow.

"A long day," he said.

"It will be longer yet," muttered Togi. "They can sense how close they are to taking the wall."

"Yes. How is the arm?"

"All right," answered Togi. "Where now?"

"Hogun said to fill in where we're needed."

"That could be anywhere. I'm for the gate. Coming?"

"Why not?" answered Gilad, smiling.

Rek and Serbitar cleared a section of battlements, then raced to join Orrin and his group. All along the wall the defensive line was bending. But it held.

"If we can hold out until they re-form for another charge, we may yet have time to get everyone back behind Valteri," yelled Orrin as Rek fought his way alongside.

For another hour the battle raged, then the huge bronze head of the battering ram breached the timbers of the gate. The great beam at the center sagged as a crack appeared; then, with a tearing groan, it slid from its sockets. The ram was withdrawn slowly to clear the way for the fighting men beyond.

Gilad sent a runner to the battlements to inform Rek or either of the gans, then drew his sword and waited with fifty others to hold the entrance.

As he rocked his head from side to side to ease the aching muscles of his shoulders, he glanced at Togi. The man was smiling.

"What is so funny?"

"My own stupidity," answered Togi. "I suggested the gates to get a bit of rest. Now I'm going to encounter death."

Gilad said nothing. Death! His friend was right: There would be no escape to Wall Five for the men at the gate. He felt the urge to turn and run and suppressed it. What did it matter, anyway? He had seen enough of death in the last few weeks. And if he survived, what would he do, where would he go? Back to the farm and a dull wife? Grow old somewhere, toothless and senile, telling endlessly boring stories of his youth and courage?

"Great gods!" said Togi suddenly. "Just look at that!"

Gilad turned. Coming slowly toward them across the grass was Druss, leaning on the girl outlaw, Caessa. He staggered and almost fell, but she held him. As they came closer, Gilad swallowed back the horror he felt. The old man's face had a sunken look; it was pallid and tinged with blue, like a two-day-old corpse. The men stepped aside as Caessa steered Druss to the center of the line, then she drew a short sword and stood with him.

The gates opened, and the Nadir poured through. Druss, with great effort, drew Snaga. He could hardly see through the mists of pain, and each step had been a new agony as the girl had brought him forward. She had dressed him carefully, crying all the while, then helped him to his feet. He himself had begun to weep, for the pain was unbearable.

"I can't make it," he had whimpered.

"You can," she had told him. *"You must."*

"The pain . . ."

"You have had pain before. Fight through it."

"I cannot. I'm finished."

"Listen to me, damn you! You are Druss the Legend, and men are dying out there. One last time, Druss. *Please.* You mustn't give up like an ordinary man. *You are Druss.* You can do it. Stop them. You must stop them. My mother's out there!"

His vision cleared momentarily, and he saw her madness. He could not understand it, for he knew nothing of her life, but he sensed her need. With an effort that tore an agonizing scream from him, he bunched his legs beneath himself and stood, clamping a huge hand to a shelf on the wall to hold himself upright. The pain grew, but he was angry now and used the pain to spur himself on.

Druss took a deep breath. "Come on, little Caessa, let's find your mother," he said. "But you will have to help me; I'm a little unsteady."

The Nadir swept through the gates and onto the waiting

blades of the Drenai. Above them, Rek received word of the calamity. For the moment the attack on the wall had ceased as men massed below in the gate tunnel.

"Back!" he shouted. "Get to Wall Five." Men began to run across the grass, through the deserted streets of outer Delnoch, streets that Druss had cleared of people so many days before. There would be no killing ground now between walls, for the buildings still stood, haunted and empty.

Warriors raced for the transient security of Wall Five, giving no thought to the rear guard at the broken gate. Gilad did not blame them and, strangely, had no wish to be with them.

Only Orrin, as he ran, noticed the rear guard. He turned to join them, but Serbitar was beside him, grasping his arm. "No," he said. "It would be useless."

They ran on. Behind them the Nadir breasted the wall and raced in pursuit.

In the gateway the carnage continued. Druss, fighting from memory, hacked and slashed at the advancing warriors. Togi died as a short lance hammered into his chest; Gilad did not see him fall. For Caessa the scene was different: There were ten raiders, and Druss was battling against them all. Each time he killed a man, she smiled. Eight . . . Nine . . .

The last of the raiders, a man she could never forget, for he had killed her mother, came forward. He had a gold earring and a scar running from eyebrow to chin. Lifting her sword, she hurled herself forward, ramming the blade into his belly. The squat Nadir toppled backward, pulling the girl with him. A knife sliced between her shoulder blades. But she did not feel it. The raiders were all dead, and for the first time since childhood she was safe. Her mother would come out of the trees now and take her home, and Druss would be given a huge meal, and they would laugh. And she would sing for him. She would . . .

Only seven men still stood around Druss and the Nadir surrounded them. A lance thrust out suddenly, crushing Druss's ribs and piercing a lung. Snaga lashed back a murderous reply, cutting the lancer's arm from his shoulder. As he fell, Gilad sliced his throat. Then Gilad himself fell, piorood through the back, and Druss stood alone. The Nadir fell back as one of their captains moved forward.

"Remember me, Deathwalker?" he said.

Druss tore the lance from his side, hurling it away from him.

"I remember you, lardbelly. The herald!"

"You said you would have my soul, yet I stand here and you die. What think you of that?"

Suddenly Druss lifted his arm to fling Snaga forward, and the blade split the herald's head like a pumpkin.

"I think you talk too much," said Druss. He toppled to his knees and looked down to see the lifeblood flowing from him. Beside him Gilad was dying, but his eyes were open. "It was good to be alive, wasn't it, boy?"

Around them the Nadir stood, but no move was made against them. Druss looked up and pointed at a warrior.

"You, boy," he said in guttural dialect, "fetch my ax." For a moment the warrior did not move, then he shrugged and pulled Snaga from the head of the herald. "Bring it here," ordered Druss. As the young soldier advanced, Druss could see that he intended to kill him with his own weapon, but a voice barked out a command and the warrior stiffened. He handed Druss the ax and moved back.

Druss's eyes were misting now, and he could not make out the figure looming before him.

"You did well, Deathwalker," said Ulric. "Now you can rest."

"If I had just one more ounce of strength, I would cut you down," muttered Druss, struggling with his ax. But the weight was too great.

"I know that. I did not know Nogusha carried poison on his blade. Will you believe that?"

Druss's head bowed, and he toppled forward.

Druss the Legend was dead.

◊ 28 ◊

SIX HUNDRED DRENAI warriors watched silently as the Nadir gathered about the body of Druss and lifted it gently, bearing it back through the gates he had striven to hold. Ulric was the last man to pass the portals. In the shadow of the broken timbers he turned, his violet eyes scanning the men at the wall, stopping at last to rest on a figure of bronze. Ulric lifted his hand as if in greeting, then slowly pointed at Rek. The message was clear enough.

First the legend, now the earl.

Rek made no reply but merely watched as the Nadir warlord strode into the shadows of the gate and out of sight.

"He died hard," said Hogun as Rek turned and sat back on the ramparts, lifting his helm visor.

"What did you expect?" asked Rek, rubbing tired eyes with weary fingers. "He lived hard."

"We will follow him soon," said Hogun. "There's not a day's fighting left in the men we have. The city is deserted now: even the camp baker has left."

"What of the council?" asked Rek.

"Gone, all of them. Bricklyn should be back in the next day or two with words from Abalayn. I think he will be bringing his message directly to Ulric—he'll be based in the keep by then."

Rek did not answer; there was no need. It was true: The battle was over. Only the massacre remained.

Serbitar, Vintar, and Menahem approached silently, their white cloaks tattered and bloody. But there was no mark of wounds upon them. Serbitar bowed.

"The end is come," he said. "What are your orders?"

310

Rek shrugged. "What would you have me say?"

"We could fall back to the keep," offered Serbitar, "but we have not enough men to hold even that."

"Then we will die here," said Rek. "One place is as good as another."

"Truly," said Vintar gently. "But I think we have a few hours grace."

"Why?" asked Hogun, loosening the bronze brooch at his shoulder and removing his cloak.

"I think the Nadir will not attack again today. Today they have slain a mighty man, a legend even among their ranks. They will feast and celebrate. Tomorrow, when we die, they will feast again."

Rek removed his helm, welcoming the cool breeze on his sweat-drenched head. Overhead the sky was clear and blue, the sun golden. He drew in a deep breath of clear mountain air, feeling its power soaking into tired limbs. His mind flew back to days of joy with Horeb in the inn at Drenan, long-gone days, never to be revisited. He swore aloud, then laughed.

"If they don't attack, we should have a party of our own," he said. "Gods, a man can die but once in a lifetime! Surely it's worth celebrating." Hogun grinned and shook his head, but Bowman, who had approached unnoticed, clapped Rek on the shoulder.

"Now, that is my kind of language," he said. "But why not do it properly, go the whole way?"

"The whole way?" asked Rek.

"We could join the Nadir party," said Bowman. "Then they would have to buy the drinks."

"There's some truth in that, Earl of Bronze," said Serbitar. "Shall we join them?"

"Have you gone mad?" said Rek, looking from one to the other.

"As you said, Rek, we only die once," suggested Bowman. "We have nothing to lose. Anyway, we should be protected by the Nadir laws of hospitality."

"This is insanity!" said Rek. "You're not serious?"

"Yes, I am," said Bowman. "I think I would like to pay my last respects to Druss. And it will make a grand exit for Nadir poets to sing about in later years. Drenai poets are almost bound to pick it up, too. I like the idea; it has a certain poetic beauty to it. Dining in the dragon's lair."

"Damn it, I'm with you, then," said Rek. "Though I think my mind must be unhinged. When should we leave?"

Ulric's ebony throne had been set outside his tent, and the Nadir warlord sat upon it dressed in eastern robes of gold thread upon silk. Upon his head was the goatskin-fringed crown of the Wolfshead tribe, and his black hair was braided after the fashion of the Ventrian kings. Around him, in a vast circle many thousands strong, sat his captains; beyond them were many other circles of men. At the center of each circle Nadir women danced in a frenzy of motion in tune to the rippling rhythms of a hundred drums. In the circle of captains the women danced around a funeral pyre ten feet high on which lay Druss the Legend, arms crossed and ax upon his chest.

Outside the circles, countless fires blazed and the smell of burning meat filled the air. Everywhere camp women carried yokes bearing buckets of Lyrrd, an alcohol brewed from goat's milk. Ulric himself drank Lentrian red in honor of Druss. He did not like the drink; it was too thin and watery for a man reared on the more potent liquors brewed on the northern steppes. But he drank it anyway. It would be bad manners to do less, for the spirit of Druss had been invited among them: A spare goblet was filled to the brim beside Ulric's own, and a second throne had been set to the right of the Nadir warlord.

Ulric stared moodily over the rim of his goblet, focusing his gaze on the body atop the pyre.

"It was a good time to die, old man," he said softly. "You will be remembered in our songs, and men will talk of you around our camp fires for generations to come."

The moon shone brightly in a cloudless sky, and the stars gleamed like distant candles. Ulric sat back and gazed into eternity. Why this black mood? What was the weight his soul carried? Rarely before had he felt this way, and certainly never on the eve of such a victory.

Why?

His gaze returned to the body of the axman.

"You have done this to me, Deathwalker," he said. "For your heroics have made me the dark shadow."

In all legends, Ulric knew, there were bright heroes and dark, dark evil. It was the very fabric of each tale.

"I am not evil," he said. "I am a warrior born, with a people to protect and a nation to build." He swallowed another mouthful of Lentrian and refilled his goblet.

"My lord, is something wrong?" asked his carle-captain, Ogasi, the thickset steppe rider who had slain Virae.

"He accuses me," said Ulric, pointing to the body.

"Shall we light the pyre?"

Ulric shook his head. "Not until midnight. The gates must be open when he arrives."

"You do him great honor, lord. Why, then, does he accuse you?"

"With his death. Nogusha carried a poisoned blade. I had the story from his tent servant."

"That was not at your command, lord. I was there."

"Does it matter? Am I no longer responsible for those who serve me? I have tainted my legend in order to end his. A dark, dark deed, Ulric Wolfshead."

"He would have died tomorrow anyway," said Ogasi. "He lost only a day."

"Ask yourself, Ogasi, what that day meant. Men like Deathwalker come perhaps once in twenty lifetimes. They are rare. So what is that day worth to ordinary men? A year? Ten years? A lifetime? Did you see him die?"

"I did, lord."

"And will you forget it?"

"No, lord."

"Why not? You have seen brave men die before."

"He was special," said Ogasi. "Even when he fell at the last, I thought he would rise. Even now some of the men cast fearful glances at his pyre, expecting to see him stand again."

"How could he have stood against us?" asked Ulric. "His face was blue with gangrene. His heart should have stopped long since. And the pain . . ."

Ogasi shrugged. "While men compete in war, there will be warriors. While there are warriors, there will be princes among warriors. Among the princes will be kings, and among the kings an emperor. You said it yourself, my lord. Such as he come once in twenty lifetimes. You would expect him to die in his bed?"

"No. I had thought to let his name die. Soon I will control the mightiest empire known to men. History will *be* as I write it.

"I could erase him from the memory of men or, worse still, sully his name until his legend reeks. But I shall not. I will have a book written about his life, and men shall know how he thwarted me."

"I would expect nothing less from Ulric," said Ogasi, his dark eyes gleaming in the firelight.

"Ah, but then you know me, my friend. There are others among the Drenai who will be expecting me to dine on Druss's mighty heart. Eater of babies, the plague that walks, the barbarian of Gulgothir."

"Names you yourself invented, my lord, I think."

"True. But then, a leader must know all the weapons of war. And there are many which owe nothing to the lance and sword, the bow and the sling. The word steals men's souls, while the sword kills only their bodies. Men see me and know fear. It is a potent device."

"Some weapons turn on their users, my lord. I have—" The man suddenly stuttered to silence.

"Speak, Ogasi! What ails you?"

"The Drenai, my lord! They are in the camp!" said Ogasi, his eyes wide in disbelief. Ulric spun in his chair. Everywhere the circles were breaking as men stood to watch the Earl of Bronze striding toward the Lord of the Nadir.

Behind him in ranks came sixteen men in silver armor, and behind them a legion gan walking beside a blond warrior bearing a longbow.

The drums petered to silence, and all eyes swung from the Drenai group to the seated warlord. Ulric's eyes narrowed as he saw that the men were armed. Panic welled in his breast, but he forced it down, his mind racing. Would they just walk up and slay him? He heard the hiss of Ogasi's blade leaving its scabbard and raised a hand.

"No, my friend. Let them approach."

"It is madness, lord," whispered Ogasi as the Drenai drew nearer.

"Pour wine for our guests. The time to kill them will come after the feast. Be prepared."

Ulric gazed down from his raised throne into the gray-blue eyes of the Earl of Bronze. The man had forsaken his helm but otherwise was fully armored, the great sword of Egel hanging at his side. His companions stood back, awaiting events. There was little sign of tension, though the legion general Ulric knew as Hogun had his hand resting lightly on his sword hilt and was watching Ogasi keenly.

"Why are you here?" asked Ulric. "You are not welcome in my camp."

The earl looked slowly about him and then returned the gaze of the Nadir warlord.

"It is strange," he said, "how a battle can change a man's perspective. First, I am not in your camp, I am standing on Delnoch ground, and that is mine by right—it is you who are on *my* lands. Be that as it may, for tonight you are welcome. As to why I am here. My friends and I have come to bid farewell to Druss the Legend—Deathwalker. Is Nadir hospitality so poor that no refreshment is offered us?"

Ogasi's hand strayed toward his sword once more. The Earl of Bronze did not move.

"If that sword is drawn," he said softly, "I will remove his head."

Ulric waved Ogasi back.

"Do you think to leave here alive?" he asked Rek.

"If I so choose, yes," replied the earl.

"And I have no say in this matter?"

"None."

"Truly? Now you intrigue me. All around you are Nadir bowmen. At my signal your bright armor will be hidden by black-shafted arrows. And you say I cannot?"

"If you can, then order it," demanded the earl. Ulric moved his gaze to the archers. Arrows were ready, and many bows were already bent, their iron points glittering in the firelight.

"Why can I not order it?" he asked.

"Why have you not?" countered the earl.

"Curiosity. What is the real purpose of your visit? Have you come to slay me?"

"No. If I wished, I could have slain you as I killed your shaman: silently, invisibly. Your head would now be a worm-filled shell. There is no duplicity here. I came to honor my friend. Will you offer me hospitality or shall I return to my fortress?"

"Ogasi!" called Ulric.

"My lord?"

"Fetch refreshments for the earl and his followers. Order the archers back to their fires and let the entertainment continue."

"Yes, lord," said Ogasi dubiously.

Ulric gestured the earl to the throne at his side. Rek nodded and turned to Hogun. "Go and enjoy yourselves. Return for me in an hour."

Hogun saluted, and Rek watched his small group wander off around the camp. He smiled as Bowman leaned over a seated Nadir and lifted a goblet of Lyrrd. The man stared when he saw his drink disappear, then laughed as Bowman drained it without a splutter.

"Damn good, hey?" said the warrior. "Better than that red vinegar from the south."

Bowman nodded and pulled a flask from his hip pouch, offering it to the man. Suspicion was evident in the hesitant way the Nadir accepted the flask, but his friends were watching.

Slowly he removed the top, then took a tentative sip, followed by a full-blown swallow.

"This is damn good, too," said the man. "What is it?"

"They call it Lentrian fire. Once tasted, never forgotten!"

The man nodded, then moved aside to make a place for Bowman.

"Join us, longbow. Tonight no war. We talk, yes?"

"Decent of you, old horse. I think I will."

Seated on the throne, Rek lifted Druss's goblet of Lentrian red and raised it toward the pyre. Ulric also raised his goblet, and both men silently toasted the fallen axman.

"He was a great man," said Ulric. "My father told me tales of him and his lady. Rowena, wasn't it?"

"Yes, he loved her greatly."

"It is fitting," said Ulric, "that such a man should know great love. I am sorry he is gone. It would be a fine thing if war could be conducted as a game where no lives were lost. At the end of a battle combatants could meet—even as we are doing—and drink and talk."

"Druss would not have had it so," said the earl. "Were this a game where the odds mattered, Dros Delnoch would already be yours. But Druss was a man who could change the odds and make nonsense of logic."

"Up to a point, for he is dead. But what of you? What manner of man are you, Earl Regnak?"

"Just a man, Lord Ulric—even as you."

Ulric leaned closer, his chin resting on his hand. "But then, I am not an ordinary man. I have never lost a battle."

"Nor yet have I."

"You intrigue me. You appear from nowhere, with no past, married to the dying earl's daughter. No one has ever heard of you, and no man can tell me of your deeds. Yet men die for you as they would for a beloved king. Who are you?"

"I am the Earl of Bronze."

"No. That I will not accept."

"Then what would you have me say?"

"Very well, you are the Earl of Bronze. It matters not. Tomorrow you may return to your grave—you and all those who follow you. You began this battle with ten thousand men; you now boast perhaps seven hundred. You pin your faith on Magnus Woundweaver, but he cannot reach you in time, and even if he did, it would matter not. Look about you. This army is bred on victory. And it grows. I have four armies like this. Can I be stopped?"

"Stopping you is not important," said the earl. "It never was."

"Then what are you doing?"

"We are *trying* to stop you."

"Is this a riddle which I should understand?"

"Your understanding is not important. It may be that destiny intends you to succeed. It may be that a Nadir empire will prove vastly beneficial to the world. But ask yourself this: Were there no army here when you arrived, save Druss alone, would he have opened the gate to you?"

"No. He would have fought and died," said Ulric.

"But he would not have expected to win. So why would he do it?"

"Now I understand your riddle, Earl. But it saddens me that so many men must die when it is futile to resist. Nevertheless I respect you. I will see that your pyre is as high as that of Druss."

"Thank you, no. If you do kill me, lay my body in a garden beyond the keep. There is already a grave there, surrounded by flowers, within which lies my wife. Put my body beside it."

Ulric fell silent for several minutes, taking time to refill the goblets.

"It shall be as you wish, Earl of Bronze," he said at last. "Join me in my tent now. We shall eat a little meat, drink a little wine, and be friends. I shall tell you of my life and my dreams, and you may talk of the past and your joys."

"Why only the past, Lord Ulric?"

"It is all you have left, my friend."

◊ 29 ◊

AT MIDNIGHT, AS the flames from the funeral pyre blazed against the night sky, the Nadir horde drew their weapons, holding them aloft in silent tribute to the warrior whose soul, they believed, stood at the gates of paradise.

Rek and the company of Drenai followed suit, then he turned and bowed to Ulric. Ulric returned the bow, and the company set off to return to the postern gate of Wall Five. The return journey was made in silence, each man's thoughts his own.

Bowman thought of Caessa and of her death at Druss's side. He had loved her in his way, though he had never spoken of it. To love her was to die.

Hogun's mind reeled with the awesome picture of the Nadir army seen from close range, numberless and mighty. Unstoppable!

Serbitar thought of the journey he would make with the remnants of the Thirty at dusk on the morrow. Only Arbedark would be missing, for they had convened the night before and declared him an abbot. Now he would journey from Delnoch alone to found a new temple in Ventria.

Rek fought against despair. Ulric's last words echoed again and again in his mind:

"Tomorrow you will see the Nadir as never before. We have paid homage to your courage by attacking only in daylight, allowing you to rest at night. Now I need to take your keep, and there will be no rest until it falls. Day and night we will come at you until none are left alive to oppose us."

Silently the group mounted the postern steps, making its way to the mess hall. Rek knew sleep would not come to him this night. It was his last night upon the earth, and his tired body summoned fresh reserves so that he could taste life and know the sweetness of drawing breath.

The group sat around a trestle table, and Rek poured wine. Of the Thirty, only Serbitar and Vintar remained. For many minutes the five men said little, until at last Hogun broke the uncomfortable silence.

"We knew it would come to this, did we not? There was no way to hold indefinitely."

"Very true, old horse," said Bowman. "Still, it is a trifle disappointing, don't you think? I must own that I always kept alive a small hope that we would succeed. Now that it is gone, I feel a tiny twinge of panic." He smiled gently and finished his drink with a single swallow.

"You are not pledged to stay," said Hogun.

"True. Perhaps I will leave in the morning."

"I don't think you will, though I don't know why," said Hogun.

"Well, if truth be told, I promised that Nadir warrior, Kaska, that I would have another drink with him once they took the keep. Nice chap—if a trifle maudlin in his cups. He has six wives and twenty-three children. It is a wonder he has the time to come to war."

"Or the strength!" added Hogun, grinning. "And what of you, Rek. Why do you stay?"

"Hereditary stupidity," answered Rek.

"That is not enough," said Bowman. "Come on, Rek— the truth, if you please."

Rek scanned the group swiftly, noting the fatigue on all their faces and realizing for the first time that he loved them all.

His eyes met Vintar's, and understanding flowed between them. The older man smiled.

"I think," said Rek, "that only the Abbot of Swords can answer that question—for all of us."

Vintar nodded and closed his eyes for several moments. All the men knew he was searching their hearts and minds, yet there was no fear, no embarrassment, no desire any longer to be alone.

"All things that live must die," said Vintar. "Man alone, it seems, lives all his life in the knowledge of death. And yet there is more to life than merely waiting for death. For life to have meaning, there must be a purpose. A man must pass something on—otherwise he is useless.

"For most men that purpose revolves around marriage and children who will carry on his seed. For others it is an ideal—a dream, if you like. Each of us here believes in the concept of honor: that it is man's duty to do that which is right and just, that might alone is not enough. We have all transgressed at some time. We have stolen, lied, cheated—even killed—for our own ends. But ultimately we return to our beliefs. We do not allow the Nadir to pass unchallenged because we cannot. We judge ourselves more harshly than others can judge us. We know that death is preferable to betrayal of that which we hold dear.

"Hogun, you are a soldier and you have faith in the Drenai cause. You have been told to stand and will do so without question. It would not occur to you that there were any alternatives but to obey. And yet you understand when others think differently. You are a rare man.

"Bowman, you are a romantic and yet a cynic. You mock the nobility of man, for you have seen that too often nobility gives way to more base desires. Yet you have secretly set yourself standards which other men will never understand. You, more than any of the others, desire to live. The urge is strong in you to run away. But you will not, not as long as a single man stands to defend these walls. Your courage is great.

"Rek, you are the most difficult to answer for. Like Bowman, you are a romantic, but there is a depth to you which I have not tried to plumb. You are intuitive and intelligent, but it is your intuition that guides you. You know it is right that you stay—and also senseless that you stay. Your intellect tells you that this cause is folly, but your intuition forces you to reject your intellect. You are that rare animal, a born leader of men. And you cannot leave.

"All of you are bound together in chains a thousand times stronger than steel.

"And finally there is one—who comes now—for which all I have said remains true. He is a lesser man than any here and yet a greater, for his fears are greater than yours, and yet he also will stand firm and die beside you."

The door opened, and Orrin entered, his armor bright and freshly oiled. Silently he sat among them, accepting a goblet of wine.

"I trust Ulric was in good health," he said.

"He has never looked better, old horse," answered Bowman.

"Then we will give him a bloody nose tomorrow," said the general, his dark eyes gleaming.

The dawn sky was bright and clear as the Drenai warriors ate a cold breakfast of bread and cheese, washed down with honeyed water. Every man who could stand manned the walls, blades to the ready. As the Nadir prepared to advance, Rek leapt to the battlements and turned to face the defenders.

"No long speeches today," he shouted. "We all know our plight. But I want to say that I am proud, more proud than I could ever have imagined. I wish I could find words . . ." He stammered to silence, then lifted his sword from its scabbard and held it high.

"By all the gods that ever walked, I swear that you are the finest men I ever knew. And if I could have chosen the end of this tale and peopled it with heroes of the past, I would not change a single thing. For no one could have given more than you have.

"And I thank you.

"But if any man here wishes to leave now, he may do so. Many of you have wives, children, others depending on you. If that be the case, leave now with my blessing. For what we do here today will not affect the outcome of the war."

He leapt lightly to the ramparts to rejoin Orrin and Hogun.

Farther along the line a young cul shouted: "What of you, Earl of Bronze? Will you stay?"

Rek stepped to the wall once more. "I must stay, but I give you leave to go."

No man moved, though many considered it.

The Nadir war cry rose, and the battle began.

Throughout that long day, no toothold could be gained by the Nadir and the carnage was terrible.

The great sword of Egel lunged and slew, cleaving armor, flesh, and bone, and the Drenai fought like demons, cutting and slaying ferociously. For these, as Serbitar had predicted so many weeks ago, were the finest of the fighting men, and death and fear of death had no place in their minds. Time and again the Nadir reeled back, bloodied and bemused.

But as dusk approached, the assault on the gates strengthened and the great barrier of bronze and oak began to buckle. Serbitar led the last of the Thirty to stand, as Druss had done, in the shadow of the gate porch. Rek raced to join them, but a withering mind pulse from Serbitar ordered him back to the wall. He was about to resist when Nadir warriors scrambled over the ramparts behind him. Egel's sword flashed, beheading the first, and Rek was once more in the thick of battle.

In the gateway Serbitar was joined by Suboden, the captain of his Vagrian bodyguard. Only some sixty men were still alive out of the force that had originally arrived.

"Go back to the walls," said Serbitar.

The fair-haired Vagrian shook his head. "I cannot. We are here as your carle-guard, and we will die with you."

"You bear me no love, Suboden. You have made that plain."

"Love has little to do with my duty, Lord Serbitar. Even so, I hope you will forgive me. I thought your powers were demon-sent, but no man possessed would stand as you do now."

"There is nothing to forgive, but you have my blessing," Serbitar told the blond carle-captain.

The gates splintered suddenly, and with a roar of triumph the Nadir burst through, hurling themselves upon the defenders spearheaded by the white-haired templar.

Drawing a slender Ventrian dagger, Serbitar fought two-handed, blocking, stabbing, parrying, and cutting. Men fell before him, but always more leapt to fill the breach he created. Beside him the slim Vagrian carle-captain hacked and hammered at the oncoming barbarians. An ax splintered his shield, but hurling aside the fragments, he took a double-handed grip on his sword, bellowed his defiance, and launched himself forward. An ax crushed his ribs, and a lance tore into his thigh. He fell into the seething mass, stabbing left and right. A kick sent him sprawling to his back, and three spears buried themselves in his chest. Feebly he sought to lift his sword one last time, but an iron-studded boot stamped on his hand, while a blow from a wooden club ended his life.

Vintar fought coolly, pushing himself alongside the albino, waiting for the arrow he knew would be loosed at any second. Ducking beneath a slashing sword, he disemboweled his opponent and turned.

In the shadows of the sundered gates an archer drew back on his string, his fingers nestling against his cheek. The shaft leapt from the bow to take Vintar in the right eye, and he fell against the Nadir spears.

The remaining defenders fought in an ever-tightening circle as dusk deepened into night. The Nadir cries were silenced now, the battle tense and silent but for the sounds of steel on steel on flesh.

Menahem was lifted from his feet by the force of a stabbing spear that tore into his lungs. His sword whistled down toward the neck of the kneeling lancer—and stopped.

Lightly he touched the blade to the man's shoulder. Unable to believe his luck, the warrior dragged his spear free and buried it once more in the priest's chest.

Now Serbitar was alone.

Momentarily the Nadir fell back, staring at the blood-covered albino. Much of the blood was his own. His cloak was in tatters, his armor gashed and dented, his helm long since knocked from his head.

He took three deep shuddering breaths, looked inside himself, and saw that he was dying. Reaching out with his mind, he sought Vintar and the others.

Silence.

A terrible silence.

It was all for nothing, then, he thought as the Nadir tensed for the kill. He chuckled wryly.

There was no Source.

No center to the universe.

In the last seconds left to him he wondered if his life had been a waste.

He knew it had not. For even if there was no Source, there ought to have been. For the Source was beautiful.

A Nadir warrior sprang forward. Serbitar flicked aside his thrust, burying his dagger in the man's breast, but the pack surged in, a score of sharp blades meeting inside his frail form. Blood burst from his mouth, and he fell.

From a great distance came a voice:

"Take my hand, my brother. We travel."

It was Vintar!

The Nadir surged and spread toward the deserted Delnoch buildings and the score of streets that led to Geddon and the keep beyond. In the front line Ogasi raised his sword, bellowing the Nadir victory chant. He began to run, then skidded to a halt.

Ahead of him on the open ground before the buildings stood a tall man with a trident beard, dressed in the white robes of the Sathuli. He carried two tulwars, curved and deadly. Ogasi advanced slowly, confused.

A Sathuli within the Drenai fortress?

"What do you do here?" yelled Ogasi.

"Merely helping a friend," replied the man. "Go back! I shall not let you pass."

Ogasi grinned. So the man was a lunatic. Lifting his sword, he ordered the tribesmen forward. The white-robed figure advanced on them.

"Sathuli!" he yelled.

From the buildings came a mighty answering roar as three thousand Sathuli warriors, their white robes ghostly in the gathering darkness, streamed to the attack.

The Nadir were stunned, and Ogasi could not believe his eyes. The Sathuli and the Drenai were lifelong enemies. He knew it was happening, but his brain would not drink it in. Like a white tide on a dark beach, the Sathuli front line crashed into Nadir.

Joachim sought Ogasi, but the stocky tribesman was lost amid the chaos.

The savage twist to events, from certain victory to certain death, dismayed the tribesmen. Panic set in, and a slow

withdrawal became a rout. Trampling their comrades, the
Nadir turned and ran with the white army at their backs,
harrying them on with screams as bestial as any heard on
the Nadir steppes.

On the walls above, Rek was bleeding from wounds in
his upper arms and Hogun had suffered a sword cut to his
scalp, blood running from the gash and skin flapping as he
lashed out at his attackers.

Now Sathuli warriors appeared on the battlements and
once more the Nadir fled their terrible tulwars, backing to
the walls and seeking escape down the ropes.

Within minutes it was over. Elsewhere on the open
ground small pockets of Nadir warriors were surrounded
and dispatched.

Joachim Sathuli, his white robes stained with crimson,
slowly mounted the rampart steps, followed by his seven
lieutenants. He approached Rek and bowed. Turning, he
handed his bloody tulwars to a dark-bearded warrior. Another man passed him a scented towel. Slowly, elaborately,
he wiped his face and then his hands. Finally he spoke.

"A warm welcome," he said, his face unsmiling but his
eyes full of humor.

"Indeed," said Rek. "It is lucky the other guests had to
leave; otherwise there would not have been any room."

"Are you so surprised to see me?"

"No, not surprised. Astonished sounds more accurate."

Joachim laughed. "Is your memory so short, Delnoch?
You said we should part as friends, and I agreed. Where
else should I be in a friend's hour of need?"

"You must have had the devil's own task convincing
your warriors to follow you."

"Not at all," answered Joachim, an impish gleam in his
eyes. "Most of their lives they have longed to fight inside
these walls."

The tall Sathuli warrior stood on the high walls of Geddon,
gazing down at the Nadir camp beyond the deserted battlements of Valteri. Rek was asleep now, and the bearded
prince strode the walls alone. Around him were sentries and
soldiers of both races, but Joachim remained solitary.

For weeks Sathuli scouts atop the Delnoch range had

watched the battle raging below. Often Joachim himself had scaled the peaks to view the fighting. Then a Nadir raiding party had struck at a Sathuli village, and Joachim had persuaded his men to follow him to Delnoch. Added to this, he knew of the traitor who dealt with the Nadir, for he had witnessed a meeting in a high, narrow pass between the traitor and the Nadir captain, Ogasi.

Two days later the Nadir had tried to send a force over the mountains, and the Sathuli had repulsed it.

Joachim heard the news of Rek's loss with sadness. Fatalistic himself, he could still share the feelings of a man whose woman had died. His own had died in childbirth two years before, and the wound was still fresh.

Joachim shook his head. War was a savage mistress but a woman of power nonetheless. She could wreak more havoc in a man's soul than time.

The Sathuli arrival had been timely and not without cost. Four hundred of his men were dead, a loss scarcely bearable to a mountain people who numbered a mere thirty thousand, many of those being children and ancients.

But a debt was a debt.

The man Hogun hated him, Joachim knew. But this was understandable, for Hogun was of the legion and the Sathuli had spilled legion blood for years. They reserved their finest tortures for captured riders. This was an honor, but Joachim knew the Drenai could never understand. When a man died, he was tested—the harder the death, the greater the rewards in paradise. Torture advanced a man's soul, and the Sathuli could offer no greater reward to a captured enemy.

He sat upon the battlements and stared back at the keep. For how many years had he longed to take this fortress? How many of his dreams had been filled with pictures of the keep in flames?

And now he was defending it with the lives of his followers.

He shrugged. A man with his eyes on the sky did not see the scorpion below his feet. A man with his eyes on the ground did not see the dragon in the air.

He paced the ramparts, coming at last to the gate tower and the stone inscription carved there: GEDDON.

The wall of death.

The air was thick with the smell of death, and the morning would see the crows fly in to the feast. He should have killed Rek in the woods. A promise to an unbeliever was worth nothing, so why had he kept it? He laughed suddenly, accepting the answer: Because the man had not cared.

And Joachim liked him.

He passed a Drenai sentry who saluted him and smiled. Joachim nodded, noting the uncertainty of the smile.

He had told the Earl of Bronze that he and his men would stay for one more day and then return to the mountains. He had expected a plea to remain—offers, promises, treaties. But Rek had merely smiled.

"It is more than I would have asked for," he said.

Joachim was stunned, but he could say nothing. He told Rek of the traitor and of the Nadir attempt to cross the mountains.

"Will you still bar the way?"

"Of course. That is Sathuli land."

"Good! Will you eat with me?"

"No, but I thank you for the offer."

No Sathuli could break bread with an unbeliever.

Rek nodded. "I think I will rest now," he said. "I will see you at dawn."

In his high room in the keep Rek slept, dreaming of Virae, always of Virae. He awoke hours before dawn and reached out for her. But the sheets beside him were cold, and as always, he felt the loss anew. On this night he wept long and soundlessly. Finally he rose, dressed, and descended the stairs to the small hall. The manservant Arshin brought him a breakfast of cold ham and cheese, with a flagon of cold water laced with honey mead. He ate mechanically until a young officer approached with the news that Bricklyn had returned with dispatches from Drenan.

The burgher entered the hall, bowed briefly, and approached the table, laying before Rek several packages and a large sealed scroll. He seated himself opposite Rek and asked if he could pour himself a drink. Rek nodded as he opened the scroll. He read it once, smiled, then laid it aside and looked across at the burgher. He was thinner and perhaps even grayer than the first time Rek had seen him. He was still dressed in riding clothes, and his green cloak was dust-covered. Bricklyn drained the water in two swallows and refilled his cup; then he noticed Rek's eyes upon him.

"You have seen the message from Abalayn?" he asked.

"Yes. Thank you for bringing it. Will you stay?"

"But of course. Surrender arrangements must be made, and Ulric welcomed to the keep."

"He has promised to spare no one," said Rek softly.

Bricklyn waved his hand. "Nonsense! That was war talk. Now he will be magnanimous."

"And what of Woundweaver?"

"He has been recalled to Drenan, and the army disbanded."

"Are you pleased?"

"That the war is over? Of course. Though I am naturally saddened that so many had to die. I hear that Druss fell at Sumitos. A great shame. He was a fine man and a magnificent warrior. But it was as he would have wished to go, I am sure. When would you like me to see Lord Ulric?"

"As soon as you wish."

"Will you accompany me?"

"No."

"Then who will?" asked Bricklyn, noting with pleasure the resignation mirrored in Rek's face.

"No one."

"No one? But that would not be politic, my lord. There should be a deputation."

"You will travel alone."

"Very well. What terms shall I negotiate?"

"You will negotiate nothing. You will merely go to Ulric and say that I have sent you."

"I do not understand, my lord. What would you have me say?"

"You will say that you have failed."

"Failed? In what? You speak in riddles. Are you mad?"

"No. Just tired. You betrayed us, Bricklyn, but then, I expect nothing less from your breed. Therefore, I am not angry. Or vengeful. You have taken Ulric's pay, and now you may go to him. The letter from Abalayn is a forgery, and Woundweaver will be here in five days with over fifty thousand men. Outside there are three thousand Sathuli, and we can hold the wall. Now be gone! Hogun knows that you are a traitor and has told me that he will kill you if he sees you. Go now."

For several minutes Bricklyn sat stunned, then he shook his head. "This is madness! You cannot hold! It is Ulric's day, can you not see it? The Drenai are finished, and Ulric's star shines. What do you hope to achieve?"

Rek slowly drew a long, slender dagger and placed it on the table before him.

"Go now," he repeated quietly.

Bricklyn rose and stormed to the door. He turned in the doorway.

"You fool!" he spit. "Use the dagger on yourself, for what the Nadir will do when they take you will make merry viewing." Then he was gone.

Hogun stepped from behind a tapestry-covered alcove and moved to the table. His head was bandaged, and his face pale. In his hand he held his sword.

"How could you let him go, Rek? How?"

Rek smiled. "Because I couldn't be bothered to kill him."

◇ 30 ◇

THE LAST CANDLE guttered and died as a light autumn wind billowed the curtains. Rek slept on, head resting on his arms at the table where only an hour before he had sent Bricklyn to the Nadir. His sleep was light but dreamless. He shivered as the room became cooler, then awoke with a start in the darkness. Fear touched him, and he reached for his dagger. He shivered again. It was cold . . . so cold. He glanced at the fire. It was blazing, but no heat reached him. He stood and walked toward it, squatting in front of it and opening his hands to the heat. Nothing. Confused, he stood once more and turned back to the table, and then the shock hit him.

Head resting on his arms, the figure of Earl Regnak still slept there. He fought down panic, watching his sleeping form, noting the weariness in the gaunt face, the dark-hollowed eyes, and the lines of strain about the mouth.

Then he noticed the silence. Even at this late hour of deepest darkness some sounds should be heard from sentries or servants or the few cooks preparing the morning's breakfast. But there was nothing. He moved to the doorway and beyond into the darkened corridor, then beyond that into the shadow of the portcullis gate. He was alone. Beyond the gate were the walls, but no sentries paced them. He walked on in the darkness, and the clouds cleared and the moon shone brightly.

The fortress was deserted.

From the high walls of Geddon he looked to the north. The plain was empty. No Nadir tents were pitched there.

So he was truly alone. Panic left him, and a deep sense

331

of peace covered his soul like a warm blanket. He sat on the ramparts, gazing back at the keep.

Was this a taste of death? he wondered. Or merely a dream? He cared not. Whether a foretaste of tomorrow's reality or the result of a needed fantasy was immaterial. He was enjoying the moment.

And then, with a deep sense of warmth, he knew that he was not alone. His heart swelled, and tears came to his eyes. He turned, and she was there: Dressed as he had first seen her, with a bulky sheepskin jerkin and woolen trews, she opened her arms and walked into his embrace. He held her tightly to him, pressing his face into her hair. For a long time they stood thus while deep sobs racked his body. Finally the crying subsided, and he gently released her. She looked up at him and smiled.

"You have done well, Rek," she said. "I am so proud of you."

"Without you it is meaningless," he said.

"I wouldn't change anything, Rek. If they told me that I could have my life again but not meet you, I would refuse. What does it matter that we had only months? What months they were!"

"I never loved anyone as I loved you," he said.

"I know."

They talked for hours, but the moon shone from the same place and the stars were static, the night eternal. Finally she kissed him to stem his words.

"There are others you must see."

He tried to argue, but she held her fingers to his mouth. "We will meet again, my love. For now, speak to the others."

Around the walls was now a mist, swirling and thick. Overhead the moon shone in a cloudless sky. She walked into the mist and was gone. He waited, and soon a figure in silver armor came toward him. As always he looked fresh and alert, his armor reflected the moonlight, and his white cloak was spotless. He smiled.

"Well met, Rek," said Serbitar. They clasped hands in the warrior's grip.

"The Sathuli came," said Rek. "You held the gate just long enough."

"I know. Tomorrow will be hard, and I will not lie to you. All futures have I seen, and in only one do you survive the day. But there are forces here which I cannot explain to you, and even now their magic is at work. Fight well!"

"Will Woundweaver arrive?" asked Rek.

Serbitar shrugged. "Not tomorrow."

"Then we will fall?"

"It is likely. But if you do not, I want you to do something for me."

"Name it," said Rek.

"Go once more to Egel's room, where there is a last gift for you. The servant Arshin will explain."

"What is it? Is it a weapon? I could use it tomorrow."

"It is not a weapon. Go there tomorrow night."

"Serbitar?"

"Yes, my friend."

"Was all as you dreamed it would be? The Source, I mean?"

"Yes! And so much more. But I cannot speak of it now. Wait for a while longer. There is another who must speak with you."

The mist deepened, and Serbitar's white form drew back until he merged and was gone.

And Druss was there. Mighty and strong, his black jerkin glistening, his ax at his side.

"He gave me a fine send-off," said Druss. "How are you, boy? You look tired."

"I am tired but all the better for seeing you."

Druss clapped him on the shoulder and laughed.

"That Nogusha used a poisoned blade on me. I tell you, laddie, it hurt like hell. Caessa dressed me. I don't know how she got me to my feet. Still ... she did."

"I saw it," said Rek.

"Aye, a grand exit, was it not? That young lad Gilad fought well. I have not seen him yet, but I expect I shall. You're a good boy, Rek. Worthy! It was good to know you."

"And you, Druss. I never met a better man."

"Of course you did, boy. Hundreds! But it's nice of you to say it. However, I didn't come here to exchange compli-

ments. I know what you are facing, and I know tomorrow
will be hard—damned hard. But don't give ground. Do not
retreat to the keep. Whatever happens, hold the wall. Much
rests on it. Keep Joachim beside you; if he dies, you are
finished. I must go. But remember. *Hold the wall. Do not
retreat to the keep.*"

"I will remember. Good-bye, Druss."

"Not good-bye. Not yet," said Druss. "Soon."

The mist moved forward, enveloping the axman and
sweeping over Rek. Then the moonlight faded, and dark
descended on the Earl of Bronze.

Back in the keep Rek awoke. The fire still burned, and
he was hungry again.

In the kitchens Arshin was preparing breakfast. The old
man was tired, but he brightened when Rek walked in.

He liked the new earl and remembered when Virae's father, Delnar, had been a young man, proud and strong.
There seemed a similarity, but perhaps, Arshin thought, the
long years had distorted his memory.

He handed the earl some toasted bread and honey, which
he wolfed down, following it with watered wine.

Back in his quarters Rek buckled his armor into place
and made his way to the battlements. Hogun and Orrin
were already there, supervising the barricade within the
gate tunnel.

"This is the weak spot," said Orrin. "We should retire to
the keep. At least the gates will hold for some hours."

Rek shook his head. "We will stand on Geddon. There
must be no retreat."

"Then we shall die here," said Hogun. "For that barricade will hold them not at all."

"Perhaps," said Rek. "We shall see. Good morning,
Joachim Sathuli."

The bearded warrior nodded and smiled. "You slept well,
Earl of Bronze?"

"Well, indeed. I thank you for giving us this day of your
time."

"It is nothing. The payment of a small debt."

"You owe me nothing. But I tell you this: If we survive
this day, there shall be no more war between us. The rights
to the high Delnoch passes are mine, though you dispute

the rights of the Drenai to them. Therefore, before these witnesses, I give them to you.

"There is also a scroll bearing my seal at the keep. When you leave tonight, you shall have it. A copy will go to Abalayn in Drenan.

"I know that the gesture will have little meaning if the Nadir win through today, but it is all I can do."

Joachim bowed. "The gesture is enough in itself."

The talk ceased as the Nadir drums sounded and the warriors of Dros Delnoch spread out along the wall to receive the attackers. Rek lowered his helm visor and drew the sword of Egel. Below, in the barricaded gate tunnel, stood Orrin and one hundred warriors. The tunnel was only twenty feet wide at the center, and Orrin reckoned to hold it for the greater part of the morning. After that, with the barricades torn down, the sheer weight of the Nadir horde would push them back into the open ground behind the ramparts.

And so the last bloody day began at Dros Delnoch.

◇ 31 ◇

WAVE AFTER WAVE of screaming tribesmen scaled ropes and ladders throughout the morning, finding that only cold, terrible death awaited them under the slashing swords and tulwars of the defenders. Men fell screaming to the rocks below the walls or died trampled beneath the feet of battling men on the ramparts. Side by side, Sathuli and Drenai brought death to the Nadir.

Rek cut and slashed two-handed, the sword of Egel cleaving the ranks of the Nadir like a scythe through wheat. Beside him Joachim fought with two short swords, whirling and killing.

Below, Orrin's men were being pushed slowly back into the wider section of the tunnel, though the Nadir paid dearly for every inch of ground.

Blocking a thrusting lance, Orrin backhanded a slashing cut to a warrior's face. The man disappeared in the milling mass, and another attacker took his place.

"We can't hold!" yelled a young officer to Orrin's right.

Orrin had no time to answer.

Suddenly the leading Nadir warrior screamed in horror, pushing back into his comrades. Others followed his gaze, looking back beyond the Drenai at the tunnel mouth.

A gap opened between the Drenai and the Nadir and widened as the tribesmen turned and fled down into the open grounds between Valteri and Geddon.

"Great gods of Missael!" said the officer. "What's going on?" Orrin turned and saw what had filled the Nadir with terror.

Behind them in the darkened tunnel stood Druss the Legend, Serbitar, and the Thirty. With them were many departed warriors. Druss's ax was in his hand, and the joy of battle was in his eyes. Orrin swallowed, then licked his lips. He replaced his sword in its scabbard at the third attempt.

"I think we will leave them to hold the tunnel," he said. The remaining men bunched behind him as he walked toward Druss.

The ghostly defenders appeared not to notice them, their eyes fixed on the tunnel beyond. Orrin tried to speak to Druss, but the old man just stared ahead. When Orrin reached out a shaking hand and tried to touch the axman, his hand met nothing, only cold, cold air.

"Let us get back to the wall," he said. He closed his eyes and walked blindly through the ranks of the spirits. By the time he reached the tunnel mouth, he was shivering. The other men with him said nothing.

No one looked back.

He joined Rek on the wall, and the battle continued. Moments later, during a brief lull, Rek shouted: "What's happening in the tunnel?"

"Druss is there," replied Orrin. Rek merely nodded and turned again as fresh Nadir warriors breasted the ramparts.

Bowman, bearing a short sword and buckler, fought beside Hogun. Though not as skilled with the blade as with the bow, he was no mean warrior.

Hogun blocked an ax blow, and his sword snapped. The ax head crushed his shoulder, burying itself in his chest. He hammered the broken sword into the belly of the axman and fell with him to the ground.

A lance licked out, spearing the legion general's back as he struggled to rise. Bowman's short sword disemboweled the lancer, but more Nadir pressed forward and Hogun's body was lost in the melee.

By the gate tower Joachim Sathuli fell, his side pierced by a thrown spear. Rek half carried him beyond the ramparts but had to leave him, for the Nadir had almost broken through. Joachim gripped the spear with both hands, sweat breaking out on his forehead, and examined the wound. The point had passed through just above the right hip and broken the skin of his back. The head, he knew, was barbed, and there would be no drawing it out. He gripped

the spear more firmly, rolled to his side, then pushed it farther into the wound until the whole of the spear head
cleared his back. He passed out for several minutes, but the
gentle touch of a hand roused him. A Sathuli warrior
named Andisim was beside him.

"Remove the head of the spear," Joachim hissed.
"Quickly!"

Wordlessly the man took his dagger and as gently as pos-
sible levered the spear head from the shaft. At last it was
done. "Now," whispered Joachim, "pull the shaft clear."
Standing above him, the man slowly withdrew the spear as
Joachim grunted against the agony. Blood gushed out, but
Joachim ripped his robe and plugged the wound, allowing
Andisim to do the same for the hole in his back.

"Get me to my feet," he ordered, "and fetch me a tulwar."

Beyond the walls of Eldibar, within his tent, Ulric
watched the sands fall in the huge glass. Beside him was
the scroll he had received that morning from the north.

His nephew Jahingir had declared himself khan—
overlord of the north. He had slain Ulric's brother, Tsubodi,
and taken Ulric's mistress, Hasita, as a hostage.

Ulric could not blame him and felt no anger. His family
was born to lead, and blood ran true among them.

But he could not dally here and so had set the glass. If
the wall had not fallen by the time the sand ran out, he
would lead his army north again, win back his kingdom,
and return to take Dros Delnoch on another day.

He had received the message about Druss holding the
tunnel and had shrugged. Alone once more, he had smiled.

So, not even paradise can keep you from the battle, old
man!

Outside his tent stood three men bearing rams' horns,
waiting for his signal. And the sands flowed on.

On the wall of Geddon the Nadir broke through to the
right. Rek screamed for Orrin to follow him and cut a path
along the ramparts. To the left more Nadir gained the ramparts, and the Drenai fell back, leaping to the grass and reforming. The Nadir swarmed forward.

The day was lost.

Sathuli and Drenai waited, swords ready, as the Nadir

massed before them. Bowman and Orrin stood beside Rek, and Joachim Sathuli limped toward them.

"I'm glad we are offering you only one day," grunted Joachim, clutching the bloody bandage wedged into his side.

The Nadir spread out before them and charged.

Rek leaned on his sword blade, breathing deeply and saving what was left of his strength. There was no longer the energy inside him to promote a baresark rage, or the will.

All his life he had feared this moment, and now that it was upon him, it was as meaningless as dust upon the ocean. Wearily he focused his gaze on the charging warriors.

"I say, old horse," muttered Bowman, "do you think it's too late to surrender?"

Rek grinned. "Just a little," he said. His hands curled around the sword hilt, he twisted his wrist, and the blade hissed into the air.

The front ranks of the Nadir were less than twenty paces from them when the sound of distant rams' horns echoed up from the valley.

The charge slowed . . .

And stopped. Less than ten paces apart, both sides stood listening to the insistent wailing.

Ogasi cursed and spit, sheathing his sword. He stared sullenly into the astonished eyes of the Earl of Bronze. Rek removed his helm and plunged his sword into the ground before him as Ogasi stepped forward.

"It is over!" he said. He lifted his arm, waving the Nadir back to the walls. Then he turned. "Know this, you round-eyed bastard. It was I, Ogasi, who slew your wife."

It took a few seconds for the words to register, then Rek took a deep breath and removed his gauntlets.

"Do you think it matters amid all this," said Rek, "to know who fired one arrow? You want me to remember you? I shall. You want me to hate you? I cannot. Maybe tomorrow. Or next year. Maybe never."

For a moment Ogasi stood silent, then he shrugged.

"The arrow was meant for you," he said, weariness settling on him like a dark cloak. Turning on his heel, he fol-

lowed the departing warriors. Silently they climbed down
the ladders and ropes; none took the path through the gate
tunnel.

Rek unbuckled his breastplate and walked slowly to the
tunnel mouth. Coming toward him were Druss and the
Thirty. Rek lifted a hand in greeting, but a wind blew and
the warriors vanished into mist and were gone.

"Good-bye, Druss," he said softly.

Later that evening Rek bade farewell to the Sathuli and
slept for several hours, hoping for another meeting with
Virae. He awoke refreshed but disappointed.

Arshin brought him food, and he ate with Bowman and
Orrin. They said little. Calvar Syn and his orderlies had
found Hogun's body, and the surgeon was laboring to save
the hundreds of wounded men now being carried to the
Geddon hospital.

Rek made his way to his room around midnight and removed his armor; then he remembered Serbitar's gift. He
was too tired to care, but sleep would not come, so he rose
and dressed, took a torch from a wall bracket, and made his
way slowly down into the bowels of the keep. The door to
Egel's room was closed once more, but it opened to him as
before.

The lights blazed within as Rek placed his torch against
the wall and stepped inside. His breath caught in his throat
as he gazed on the crystal block. Within it lay Virae! Upon
her body was no mark, no arrow wound; she lay naked and
peaceful, seemingly asleep, floating within the transparent
crystal. He walked to the block, reached inside, and touched
her. She did not stir, and her body was cold. Stooping, he
lifted her clear and placed her on a nearby table. Then he removed his cloak, wrapped it around her, and lifted her again.
Gathering up the torch, he made his slow way back to his
room above the keep hall.

He summoned Arshin, and the old retainer blanched as
he saw the still form of the earl's wife. He looked at Rek,
then gazed at the floor.

"I am sorry, my lord. I do not know why the white-
haired one placed her body in the magic crystal."

"What happened?" asked Rek.

"The prince Serbitar and his friend the abbot came to see

me on the day she died. The abbot had had a dream, he said. He would not explain it to me, but he said it was vital that my lady's body be placed within the crystal. He said something about the Source . . . I didn't understand it. I still don't, my lord. Is she alive or dead? And how did you find her? We laid her upon this crystal block, and she gently sank into it. Yet when I touched it, it was solid. I understand nothing anymore." Tears welled in the old man's eyes, and Rek moved to him, placing a hand on his bony shoulder.

"It is all hard to explain. Fetch Calvar Syn. I will wait here with Virae."

A dream of Vintar's—what could it mean? The albino had said that there were many tomorrows and that no one could ever tell which would come to pass. But he had obviously seen one in which Virae lived and had ordered her body to be preserved. And somehow the wound had been healed inside the crystal. But did that mean she would live?

Virae alive!

His mind reeled. He could neither think nor feel, and his body seemed numb. Her death had all but destroyed him, yet now, with her here once more, he was afraid to hope. If life had taught him anything, it had shown him that every man had a breaking point. He knew he was now facing his. He sat by the bed and lifted her cold hand, his own hand shaking with tension, and felt for a pulse. Nothing. Crossing the room, he fetched another blanket and covered her, then went to work building a fire in the hearth.

It was nearly an hour before he heard Calvar Syn on the stairs outside. The man was cursing Arshin loudly. Wearing a stained blue tunic and a blood-covered leather apron, the surgeon stepped into the room.

"What fool nonsense is this, Earl?" he thundered. "I have men who are dying for want of my skills. What . . ." He stammered to silence as he saw the girl in the bed. "So, the old man was not lying. Why, Rek? Why have you brought her body back?"

"I don't know. Truly. Serbitar came to me in a dream and told me he had left a gift for me. This is what I found. I don't know what's happening. Is she dead?"

"Of course she's dead. The arrow pierced her lung."

"Look at her, will you. There's no wound."

The surgeon pulled back the sheet and lifted her wrist. For several moments he stood in silence. "There is a pulse," he whispered, "but it is faint and very, very slow. I cannot wait with you. There are men dying. But I will return in the morning. Keep her warm; that's all you can do."

Rek sat beside the bed, holding her hand. Sometime, though he knew not when, he fell asleep beside her. The dawn broke bright and clear, and the rising sun's light entered the eastern window, bathing the bed in golden light. At its touch, Virae's cheeks gained color and her breathing deepened. A soft moan came from her lips, and Rek was instantly awake.

"Virae? Virae, can you hear me?"

Her eyes opened, then closed again, her lashes fluttering.

"Virae!" Once more her eyes opened, and she smiled.

"Serbitar brought me back," she said. "So tired . . . Must sleep." She turned over, hugged the pillow, and fell asleep just as the door opened and Bowman stepped inside.

"Gods, it's true, then," he said.

Rek ushered him from the room into the corridor.

"Yes. Somehow Serbitar saved her. I cannot explain it. I don't even care how it happened. What is going on outside?"

"They've gone! All of them—every damned one of them, old horse. The camp is deserted; Orrin and I have been there. All that's left is a Wolfshead standard and the body of that burgher Bricklyn. Can you make any sense out of it?"

"No," said Rek. "That standard means that Ulric will return. The body? I can't say. I sent him to them. He was a traitor, and obviously they had no more use for him."

A young officer came running up the spiral stairs.

"My lord! There is a Nadir rider waiting at Eldibar."

Rek and Bowman walked together to Wall One. Below them on a gray steppe pony sat Ulric, Lord of the Nadir, dressed in fur-rimmed helmet, woolen jerkin, and goatskin boots. He looked up as Rek leaned over the ramparts.

"You fought well, Earl of Bronze," he shouted. "I came to bid you farewell. There is civil war in my own kingdom, and I must leave you for a while. I wanted you to know that I shall return."

"I will be here," said Rek. "And next time your reception will be even warmer. Tell me, why did your men retire when we were beaten?"

"Do you believe in fate?" asked Ulric.

"I do."

"Then let us call it a trick of fate. Or perhaps it was a cosmic jest, a joke played by the gods. I care not. You are a brave man. Your men are brave men. And you have won. I can live with that, Earl of Bronze. A poor man would I be if I could not. But for now, farewell! I shall see you again in the spring."

Ulric waved, turned his pony's head, and galloped off into the north.

"Do you know," said Bowman, "although it may sound grotesque, I think I like the man."

"Today I could like anybody," said Rek, smiling. "The sky is clear, the wind is fresh, and life tastes very fine. What will you do now?"

"I think I will become a monk and devote my entire life to prayer and good works."

"No," said Rek. "I mean, what will you do today?"

"Ah! Today I'll get drunk and go whoring," said Bowman.

Throughout the long day Rek periodically visited the sleeping Virae. Her color was good, her breathing deep and even. Late in the evening, as he sat alone in the small hall before a dying fire, she came to him, dressed in a light green woolen tunic. He stood and took her into his arms, kissed her, then sat down in the leather chair and pulled her to his lap.

"The Nadir have really gone?" she asked.

"They have indeed."

"Rek, did I truly die? It seems like a dream now. Hazy. I seem to remember Serbitar bringing me back and my body lay in a glass block beneath the keep."

"It was not a dream," said Rek. "Do you remember coming to me as I fought the giant worm and a huge spider?"

"Vaguely. But it's fading even as I remember it."

"Don't worry about it. I will tell you everything during the next fifty years or so."

"Only fifty years?" she said. "So you will desert me when I'm old and gray?"

The sound of laughter echoed through the keep.

Epilogue

ULRIC NEVER RETURNED to Dros Delnoch. He defeated Jahingir in a pitched battle at Gulgothir Plain and then took his army to invade Ventria. During the campaign he collapsed and died. The tribes fled back to the north, and without his influence Nadir unity was broken. Civil war came once more to the north, and the people of the rich southlands breathed again.

Rek was welcomed as a hero in Drenan but soon tired of the city life and returned with Virae to Delnoch. Their family grew over the years, with three sons and two daughters. The sons were Hogun, Orrin, and Horeb. The daughters were Susay and Besa. Grandfather Horeb brought his family from Drenan to Delnoch, taking over the inn of the traitor Musar.

Orrin returned to Drenan and resigned from the army. His uncle Abalayn retired from public life, and Magnus Woundweaver was elected to lead the council. He chose Orrin as his deputy.

Bowman remained at Delnoch for a year, then traveled to Ventria to fight the Nadir once more. He did not return.

THE KING
BEYOND
THE GATE

Book Two of *The Drenai Saga*

by David Gemmell

Published by Del Rey Books.
Available wherever books are sold.

Read on for a preview of
THE KING BEYOND THE GATE...

Prologue

THE TREES WERE laced with snow, and the forest lay waiting below him like a reluctant bride. For some time he stood among the rocks and boulders, scanning the slopes. Snow gathered on his fur-lined cloak and on the crown of his wide-brimmed hat, but he ignored it, as he ignored the cold seeping through his flesh and numbing his bones. He could have been the last man alive on a dying planet.

He half wished that he were.

At last, satisfied that there were no patrols, he moved down from the mountainside, placing his feet carefully on the treacherous slopes. His movements were slow, and he knew the cold to be a growing danger. He needed a campsite and a fire.

Behind him the Delnoch range reared under thickening clouds. Before him lay Skultik forest, an area of dark legend, failed dreams, and childhood memories.

The forest was silent, save for the occasional crack of dry wood as thickening ice probed the branches or the silky rushing of snow falling from overburdened boughs.

Tenaka turned to look at his footprints. Already the sharp edges of his tracks were blurring, and within minutes they would be gone. He pushed on, his thoughts sorrowful, his memories jagged.

He made camp in a shallow cave away from the wind and lit a small fire. The flames gathered and grew, red shadow dancers swaying on the cave walls. Removing his woolen gloves, he rubbed his hands above the blaze; then he rubbed his face, pinching the flesh to force the blood to flow. He wanted to sleep, but the cave was not yet warm enough.

The Dragon was dead. He shook his head, and closed his eyes. Ananais, Decado, Elias, Beltzer. All dead. Betrayed because they believed in honor and duty above all else. Dead because they believed that the Dragon was invincible and that good must ultimately triumph.

Tenaka shook himself awake, adding thicker branches to the fire.

"The Dragon is dead," he said aloud, his voice echoing in the cave. How strange, he thought. The words were true, yet he did not believe them.

He gazed at the fire shadows, seeing again the marbled halls of his palace in Ventria. There was no fire there, only the gentle cool of the inner rooms, the cold stone keeping at bay the strength-sapping heat of the desert sun. Soft chairs and woven rugs; servants bearing jugs of iced wine, carrying buckets of precious water to feed his rose garden and ensure the beauty of his flowering trees.

The messenger had been Beltzer. Loyal Beltzer, the finest bar-ranking warrior in the wing.

"We are summoned home, sir," he had said, standing ill at ease in the wide library, his clothes sand-covered and travel-stained. "The rebels have defeated one of Ceska's regiments in the north, and Baris has issued the call personally."

"How do you know it was Baris?"

"His seal, sir. His personal seal. And the message: 'The Dragon calls.' "

"Baris has not been seen for fifteen years."

"I know that, sir. But his seal . . ."

"A lump of wax means nothing."

"It does to me, sir."

"So you will go back to Drenai?"

"Yes, sir. And you?"

"Back to what, Beltzer? The land is in ruins. The Joinings are undefeatable. And who knows what foul, sorcerous powers will be ranged against the rebels? Face it, man! The Dragon was disbanded fifteen years ago, and we are all older men. I was one of the younger officers, and I am now forty. You must be nearer fifty—if the Dragon still survived, you would be in your pension year."

"I know that," Beltzer said, drawing himself stiffly to attention. "But honor calls. I have spent my life serving the Drenai, and now I cannot refuse the call."

"I can," said Tenaka. "The cause is lost. Give Ceska time and he will destroy himself. He is mad. The whole system is falling apart."

"I am not good with words, sir. I have ridden two hundred miles to deliver the message. I came seeking the man I served, but he is not here. I am sorry to have troubled you."

"Listen, Beltzer!" Tenaka said, as the warrior turned for the door. "If there was the smallest chance of success, I would go with you gladly. But the thing reeks of defeat."

"Do you not think I know that? That we all know it?" said Beltzer. And then he was gone.

The wind changed and veered into the cave, gusting snow to the fire. Tenaka cursed softly. Drawing his sword, he went outside, cutting down two thick bushes and dragging them back to screen the entrance.

As the months had passed, he had forgotten the Dragon. He had estates to minister, matters of importance in the real world.

Then Illae had fallen sick. He had been in the north, arranging cover patrols to guard the spice route, when word had reached him, and he had hurried home. The physicians said that she had a fever that would pass and that there was no cause for concern. But her condition worsened. Lung blight, they told him. Her flesh melted away until at last she lay in the wide bed, her breathing ragged, her once beautiful eyes shining with the image of death. Day after day he sat beside her, talking, praying, begging her not to die.

And then she had rallied, and his heart leapt. She had been talking to him about her plans for a party and had stopped to consider whom to invite.

"Go on," he had said. But she was gone. Just like that. Ten years of shared memories, hopes, and joys vanished like water on the desert sand.

He had lifted her from the bed, stopping to wrap her in

a white woolen shawl. Then he had carried her into the rose garden, holding her to him.

"I love you," he kept saying, kissing her hair and cradling her like a child. The servants had gathered, saying nothing, until after an hour two of them had come forward and separated them, leading the weeping Tenaka to his room. There he found the sealed scroll that listed the current state of his business investments, and beside it a letter from Estas, his accountant. This letter contained advice about areas of investment, with sharp political insights into places to ignore, exploit, or consider.

Unthinkingly he had opened the letter, scanning the list of Vagrian settlements, Lentrian openings, and Drenai stupidities until he came to the last sentences:

Ceska routed the rebels south of the Sentran Plain. It appears he has been bragging about his cunning again. He sent a message summoning old soldiers home; it seems he has feared the Dragon since he disbanded it fifteen years ago. Now his fears are behind him—they were destroyed to a man. The Joinings are terrifying. What sort of world are we living in?

"Living?" Tenaka said. "No one is living—they are all dead."

He stood up and walked to the western wall, stopping before an oval mirror and gazing at the ruin of his life.

His reflection stared back at him, the slanted violet eyes accusing, the tight-lipped mouth bitter and angry.

"Go home," said his reflection, "and kill Ceska."

◊ 1 ◊

THE BARRACKS BUILDINGS stood shrouded in snow, the broken windows hanging open like old, unhealed wounds. The square once trodden flat by ten thousand men was now uneven as the grass pushed against the snow above it.

The Dragon herself had been brutally treated: her stone wings smashed from her back, her fangs hammered to shards, and her face daubed with red dye. It seemed to Tenaka as he stood before her in silent homage that she was crying tears of blood.

As Tenaka gazed at the square, memory flashed bright pictures to his mind: Ananais shouting commands to his men, contradictory orders that had them crashing into one another and tumbling to the ground.

"You dung rats!" the blond giant bellowed. "Call yourselves soldiers?"

The pictures faded against the ghostly white emptiness of reality, and Tenaka shivered. He moved to the well, where an old bucket lay, its handle still tied to a rotting rope. He dropped the bucket into the well and heard the ice break, then hauled it up and carried it to the Dragon.

The dye was hard to shift, but he worked at it for almost an hour, scraping the last traces of red from the stone with his dagger.

Then he jumped to the ground and looked at his handi-work.

Even without the dye she looked pitiful, her pride broken. Tenaka thought once more of Ananais.

"Maybe it is better you died rather than living to see this," he said.

It began to rain, icy needles that stung his face. Tenaka scooped his pack to his shoulder and ran for the deserted barracks. The door hung open, and he stepped inside the old officers' quarters. A rat scurried into the dark as he passed, but Tenaka ignored it, pushing on to the wider rooms at the rear. He dumped his pack in his old room and then chuckled as he saw the fireplace: It was stacked with wood, the fire laid.

On the last day, knowing that they were leaving, someone had come into his room and laid the fire.

Decado, his aide?

No. There was no romantic element in his makeup. He was a vicious killer, held in check only by the iron discipline of the Dragon and his own rigid sense of loyalty to the regiment.

Who else?

After a while he stopped scanning the faces his memory threw at him. He would never know.

After fifteen years the wood should be dry enough to burn without smoke, he told himself, and placed fresh tinder below the logs. Soon the tongues of flame spread, and the blaze took hold.

On a sudden impulse he moved to the paneled wall, seeking the hidden niche. Where once it had sprung open at the touch of a button, now it creaked on a rusted spring. Gently he prized open the paneling. Behind was a small recess created by the removal of a stone slab many years before the disbanding. On the back wall, in Nadir script, was written:

> Nadir we,
> Youth born,
> Bloodletters,
> Ax wielders,
> Victors still.

Tenaka smiled for the first time in months, and some of the burden he carried was lifted from his soul. The years swept away, and he saw himself once more as a young man, fresh from the steppes, arriving to take up his commission with the Dragon, felt again the stares of his new brother officers and their scarcely veiled hostility.

A Nadir prince in the Dragon? It was inconceivable; some even thought it obscene. But his *was* a special case.

The Dragon had been formed by Magnus Woundweaver after the First Nadir War a century before, when the invincible warlord Ulric had led his hordes against the walls of Dros Delnoch, the most powerful fortress in the world, only to be turned back by the Earl of Bronze and his warriors.

The Dragon was to be the Drenai weapon against future Nadir invasions.

And then, like a nightmare come true—and while memories were still fresh of the Second Nadir War—a tribesman had been admitted to the regiment. Worse, he was a direct descendant of Ulric himself. And yet they had no choice but to allow him his saber.

For he was Nadir only on his mother's side.

Through the line of his father he was the great-grandson of Regnak the Wanderer: the Earl of Bronze.

It was a problem for those who yearned to hate him.

How could they visit their hatred upon the descendant of the Drenai's greatest hero? It was not easy for them, but they managed it.

Goat's blood was daubed on his pillow, scorpions hidden in his boots. Saddle straps were severed, and finally a viper was placed in his bed.

It almost killed him as he rolled on it, its fangs sinking into his thigh. Snatching a dagger from his bedside table, he had killed the snake and then slashed a cross-cut by the fang marks, hoping the rush of blood would carry the venom clear. Then he lay very still, knowing any movement would accelerate the poison in his system. He heard footsteps in the corridor and knew it was Ananais, the officer of the guard, returning to his room after completing his shift.

He did not want to call out, for he knew Ananais disliked him. But neither did he want to die! He called Ananais' name, the door opened, and the blond giant stood silhouetted in the doorway.

"I have been bitten by a viper," said Tenaka.

Ananais ducked under the doorway and approached the bed, pushing at the dead snake with his boot. Then he looked at the wound in Tenaka's leg.

"How long ago?" he asked.

"Two, three minutes."

Ananais nodded. "The cuts aren't deep enough."

Tenaka handed him the dagger.

"No. If they *were* deep enough, you would sever the main muscles."

Leaning forward, Ananais put his mouth over the wound and sucked the poison clear. Then he applied a tourniquet and left to get the surgeon.

Even with most of the poison flushed out, the young Nadir prince almost died. He sank into a coma that lasted four days, and when he awoke, Ananais was at his bedside.

"How are you feeling?"

"Good."

"You don't look it. Still, I am glad you're alive."

"Thank you for saving me," said Tenaka as the giant rose to leave.

"It was a pleasure. But I still wouldn't want you marrying my sister," he said, grinning as he moved to the door. "By the way, three young officers were dismissed from the service yesterday. I think you can sleep soundly from now on."

"I shall never do that," Tenaka said. "For the Nadir, that is the way of death."

"No wonder their eyes are slanted," said Ananais.

Renya helped the old man to his feet, then heaped snow on the small fire to kill the flames. The temperature plummeted as the storm clouds bunched above them, grim and threatening. The girl was frightened, for the old man had ceased shivering and now stood by the ruined tree, staring vacantly at the ground by his feet.

"Come, Aulin," she said, slipping her arm around his waist. "The old barracks are close by."

"No!" he wailed, pulling back. "They will find me there. I know they will."

"The cold will kill you," she hissed. "Come on."

Meekly he allowed her to lead him through the snow.

She was a tall girl and strong, but the going was tiring and she was breathing heavily as they pushed past the last screen of bushes before the Dragon Square.

"Only a few more minutes," she said. "Then you can rest."

The old man seemed to gain strength from the promise of shelter, and he shambled forward with greater speed. Twice he almost fell, but she caught him.

She kicked open the door of the nearest building and helped him inside, removing her white woolen burnoose and running a hand through her sweat-streaked, close-cropped black hair.

Away from the biting wind, she felt her skin burning as her body adjusted to the new conditions. She unbelted her white sheepskin cloak, pushing it back over her broad shoulders. Beneath it she wore a light blue woolen tunic and black leggings partially hidden by thigh-length boots, sheepskin-lined. At her side was a slender dagger.

The old man leaned against a wall, shaking uncontrollably.

"They will find me. They *will*!" he whimpered. Renya ignored him and moved down the hallway.

A man came into sight at the far end, and Renya started, her dagger leaping to her hand. The man was tall and dark and dressed in black. By his side was a longsword. He moved forward slowly yet with a confidence Renya found daunting. As he approached, she steadied herself for the attack, watching his eyes.

They were, she noticed, the most beautiful violet color and slanted like those of the Nadir tribesmen of the north. Yet his face was square-cut and almost handsome, save for the grim line of his mouth.

She wanted to stop him with words, to tell him that if he came any closer she would kill him. But she could not. There was about him an aura of power, an authority that left her no choice but to respond.

And then he was past her and bending over Aulin.

"Leave him alone!" she shouted. Tenaka turned to her.

"There is a fire in my room. Along there on the right," he said calmly. "I will take him there." Smoothly he lifted the old man and carried him to his quarters, laying him on the narrow bed. He removed the man's cloak and boots and began to rub gently at his calves where the skin was blue and mottled. Turning, he threw a blanket to the girl. "Warm this by the fire," he said, returning to his work. After a while he checked the man's breathing: It was deep and even.

"He is asleep?" she asked.

"Yes."

"Will he live?"

"Who can say?" said Tenaka, rising and stretching his back.

"Thank you for helping him."

"Thank you for not killing me," he answered.

"What are you doing here?"

"Sitting by my fire and waiting for the storm to pass. Would you like some food?"

They sat together by the blaze, sharing his dried meat and hardcake biscuits and saying little. Tenaka was not an inquisitive man, and Renya intuitively knew he had no wish to talk. Yet the silence was far from uncomfortable. She felt calm and at peace for the first time in weeks, and even the threat of the assassins seemed less real, as if the barracks were a haven protected by magic, unseen but infinitely powerful.

Tenaka leaned back in his chair, watching the girl as she in turn gazed into the flames. Her face was striking, oval-shaped with high cheekbones and wide eyes so dark that the pupils merged with the irises. Overall the impression he gained was one of strength undermined by vulnerability, as if she held a secret fear or was tormented by a hidden weakness. At another time he would have been attracted by her. But when he reached inside himself, he could find no emotions, no desire . . . No life, he realized with surprise.

"We are being hunted," she said at last.

"I know."

"How would you know?"

He shrugged and added fuel to the fire. "You are on a road to nowhere, with no horses or provisions, yet your clothes are expensive and your manner cultured. Therefore, you are running away from something or someone, and it follows that they are pursuing you."

"Does it bother you?" she asked him.

"Why should it?"

"If you are caught with us, you will die, too."

"Then I shall not be caught with you," he said.

"Shall I tell you why we are hunted?" she inquired.

"No. That is of your life. Our paths have crossed here, but we will both go on to separate destinies. There is no need for us to learn of one another."

"Why? Do you fear it would make you care?"

He considered the question carefully, noting the anger in her eyes. "Perhaps. But mainly I fear the weakness that follows caring. I have a task to do, and I do not need other problems in my mind. No, that is not true—I do not *want* other problems in my mind."

"Is that not selfish?"

"Of course it is. But it aids survival."

"And is that so important?" she snapped.

"It must be; otherwise you would not be running."

"It is important to him," she said, pointing at the man in the bed. "Not to me."

"He cannot run from death," said Tenaka softly. "Anyway, there are mystics who maintain there is a paradise after death."

"He believes it," she said, smiling. "That is what he fears."

Tenaka shook his head slowly, then rubbed his eyes.

"That is a little too much for me," he said, forcing a smile. "I think I will sleep now." Taking his blanket, he spread it on the floor and stretched himself out, his head resting on his pack.

"You are Dragon, aren't you?" said Renya.

"How did you know?" he asked, propping himself on one elbow.

"It was the way you said 'my room'."

"Very perceptive." He lay down and closed his eyes.

"I am Renya."

"Good night, Renya."

"Will you tell me your name?"

He thought of refusing, considering all the reasons why he should not tell her.

"Tenaka Khan," he said. And slept.

Life is a farce, Scaler thought as he hung by his fingertips forty feet above the stone courtyard. Below him a huge Joining sniffed the air, its shaggy head swinging ponderously from side to side, its taloned fingers curled around the hilt of the saw-edged sword. Snow swept in icy flurries, stinging Scaler's eyes.

"Thanks very much," he whispered, transferring his gaze to the dark, pregnant storm clouds above. Scaler was a religious man who saw the gods as a group of Seniles, eternals playing endless jokes on humanity with cosmic bad taste.

Below him the Joining sheathed its sword and ambled away into the darkness. Taking a deep breath, Scaler hauled himself over the windowsill and parted the heavy velvet curtains beyond. He was in a small study furnished with a desk, three chairs of oak, several chests, and a row of bookshelves and manuscript holders. The study was tidy, obsessively so, Scaler thought, noting the three quill pens placed exactly parallel at the center of the desk. He would have expected nothing less of Silius the Magister.

A long silvered mirror framed in mahogany was fixed to the far wall, opposite the desk. Scaler advanced toward it, drawing himself up to his full height and pulling back his shoulders. The black face mask, dark tunic, and leggings gave him a forbidding look. He drew his dagger and dropped into a warrior's crouch. The effect was chilling.

Perfect, he told his reflection. I wouldn't want to meet you in a dark alley! Replacing the dagger, he moved to the study door and carefully lifted the iron latch, easing the door open.

Beyond was a narrow stone corridor and four doors: Two on the left and two on the right. Scaler padded across to the farthest room on the left and slowly lifted the latch. The door opened without a sound, and he moved inside, hugging the wall. The room was warm, though the log fire in the grate was burning low, a dull red glow illuminating the curtains around the large bed. Scaler moved forward to the bed, pausing to look down on fat Silius and his equally fat mistress. He lay on his stomach, she on her back; both were snoring.

Why am I creeping about? he asked himself. *I could have come in here beating a drum.* He stifled a chuckle, found the jewel box in its hidden niche below the window, opened it, and poured the contents into a black canvas pouch tied to his belt. At full value they would keep him in luxury for five years. Sold, as they must be, to a shady dealer in the southern quarter, they would keep him for barely three months, or six if he did not gamble. He thought of not gambling but it was inconceivable. Three months, he decided.

Retying his pouch, he backed out into the corridor and turned . . .

Only to come face to face with a servant, a tall, gaunt figure in a woolen nightshirt.

The man screamed and fled.

Scaler screamed and fled, hurtling down a circular stairway and cannoning into two sentries. Both men tumbled back, shouting as they fell. Scaler hit the floor in a tumbler's roll, came to his feet, and sprinted left, the sentries close behind. Another set of steps appeared on his right, and he took them three at a time, his long legs carrying him at a terrifying speed.

Twice he nearly lost his footing before reaching the next level. Before him was an iron gate, locked, but the key hung from a wooden peg. The stench from beyond the gate brought him to his senses, and fear cut through his panic.

The Joinings' pit!

Behind him he could hear the sentries pounding down the stairs. He lifted the key, opened the gate, and stepped inside, locking it behind him. Then he advanced into the darkness, praying to the Seniles to let him live for a few more of their jests.

As his eyes grew accustomed to the darkness of the corridor, he saw several openings on either side; within, sleeping on straw, were the Joinings of Silius.

He moved on toward the gate at the far end, pulling off his mask as he did so.

He was almost there when the pounding began behind him and the muffled shouts of the sentries pierced the silence. A Joining stumbled from its lair, blood-red eyes fastening on Scaler; it was close to seven feet tall, with huge shoulders and heavily muscled arms covered with black fur. Its face was elongated, sharp fangs lining its maw. The pounding grew louder, and Scaler took a deep breath.

"Go and see what the noise is about," he told the beast.

"Who you?" it hissed, the words mangled by the lolling tongue.

"Don't just stand there—go and see what they want," Scaler ordered sharply.

The beast brushed past him, and other Joinings came into the corridor and followed it, ignoring Scaler. He ran to the gate and slipped the key in the lock. As it turned and the gate swung open, a sudden bellowing roar blasted in the confines of the corridor. Scaler twisted round to see the Joinings running toward him, howling ferociously. With shaking fingers he dragged free the key and leapt through the opening, pulling the gate shut behind him and swiftly locking it.

The night air was crisp as he ran up the short steps to the western courtyard and on to the ornate wall, scaling it swiftly and dropping into the cobbled street beyond.

It was well after curfew, so he hugged the shadows all the way to the inn, then climbed the outer trellis to his room, rapping on the shutters.

Belder opened the window and helped him inside.

"Well?" asked the old soldier.

"I got the jewels," stated Scaler.

"I despair of you," said Belder. "After all the years I spend on you, what do you become? A thief!"

"It's in the blood," said Scaler, grinning. "Remember the Earl of Bronze?"

"That's legend," replied Belder. "And even if it's true, not one of his descendants has ever lived a less than honourable life. Even that Nadir spawn Tenaka!"

"Don't speak ill of him, Belder," Scaler said softly. "He was my friend."